Also by Dennis Bock

Olympia
The Ash Garden

THE COMMUNIST'S DAUGHTER

DENNIS BOCK

THE COMMUNIST'S DAUGHTER

A NOVEL

A Phyllis Bruce Book
HarperCollins*PublishersLtd*

A Phyllis Bruce Book, published by
HarperCollins Publishers Ltd

First Edition.

HarperCollins Publishers Ltd
2 Bloor Street East, 20th Floor
Toronto, Ontario, Canada
M4W 1A8

www.harpercollins.ca

Library and Archives Canada Cataloguing in Publication

Bock, Dennis
The communist's daughter : a novel /
Dennis Bock.—1st ed.

"A Phyllis Bruce book".
ISBN-13: 978-0-00-200528-9
ISBN-10: 0-00-200528-X

1. Bethune, Norman, 1890–1939—
Fiction. 2. Sino-Japanese Conflict,
1937–1945—Fiction. I. Title.

PS8553.O42C64 2006   C813'.54
C2006-901089-7

RRD 9 8 7 6 5 4 3 2 1

Printed and bound in Canada

Set in Minion

FOR MY MAGNIFICENT SONS, ADAM AND OLIVER

The enclosed manuscript was found at Huang-shih
K'ou, Hopei Province. It was likely written in the
Chin-ch'a-chi Border Region, north China, sometime
between May 1938 and November 1939. Included among
its 448 pages were numerous medical illustrations,
a telegram, a newspaper clipping, a personal letter
and drawings.

Each member of the committee will be asked to
provide recommendations regarding suitability
for translation and wide distribution throughout
the territories of the Border Regions.

Recommendations will be considered and incorporated
into the final report made by this Office.

Major Lu Ting-yi,
Director of the Propaganda Department of the
  Central Committee of the Chinese Communist
  Party,Yan'an, Shensi Province

ENVELOPE ONE

I t is my hope that your understanding will win out against any mistrust or anger you may harbour against me when you finally read this. It is so easy to feel anger, and Lord knows I deserve a good dose of it. But I am trying, and you will see I have been trying for quite some time. I also hope that you will read this many years from now, when you are grown, at a time when this story will be long past. With an adult's eyes it is more likely that you will see this letter for what it is, and know the regret and tenderness I feel as I compose this history for you. Of course, I know I have no control over any of this, yet still I hope. The dead must relinquish so much.

Heaven forbid these pages return to you without me, but allowing for such a possibility I give you my word absolutely that I will recount my life as faithfully as I recall it, nothing added, nothing lost.

Will I be dead? That is certainly the way things seem to go around here, but it is not my intention to go off and die any time soon. You may also take some consolation in knowing that we Bethunes are fighters, first and foremost, and never go down without a mighty struggle. For a man nearing fifty I have got a good bit of life left in me.

The reality is that you have missed every word of the story I will tell, and I cannot change that fact. When such a small miracle as you awaited, I chose to look elsewhere for purpose. I chose to leave you behind, and that is the sadness in my life. I feel there is no adequate apology a father can offer his child for something like that, but it is my hope to tell you a little about the world as it was before you came into it, and about the terrible forces that pulled me away from you once you finally did. And to tell you why I came to this faraway country. One's journey through life is fraught with contradictions and compromises. I see that now, and perhaps one day you will see it too.

*

There is a boy here in north China with me named Ho. You would like him. The plain truth is that nothing would get done around here without him. He is my vigilant sentry, my water boy, my trusted valet, my cook, my barber. He is the one who provides me with everything I need. When he saw the state of this typewriter ribbon (I had been using the old Remington portable to write up a number of medical reports) he dipped it in some oil he found dripping from the belly of a wounded generator hidden behind the hospital (which was, not so long ago, a Buddhist temple), and lo, by nightfall, it was set for another ten or fifteen pages. It has since become part of his morning ritual.

The reason I mention this so early on is that whatever it is that he puts into this customized ink of his reminds me of a perfume I once purchased for your mother in Madrid, before the war in China came to take me away. A whiff of lavender and mint that is my own Proustian delight. As I work, these keys release small shock waves of that perfume into the air, making this letter—for brief periods at least—an almost pleasant walk down memory lane. I imagine these additives, whatever they are, are meant only to suppress the oil's natural foul composition, and perhaps to deepen the colour of the imprint of these letters. It works surprisingly well, I must say. Every morning I find the Remington stripped of its ribbon, and every morning Ho comes to me with my breakfast of millet or steamed rice and tea, his hands stained the same colour as these pages.

*

I do not have much idle time here, but what little there is I spend trying to make some sense of the fates that have shaped me into the man I am. I'll admit to finding this quite a task. I often think about your mother and see now that she was not so unlike my own mother, how they shared a common desire to improve the world they lived in. I also think about who you will be when you finally read this. I like to imagine the glow of understanding that will light up your face as you move deeper into the history of your father's people and your own miraculous beginning. And I like to imagine that I will soon be home to see you, that peace will descend upon us, that there will be no need for these writings other than to help recall the vicious events that took place before this war made things right.

My first memory is of my mother stepping out of a baker's shop, me in one arm, a bag of cinnamon buns in the other.

I was four years old. It was looking to be a fine day, as I had earned one of those buns for my good behaviour that morning. I was stuffing it into my mouth, nestled there in the cradle of my mother's arm, when she suddenly turned on her heel and swung her shopping bag at a man who was entering the shop just as we were leaving. The man fell—he must have been old, certainly caught unawares—and as my mother stood over him I munched away happily, thinking this was some sort of panto-mime enacted for my amusement. The baker came out from behind his counter and stepped into the game. His apron was white. He was a large man and wore a pleated hat. I remember thinking that it looked like a mushroom. More, I said, and the baker with the mushroom hat raised the man by the collar and threw him out the door.

This early memory, though I include it here, is not typical of your grandmother, for she was, in faith and in deed, a woman devoted to the Lord and to the improvement of His world. She was a warm and loving mother, gentle as a lamb, but a fighter, too, who wouldn't turn the other cheek when confronted by the ugliness of disrespect-ful men. It was your grandmother who taught me and my brother and sister that things could be made better by virtue of regular Bible study and a calm spiritual persistence, and that our highest calling was to commit ourselves to the betterment of our small corner of the world. This was a first lesson in life and one I carry with me to this day, greying sinner that I am. She instilled within me the impulse to make the most of what I had been given. We are all given talents, she would say. Each of us to our own abilities.

Every Sunday in the parlour, she told us one of Jesus's par-ables. I remember my mother's soft hand on my head as she read through Matthew. The Parable of the Talents has stayed with me.

You might know it. One man hoards his gifts while others bring them out into the world to gain strength and knowledge. Her hand lifted from my head and gently touched the open Bible.

"And what does this mean?" she asked softly.

"That it is God's will for us to make the most of what we're given," I said.

"Yes, and that what you're given belongs not to you, Norman, but to the Lord, who has favoured us all with a special gift, each of us in our own way. You are now the keeper of these talents, Norman, and you have many of them. You must not bury your gifts but share them with others."

I told your mother about these Bible lessons, more than forty years after the fact. I told your mother that I had taken my Presbyterian upbringing very seriously. That I saw life as a series of lessons, of morally correct or incorrect choices. That the decision to lead a good life was yours. I still feel it in me, I told her, even now. She sat on a stool before me. We were in Madrid. The war there was on then, and still is.

"Turn your shoulder toward me, please," I said. I thought of myself as something of a weekend painter, if that's the right expression. It was a quiet night at the Hotel Santander.

Your mother said, "Yes, I know that about you, Norman. I can see how you are."

"Move the shoulder a little more, please."

She said, "There's no other place I'd rather be than here, at this very moment, with you."

I was silent for a moment, then said, "I don't know if I'll ever get your skin right. You're like a snowflake. You're the whitest thing I've ever seen."

"I am your Swedish princess." She shifted the blanket on her shoulder and tossed her hair. She spoke English very well. "Did you ever believe you'd find someone here? In the middle of this stupid war?"

"No, I did not," I said.

And she said, "Does being happy diminish your sense of purpose, Norman?"

And I said, "I've always had purpose. What I never had was peace."

I have thought about that conversation often, and I can still say with confidence that the look your mother gave me on that night told me she would never expect to hear another truth so full of sadness as that one, not as long as she lived.

★

Today was a difficult day and it is late now. I need sleep very badly. We've had little water, and in this heat that's something to worry about. Most mornings Ho replenishes my cistern. I hear him pass my door just after first light on his way down to the river. Sometimes he's singing to himself. When he came back empty-handed this morning I knew something was wrong. Last night we heard the fighting up near Chin-kang K'u, a village in the clouds. Ho found the stream running a deep red. When I went out to see for myself, I watched the limpid pink water slipping over the felt-green rocks like a cool summer lemonade. An hour later, a second stain came, lighter still, from the executions that followed.

Sepsis, starvation and tuberculosis are the three main killers here, after the Japanese. How desperate this place is, how wrenching its agonies. I wish you could understand, and somehow at the same time I hope you never will. But I am glad for the silence of writing. This is my one respite, though it is difficult to find the time. Today I operated on 7 wounded, two of whom were no older than seventeen. Another 126 are yet to be seen to. The odds are overwhelming. I am alone here but for two under-trained assistants, both too recent to medicine to be of any real help. General conditions in Shansi Province are ghastly. We have few supplies. Without complaint the wounded lie dying in their ragged and filthy uniforms. In the heat of the day they are covered by flies and lice and dust, sweating away the last of their strength, and in the cold of these mountain nights, without blankets or fire, they live moment to moment in shivering agony for lack of morphine or nitrous oxide. The small houses of this village offer scant comfort. There are no windowpanes and there is not enough fuel for fires. This landscape is almost barren of trees but for a few willows at the bottom of a steep valley to the east, practically impassable from here. I am afraid for these men, perhaps more so than they are for themselves. I have never seen a breed of men as tough as these peasants of north China.

It seems to me that religion figured out long ago that the central tenets of belief must be embodied within a single entity. Let one man bear the burden of perfection and suffering. Since arriving to China from Spain I have come to the conclusion that the absence of a leader in the Spanish War amounts to a grave danger that might possibly doom that struggle to failure. That is not the case here, I can say with some authority, and I will try to help you understand why. This is one thing these men do have, an embodiment of their ideals. Perhaps the new Spanish Christ has risen since I left Madrid, and with all my heart I hope that is the case.

*

The first thing that struck me about your mother was the paleness of her skin. I don't think I ever did get it right in that painting. Her beauty demanded a greater talent than I was able to muster. Her eyes were hazel and streaked with gold, for one. I have never seen anything like it. One day you will see it in her portrait. It's like trying to hide a lit candle under a bushel; the light escapes through the cracks no matter what. Her hair was blond, cut just above the shoulder, and parted at the side. Her bangs curled from right to left, as if rebelling against those conservative Catholic hairstyles that had become all too common in Madrid. Her nose was long and delicate and sat perfectly above a wide half-smile that only barely concealed a wry pout, which, the beauty that she was, never failed to pull my attention from whatever was happening around us.

Well, journalists from England, Norway and America had started coming around to see about the blood-transfusion work that we were doing in Spain. The clinic was attracting a fair bit of attention, I can say without presuming too much. Even a film producer came with the idea of making a documentary, which I did in fact agree to. One January afternoon, in walked the English journalist Frank Pitcairn. He'd come to conduct interviews for the story he was going to write about me. At first I thought your mother was his assistant, perhaps an interpreter.

She smiled and said with her distinctive Swedish accent, "This is all very impressive, Doctor Bethune."

She wore a short leather coat—a flyer's jacket, I think it was, the type with a high fur collar—and dark slacks. She carried herself with remarkable confidence.

"And you are?" I said.

"Kajsa von Rothman," she said, extending her hand. We were foreigners. We did not touch cheeks the way the Spanish did.

Only a few weeks before, a fifteen-room flat at number 36 Príncipe de Vergara Street, Madrid, had been given over to my transfusion unit by the Ministry of War. Before then it had been occupied by a German diplomat named Koll. Of course, he'd gone running with the rest of the Fascists once Madrid declared itself with the Republic. I remember the portrait of himself he left hanging on the wall between the French doors overlooking the street—left there, I can only guess, in some final gesture of defiance or megalomania, or a bit of both. It was a sad reminder that this address had once been a hotbed of attachés, emissaries, dignitaries—Fascists come to enjoy its lush surroundings while discussing the glories of totalitarianism. Brandy and cigars in the library—consisting of some eight thousand volumes, mostly German—furnished with Aubusson carpets and gold brocade curtains. It must have been a fine time while it lasted.

Within days of occupying the abandoned consulate we opened our doors to the public. It was a remarkable turnout. I am obliged to report here that the Spanish put these Chinese peasants to shame in that regard. When I arrived in north China, little more than a year later, the locals were terrified by the very thought of a blood donation. In Madrid, though, young mothers, old ladies and even children formed a line that reached down the block, well past the cinema, at the time running an inspiring government propaganda film whose name has not stayed with me. The old Prussian's liquor cabinets were now stocked with medical equipment and canned food stuffs. We produced our serums and improved our instruments in a small room where the diplomat had once kept his stiff shirts and top hats.

As I walked the journalist and this elegant associate of his through the rooms of the clinic, I explained the process of transfusing, storing and transporting blood. I showed them the stations where we worked and provided statistics, details and a few simple medical anecdotes he might find useful for his *Daily Worker* article. I introduced the staff, among them the Castilian doctor Antonio Calebras, a talented man, though consumed by an odd inferiority he overcompensated for through a haughty impatience with foreigners and their near-universal inability to master the language that came to him so effortlessly. It always seemed to me that he felt we were crashing his war. I attempted to avoid him most days, but often this proved impossible. We regarded one another with a fair bit of contempt, I should think. He offered the two visitors a limp hand, the very portrait of the noble Iberian. I believe Kajsa's Spanish surprised him. The way it held his attention was unusual, though I suspect her beauty may have had something to do with that. He was a little man with black, slicked-back hair. In fact he looked a bit like photographs of the Andalusian poet García Lorca. Appearances being shallow, however, Dr. Calebras certainly did not possess the great artist's sense of poetic fraternity and political idealism.

"Do you have an average travel time," the woman asked, "based on your trips up to the Guadarrama Pass?" I now presumed your mother was another journalist, asking a question like that.

They called for a second interview the following morning, and after some persuading I agreed. It was mid-evening when I arrived at the Cervecería Alemana. It was my first break in eighteen hours. I could have worked another eighteen and still left things unfinished. Kajsa was standing at the bar with Pitcairn and leafing through a Spanish newspaper. She was more beautiful than she had seemed the day before. She wore the same jacket but different trousers, I think. She pushed her thick bangs back over the top of her head, folded her newspaper under her arm and greeted me with a handshake. Pitcairn slapped my back and thanked me for making time for him.

They began by having me describe my day, which had begun with a visit to half a dozen basement hospitals. Then came meetings with officials from the Ministry of War regarding supplies, I said, that were rarely available. I had performed three surgeries that day as well, and spent three hours on blood collection and storage.

When I finished speaking I turned to Kajsa. "You're with the *Daily Worker,* I take it?"

"Oh, I tried my hand at writing when I was a student," she said. "I've got more sense in my head now."

"Good sense and ideals," I said, "don't often go hand in hand."

She said she was with the *Mujeres Libres,* the Free Women of Spain. This was an organization of anarchist women that helped get prostitutes off the streets. They pulled them up from their misery and found them honourable work in the textile industry or in the city orphanages. The bombing raids made sure there were always lots of motherless children for the reformed ladies of the night to take care of. "From a life of hell to a life of helping," she said. She'd been studying in London but left university when she saw how pointless it was when compared with the real issue. When I asked what she considered this to be, she said, without a pause, "Nihilism. A passion for destruction."

"I see you have read Turgenev," I said.

"Would you both please stop?" Pitcairn said. "We're not dead yet. So let's forget about gloom and doom and the class struggle, shall we? I'm a bit done with the revolution for tonight."

Soon after exiting the café we found a long, narrow street lined with bars and anaemic plane trees that barely reached past the first balcony of the adjacent buildings. This was Huertas Street. I think your mother called it "charming," or something along those lines, and it was. In a tavern called Casa Alberto I drank my first glass of absinthe. It was green and turned milky white when the water was added. I didn't like it much. "Go on," she said. Its taste and effects seemed terrifically overrated. I drank another, impatiently. Your mother, who wasn't a drinker, told me to send it back when I said it tasted more like formaldehyde than liquor, but it wasn't that bad and I drank it anyway.

All the bars were busy. It was close to midnight. I was feeling the alcohol by now. The street seemed to be moving in slow motion. Groups of people were singing, chanting in deep, low voices, marching up and down the street like lumbering elephants. It seemed an entire neighbourhood of drunkenness. The smell of black tobacco was on everyone's clothing. I remember a blanket of smoke hanging over the street. Some of the bars were reserved for quiet old men who played dominoes and listened to radio reports of the war and watched the young people through the windows. Heads turned when we walked in. I was not as young as the rest of the crowd but not so old, either. No one said anything to us. I was used to that by then. In these bars nobody liked seeing a new face. It was understandable, your mother said, even healthy, to be suspicious of strangers in times like these.

*

This evening Ho passed before my door, propped open to permit the breeze, and stopped. He may have seen my foot protruding from behind this desk, hunched over as I was and thinking about where to go with this story. I rolled another sheet into the Remington. Off he walked to the sound of my clacking.

*

I remember rumours were an ongoing source of debate and discussion. They became something of a fascination and a pastime, I think. For some months it was said that the French would not buckle under British pressure to reverse their promise of military aid, and that the Americans would enter the war within six months. People spoke of Mussolini with ridicule and of Hitler with fear and of the devilish Moors with such a grinding racial hatred that I myself began to feel it. Up at the front, during the lulls in fighting, the urge to talk grew, and spies were a frequent topic. Emilio Mola, the Fascist general, spearheading four columns of soldiers at Madrid's southeastern flank, had proclaimed that a fifth column of sympathizers was said to be waiting quietly, patiently, in the heart of the capital. Soon this was considered fact, though nothing was known for certain.

Entering the world of gossip and rumour was a common rite of passage that greatly relieved the tedium. At the front there was only waiting and fighting and talking. Women and prostitutes also figured in these conversations, until some remark unwittingly reminded the men of the rapes they'd seen or had themselves committed. Then the jocularity was sucked out of the air as if fire had suddenly stolen oxygen from their lungs, and they would return to their silent stares and memories as the war again became real. Most days, recollections of my own experiences many years before, in Belgium during the Great War, came to me. I never spoke of them, not to your mother and not to these young men. Stories of another war to end all wars would do no one any good. Your mother knew enough to guess what I'd seen before coming to Spain.

*

I have been thinking about the night your mother and I spent in a bomb shelter. It was our first night together, and a very strange night, indeed. I'm sure she would tell you the same. I can close my eyes and still smell the dankness in the air, and feel the closeness of those arched brick passageways we moved through under the city. Most of us spent a fair bit of time in cellars and basements in Madrid, but this night was unusual and I think you should know about it.

Frank Pitcairn had led us into a bar called Los Gabrieles, where colourful mosaic advertisements for brandies and biscuits and sherries covered the walls. It was probably close to one o'clock in the morning when the loud, high whine of an air-raid siren came through the door and all conversations stopped. People made for the basement. Your mother seemed oddly calm, I thought. Could she be so used to this, already? I carried my drink outside and watched the streets being vacated as people ran for the safety of doorways. She followed casually behind. I did not hear the planes, but when the explosions began, the last of the drinkers and the staff quickly headed below for shelter. Your mother and I followed and walked through a long hallway, past the washrooms and down a narrow, dimly lit set of stairs. The air grew thin and dank as we descended the steps, and the thud of the exploding bombs grew muted.

Upon entering this basement I saw quickly enough that it was unlike any other shelter I had seen in Madrid, or anywhere else for that matter. It was a magnificent labyrinth, an intricate series of rooms linked by a main tunnel that branched off into smaller, darker tunnels that ran even farther beneath the city. Rooms waited at the end of four of the tunnels, each one representing, in miniature, a stage of a bullfight. Like the bar upstairs, they were decorated with ceramic tiles, depicting scenes that took up an entire wall. The mosaic of the first room we entered was that of a vestiary. On one wall the tile showed the bullfighter's brightly decorated suit of lights, gold with red sequins along the arms and legs. The room was crowded with customers from upstairs, people still holding their drinks. We found the main tunnel again and walked through the dank air to the chapel, where the matador pauses for a word with his Maker before entering the ring. The scene was well lit by the open window portrayed in the mosaic, and visible in its frame was a bright day, with the Virgin Mary hovering in the centre. Radiance emanated from her outstretched hands. The ceramic also showed a desk, on which sat a Bible propped up against a stack of books, an unlit candle, notepaper and a fountain pen. This room, too, was full of people. We exited and continued down along the main tunnel.

We entered a circular room constructed to represent the main bullring, the *plaza de toros*. It was less than ten paces across and also near capacity. The tiles showed stands filled with people facing us, creating the perception that we ourselves were the main attraction and not some hapless bull and matador. The bombs falling outside, perhaps ten blocks away, sounded as dull thuds over our heads. The room shook with the force of the distant explosions. Tiles scattered on the dirt floor had been shaken loose by previous bombardments—or this one, it's impossible to say.

Frank had found a seat and sat with his back to the wall, talking quietly with an old man. Your mother and I continued along the main tunnel to the fourth and last room.

She said, "This would be absurd if it wasn't so terrifying."

*

Absurd moments in Madrid, there are plenty of those to choose from, and I shouldn't be so surprised. I suppose that is the nature of war. I remember my first encounter with the absurd very well. It was on my first morning in Madrid, in early November of 1936, a few months before I met your mother. I recall taking my breakfast at the hotel cafeteria on the Gran Vía, Madrid's principal east–west thoroughfare, only a few doors up from a bar called the Museo Chicote. I knew very few people in the city at the time and had brought with me nothing but my few items of luggage, a small amount of cash in the form of American Express orders and safe-conduct papers issued to me by the Spanish Embassy in Paris. I had begun walking east along the Gran Vía when an annoying little creature approached from behind and grabbed me by the elbow. Of course, I had no idea what this man was trying to tell me. He spoke very fast and I didn't understand any Spanish. I was just then indicating to him the impasse, shaking my head and gently but firmly pulling away, when his free hand casually slipped under his coat. He patted something there and raised an eye. It was a gesture he might have picked up at the movie house just down the road.

Having no option but to take his lead I followed him the few steps back to my hotel, where he rang the service bell and waited for the lady to appear at her desk. She was, I know now, a typical *patrona* of the type you find all over that country—efficient and powerful in the small world of her clean hallways and uncomfortable, tubular pillows, loud, talkative and helpful. She helped me understand the gist of the man's complaint. It seemed he was connected in some form to the security apparatus of the Republican government, and that he'd heard me, while conversing with another hotel guest, say "Fascist." He had not liked how I'd spoken the word. Perhaps had I spat it in disgust he might have waived his suspicions and bought me a brandy. It's no secret, of course, that small men tend to puff themselves up, but I was to learn just how much they can do so when acting on behalf of powerful organizations and, moreover, carrying a sidearm. As I was thinking this, the other reasons for his stopping me came out, and at first I could only believe that the proprietress had translated incorrectly. He had not liked the fact that I was well dressed and wore a moustache. Fascists, I've since learned, wear Abercrombie & Fitch and sport trimmed facial hair, not Socialists or Communists or Marxists. This was beyond ludicrous, but, reading an unmistakable excitability in the man, I chose the cautious route. I had the lady explain that I had just arrived to the country, as my papers would indicate, supported the Republican cause, and would soon be donning the appropriate clothing. I did not, however, mention what I had planned for my moustache.

I watched his enthusiasm wane slightly when the landlady produced my passport from her desk drawer. With his permission I retrieved my safe-conduct papers from my breast pocket. He studied both documents, overly carefully, I thought, guessing that he was not much more than an illiterate thug looking for something to keep him occupied before lunch. He returned the documents, nodded slightly and, with a tinge of regret in his eyes, told the landlady I was free to go. I supposed that was the end of it. I took the lift to my room to splash some water on my face and shake off this ridiculous scare. It was an inconvenience more than anything else, but also a reminder that certain aspects of security were not to be taken for granted in a city ringed by Fascists and said to be brimming with spies.

Not five minutes later, as I was preparing to resume my day, a knock sounded at the door. Here stood another man, dressed in a black leather coat—very impressive and fit, quite handsome, and bearing a briefcase. With him were five guards, each armed with a carbine. This man, too, demanded to see my documents. Apparently his colleague had scampered down the road to get some help. One of the guards, instructed to descend for the passport, returned a moment later. The man in the leather coat sat down on the bed, briefcase on his lap, and began flipping through its pages. Two guards stood barring the door. I heard others in the hallway, their voices striking a chord of boredom, and the man on my bed looked up and shook his head, as if annoyed by their banal conversation. While a suspect, and perhaps a spy, I still might understand the superior regrets of an important man obliged to spend a whole war in the company of bumpkins. But this handsome, haughty police officer wasn't having such a good day, either, and seemed just as let down as his predecessor had been. My status was unimpeachable. He stood up, organized his minions with a short bark, and finally I was left in peace. For a few minutes I watched from the window, hoping to see them leave, but saw nothing but a busy street teeming with mules and military vehicles and pedestrians.

Then another knock at the door. This time a friendly face greeted me. Henning Sorensen was a Canadian associate of mine with whom I would soon travel (I did not know this yet) up to Paris and London in search of a car and various instruments, gadgets and chemicals we would need to get our clinic up and running. He had been in Spain for a number of weeks, preparing the groundwork, and spoke a bit of Spanish. Shortly before departing for Europe I'd been entrusted with a letter from his sweetheart back in Montreal, and after explaining my encounter with the secret police, I retrieved it from my luggage and handed it to him. Just then the man with the briefcase swooped through the door, accompanied by his bored, grunting men. Greatly enjoying his line of work, he snatched the letter out of Sorensen's hand while his guards aimed their rifles directly at us. Greedily, he ripped the letter open, clearly believing he'd smashed a ring of Fascist plotters until he read, "My dearest darling . . ." With that there was nothing left for him but a quiet retreat.

It was a ridiculous episode, but again, a reminder. Sorensen and I watched them leave the building, walk up Gran Vía and disappear into the crowd of vehicles and mules. We descended to the street not long after, looking to soothe our nerves with a drink at the Museo Chicote, though not before I changed my clothes and shaved off my moustache.

*

I remember the tunnel growing narrower and deeper. The things we remember! Your mother's hand brushed against mine. I remember that so well. I felt like a schoolboy! What did I do? I pretended not to notice, of course. I did not move my hand but stretched my fingers out in case her touch might come again. A moment later we entered a small infirmary that was not as crowded as the other rooms had been, situated at the confused and narrow end of the tunnel. It was the end of our journey, and the bullfighter's. The mosaic of this last room represented an operating theatre. Well, I said, at last something I understand. Perhaps the fallen bull-fighter had already been gored and was now being carried down to the infirmary, for three doctors and a nurse stood at the ready, all looking very concerned, as well as a solemn-looking priest with long, thin El Greco hands and an old, grey face. The portraits were beautifully rendered and close to life-sized. The artist had required nine tiles to depict the surgeon's rib-spreaders, laid out on the table beside a stethoscope and various cutting instruments. Their smocks were still shiny white.

This last room was the dimmest of the four, with only one electric light hanging from the stuccoed ceiling. The air was stale and damp. Two unoccupied stools sat in front of the mural. The three people in the room were sitting against the opposite wall, looking at the medical scene, and now us, while sipping from the glasses they had brought with them from the bar. They were Spanish. I gestured to the stools, and one man nodded and shrugged. We sat down and listened to the not-so-distant bombs pounding through the walls. After a few minutes Kajsa stood and said, "Take my hand."

I did, and rose to my feet, saying, "I think we're at the end of the line here."

She led me out of the room and into a smaller side tunnel. We moved down it perhaps ten feet, crouching, and stopped in front of a chair on which sat a wooden crate full of empty bottles. This alcove had, I supposed, been used for storage.

She moved the crate and chair, then pulled open the small door hidden behind. "What about this? Where do you think this goes?"

"A trap door leading down from the bar?"

"Well . . ." she said, but without finishing her thought she slipped inside.

I lit a match, stepped in after her and looked down a steep set of narrow stairs.

It's difficult to understand the impulse that told me to follow your mother like that, but I did. I suppose I already felt drawn to her, though I was trying to resist it. As I've said, it was a very unusual night. We walked, slightly hunched, down the stairs and along a cramped passageway for twenty or thirty paces before another explosive thud shook us. We journeyed deeper under the city. I struck match after match and walked slowly so as not to extinguish the flame. Occasionally, out of the dark appeared a crate or box or shovel or a bundle of clothing. It was difficult to guess from such objects who came down here, when they last had or why. There was no one in sight. We shouted out but heard no one answer.

We found no rooms off the tunnel, as there had been in the basement of the bar. It was just a narrow passageway, bricked in a low arch like a wine cellar. The path must have curved gently, for we'd entered it, I was almost certain, in a westward direction and now, if I had any sense of orientation left, were heading east toward the Retiro Park and the Prado Museum. It was difficult to tell since we couldn't see farther than a few feet in front of us. As we walked, the walls of brick around us grew silent. The bombs had stopped falling.

"I think it's this way," she said.

"Why? This might go on for miles."

"We just follow the wall," she said. "It'll lead us out somewhere."

We walked for some time, and then I struck the last match. We were walking side by side and I looked at her face in the dim light. The dying flame disappeared into my fingertips, and a perfect dark surrounded us. We heard only our quiet breathing and footfalls. When she lit a cigarette lighter, we saw a large door, pushed it open, went down another series of stairs hewn from the rock and entered a large, frescoed room with dozens of niches carved into the walls at different heights. Each one, not much more than a small ledge, held a funeral urn.

Kajsa let the light die. "Listen," she said.

The silence and darkness were total. We waited a minute or two, listening for vibrations coming down from the streets above. The flame flicked on again and we passed under a low overhang and through another short tunnel into a second frescoed room, also devoted to the ashes of the dead. But each of these urns, instead of resting in a niche, had been afforded its own small vestibule with a bench in front. People construct the strangest shrines to honour their dead. I remember thinking that. A cross on a hill. A pyramid. The hushed reverence for the dead spirals out of control to establish these odd fabrications of rock and clay. There is something beautiful in that. But also something very, very lonely.

*

I am beginning to understand that Ho is a very odd boy. I never required thanks after I took him on, only discipline. That he seems as aloof as a cat is fine with me. He is a beautiful child, his dark-gold skin not yet hardened into the tawny hide of these mountain dwellers. The future awaits. He does not limp or scowl or weep at night, at least that I know. May his dreams carry him off through the dark.

There are worse places for dreams, I suppose. I imagine myself at his age, caught in this vile nightmare. How would I have stood up to the test? It is not a thought I like to contemplate. These children are amazingly tough and have earned my silent reverence. What did my father use to say? Children are the heritage of the Lord.

*

While I am thinking about it I will tell you about another encounter you might rightly call absurd. It was on a warm, overcast day in April of that same year, 1937, just over a year ago, though in memory it belongs to a different century. I was walking toward the Gran Vía in good spirits. The unit by then was collecting and distributing between one-half and three-quarters of a gallon of blood per day, and, on average, performing three transfusions in either Madrid or the hills north of the city. I had left the clinic before the usual hour, giving myself an extra few minutes to pick out a gift for your mother. What I had planned for that afternoon, beyond the purchase, was a brief shortwave radio address. The demands on my time were enormous then, but the address would be transmitted to North America and therefore be well worth the effort. It was, of course, an exercise relating to the war. I had been approached by the Spanish government, through the Ministry of War, and had agreed to their request.

We'd returned only the day before from the front lines near Guadalajara, forty miles northeast, where we had photographed bridges, roads and various other points of interest as regards communications. This trip alone would give me ample fodder for my radio address. But so would Madrid, I remember thinking. I could talk about the indiscriminate bombing of its neighbourhoods and the wanton killing of innocent women and children. It was known that the Fascist bombs falling over Madrid carried, as well as high explosives, hundreds of rounds of ammunition, much like the French 75 mm shells of the Great War, in order to inflict as many civilian casualties as possible. Too many times I had seen the angelic, blood-spattered faces of children. Too many times had their small, crushed bodies been placed before me on my operating tables.

I would say this was no longer war as we had once known it to be. The Fascist war was directed at the women and children of this great society. If you were once neutral, believing this an isolated struggle between two abstractions, the carnage *demanded* that you think again. Ours was a struggle against a murderous machine that would not stop killing until the machine itself was destroyed. I remember how your mother's thinking had begun to influence my own. This was a fight against nihilism, I would say, a fight for the very existence of hope. The machine was run by the mad dictators Hitler and Mussolini and Franco. Never before in history had the nations of the world had so much at stake. Never before had these nations been so united against such bloodthirsty fanaticism.

Apart from a single patrol plane flying over the city that afternoon, the atmosphere was calm and relaxed. Buses ran, the cafés were busy, the streets alive with workers on their way home for the afternoon siesta. The street I walked along, Valverde Street, was relatively quiet. The clock at the top of the Telefónica building, which had just come into view, read one-thirty. Up there, beside the clock, two men stood with a 20 mm AA Oerlikon gun, waiting for the next group of Heinkels or the big Italian Capronis to power in from the south. For a moment the war might have been a thousand miles off. The smell of cooking meat and olive oil and wood and coal-burning fires filled the air. Seeing and smelling this I realized I hadn't eaten that day, and, wondering if I might steal ten minutes out of my schedule, I saw the green door of a restaurant, with *El Escondido* stencilled over the big plate-glass window, open directly across from me. A man staggered out, bleeding from a cut above his eye and supported by two others dressed in black leather jackets. Another man followed. These three looked to be of the same ilk as those who had harassed me on my first day here—overeager, bored, stupid brutes.

Of course, it was quite possible that the man they'd apprehended was of legitimate political interest; yet it was just as likely, elaborating from my own experience, that he had failed to sneer deeply enough, or spit in disgust, when speaking of Fascism, or that an acquaintance with some axe to grind had denounced him as a member of the Fifth Column. When they put him in the car idling at the curb, they were careful to push his head down gently, almost gingerly, under the rim of the open door. It was an oddly caring gesture. I looked into the man's eyes as his head went under. Then all the doors closed and the car started off down the street, stopped briefly for traffic, turned left and was gone.

A half block up along the Gran Vía I found the perfume shop that had been recommended to me. I made my purchase quickly enough, scented with lavender and mint, and was again on my way. Another ten minutes of walking brought me to the address I was looking for, an old building adjacent to a small dirt square and a crater hole covered over in planking. There was a hardware store and a small café at street level. I followed the stairs up to the third floor and knocked at number 3D. The door was opened by a thin, pale young man who looked terribly deprived of sleep, with large dark circles under his eyes. He introduced himself as Paco, then led me down a long hallway to a large room, where I met the producer of the radio program. Jorge looked to be in his mid-thirties, and he asked me how I was, if I'd had any trouble finding the place, then offered me a glass of wine. It was their lunchtime, he said, and would I join them? He produced a loaf of bread and a wheel of cheese from under a desk. His English was precise but very accented. His reading skills, he explained, were superior to his conversational ones. "We have time to eat something," he said, and gestured at the control panel behind him. "I will explain this later. Please sit."

He cut pieces of cheese from the wheel and laid them out on a plate. He did this very delicately and rapidly. His thin fingers shook only slightly and he moved them quickly so I wouldn't notice that he no longer had fingernails. They'd been bitten down to nothing. I had seen this many times in Madrid. His voice was smooth and clear, and after dividing the cheese he pulled a large red sausage from a bag under his desk, then slid the sausage and knife over the desk. His colleague joined us, and we tore the stick of bread into three pieces. I was very hungry, I told them, and would have eaten something on Valverde Street but for the commotion I'd witnessed at the restaurant, the man being taken away.

"Do you think they were police?" I asked. "They put him in a car and drove him off."

"Yes. Probably."

"What do they do to these men?"

He put a finger-gun to his temple and pulled the trigger.

"He didn't look like a spy."

"Tell me," he said, "what does a spy look like?"

"But what if he's a cook or a dishwasher, just any man?"

"Then he has a big problem. But if he has nothing to hide, a release will be granted—unless they shoot him before they understand their mistake."

When we finished eating we turned our attention to the business at hand. I spoke my address into the radio-microphone. It went well, though my hands shook as I read from my notes. Afterwards Jorge thanked me, and assured me I shouldn't worry so much about innocent men getting into trouble. Naturally, there would always be casualties of this sort. Still, walking home, I couldn't help but wonder about the man I'd seen being ushered into the car, the hand tucking him in so gently. The restaurant on Valverde Street was quiet now. Only a few old men were there. It all looked very normal.

★

I remember digging in the dirt as a boy. I suppose that's not so unusual. Girls skip rope, boys get themselves dirty any way they can. So there I was, digging a hole and putting a cat down there and covering it up with a sheet of wood. This old tom was more trusting than your average cat and didn't seem to mind. I put him in, slid the plywood over his head and heard a few meows, but that was it. The hole was a foot or so deep. On such a hot day he might even have enjoyed the coolness. There was room enough for a cat twice his size to circle around, roll over and have a nice nap. A few minutes later I pulled the wood away and bent down to haul him up into the sunlight. The look he gave me made me feel very stupid, the typical cat look laden with boredom. He was through doing me favours. Then he lifted up his tail, showing me his hindquarters, and sauntered off.

Well, today I remembered that episode because the tunnel your mother and I got trapped in has been winding through my dreams these last few nights. I am thinking about it now, and what strikes me is how long we were down there and how different everything seemed to me. Of course, I found out exactly how long and how different when it was all over, but just then it was difficult to tell. I remember thinking there was no such thing as time down there, and no such person as Norman Bethune. It was a strange feeling. We walked for what seemed hours, these odd thoughts circling round in my head and doubling back again. Being underground can play tricks on your perceptions. I have never been fond of it. Being underground strikes me as very unnatural. We walked forever, it seemed. Your mother and I didn't talk much. I suppose we were a bit too outside ourselves for words. We passed through doors and small rooms of no description, mostly empty except for discarded construction tools and gardening implements, shovels and pickaxes and so on, and then I began to wonder if it was possible to die down here in this maze of darkness with this beautiful stranger. Could these tunnels loop back upon themselves? Had that necropolis represented more than the memory of the dead?

We felt the walls and on we walked, using the flame only when we became unsure of our footing or when we found another door.

Your mother reached for my hand in the dark. I couldn't help smiling. The world was ending and here I was, smiling because a pretty girl was holding my hand. The Lord's mysterious ways, as my mother would say. I felt the walls with the other hand, reading them as I read the inside of an open chest or abdomen. Now we were inside the entrails, and here I was smiling. I said, "Light, please," and your mother lit up the cup of her hand, and then the lighter failed and the darkness grew deeper. I stopped. "Try again," I said, but that was the end of our seeing. Neither of us let go of the other's hand from that point on, and my smile fell away. After twenty paces I tripped over a shovel, almost bringing her down with me. Ten paces farther, I tripped over a bag of sand. We rounded a corner, then another, and finally stumbled onto more stairs, at the top of which was a storage room with a vertical sliver of light showing in the corner of a door at the far end. When I pushed the door open, dimly lit stairs and a handrail led us up to where the grey morning flashed before us. We had walked under the city to the Retiro Park, a distance of some ten or twelve blocks.

We stood in the early-morning light blinking at the Crystal Palace, a great glass structure set near the west end of the grounds and empty but for the light filtering through its panes. No one else was present. The park was ours. In the heart of the city, volunteers and Civil Defence teams were looking for survivors and extracting the dead from heaps of rubble. But we saw only ginkgo and birch and plane trees, benches and sky, tree sparrows and chickadees and white wagtails watching us from their branches. Behind us, encompassing the door we had emerged from, was a large rock garden on the edge of a small, mist-covered pond in front of the palace. The ducks floating on its calm surface were still sleeping, heads tucked under their wings. After the tunnels, the air was fresh. We saw no planes, no wisps of smoke from the bombings. The sky was quiet. Testing the door, we pushed through and stood there in the Crystal Palace and toasted with imaginary champagne an imaginary end of the war. It is something I thought you should know, and something to think about, that the first night I spent with your mother was under a burning city.

★

This morning I was awakened by the sound of shuffling outside my hut. The boots making most of it belonged to five Japanese prisoners as ragged and hungry and young as the Chinese escorting them past my door. It is hard to imagine such men committing themselves to this wicked enterprise without being grossly coerced and manipulated. I cannot explain it, how people and nations rise up in the name of evil. I can tell you for certain, though, that these Japanese boys come not from the wealthy families of the generals and robber-barons they fight for here but from the unemployed and working classes they've been tricked into fighting against. On both sides, it is a sad waste of youth.

I have been thinking lately how to express my thoughts, not simply my needs, to Ho. I'm sure he is a clever boy in his own language. Jean Ewen—the nurse here (before she left)—told me only that he had family in Yan'an and enjoyed reciting the poems of Liu Bang of the Han Dynasty. It goes without saying that I'm unfamiliar with Han Dynasty poetry, so at least in my eyes, this marks this youngster as special. The things we don't know perhaps impress us more than they should. Be that as it may, his practical abilities are what make the difference. With a straight razor, for example. On Sunday mornings the young poet sits me down and applies a steaming towel to my face with the strict authority of a Turkish barber. A smoother shave I have never known. Without a word he flutters about my head like a pigeon on a statue, efficiently hacking off a week's worth of grey whiskers. In all this time—nine months and counting—I am relieved to report that he has never drawn blood, not so much as a nick or scratch. It is difficult now, tonight, as I exhaust this ribbon of its voice, to imagine a time when my beard could do without his clever, wordless razor.

★

It occurs to me, before we proceed any further, that you might be interested to know something of the Bethune history. Let me assure you that it is not my intention to speak harshly of anyone in this family, least of all your paternal grandfather. But let me say also that fairness and truth shall reign, that is my promise to you. He was, in the end, only a man; and, as such, his decent character and natural goodness waged a silent war with the anger he carried within him. Over time that war spread, as does this present war in China, to consume the life and thoughts of his older son, your absent father.

My mother and father were introduced in 1883 in Hawaii— that flowery paradise so unlike these sparse mountains—by the charismatic preacher of a church that had wrenched her all the way from Plymouth to do its Christian work, namely, to bring salvation to the heathens. Apparently it did not take my father, a traveller in search of business opportunities, long to see the light as well. A coconut might have fallen from a nearby tree, or perhaps a bird sang hidden somewhere in its palm fronds, a sign to a young man looking to change his fortunes. We can only imagine.

I am told that my father, Malcolm Nicolson Bethune, a Canadian, timidly shook the hand of the evangelical English missionary Elizabeth Ann Goodwin in that paradise on earth, by then an Eden in decline, an island of lost promise. That he took her hand, made her his, and that together they sailed for Canada.

But did my dear mother know what she was getting into? Knowing her as only a son can, now an adult older and wiser than the innocent evangelist she was then, and bracketed by my own failures in love that we'll get to later, I can only answer that no, she did not. It is true that her tutelage only strengthened my father's sanctimony. He was a machine waiting to be tooled, to be sure. But did she know to what extent he would embrace this new salvation? My mother, I believe, lived to regret it.

Once married and back home, in the village of Gravenhurst, Ontario, he became minister of the Knox Presbyterian Church at number 315 Muskoka Road, though in the years to come we would move constantly. This is where your father comes into the picture. A village known as the sawdust city, Gravenhurst smelled of amputated trees and manure. But its greatest promise, this new job, was my father's rock-solid guarantee of a lifetime of rectitude. He was respected, as were all men of the cloth in his day, and both feared and hated by all but the most forgiving of souls.

His father before him—whose profession and name, Henry Norman Bethune, I proudly share—was, in 1850 in Toronto, a founding member of the Trinity College Medical School, a good man and a disappointed father. I never heard that truth spoken openly and neither will you, but at the age of seven I saw in his eyes, as his fingers delicately picked at the tired sheets, the regret of a defeated man. After he died they tied his jaw shut with a red handkerchief and took him away: my first experience of death. His secret grief soon became my silent companion. And your grandfather, my dad, was free to do as he pleased, now that the only authority on this earth greater than his had been silenced forever.

My father was a sedentary, slow-moving man. We lived in a quiet house. I recall the nature of his fierce concentration, which the whole house was taught to respect, and those moments when he would emerge from his study and stare off into space. It always seemed to me that he was plotting some exquisite *coup de grâce* against all the unbelievers surrounding him. He was a strong man, both of body and spirit, though as I recall his only two forms of physical exercise—the first powered by a steady stride, the second by those unaccountably gnarled fists—were his twice daily walks to church and the vigorous thrashings he doled out to his children.

I was carefree before the troubles between me and my father began. We were well loved and warm and fed, my siblings and I, and in this silence I now thank my mother and father for basic comforts that in those days we all took for granted. I can say we benefited from the favours that came to the family of a respected man of God. I suppose you might even argue that God has not failed me in that sense. In fact, I'll admit that I enjoyed time spent with my father. So you see, it was not all fire and brimstone. I took pride in his strength and the respect he commanded in town and enjoyed the family histories he regaled us with as we gathered by the kitchen fire on a cold winter's night. He was at times a warm man, and he held us close in his big arms as he told stories of the world he'd seen before crossing over to the Lord—of Hawaii and the prairies of Canada, the Maritime provinces and other places he'd been to and ultimately renounced for the small world we now inhabited. The Lord was All and All was the Lord, he would say, Amen. What a grand spectacle and delight was Creation. You will see it one day, God willing, he would say. Our mother looked on, a contented woman at those times, I'm sure, busying herself with needle and thread or reading Shakespeare and Ibsen and Saint Theresa. These were fine moments, and to this day I cherish their memory.

My mother, a woman of great imagination, never failed to encourage the natural curiosity that was brewing deep down inside me. She left books on my bedside table and two or three days later would sit with me and listen patiently as I described the adventures of Tom Sawyer or Jim Hawkins or White Fang. Evenings, when the house was quiet, you would find her reading at the kitchen table over a cup of tea, as I was in my bedroom, the covers pulled to my chin. We were both very bookish then. I still remember the magic spell a volume from her evangelical days cast over me, a large, musty old thing that told the story of a Catholic missionary's travels through Mongolia. She hadn't said a word about it, but one evening I found it under my pillow. There was no telling what my father would have thought of all those Catholics and Buddhists traipsing through the clouds together; it was best not to invite scrutiny. She was eager, I think, to have me pick up where she left off. The world of the mind, of travel, of good works. The great world awaited me, as it had awaited her in her day, in all its glory and sin, before motherhood overcame her.

ENVELOPE TWO

I should tell you that my scientific nature began to manifest itself at an early age. I wonder if we will have that in common, this interest in the workings of the natural world. For my tenth birthday I was given a jackknife, so I suppose my parents had me figured out by then. My experiments with this handy tool were in the beginning barely a step ahead of the frog hunting and ant burning of my peers. But one day, early the following summer, the single most important idea of my young life leapt out at me from the bony cavity of a battered and eyeless gull—at first glance no different from any other dead animal, yet my interest in it would fire the opening salvo in the war between father and son.

We were living in Owen Sound then, a small community northwest of Toronto that clings for life to the southern tip of Georgian Bay. It was lovely and wild, the bay, changing from day to day, hour to hour, its rocky edge a rich playground of delight and discovery for a boy my age. It seemed to me possessed by rebellious spirits I couldn't help but identify with. I felt its moods, I believed, and it felt mine. Such was my fanciful imagination. In any case, it was a sunny afternoon, with only a spot of cloud hanging in the east. The bird was nestled snugly in an open tomb of cracked shale and warped driftwood and pulsating with maggots. I recall the feeling that overcame me, even now as I write, so many years later—the feeling of something turning inside me, some new and unusual consciousness. I cannot say what it was in this animal that coaxed such trembling from my fingertips, such pure excitement. Perhaps overnight I had turned the right age to finally appreciate the breadth of my world and its unsubtle avian tragedies. Whatever the reason, it was as if a thunderbolt had struck me between the eyes. I realized in an instant that I was completely alone in the world, and that all that my father had taught us about the Good Book and angels and the Resurrection was lies.

After hacking at it with my jackknife, I decided not to bury the bird behind the cedar woodpile, pray for it or utter a child's fairy tale of last rites, as I usually did. No, I left it right where I'd found it and visited it day after day, watching it wither before my eyes. I didn't study the bird's inner workings but instead focused on its descent into nothingness. It was a remarkable experience, for my curiosity burned with the meaning of life itself.

Every day the gull grew smaller and the maggots grew fatter and more numerous, and then it was the maggots' turn to die. One day, it stood to reason, my turn would come. Before the next rainstorm the bird was no more than a hollow shack of bones and feathers. For so long my quiet neighbourhood, including that rocky shoreline, had been ruled by my father's silent God; and now, suddenly, it was not. I fail to describe adequately the force such a revelation had on my young mind. Perhaps one day you will have such a moment yourself and understand what I am talking about.

*

One early evening, at the end of a glorious summer's day, the dinner bell rang. As we took our seats at the kitchen table, I felt somehow that my life was about to change, that poor bird doubtless having prepared me for the impending confrontation. My father's sharp hands formed a spire in front of his face. His moustache back then was as bushy as a raccoon's tail. "Let us pray," he said, and we did.

> *O Divine Master, grant that I may not so much*
> *seek to be consoled as to console,*
> *not so much to be understood as to understand,*
> *not so much to be loved as to love;*
> *for it is in giving that we receive,*
> *it is in pardoning that we are pardoned,*
> *it is in dying that we awake to eternal life.*

He then asked God to bless our food, and continued with a brief prayer for each of us, speaking our names in the tired crescendo I knew so well from his sermons. The secret I held—the second, really, the first being that look in my dying grandfather's eyes—had practically throbbed against the bones in my skinny chest as we spoke the words of Saint Francis of Assisi. We prayed along with my father—myself, mother, brother and sister—and when we finished we offered a humble Amen, then set to eating our chicken and green beans and potatoes—a meal I remember so clearly—in silent gratitude.

I don't pretend to blame him for the violence that followed. My impertinence and love of words often outran my deference and good sense in those days, and this is something I have trouble with from time to time even now. Clearing my throat, I put down my fork and knife and stood. "Father, say a farmer's son has no taste for his father's rutabagas—what then?" My family looked up from their plates.

"Well, then, he eats carrots," said my sister, Janet, rather sensibly.

"Norman, sit down, please," my father said.

Vexed, I refused. "Nor carrots! What if he doesn't like carrots either!"

What I was trying to say—and eventually did—was that one was not required to love vegetables simply because one's father earned his living farming the fields, and though a boy's father was the minister of the church in a certain small town, he himself might be right in considering Jesus less real than a rutabaga or carrot.

My heart racing, I glowed with defiance and pride. My father's face turned pale as a sheet, then flashed bright red. His eyes narrowed. He rose like thunder from the head of the table, slammed a fist down against it—upsetting the plates and glasses—and seized my right ear in his other spade-like hand. The rest of me followed out the door and was soon sprawled upon the ground. It was a hot evening. The squirrels chattering in the overhead branches fell silent. My mother stood in the doorway, young Malcolm and Janet under either arm. None moved to help me but I could not blame them, either then or now. This was my battle.

Well, he was too angry to do anything but push my face into the ground and hold it there, grinding. It wasn't much of a fight, and I won't hide the fact that I began to cry. He lowered his mouth to my ear—this deaf one, the left—and I could feel his hot breath on my skin. I suspect it was here he saw himself for what he had become, a brute, a bully, a man who would smite a child, and he began sobbing. "Children are the heritage of the Lord," I heard him say as he collapsed over me. My mother rushed forward and lifted him off, then took me in her arms and wept and begged for mercy for her injured family. She held me, and together we wept like saplings snapped in a storm.

★

The little things you remember—sometimes it amazes me. Today Ho walked past my door with a crate of empty bottles of some sort or other, and that sound got me to thinking about Spain. This was how we got blood up to the front, after we packed the bottles in ice in the back of the Ford. I don't think I ever consciously listened to that sound at the time, but now I can remember it so clearly. After the first few trips we found ice was more reliable than the Electrolux refrigeration units I'd brought down from London. Sometimes we would stop the Ford on the way up the Guadarrama Pass, which separates the provinces of Madrid and Segovia, and there, just shy of the summit, cool the bottles in one of the streams that ran down the south face of the sierra, while we waded barefoot under the bony pines.

After thinking about it for some time I have decided that in war, the lucky man is one who has something of a serene resignation regarding his fate. It is not whether he lives or dies but that he knows he has no choice in the matter that makes the difference. That should make things a great deal easier. I'm certainly not saying I don't care one way or the other, only that death out here is too random to think otherwise. I don't want to scare you, or myself. I fully intend to keep my head down. But I suppose I am resigned, as much as is possible. You see it in the eyes of the partisans here. I think they know, each of them, that the end of the day belongs to chance. I am aware of that resignation in their eyes, since I see it every day; it is so very close to an absence, I think, that I often find myself looking again to see if I'm understanding it quite right. Well, the truth is that a man prepares himself for death up here, and the faster he does it the better off he is. That's all well and good, at least when you're surrounded by people who are out to kill you, but the nihilism your mother spoke of had claimed a part of all of us in Spain in a way it does not in China. One does not hear of suicide in China, nor is there much drunkenness. I can't say why we feel differently about it here, and perhaps this is only my own bias showing through.

In Spain I saw many men fail to find the resignation I'm talking about. You saw it when a man took his own life so that another was denied the pleasure of doing it for him. I think alcohol also helped, though it did not stop you from getting killed. I knew that well enough from my time in the Great War. Regarding matters of life and death, some men wore a strange nobility and patience, which others characterized as madness or ignorance. Some died with the fervour of the righteous. Others sought their death with a blind fury. Some didn't care either way, and those were the fortunate ones. Very few mentioned a wish to speak of God or other spiritual matters, and none asked for last communion as this was frowned upon mightily. The common expression of the time was I s——t on God or I s——t on the Virgin or I s——t in the Milk of the Virgin. I was shocked by the blasphemy at first, but in times like those you get used to so many things so very quickly.

Fewer men died after we got the clinic up and running in Madrid, a consolation I try to remember, but we were only a small group. The ones we were not able to get to lay awake and lucid as they watched their own blood spill into the earth and soak it with curious indifference and puddle deep, as if a storm of black rain had passed unseen over their heads. Many of them lay murmuring with their faces to the ground and their thoughts consumed by the furious negotiating of the dying, which on occasion you heard coming across the fields: O That I May Live One Day More, O That I Do Not Die. But this negotiation rarely prevailed, and the earth grew darker and the negotiating more frenzied. Then gradually it grew fainter, and soon there was little thinking and no negotiating, just the quiet calm of resignation as thunder and chaos pealed through the sky. Sometimes a gentle hand came out of nowhere, really, to close the eyes of the dead. When this hand failed to appear the eyes were left open to stare blankly upon the streaked ground, and some men were carried to me in this fashion, confused with those wounded but still alive.

The strange slowness of the fighting continued through February and March of 1937. We were a besieged city. The fighting at the western edge of the capital continued and we went to it almost every day. If a man fell to the earth to escape a raking of fire he might choose to close with his thumbs the sightless eyes of the fallen man beside him, if he himself believed this simple kindness might come in line with his own private negotiations with fate, this respect for the dead as payment in lieu of one's own death. But in fact there were very few men who still believed the dead could be abused or desecrated any further, and so the many who had yet to die fought on, mindless of the bodies piling up on the landscape, and instead turned their thoughts to survival, not salvation. I did not blame them one bit.

Wars never go hungry. There were always new men coming to this one—Americans, Poles, Czechs, Germans, Italians, Canadians, Britons, Dutch, each man committed to defending the legally elected government of the Spanish Republic. The war attracted the intellectuals of the world, of all classes and professions. Foreign professors fought shoulder to shoulder with local farmers. In village squares throughout the country men gathered to collect a rifle and armband and listen to an oration by a town leader, or perhaps a radio address, and organized themselves into units, and all the while believed their numbers and weapons and brotherhood were sufficient. They were moved forward singing and hopeful to meet with their brothers, whom they would assist and from whom they would inherit the worst of the fighting, and the capital would quickly enough hear of their gallantry and from tavern to tavern up and down the land their names might spread. One evening it would slip under a creaking old door back home and alert a sister or mother or father, pride and overwhelming gratitude filling the house like the arrival of a new baby, neighbours hearing of how well the boy had done in the fighting. Such thoughts were harboured in many a chest as men sat in trenches only two hundred yards distant from those who would kill each and every one of them if they should be so lucky.

*

It is late. In under four hours I will be back in the operating theatre and I will now try to sleep. But let me leave you with this thought: I wonder if, in time of war, anything can be as vivid as the imagination, anything so clear and riveting as a man's thoughts at the moment he draws his last breath. It has sharpened my own, I can say that, even through this exhaustion. I saw it over and over again in Spain—not those thoughts, no, but the men those thoughts inhabit or haunt. The imagination journeys longest when the body is tense with fear, when someone unseen lies in wait. It dreams of a moonlit dance and melancholy loves and gathers meaning and significance where before there was none. A spontaneous word, a wisp of hair—in normal life a moment gone almost before it was fully noticed. Yet only a short drive north, scattered over miles of front line and dead-dog gullies and scrub deserts of sharp mountainous terrain, the silent dreams of men took wing. It is in the silence hanging over the land that you find what is worth fighting for. Sainthoods are here for the taking.

★

Early July. The sound of insects fills the sky. China seemed a lovely country today, and so, too, on this night. We had a beautiful afternoon and early evening, and the darkness now chatters with an abundance of life that remains hidden until dark falls and then, all of a sudden, surprises you with its forceful insistence. I'm watching the faintest streak of orange-red sunset retreat beyond the eastern face of the Wu-t'ai Mountains. It is a spectacular drama—the light crawls back over miles of rock in the space of time it takes me to write this sentence. From here it's half the length of my forefinger, yet it holds within its embers the light of millions of years. That will give you a sense of the size of this country and the small place we occupy in it.

We have moved shop to General Nieh's headquarters in Wutaishan. General Nieh is the Divisional Commander of the Communist Eighth Route Army, one of the key military forces in this war against the Japanese. Conditions are generally better here than up in Shensi, where we spent some miserable weeks this past winter. General Nieh is a fine man and spares no effort in securing what medical supplies and funding he is able to for me and my assistants. I still have great concerns regarding the lack of trained medical staff. I have been sending letters back home, hoping to raise awareness, because we need all the attention we can get. Today I finished an article for *The Manchester Guardian*. Ho will send it tomorrow. With its proceeds I intend to reduce for the Chinese the burden of keeping me on, though I claim no more rations than anyone else. How I would like to pay my way! Every cent counts.

We are presently camped at the edge of a small stream whose name Mr. Tung, my translator, told me, but I've forgotten it. I find its splashing calming after these last few terrible days. I have dark circles under my eyes and am no more than skin and bone. I am told to rest more. Of course I should. This is because my nerves are showing. God help these people! The Chinese are too polite and obedient to say anything to me. They are a deferential race in the extreme but all so incredibly devoted to our work that it pains me when I'm short with them and bully them perhaps a little more than is necessary. Each man and woman pulls his or her own weight and then some. I should be grateful for that. Yet I push and push and push. It's uplifting and gratifying to see how much they give, but often I am too forceful and too angry. Nerves and exhaustion and a short temper by nature, I suppose, and these late nights with you, though you're scarcely to blame for that! Well, this trickling stream helps. Anyway, we are hunkered down here with time enough, it seems, to return to the story I want to tell you.

Why *am* I writing? I'm so very busy, and I ask myself this question night after night. I ask it now. I know it is not to spout political slogans for you or to claim idealistic affiliations. None of those may make any sense to you by the time you read this. They're just words, after all, and I'm aware that words change or lose their meaning. What do you think, for example, when I write the words "justice" and "society" and "democracy"? They are often used these days, and so they should be. But will they mean anything to you twenty or forty years on? Probably not, and maybe that's for the better. Maybe there will no longer be any need of them. Maybe we will have accomplished what we set out to do. When my dear old mother raised me we had no such words. She said only, Do unto him, Norman, as you would have him do unto you. You see how complicated this has become?

I remember thinking this on a particular day in Montreal. I had just returned home from a full night and day at Sacre-Coeur Hospital. Not long out of my marriage, I passed before the hallway mirror and glimpsed a tired and conflicted man. I was taken with the desire to examine my heart. Do unto him, I thought. The odd thing was that I didn't know what it was I was in need of. I saw traces of my wife, Frances, wherever I looked. A portrait of her I had painted during our days in Detroit. A novel I had read aloud to her years before. An old Eaton's chair, worn, comfortable and entirely out of place. I found blame and regret in each of these, but no connection to myself. Soon, too exhausted to continue, I switched on the shortwave radio hoping to catch the opera from London and thus calm myself before bed. Do unto him, I thought, as you would have him do unto you. This seemed to me a baffling riddle.

But the signal did not come clear. I picked up the crackling transmitter, shifted it, shook it, held it upside-down. I practically stood on my head to get a proper sound out of that rickety old box. In fact I put myself into all sorts of contortions trying to coax the signal but still nothing came through, just a crackling, hissing blur. Do unto him, I thought. Finally I leaned out the window, hoping this might help, and it was then that I heard through the background noise the terrible news of war in Spain.

★

Tonight I am thinking about your mother and that morning she and I emerged from those tunnels. It was almost as if the war had ended for me, as if the world *had* changed, for the better, as well as something inside me. Soon, when I could manage, between surgeries in various neighbourhoods and trenches and running the administrative affairs at the clinic, we began sharing our nights together in hotel rooms not far from where those bombs had first driven us underground.

We stayed at the Hotel Santander, a fourth-floor pension with a lift that sank noticeably when you stepped into it, then creaked and popped as the cables over your head dragged you up through the building's sour old innards. The pension smelled of the woodsmoke that rose from the chimneys in the neighbourhood, of bleach, of the lentils brewing in the family kitchen down the hall where a radio played most of the day behind a beaded curtain. It smelled of hand-rolled cigarettes, of oil paints and turpentine and of coffee brought up from the bar downstairs.

In the morning we would walk east on Huertas or on Cervantes Street to the Plaza Cánovas del Castillo, where we'd part with a discreet touch. Smiling, I'd walk past sandbagged fountains, uprooted cobblestones, blown-out buildings. I was a man in love. I remember your mother's scent following me as I joined the bustle along the Paseo del Prado and then slipped into the quiet Retiro Park to walk past its shimmering, steaming ponds, among its trees and morning strollers, thinking what a gift the world was to those who chose to see, and up I walked to the Crystal Palace and Vergara Street on the other side of the park, where the clinic and its empty bottles and cold syringes awaited me.

Early in March your mother had taken the paints and brushes and canvas from one of the studios at the Prado where the restorers had worked before the war began. That month the fighting at the western fringes of the city went on without stop, but the city itself often fell quiet and we could almost pretend the war never was. On nights such as those she sat in the chair by the window overlooking the street and allowed me to resume my work on her portrait. She said the restorers had abandoned their work after the first bomb punched a hole through the roof of the seventeenth-century Italian Room. "No one else is using them," she said. "So I thought, 'Happy Birthday, Norman.'"

I dragged my thumb over the bristles and said, "Forty-eight years old."

They were excellent brushes. I hadn't held a paintbrush since coming over to Europe.

"What about this?" she said, pulling the blanket from the bed and draping it over her shoulders. It was past midnight.

"I like it."

The blanket slipped to reveal a perfect white shoulder.

"You'd rather stick to saving lives?" she said.

"I prefer the artist's life."

She waited before saying, "Wrong war, then."

I found a piece of charcoal in the tin of paints and used it to begin sketching. "In what war was the painting any better than this?"

"There must have been one. The Napoleonic, maybe."

"Goya liked that one. Shoulder, please."

She adjusted the blanket.

"This lighting's too romantic," I said. "Too many shadows. Turn your head a little. A little to the left."

"We can't have people thinking you're a romantic, can we?"

"I would certainly be ruined."

"So would I," she said.

★

The war always came back soon enough. You'd almost have forgotten it, then the sound of planes would come over the city. Usually it was difficult to tell how many. We got a better sense when the bombs started falling. You'd hear them out there, even if they were falling up in the north end near the Estrecho metro stop.

"Three or four," she said the first night I took her up with me.

"More than that," I said.

Then she said, "I'll bet that's Cuatro Caminos."

"I'll take you to a shelter. Then I'll go up there."

"I want to see it."

"It's nothing to see," I said.

When she insisted we left the hotel and walked to Sol and flagged down a truck carrying eight or ten boys from one of the Socialist youth groups. This is a memory that troubles me still. They circled around, waiting for a raid, then went up there with picks and shovels and buckets and dug people out of the rubble. I told them I was a doctor. They gave us a hand up. The driver took Alcalá Street to Recoletos and turned on Raimundo. It was a fifteen-minute drive. The city was dark, no lights whatsoever, and felt abandoned, dark and quiet but for the far-off pounding in a distant neighbourhood. We drove in silence. There were very few vehicles on the roads.

Continuing up Raimundo Street we saw a glowing mist rising over a horizon of squat buildings. It became a leaping mass of flames a little way up Bravo Murillo. The planes were gone now but had set a dozen buildings afire. There was only the sound of the fires and gas explosions and the confusion of people crying and screaming. Teams were already going through the wreckage. The boys we'd ridden with started clearing rubble with their pickaxes and shovels. When they pulled away part of a wall of a music store they found a small girl pinned under a piano and bookshelf and rough wood beams. She was not conscious. A man came and claimed her as his daughter, calling her name again and again. The flames from the burning buildings glowed off the piano top like a candelabra. The man finally permitted us to move his daughter to the aid station two blocks up Bravo Murillo, where she died just before first light.

By then the fires were under control. The rest of the wounded had been taken to hospitals around the city. I would see them later in the day as I made my rounds. I often visited ten or twelve hospitals per day. On a side street up Bravo Murillo I saw Kajsa sitting on the curb beside an old woman. I walked down and waited just out of earshot. The old woman was rolling rosary beads between her fingers. They would be worn to nothing before the end of the war. The morning light filtered through the blue smoke of the smouldering fires. The whole neighbourhood seemed shrouded in the deep blue light of an old forest.

I waited for your mother to finish comforting the woman, then we walked back to the centre of town. Away from there, the city was back to normal. Cafés rolled open their shutters, jewellers and fruit-sellers swept their storefront sidewalks. Automobiles and military vehicles drove through the streets without urgency. The sky was clean and pure again. You wouldn't have known there was a war on for a thousand miles in any direction.

That is what it was like to live in a besieged city. The war flew in upon us from the front lines and from the Nationalist airfields to the south, most often at night, but also first thing, or at midday, or at the hour of the siesta or the afternoon stroll. Sometimes it was predictable. Three or four days running the same three planes came overhead, the Italian Capronis, each marked with its identification number under the left wing. They cut the sky in perfect thirds. These were men of ritual. Other times seemed to bring no pattern to the brutality. After a stretch of quiet days the bombs always fell again.

Kajsa found more paint. No one would miss it, she said. Occasionally she went down to the Prado to pick up the new announcement posters from the printing presses in one of the basements there. She was always going, always busy. During the day she worked with the prostitutes in the same Madrid neighbourhoods that we went to at night when the planes came. I thought you might like to know that she gave of herself in this world.

★

One day the room smelled of figs that she'd bought on the steps of the San Miguel market from a little old man, she said, "who subsists on bread and water. He probably eats scraps gathered up from abandoned market stalls. Maybe a few of his own figs. And he's made happy with a couple of extra centimos."

"Do you deny him that?" I asked. Your mother seemed troubled, and I couldn't understand why.

No, she did not. In fact she'd emptied her purse into his hand.

He shook his head, she told me. "No, no. Not that much. Only three of these," he said, picking out the coins, "only this."

When she insisted he grew angry. He began to shout, "I am no beggar! The pretty American believes I am a beggar!" Every beautiful foreigner in Madrid was thought to be an American.

She told me this as I sat on the bed eating the old man's figs. It was something that troubled your mother more than I was able to understand at the time.

"Spanish pride," she concluded.

How would he have seen her, that old man, I wondered, this beautiful "American" in the midst of all that chaos? He would not have seen condescension in her, or pity. That was not possible. Your mother was a generous soul. She stopped people in the street. She asked questions. The smile she wore, and her soft brown eyes, perfect comprehension, would have revealed that this woman's proffered gift was a simple, pure, muted gesture. I cannot imagine otherwise.

"I suppose you could be his daughter," I said. "He would not take alms from his daughter. That would make him weak."

The figs sat in their paper cone on the night table. In the street below we could hear the neighbourhood beginning its ritual evening stroll.

"The street's filling up. Do you want to go down for a walk?"

"I don't even remember why I'm here," she said.

I rolled a cigarette and lit it. "I don't believe that." It was a cool evening. I opened the ceiling-high double windows. The crowds streamed by below. "You know more about it than I do."

"Maybe I'm just worn down," she said.

"I think that's it."

"I'm dizzy a lot. Spells."

"Headaches?"

"No," she said.

I checked her. I knelt down before her and looked into her eyes. They were not so different from those I looked into a hundred times a day.

"Exhaustion," I said. "Stress. Tell me if it gets worse."

★

That night we were awakened in the dark by the sound of a single rifle shot, not very far off. Perhaps a block up the street. We lay together, silently, listening, waiting for the night's emptiness to return. I wasn't able to sleep after that and I just kept waiting, but there was no second shot. I rose from the bed and sat in the dark beside the half-finished portrait near the window. I rolled a pinch of tobacco into the small yellow paper and smoked and looked down at the street below, waiting for someone to pass. She didn't speak but watched me watch the empty street. I wondered what had made her say that, about her not remembering why she'd come. She couldn't mean it. You know why you're here, I thought, but I didn't say that.

Instead I began to talk about my life.

Your mother said nothing, asked nothing. She lay staring up at the ceiling. When I stopped talking I sat and listened to her breathing and studied her eyes and the lonely silhouette of her body curled under the blanket. It was cold in the room. I didn't need her to explain.

I slipped back into the bed and felt her hands. The morning brought its first pale shadows to the window and the room began to expand and take shape, and the magic of the world was swallowed up by the light of morning.

What was it that I felt with your mother in our small room at the Hotel Santander? What did I begin to feel? Again and again we'd awaken together deep in the night. It was as if we had become other people and re-entered the world at a different angle, a perfect tilt that helped correct for the terrors we both knew. We became, each for the first time in our lives, ourselves. One night, after weeks of this, your mother surprised me.

She said, "Sometimes I am afraid to sleep."

"I'm afraid of more than that," I said.

"Death?" she said.

"I am not afraid of dying. That will be easier than the part that comes before it."

She watched me. "I said 'death,' not 'dying.'"

"No," I said.

The blanket moved slightly. Cigarette smoke rose silently in the dark. I sat without moving.

"I am afraid that I'm more than I can be. More than I'm able to be. Alone with you I am no longer the man I'm supposed to be."

"You're much more than that."

"No, I'm like a little boy, an insecure snot-nosed brat. I'm scared senseless."

"A little boy who will grow up to be a great man."

"He doesn't know that yet. The boy is still afraid of his father's thrashings. Displeasing those around him. Of *failing*. And it's only you who reminds him of this. You remind him that he must make himself new every morning."

She sat upright and placed her bare feet on the floor. She reached over and took the lit cigarette from my fingers. She looked at it, then inhaled. She leaned forward, I thought to kiss me, but instead she brought the cigarette close to my skin. She held it there, embracing me. I felt the ember hovering above my neck.

"Are you afraid now?"

"No."

"This is real," she whispered. "Are you afraid now?"

"No."

She sat back on the bed. "Of course not." She raised the ember to her own neck. "But you are afraid for others. See? You flinched. Is it as a doctor that you're afraid for me? Or as a man?"

"It's the same thing," I said.

"Just like the boy and the man are one and the same." She nodded. "This is who you are. That's what I know about you."

*

High summer. The fighting in these hills continues. Our lack of supplies is perhaps our greatest gift to the Japanese. That and the shortage of properly trained medical staff. I have begun producing surgical drawings here in my free time. (What free time is that? I should ask myself.) "Surgical Fixation of Complex Femur Fractures" is my latest. We're getting a lot of these, you see. One drawing is worth ten demonstrations, and in a place like this, where language is a complicating barrier, it's a shame I didn't begin using these drawings much sooner. Presently I shall start in on "Surgical Fixation of Bilateral Lower Leg Fractures." I have found it difficult to avoid smudging the drawings and must take greater care. It helps to draw with a cloth between the forearm and paper. We shall see how that goes.

*

I have mentioned the fact that we saw a fair number of journalists at the clinic. Well, the filmmakers Kline and Karpathi were among them, though they weren't exactly journalists but, I suppose, propagandists. They proposed making a documentary about the clinic that could be used to raise money. One afternoon I made time for them. They told me they wanted to employ a strategy of contrasts, that they wanted something beautiful and uplifting, something that would bring the message home to people who knew little or nothing about the struggle over there. They needed my help, they said, because I was representative of the sort of international solidarity that was required. Once it was done, someone would take the film around North America, raising awareness and donations. They wanted a roller coaster of emotions, they said. A beautiful landscape. An orphaned child sifting through rubble. Some shocking contrast. A collage of images that would mould a political aesthetic and present an undeniable truth regarding the oppressors, Good and Evil, Us and Them. Nothing chronological, nothing like a "News of the World" trailer at the front end of a Clark Gable picture. They thought that beginning with an image of a painting by the great Goya might position the film correctly, allowing one fine moment of beauty and horror to stand for all that is noble and depraved in man.

That was what they talked to me about that afternoon: the struggle for man's dignity in the face of death. And then the reversal: a painting flipped on its side as it was walked out of the Prado, then a victim carried on a stretcher from a bombed building. It didn't take much to convince me. Karpathi followed us around Madrid and up into the hills for more than three weeks. Synchronous sound shooting proved too difficult, but the music and commentary could be added later.

★

One morning your mother sat leafing through a month-old issue of LIFE magazine. She looked over her shoulder at where I was straightening my jacket in the mirror, preparing to leave. "Will you take me with you?" she said.

This was a week or so after the bombing raid on Cuatro Caminos. I looked at her reflection. "To sit in a car all day long?"

I'd told her the night before that Sorensen and I would be driving out that day to the Guadalajara front to take a look at some roads and bridges and deliver ten pint bottles of preserved blood.

She said, "I am suffocating in this city."

"It's not such a good idea. It's dangerous."

She turned back to her magazine. I thought that was the end of it.

"What about your work?"

"It will not miss me today," she said.

I crossed to the window, raised the blind and watched the street below. She seemed uninterested now. This part of the city had largely escaped the bombing runs of the past months. The Italian fliers had concentrated their efforts on the working-class neighbourhoods. Here, near the heart of the banking centre, they'd been more careful, though bombs still flew out of the sky with frightening randomness. You couldn't walk far in any direction without coming across towering heaps of rubble, but along San Jerónimo Street the buildings stood untouched. A bright winter sun shone down over the canyon of dirty white and beige buildings. The street below was busy.

Under an hour later, near ten o'clock, we collected Sorensen and Calebras at the clinic. They each gave me a puzzled look when they saw Kajsa. Though Sorensen said nothing, I knew he was annoyed. In France that November I had put my foot down regarding Moran Scott, a friend of Hazen Sise, our driver and utility man, who'd wanted to cross the border back into Spain with us. This lady friend of his had wanted to come along. I'd let Sise and Scott know that we were not a taxi service, fact one. And fact two: I was not willing to assume the responsibility of delivering a civilian through hostile territory. In any case, his reservations about Kajsa's presence were of no concern to me.

Dr. Calebras was another matter. As we prepared to leave, he'd been looking over his shoulder, waiting for Kajsa to step away. "Doctor," he said, finally.

Sorensen came over to translate. "He thinks you're taking liberties not entitled to you. He thinks the woman should stay. She doesn't belong on such a trip. He says she's a liability."

"Tell him I have taken his protest under consideration. Tell him we leave in five minutes. With or without him."

Neither he nor Sorensen spoke as we loaded the vehicle with supplies: a lunch of bread, cheese and omelettes prepared for us by our cook, Maria, a lady from the neighbourhood; the Leica IIIa, given to the unit by the Syndicate of Spanish Photographers; three tin boxes of medical supplies; and the pint bottles of blood, packed in a wire basket and ice. Finally, nearing eleven o'clock, we set out. Alcalá de Henares is just forty miles east of Madrid and we arrived in under an hour, then recorded the state of the roads and bridges leading into town.

Kajsa and I waited near the car while Sorensen walked upriver to get a photograph of the eastern side of the bridge. Calebras sat in the back seat, beside the packed blood. It was a cold day, bright, with few clouds in the sharp sky. The river was shallow at this point, only a foot or two at its deepest, but the bank was so broad and muddy that it would prove next to impossible to cross in our vehicle if the bridge were to suffer damage. We watched him walk upstream along the bank. I turned to my notebook and jotted down the travel time from Madrid. This information would prove critical for future operations along the front line. I hollered over to Sorensen that he should get the bridge from the west, as well. He walked downriver and another twenty-five yards beyond the bridge, took the shot, then started back, found a path and came up onto the road.

"We don't need this, Beth," he said. "I think you should talk to Calebras."

I smiled, then rapped the hood with my knuckles. "Leave it alone. Get in."

We drove through Alcalá de Henares, stopping to assess

the condition of the bridge leading out to the Guadalajara road. On the open road we made good time, averaging sixty miles per hour. Calebras sat in the back silently watching the view, bouncing with the packed blood. The road was still in excellent shape. It was paved, very unlike the irregular Burgos road, but there were plenty of bumps he could feel back there. Kajsa looked splendid sitting between me and Sorensen. Sorensen was a very serious man at the wheel and didn't once take his eyes off the road. The Leica sat on the dash. The flat landscape rolled by. Some stone outbuildings, not much more than shacks, could be seen now and again, but very little else on these lovely, unbroken plains. A Spanish farmer did not live on or own the land he farmed but arrived to it as a factory worker might. He worked it but received no profit from it, only subsistence, and in effect was an indentured slave. You could drive for hours through groves of olive or corn or wheat fields and see not a single farmhouse, only stone fences or outbuildings where someone kept his tools. This was a system as old as time.

Fifty miles north, the Guadarrama range was capped by late-winter snows. Soon we came upon a slow-moving convoy of gasoline trucks, supply wagons and carts pulled by automobiles and donkeys. Sorensen was forced to drive on the shoulder of the road. Shortly after that we saw a long line of transport trucks loaded with Republican soldiers, their bayonets fixed, staring off to those same, unchanging mountains. A significant mobilization seemed to be in progress. I counted fifteen personnel transports, and each one cheered us as we sped past. Blow the horn, I told Sorensen, let them know we're here. As we passed we heard various languages as the International Brigades called to us. Their shouts grew more enthusiastic when Kajsa leaned over my lap and out the window. I held her by the belt. When we heard German, and saw these men's helmets, I knew they were the shock troops of the Thaelmann Battalion, Socialists, Communists and anarchists who'd escaped their own country to fight against Fascism here in Spain. The men waved and thrust their weapons in the air and hollered and blew kisses at Kajsa.

"How wonderful!" she cried, tucking her head back in the compartment, the rapturous curl in her bangs leaping in the wind. "Oh, those boys are marvellous, aren't they? Each and every one of them. It's impossible to lose. Say it, Calebras, your country can't lose when all the world is here! Germans, Poles, Yugoslavs!"

"Even a Swede!" I said.

He nodded and smiled thinly at her with an evident disgust that I couldn't understand. Minutes later there appeared a large cloud of dust on the horizon. This was the reason for the troops' enthusiasm and confidence. As we approached from behind we saw the column, still unsure as to what it was we were witnessing, and the first of a long line of tanks came into view. We felt the ground rumbling beneath our car and the air filled with the roar and smell of diesel engines. They were Soviet T-26s. That is a very impressive machine to see right before your eyes, I can tell you, and a very terrible one, too. We sped past, honking. Kajsa took up the Leica from the dashboard, leaned out the window, waving, and then started snapping. She cheered and hollered into the din and we drove on, knowing nothing of how this moment had changed our lives forever.

*

Today I performed a double amputation. A land mine took this boy's legs out from under him. He may have been twenty years old. Unfortunately not such a rare occurrence in these parts. But today I considered what an obscenely apt metaphor a minefield is, and by that I mean its ability to surge up from the unknown to grab hold and twist. Isn't this so much the case of our past, our hidden lives? Well, not always hidden, sometimes simply discarded or forgotten. This poor boy, his legs blown apart, and me above him looking over my white mask to see an inkling of the hidden banalities in my own life. Perhaps I'm just too tired. Surely he needed no such lessons in the metaphysics of life. An honest man has no discarded memories, none worth dredging up. Metaphors are gratuitous out here, of that I'm sure. I was ashamed. I took from him what was left of his legs, turned away and began with the next boy. There were six more, just like him, waiting.

*

This has got me to thinking of a number of failures in my life. By which I mean my own failures that have affected people I've known.

The need to make good use of myself in the world first came under fire when I was eighteen years old. That may still be young enough to appeal to the inexperience of youth as some sort of defence for my actions, but I know that's no excuse and will therefore show you due respect and not use it here.

It was the winter I was taken on as a schoolteacher in northern Ontario, and through this posting I met someone I will do my best to tell you about. Through him you will see why I might fairly characterize this entire episode as a failure, one that started small, in that schoolhouse north of Toronto, and ended in tragedy on a dark battlefield in Belgium. You will see why it keeps coming back to me, and why it's something I need to tell you. It is something a man does not forget.

This happened in the small town of Edgely, during the bitter January of 1908 or 1909. The youthful minds I found waiting for me there seemed as harsh and ignorant as that cruel weather. From the very beginning I was thwarted, vexed, deceived, chuckled at, abused, ignored, tried, hounded, belittled and tested. Until one morning I awoke from my slumber. I remember the day with particular clarity. I'd just begun a class on prime numbers when I was greeted with a series of spitballs. I turned quickly. A buckle of laughter rose from the back row. These were restless children, I knew, but here a line had been crossed. I felt the laughter spread forward until the whole room—that is to say the entire schoolhouse—was wetting itself with laughter (pardon the expression). I stood stricken, dumbfounded and burning with anger. When I asked who was responsible there was, of course, no response. I asked a second time. The laughter retreated like an ocean tide to the back rows and there it stalled. "Hands on desks now," I ordered, then slowly walked down the aisle examining each boy, his hands and funereal smirk. As I approached the back of the class, where the laughter had both started and ended, a foot caught me. Up and over I went, tumbling to the boards. Another howl of laughter rained down over me. Cursing now, I rose to my feet and with great eagerness pulled up the guilty boy, or who I thought was the most likely culprit, by the collar. I very nearly lifted him out of his shoes as I held him against the back wall of the classroom. His eyes suggested that I had gained his undivided attention. Three times his head hit the wall and three times his yellowy eyes rolled over like broken egg yolks. I would surely have continued, for my anger felt quite intoxicating, but something came over me—common sense, most likely.

Before I was able to release the boy from my grip I felt a punch on the side of my head. Another boy was on me. I turned to face a big farm lad named Jimmy, a sullen and angry boy I'd never much liked to begin with. Without a word I laid him out with a single punch. He fell like a sack of potatoes, and silence descended over his classmates. Stepping over him, I returned to my desk and sat ramrod straight, staring down the young cretins like a regent awaiting signs of full-out rebellion. Soon the boy came to, whimpering somewhat. He moved his jaw with a hand, testing it as he returned to his seat. When the hour struck I rose silently and walked out the door, convinced that this was the end of my teaching career.

That evening I was restive. I lived with an old woman who had difficulty remembering my name, but her head for figures was fine and she never failed to remind me how much I owed her from week to week. I lay in my hard bed late into the night and wondered what the following day held in store. I had no fear of the law for I knew this community frowned upon its Constable Ryan. He was a sad drunk, they said, and kept his nose out of their business as best he could, as long as they didn't come between him and his favourite taverns. It was not the law I was concerned about.

I shaved that morning, and though it was doubtful I needed to, that is what I did. I suppose I was shoring myself up. I probably made threatening faces in the mirror, but I remember staring at myself and wondering what my face would look like cut and smashed and what hints of regret it might bear should my body be laid out on a slab awaiting identification by my parents, and what their reaction would be beyond the sorrow felt by my mother and the pity and shame felt by my father. Would I be a good-looking cadaver? I wondered. A strange thought—though it has crossed my mind a number of times since.

My heart racing, I left my landlady sitting silently in her rocking chair and marched down the single street of that village, prepared to meet whatever awaited me. I unlocked the schoolhouse—being as much custodian as headmaster, principal and teacher—and arranged my textbooks, then began pacing nervously up and down the classroom.

To my surprise, the morning proceeded without incident. I sensed no rebellion whatsoever. The boys were well behaved, better than I had ever seen them. It seemed that yesterday's confrontation was precisely what was needed to settle them down a good deal, so I thought we might make some genuine progress. We concentrated on the mathematics, then reading and history in the second and third hours, and when geography came we began with a lesson on western Europe. Only four of the twenty were able to locate that continent on the map for me. This ignorance suggested a sad state of affairs indeed. But the manner in which these boys wore their ignorance that morning was almost endearing, for they were humbled and by no means proud of their lack of knowledge. I could hardly blame them for their rowdy behaviour in a school that had managed to teach them so little.

I dismissed the boys for lunch on a positive note, liberating them a few minutes early as a reward for their co-operation. I worried that I'd misjudged their cruelty and thought badly of myself for doing so. They were a fine lot, I concluded, and the day was looking up. I returned to my lodging for a meal of barley and beet soup and three slices of dark rye and started back to my schoolhouse before half past noon.

The mood there was very much changed, with boys swarming and snickering in the schoolyard. I felt their energy from a hundred yards and slowed my pace, unable to construct a strategy to help the situation. As I stepped through the main gate the crowd of boys parted and before me stood a large man, much larger than any student and taller than me by half a head. I knew this man to look at from the village but did not know his name.

He stepped forward to meet me. Too young to be the father of a student, he perhaps was a brother of the boy I'd knocked down.

"Bethune," he said, "you need some of that thrashing you like to dole out to these helpless boys."

"I give back only what's given out."

"Well then, I've come to return what's yours."

He hit me with a fair punch to the left side of my head. I saw it coming but was still too bewildered to react. It was not possible that I should find myself standing in a schoolyard on the point of entering into a fistfight; this was not what any teacher expects, though I believed it soon enough. My vision turned white and my ears rang for a quick moment with the force of another blow. I staggered but stayed upright. When the lights cleared and my ears stopped ringing I was able to hear whoops of joy coming from the crowd that had gathered around. My students were overjoyed by the promise of my defeat.

*

All this happened quickly. I should hope you never see such a fight, but imagine if you can a man—a boy barely yet a man—strong enough, back straight, fists forward. In a fight like that instinct counts, but experience means the difference between standing and falling. After that second punch I regained myself and the shouts of joy became calls of encouragement for my opponent. I soon learned his name was Robert. Kill him, Robert, the boys shouted, make him sorry he done that to poor Jimmy, and so on. We began in earnest then, weaving and bobbing in and out. One of us threw a good punch now and then. We were circling a fair bit, looking for the invitation of a dropped fist or a missed step. It was snowing lightly and a beautiful light was shining down, and a surprising calmness came over me—akin to the elation I'd felt the day I understood myself to be alone in a Godless world, that the world was mine to make. Within a minute or two it was snowing heavily, but I finished the matter so splendidly that the new-fallen snow had not yet made a noticeable accumulation on the snow already trampled in the yard or on the slate roof of the schoolhouse and the caps of the watching boys. Their cries of encouragement were silenced when it became clear in whose favour the fight was turning. He was a large lad but in the end that did not help him. I laid him out as I had laid out his brother the day before. Serves you right, I thought. There I stood, a trace of blood on my split lip, taunting him, "Get up, you, get up, you, I'll finish you, you miserable s——t."

He was finished but I wanted more: I am ashamed to say it but it's true. I felt the surprise in the crowd's silence when I finally stopped demanding he rise to his feet, and an overwhelming pleasure, a sort of delirium, at my victory. At the same time I was overcome with shame. Is this what my idealism had turned into, the desire to stomp a man? I was the one who had finally taught the thug a lesson, the oafish brother of the boy who'd tripped me up, and by the looks of it this was something new in this town. I was not a teacher standing there now but the town bully, an enforcer, warrior and constable all in one. I was drunk with satisfaction and I was red with shame. I knew his nose was broken, I'd heard the crack. The cold air had delivered the resounding snap for the whole school to hear. It was as if the frozen branch of the greatest tree in the county had buckled under the weight of wet snow.

*

Earlier this evening I had a free moment. I carried my chair outside and watched this village from the doorway of the old ramshackle hut they've put me in and sat there like some old man waiting for his time to come. There was a chill in the air, which has become sharper in the hours since. (Thank goodness the heat has broken!) I leaned my chair back against the door frame and breathed in the smells of China. A man enjoying his peace. But for the chaos around me, that's what you might have thought, that the world had for a moment fallen still, and what a lovely thought that is. When all one has ever dreamed of accomplishing is set out before him, like a series of paintings or poems ready for cataloguing, there to speak for him once he is gone. Is that what a great artist would feel? I long to settle into the weary comfort of age. There I was, biding my time. For a moment I felt truly at ease.

*

I will tell you flat out that I myself was not a model student and so should not be so hard on those poor boys of Edgely. My dear mother, bless her heart, would take this opportunity to remind me that we are each granted our own particular skills and abilities and talents, some of us for book study, some for ploughing, some for healing the sick. When I gained entrance to the university the following year I was reminded of that fact once again. I have not forgotten it since, despite my failures by the cartload. I have always been a bit impatient, a bit impertinent, a bit hot-headed. The only crime would lie in the denial of this truth. In the lecture hall I was inattentive, openly rebellious, bored and short-tempered.

I left the university for a time, only to return again, and during the winter of my second year the Great War began. I was twenty-four years old. I recall that day with deep sorrow, though at the time I didn't know enough to see through the smoke screen of patriotic pride and glory. Within a week of the announcement, the halls and classrooms at the university were abuzz with talk of driving the Kaiser back into his hole. Oh, it was heady stuff for a boy looking to make himself into a man. We all went in for it. It was not difficult to leave the university behind. I had not excelled, and the European war offered an excuse for all of us to abandon that cloistered world and begin the great adventure of life. I signed up and for the first weeks of my enlisting was proudly occupied with the task of saving humanity from itself. Soon my enthusiasm was replaced by tedium and a longing for the comforts of home. I had never seen so many uniforms and so many people thinking identical thoughts. The army is like that. It is sure to reveal your individuality, if you have any, and stamp it out as quickly as possible. What had begun, in the spirit of good fun and adventure, at the university and in the streets of Toronto and every other Canadian town and city—and continued at Valcartier, where I enlisted, and aboard the SS *Cassandra* to England, where we would endure months of training—became a grinding routine of drills and grub and close quarters. Already the romance of war was wearing thin.

Only fools and thugs enjoyed this life. You can probably imagine. Our patriotism was orchestrated and came in waves, soon competing with a nostalgic yearning for a good home-cooked meal. Unbelievable casualty numbers circulated among us, rumours purporting wildly unrealistic sums of the dead. Ten thousand in one day, thirty thousand the next. We were officially warned to disregard such slanders, you can imagine why. Propaganda was manufactured by the Hun and directed toward King and Country, we were told. But even still you began to fear that this was indeed a war and not an adventure, though we were insulated from it by razor wire and soapbox speeches and optimistic newspaper articles regarding the outcome.

While I was at Fort Pitt, in the south of England, thousands of Canadian boys came through. Only a mild feeling of curiosity and nostalgia grew within me when I saw the boy, now a man, I had beaten in the schoolyard four or five years earlier.

"Hello, Robert," I said. He looked at me without a glimmer of recognition. I smiled and faked a left jab and still he had no idea.

"Bugger off," he said.

"How long have you been here?" I asked.

"Thirty-nine days," he said.

"Maybe we were on the same ship over, the *Cassandra*?"

"That's the one," he said. "Stinking s——t bucket."

"It'll get worse, don't worry about that," I said.

"Maybe it will," he said.

That evening at mess, I sat two men down from him and ate my supper without drawing attention to myself. I watched him. He ate with his head hanging over his plate, a horse feeding at a trough. He had no interest in the men around him. He ignored their taunts and rough jokes. But all around us were boys committed like him to their silence in the hope that it would speed their time there and maintain the peace of mind they'd brought over with them. He was determined, eating with fear and concentration. He would fill his belly and sleep and complete whatever duties he was assigned. He was a farmer allotted a single furrow and would not stray outside its narrow rut, I could tell. I was intrigued by this connection to home. I had no free time, not even for letters to my family. My concentration was fiercely set on the adventure ahead.

The presence of Robert Pearce was strangely comforting to me, though. He was a link back to something I knew, and though we'd fought, he was the one who had helped me establish myself in that town. It was through him that I had become the sheriff and the bully and the enforcer with a higher purpose. Something had happened that afternoon, something exceptional in my life, by equal measures shameful and ennobling, something beyond the bullying that I felt still. I wanted to know what that was. I studied him over the following days and weeks. But his sad eyes told me something had changed in him since we'd stood face to face.

I didn't know if it was his being there that pulled him low, or if my knocking him down years before had reduced the bully he once had been to a meek and soft man, lonely for his people and his town and the simple tasks he'd grown used to over his short life. He was maybe twenty-four, my age. He caused no trouble. He marched in a straight line like the rest of us, performed his physical exercises and his rifle work proficiently and not a whit better than was expected. It was as though he was always thinking of something else, and for the weeks I watched him I believed it was the miserable town of Edgely he was dreaming about, caught up in his idyllic boyhood.

The early morning of the day we sailed for Belgium I told him who I was. He smiled softly and said, "It was a fair fight so I don't hold nothing against you." We sat for a moment in silence as the ferry pulled out from the docks. The rumble rattled our bones. The lumps of porridge gurgled in our guts. A low murmur of voices filled the hollows of the ship.

"What are you thinking?" I said.

"I'm thinking I'll die over there."

"We all might," I said. "But there's no knowing."

"I know it," he said.

I said, "Keep your head down, Robert. That's all you can do."

The Channel whipped up, and the crossing took close to two hours.

"This is a sign," he said. "'Turn back,' it's saying."

"I don't think so, Robert, it's just weather."

We went above deck and watched England recede through the hundreds of Jacob's ladders that descended from above in gleaming columns. Though the farm lad Robert was full of dread, I felt a sense of history fill my heart and hold me in the good favour of my ancestors. I'd never been so close to war before but had heard all my father's stories of links by blood to the noble past. I knew of the Highland Scot named Angus of Combust, the Jacobite who fell in the battle of Culloden in 1745 and then dragged his wounded body to safety and, through toil and the grace of God, was able to make his way to the Isle of Skye, where he met and married Christina Campbell of the Isle of Harris who bore him a son, my great-great-grandfather John. This man, John Bethune, arrived to North Carolina as a result of the Clearances. There, as a chaplain, he fought with the Royal Highland Immigrants to put down the American rebellion, and then, with the Royal 84th Regiment, he helped defend the Citadel of Quebec against the American invaders in the winter of 1775–76. From these histories and others, I took no small measure of pride and strength in knowing I was of fighting stock, and fight I would when the time came. You see how little I knew then? How flush with romantic dreams I was! This Bethune blood had on many occasions been spilled in earlier times, and if my blood were destined to stain the soil of France and Belgium this year or the next, so be it, I thought, it would run again in the veins of future generations of great-nephews and their sons. But I did not say this. I simply said, "Robert, it's just weather."

I knew what he meant to say, though, and wasn't inclined to look down on him for his anxiety and sadness. He was a man connected to his fear. It was the simple truth. In some ways he was more truthful about the matter than I was. I would never call that cowardice, not then and especially not now. He had every right to fear the coming days. Europe was already a graveyard. He had no ancestry or lineage to warm his breast. He had only a plot in Ontario to look forward to, nothing more than hay and beans and superstitious, nonsensical ideas of poetic weather.

I wished for his sake that suddenly a great fish would leap from the water or a sunny sign would break through the clouds, but the sea was chopped by winds alone and the sky grew only darker as the lovely columns of light streaming down were choked off by great fists of cloud. When we landed at Flanders we organized ourselves and then began filing down the gangplanks loaded down with our packs. The clouds at once disgorged sheets of rain over the Channel behind us and Belgium before us, nothing but rain and more rain. Poor Robert took no heart in what he saw waiting, and later I thought he somehow had known what was coming.

It was as cold as England, and maybe as cold as northern Ontario, where the trees were white with snow now, and suddenly we were much closer to the war.

If you had been unable to imagine the fighting thoroughly enough before coming over, you saw it in the country once you arrived. The landscape was a torn carcass stretched before us like nothing I'd ever seen. Limbs hung from tree branches. Barbed wire stitched across open wounds in the earth. An arm reached out from the mud like a pathetic shrub.

I remember on our left flank we had the French 87th Territorial and the 45th Algerian Division. On our right we had the Brits. They looked as if they'd suffered ordeals a thousand times worse than our basic training. There were already ghosts in their eyes. It was quiet the first night I arrived, though, and I had occasion to pretend the worst was over. I was racked with fear and excitement, quietly hunched in a ball in an underground bunker with forty or fifty men. Its dirt walls were supported by thick lumber. A cloaked man brushed past me, looked down, and my eyes met his. It was as if he couldn't see me, not with those haunted eyes. But he *had* seen something he would never forget, I thought. Perhaps now he saw only cadavers in the uniforms around him. He had seen and smelled the unimaginable, and it would not let him go. The eyes offered a story but it was a coded, silent mystery I could make no sense of. He scurried off in the dark. To help me pass the hours that first night I recalled my father's stories of France in her glory days and our family's life there before they migrated to Scotland. On that cold first night in Belgium, the family legends provided a curious mixture of strength of purpose and impermanence. On the transport ship over, I had been buoyed by thoughts of genealogy as destiny, but as the black night deepened these family histories no longer held me in such thrall. I felt more akin to Robert the farmer than to any distant nobility.

★

It is late September. We have arrived without incident to the base of the Wu-t'ai Mountains at Sung-yen K'ou. How many villages have I slept in since arriving, how many abandoned huts have hosted my restless sleep? I am told this area of Shansi Province holds some significant religious aura. You will not be surprised that I cannot myself attest to its spiritual power, but I can tell you that it is a remarkably beautiful place. There are Buddhist temples on every hill and cliff here, it seems. I suppose I can imagine some god smiling down upon this landscape in some previous century. But be that as it may, the Eighth Route Army can use as many solid structures as they can find, and these temples of stone and mortar were built to serve the most eternal of spirits.

We have found a hospital here in thorough disarray but are whipping it into shape. I take it you know by now that in north

China "hospital" signifies nothing more than a ramshackle and incomplete assortment of medical supplies and poorly trained doctors gathered together under the nearest roof. This is what we have here, of course. I have taken to giving daily lectures on sanitation and other basics as well as tending to the wounded. I expect to stay here through the month before moving on. Twenty men of my training here would still not be enough. I have been provided a hut not far from the hospital, and Ho is hard at work turning it into something that resembles a home. He's even found a desk for the Remington. More than I can ask, really, considering.

★

The truth is that Robert Pearce was just one man among the mass of brown-uniformed men moving through snaking gorges cut into the mud and earth. I sought him out and spent time with him when I could. We met at chow on the narrow stretch between the trenches and the Regimental Aid Station. He was not a man given to words, though his eyes told me he was thinking all the time. He had impressed me with his gracious acceptance of defeat, so I tried to engage him. He was a familiar face, I suppose. Initially that is what drew me to him. I took pity on him, too, as perhaps he did on me. He was as lost as the rest of us and maybe more so, but he made no secret of it.

"I can't say I'm having a good time here, Beth," he said one day, when I saw him standing off by himself.

We all went by nicknames. Beth was the one I answered to.

"Farmer," I said, "it's not what they told us to expect, is it?"

"I believe you like it here, Beth. You're that type. It's not a world I care for."

"I like it here less than you," I said. "Do you read the Bible?" He shook his head. "Good," I said. "What do you think about?"

"I think about home. I think about trees. Here it's only mud."

"Trees," I said.

"Climbing. Sitting under. Building with. Pissing against. Blooming. Falling. Colourful leaves. Trees in all their shapes and uses. I dream of a roof of leaves over my head."

Three days later, in the evening, the Germans released poison gas from their positions. It crawled toward us like slow-moving green worms, hugging every pore of earth, cowardly in its advance. Heavier than the air we breathed, it sought low ground and was pushed forward by obliging winds.

The Algerians and Moroccans got the worst of it. When they rose in choking desperation from the gas, the artillery began—a tactic no one had seen before. If they stayed low, the poison got them; if they ran, the shells or bullets did. It was a brilliant and merciless attack. Equipped with respirators, the enemy walked among the dead and blind and breathless as an army of exterminators. This was like nothing we knew. Our communications were down but news spread along the line for miles that the Hun had changed the rules of war. Runners brought word that we were to contain the salient at all costs, despite this new weapon.

We were ordered to prepare a counter-attack. As dark fell, fifteen hundred men collected in a nearby field. It was a grim sea of mud-splattered faces. These men would move against the enemy in eight waves. We would follow behind, the members of my Field Ambulance Unit, tending to the fallen, then carrying them back to safety. It was a night of terrible anticipation. Silence was the rule, and in this silent gloom each man attempted to master his fear in his own way, and accept his coming death. Just before midnight the whistle blew and the first wave went over, then the next and the next, like a pulsing, raging heartbeat running down to its last, until No Man's Land was overrun by the living and the dead.

We began our work then, searching in teams of six in the darkness and listening for calls, groans or weeping, the organic noises of the fallen. It was not possible to run in mud as deep as that, and the shells and screaming and gunfire deafened anyone who tried, leaving him disoriented and useless to those whom he had come out in search of. Sometimes you stumbled over one of your men even before you knew what he was, not just a stump. That first night we went out more times than I could count. It was by far the dirtiest day my life had yet seen. All night long I saw things I had never imagined possible. In the ghostly green lightning of bursting shells men glowed and flickered as their flesh dropped away from them in pieces. Those men you could not help and their screams faded as the burning grew brighter.

I listened for the cries of the living, not the dying. These led down into dark holes, like a string pulling you by the guts to your own death, in hopes that you might load a man on a stretcher, all six of you committed to this one simple, near-impossible task. It felt nothing less than superhuman. Back and forth we trudged, often more than an hour for every man. We worked like machines in the mud with no time to think or feel pity. There were occasions of nausea at the sight of exploded bodies. Again and again the night lit up with cannon and flares to illuminate the sight of one of our men doubled over retching. We moved forward, avoiding a single building in the distance that was said to house a machine-gun nest. We'd advanced and taken the forward trench of the enemy with bayonet and hand-to-hand fighting, and following the capture of that ditch we stretcher-bearers descended into the pure dark to find what we could. We ignored the enemy's pleas to staunch the flow of their wounds. There was much leg- and boot-work on the dying. This was how we'd been taught to dislodge a stuck bayonet—the full force of the body, foot against shoulder to pull mightily if the blade had wedged into the chest plate or single rib. If it was stuck deep into the spinal column there was no hope for the boy, and sometimes a man came out of nowhere, without a word, and helped him die quickly, but I was not forced to do so, not yet, though I had already heard the necessity for it in inhuman groans closer to death than to life.

Through the night the fighting continued, horror upon horror. The Germans counter-attacked, having previously buttressed their forward lines with reinforcements. Waves of them came at us, and in our turn we advanced against them, and my comrades and I picked over the deep fields for the wounded who awaited us. A disembodied voice was always imploring from the darkness beyond, but too often a search party was denied permission if the position was too exposed. And so the night proceeded. Our spotters informed us as to the approximate position of a man located through sightings or his cries, then off we went like spelunkers down a dark cave.

Just days into it, we were as experienced as the French Colonials to our left and the British to our right. Distant explosions and sniper fire never let up during the lulls in fighting. Catching a moment's rest, I leaned against a wall of earth and timber and conjured thoughts of the sacrifices and the ancient battlefields of my forebears. It was my desperate attempt to find heroism in my blood. But by now I knew that it was all—the gallantry, the romance, the glory—a great deception.

*

On the seventh day we consolidated our line with the help of British reinforcements who'd arrived at the small town of St. Julien. The day broke sunny and clear. It was a great relief to feel the natural warmth on my face, but a dread, too, as the enemy's spirit would be similarly improved. Waiting for instructions to move, we played cards, wrote letters, thought about home. I wrote to my family reporting that I was alive and well, the war was proceeding apace and with luck I should be home before the end of summer. Belgium was not what I had imagined and neither was the human spirit, in fact, more noble than anything I had ever known. The common man here—the farmers and bricklayers and factory workers so in abundance along the front—possessed such dignity in these least of humane conditions that I felt honoured to be associated with them. It was horrible to witness the true horrors of war, but we all were committed to the certain victory ahead and in good spirits, our morale undaunted.

I felt obliged to include these lies for the sake of my mother and sister, whose worry preoccupied me as much as my own fate in those days. I attempted to keep my letters optimistic and descriptive in nature, highlighting my daily rituals and observations, along with a telling anecdote, such as the time one of the boys, named Bud MacFarlane, had stood a stretcher on its hand-grips and danced a waltz under a full moon. There were twenty men in the Number Two Field Ambulance, myself included—numbers enough to find characters of Bud's sort. I wrote home about some of those boys, and about a soft-spoken lad named Robert I'd met over here from my teaching days, explaining that he had no greater ambition than to return to his people back home, find a wife and raise children. As I wrote this I felt a momentary desire to claim those plain desires as my own, suspecting that my mother would find peace in such wholesome simplicity, given my perilous situation, but knowing, too, that fabricating such sentimental nonsense would do no one any good in the long run.

The Regimental Aid Station was located only three miles behind the front line. When not writing letters, we spent our time preparing for an assault, either offensive or from the enemy, organizing and stocking and making sure all was in order, from generators and surgical equipment to operating tables. Idle time was best filled with labour, an occupied mind finding fewer opportunities to dwell on the madness around us.

In fact, the solemn anticipation felt among the men before they jumped the bags and until the stretcher-bearers came forth to fetch the wounded was, in its way, less terrifying than the idle waiting. In those last moments the mind races and the body, powered by adrenalin and fear, becomes a coiled spring. Just moments behind the forward rush, the stretcher-bearers poured from the trenches into the fighting to collect the wounded and hurry them back to the Aid Post, where the surgeons worked on the boys who needed it most while many others waited. We returned again and again to No Man's Land to bring back those who could be stabilized then loaded onto horse-drawn carts and transported by lorry or tram to the Field Ambulance, where they were further cared for and eventually shipped in the space of a day or two to the clearing hospitals near the French ports, or maybe as far away as Merry Old England, if they were lucky enough to find themselves wounded out of the war.

As I say, I attempted to maintain an optimistic tone in these letters regarding my own situation, on occasion hinting at the fear and anxiety and harsh conditions, hoping that the censors would not interfere; but for the most part I wrote of my longings for home and study and the company of my family and the north woods. These letters gave me great respite and were a forum for my dreams to run free, a release from the tedium and filth and death all around me. As if from a well I drew memories of camping and fishing trips and clear air and even the confines of Edgely, Ontario, where I'd learned a thing or two about the strength of will and learning to fight with your fists. I always signed my letters "Yours with love," and those I received with such anticipation began in my mother's hand "Our dear son" or my father's "Dear Norman." Those words alone often provoked tears and I felt an impossible distance separate me from my family. It was like reading a book from a century past, with every paragraph registering the irrecoverable years and miles. Upon opening a letter, I sometimes found a man hiding behind his cloth. "Dear Norman," he would write, "It will do you good to remember the Lord's words in times like these. Every day I pray for your safe return:

> *Thou shalt not be afraid for the terror by night;*
> *nor for the arrow that flieth by day;*
> *Nor for the pestilence that walketh in darkness;*
> *nor for the destruction that wasteth at noonday.*

And with a definitive Amen, your grandfather would hurriedly sign off like a man late for his own sermon.

Of course, I preferred your grandmother's letters, filled with news of my brother, Malcolm, and sister, Janet, and of the precocious children in her Sunday School class and talk of neighbours and their pride that I was here in the fight as all good boys must be. Some letters I saved while others were lost in the chaos of those days. I remember clearly one in which your grandmother wrote that they were pinning white feathers onto the lapels of able-bodied men back home. "A league of women who make it their business to meddle," she said, and went on to describe rallies in Toronto. Though my mother was no warmonger—nor was my father, certainly—their letters were predictably patriotic. Such thinking had become almost like breathing, I supposed. I did not think badly of this, only saddened on occasion that people should have such strong opinions of things which they knew so little about. Here we saw the fighting through a different lens. We did not see "war" but only a few hundred yards of nothing, beyond which were men who wanted to kill us. It was nothing like this present war in China, since we had no ideals other than to avoid death.

In an attempt to entertain ourselves, we sometimes read aloud our letters from home—the funny or pleasant bits, in any case. When I read my mother's account of the women and their white feathers, a young French literature major from the University of Toronto made a smart remark about those old biddies taking after the decadent scatologist Rabelais and employing their white feathers in a more useful manner.

The same day I saw Robert, who'd been sent to the Aid Station after cutting his hand while sharpening a bayonet. I wrapped him up, it was not serious, and sat talking with him afterwards. He seemed peaceful and said, "Does this mean I'm going home?"

"It's not up to me, Farmer," I said, "but it's not likely. You have to be hurt worse than that."

He nodded. "That's all right, Beth. I feel it. I'm going home soon. Look at this stretch of weather."

"Good things to come," I said.

"I got a letter the other day. It was from my brother, the one you walloped in school that time. He can't wait to come over and fight the Kaiser with me. He's just turned eighteen and my mother can't keep him from coming no more. Jimmy's not a violent boy, and I don't think he'd like it here. I have a letter for him in my breast pocket that I'll send tomorrow. I'm asking him to wait on the enlisting, and promise I'll be back soon. I told him I can feel it coming."

The fighting started again the following day. It never went away but levelled off with constant ongoing skirmishes. There was always the crack of rifle fire or an exploding shell in the distance, but these seemed like waves from a distant shore. On April 29 it came as a tidal wave.

The attack began that morning at eleven o'clock. The inevitable counter-attack followed, and shortly after that we went over. Each man that day took an average two hours for the mere three hundred yards we had to travel. The mud was often past our knees. We were still going out at sunset, and the sky had a purple tinge to it when we went up for our last man, just then spotted by one of the snipers. He was lying wedged against a post, tangled in barbed wire, on a slight rise in the terrain. We followed the ears of a boy named McGraw, from Calgary, Alberta, who claimed he could hear the Kaiser sneeze in Berlin on a quiet day. It took close to an hour to locate and approach the man. The closer we came the more sure I was that he was dead and this dangerous attempt would end in futility, but from twenty yards off we saw the lump flinch. An arm wiggled, almost waving us on. "It's Farmer, I think," one of the boys said. We came closer, and it was Robert.

It was a wonder a sniper had failed to get him in such an exposed position. Maybe the gentle rise in the land had obscured him, or from the opposite angle the enemy was unable to notice the twitching that became more evident as we approached, or they were just too tired to care. Maybe they thought to let him die out there, slowly. Then I heard the whistle of a shell. McGraw called us down right then and we jumped and the shell exploded. I realized that Robert was the lure, the bait. We'd been drawn out, I remember thinking. This was the end of us. As the dirt settled I waited. The debris cleared, and I waited still. I didn't dare to call out to my friends. Crawling on my knees, chest to the ground, I found my party dead. I tested each man for signs of life but they were all gone, each one of them. I lay motionless and cried and asked God why I had survived. I spoke to God, for the last time in my life, and He did not speak back.

Then I heard a single moan. I lay flat on my stomach without moving. It seemed I waited a century. I shifted my head ever so slightly and saw Robert, removed from the fence post now—likely by the force of the mortar blast—and sprawling flat on the ground. I saw him, or what I thought was him. He was a lump of clothing staring up to the sky. I waited. I watched him. The sun behind him sank below the horizon. The sky turned a lovely pink and yellow and slowly the blues and purples dropped from the centre directly above, spreading downward slowly to the horizon like running paint washing out the colours from the sunset, and then I was alone in the night surrounded by the dead and a handful of stars.

I listened to Robert's moans. In the new dark I saw him roll his head toward me, and his eyes opened. They were small white things. I crawled toward him carrying a canteen, an aid kit and my sidearm. "Robert," I said, "it's me, Beth. Stop your groaning, they'll hear you." I examined him and found a large piece of wood piercing his left thigh. His cheek was hanging open like a second set of lips. He was missing his left ear. He was a terrible sight. I told him to shut his mouth. "I'll get you back," I said, "you can survive this. But you have to shut up. They're not far off, and they can shoot with their ears as well as their eyes."

I remember thinking it best to leave the leg as it was. I wrapped his thigh tight with a tourniquet to staunch the flow, though it seemed already to have ebbed. In the dark I hefted him up onto my shoulders and began walking. I managed perhaps ten or fifteen feet before we fell into a crater. I lay silent, trying to catch my breath, and watched the darkness above us. Our round view of the universe looked peaceful and still. I was very tired now. It was like looking up from the bottom of a well, darkness on all sides giving way to a dark sky specked with lights. It looked like a hat full of stars above us, flowers in a lady's bonnet. A sharp chill draped itself like a shawl over my shoulders. I heard pot-shots and cannon fire but it felt far removed from our situation, as harmless as distant thunder.

I whispered, "It's like a spring evening back home, Robert."

He moaned, a sound deep and throaty, almost echo-like. I didn't understand what caused it but then I realized that the hole in his face functioned as a second mouth and he was try-ing to speak as if with two voices. There was nothing I could do but keep him company in his suffering. I had no medicines to induce unconsciousness. "When you get back," I said softly, "you'll tell that brother of yours that a German hits from behind, like a woman."

He moaned again. After a minute he tried to speak but nothing comprehensible came out, only a strange murmuring through his teeth and that doubled sound as it passed through his destroyed cheek. He gave up and fell silent again. Soon I dozed. When I awoke it was full dark. The stars have closed their eyes, I thought, and now I am blind. I reached over and tapped Robert, who stirred and grunted. "It's time to start again," I whispered. His head fell forward, so I tapped him again harder.

I pulled up to the ridge of the crater and left him slightly below, protected, while I peeked out. I saw nothing, just blackness spotted by distant fires far behind the enemy's lines, or maybe they were our lines, I couldn't be sure. I slipped back into the crater, took hold of Robert and dragged him moaning up into the night. "Shut up," I said, then gripped him by the crotch and arm and stood, turning slowly in a circle to get the lay of the land. I believed I noticed the gentle incline pointing toward home and so I started. "Robert, if you know something I don't, feel free to tell me now," I said. "Because we're knee deep in s——t now, Robert." I stopped to adjust my grip, then continued. "Robert," I said, "I'll be honest with you, Robert Pearce. I wish we were standing in that schoolyard. I'd take a bleeding lip over this any day."

After a time I put him down again. I remember feeling that my legs could go no farther. I looked in all directions, again turning in a slow circle. I saw no distinguishing features, nothing on this landscape to direct me. There were no fires now, just complete blackness. I rested as long as I thought it was safe, then picked him up again. I continued in the direction I believed we'd been walking now half the night. My feet sank into the mud and each step felt like the Devil himself was grabbing hold of my foot down there. God had not answered and now Satan would, his fiery hands reaching up to grip my ankle as I struggled to raise it again.

And this with a man on my shoulders. I walked on with my burden, my friend. Suddenly the earth would open before us and down we would slide to the bottom of a bomb crater. I would catch my breath and then climb up again to the edge, hoping it was the proper side to come up on, and pull him up over the lip of mud so we could forge deeper into the night.

I hoped for a single star to break through the cloud cover, but none did. "Don't worry," I said quietly, trudging along, "and do you know why, Farmer?" I heard that raspy, echoing breathing through mouth and cheek. "There's no need to worry because we're brothers and this night will end once and for all, and we'll come out on the right side. We're brothers, after all. Not because we think alike, you and I—we couldn't be more different—and it's not because we have a common enemy who wants to see us dead, but because together we're being tested and we have no one to look to or depend on, just ourselves. We're brothers because my life is in your hands and yours is in mine, because on this night we'll find out what we have in store for us. I can say I've never been in a situation like this, Farmer, this is rock bottom as far as I'm concerned. We only have each other, and what we find out here in this wasteland will make us as close to holy as we're ever likely to get, and holy I wish to be, although you don't look to the Bible in times like these. But that doesn't change the fact that out here in this muddy, starless night, not knowing which way to go, we'll be made either holy or dead, and I much prefer the former, Robert, so just hang on. It's just as well you can't hear me because I don't know what I'm saying, but I'll keep talking anyway." His breathing rose and fell gently against the back of my neck. "Farmer, this will be a story one day. A story to tell your little brother."

The tourniquet on the upper portion of his left thigh was still tight. "You were right, that weather did mean something. I think it means you'll be out of this war in no time. This is the story of how you got out of the war. Beth carries you to safety. Won't that make a grand story? You might even beat that letter in your pocket home. You'll be having breakfast one morning with your little brother when that letter comes knocking and you'll take it from the postman's hand and think of poor me still stuck here thinking of you." I rolled him off my shoulders and sat.

I waited. I dreamed the world was full of light. Bright blue stars streaked across the sky. When I opened my eyes I saw this was not a dream. A flare had been sent up. For a few seconds I sat in full daylight in a vast ocean of mud and mounds of churned earth and the tangled bodies of men. I did not move. I watched the flare sink in the sky, and the sky slowly returned to its sombre grey, then the indifferent dark returned. We were alone in our private sea of darkness.

Just as the green glow of dying ember-tip was extinguished and I was attempting to lift Robert, I heard the crack of a German Mauser—distinct and not difficult to distinguish from a Lee-Enfield. I knew this before I felt the bullet penetrate my leg. I collapsed and thought, Thank you. Thank you for pointing me home. I gripped the leg while keeping my sights aimed in the direction opposite the one I knew the bullet had come from, for behind me was the Mauser and ahead of me was home and what I now had to do was tie off my leg below the knee without losing sight of that hole in the darkness. It pointed a straight line away from the Mauser. Assume the life of the bullet, I told myself, and continue in the direction it was travelling. I sat down, rolled Robert off, removed the tourniquet soaked with his blood and wrapped my leg. Go, I told myself, follow the bullet. The world glowed again. It was not the light of flares or bombs or fire. The night glowed ecstatically.

*

Maybe I've told you too much. I am sorry. It was not my aim to burden you with difficult tales of my life. But I'm beginning to think that's exactly where the truth lies. You take strength where you can find it, whether from the dark or the light. Those were terrible times. But they did not belong only to me. If you are to know anything about me, you will understand that. I have acted with fine intentions and failed miserably. I have given the best of myself and found that it wasn't enough. I have wished for my father's strength. I have envied his ability to pray for those things he himself could not provide or achieve, and have envied his God-like patience when it came to waiting for an answer. I have envied his faith, in the face of the horrors I've seen. Tomorrow, another day. Higher into the hills.

★

I was shipped to Southampton, England, like so many wounded out of the war, and then on to the Cambridge Military Hospital. It was there I learned to walk again. There I mastered, for the second time in my life, the baby step. And there, three days into my convalescence, it was confirmed for me that both Robert and God had been left for dead in that wasteland. It is not pleasant to dwell on this dark time, and if I'm correct in saying that the difficult tales of my life will bring forth some hard truth, you can be sure there will be a fair measure of it here.

In total I spent eleven weeks at the hospital. With great pain I waited from one day to the next for some sign. For the darkness to lift. I was wheeled about in a chair, but the windows were set high in the walls and poorly designed for viewing from that position, so I sat in the grey shadows waiting like a crippled child for his father to come and take him in his arms. Near the end of my third week I rose with a great teeth-grinding effort. Aided by a cane I managed briefly to teeter on my legs and peer down into the garden, and slowly, in ever-widening arcs as the weeks passed, I began to explore the wide polished hallways and stairwells, the lounges and cafeterias. Into my sixth week I investigated the carved granite front steps leading back into the world, and when I was ready I journeyed down to the bright lawns and their gentle slopes to the riverbed.

Standing at this window I watched the elms and the ginkgoes display their new blossoms on the grounds below, and the river grew fat and brown with the spring rains and carried away the buds of willows. I attempted to compose a letter to Robert's family but was not successful. Every afternoon I took my spot at the window and put pen to paper, yet nothing came. Both God and Robert were dead, and words, too, were dead for me. Birds came down from their branches to pick in the grass and fluttered up and off at the approach of a cheerily dressed nurse strolling with a patient on her arm. I observed the world while trying to write the correct letter, though all I could think about was that night I'd left Robert out there to die. In the dark I closed my ears to the panicked calls that issued from the nightmares of sleeping soldiers. What did they see? How I tried to dodge that question as I lay waiting for light to break through the darkness.

I watched the hushed frenzy that marked the arrival of a new man, or the ordered regimen of nurses going about their business. I visited other floors, and sometimes a nurse sent me away; others merely regarded me with a look of irritation, and some did not regard me at all. There were many young nurses whose responsibilities had been accelerated prematurely as a result of pressing need, whereas the doctors seemed too old, many having come out of retirement; but the hospital was always calm and efficient, and I was cared for with a high degree of professionalism and attention.

It is difficult to live for months in the dark without once seeing the face of an angel. Wait long enough, dream long enough, and she will come. What finally appeared to me was not an Angel of God but an angel for a young boy turned man, still young enough to hold such silly dreams but old enough to feel the crushing solitude of the place that housed him.

Such an angel came to me in the form of Agnes McGinnis, a quiet, intelligent girl from the hand-loom weaving village of Little Goven, near Glasgow. This was many years ago—you must permit me a wide berth here—but these memories of her, the lilt in the voice I can still hear in my head, suggest a lighter heart than I have attested to. Perhaps I was even younger than I knew. She was only one of many who tended to us in that ward, but she was the one I most remember, the one who raised my spirits. In practical terms, she was very good at blanket-bathing and wound-dressing. Her patients hardly noticed her going about her work. In not so practical terms, she was too fast for my liking. From the moment she snipped off the old dressing, cleaned my leg and applied the new bandage, the process rarely lasted more than two minutes. Often I simply closed my eyes. Other times we exchanged snippets of conversation. We struck up a friendship. I told her what I could of myself and my family. After I mentioned the Scots blood in my veins, she came to me every afternoon with a new story of her village—Crazy Pete, the story of the talking ducks, the day Jimmy Quinn fell down the well. She painted such a fine picture of the place that I decided to go there with her and stay a lifetime. I listened eagerly. Her eyes hinted at a future I could only long for.

As she snipped my bandages, she told me she spent her one day off a week in London, an hour and a half distant, where she liked to sit for hours in the great cavernous silence of the British Museum. She preferred Ancient Egypt above all else. She admired its gods and goddesses, each with an assigned place in the world. She went with a girlfriend, a nurse in the opposite wing to mine. They saved for the train and ate sandwiches as they watched the countryside roll by. They complained to each other about the matron, Simpson, who managed to torment all the nurses equally. I squirmed and moaned as she talked, hoping to slow her down. Her fingers raced across my leg. To keep her by my bedside longer I asked if she had a favourite part of London. Had she ever seen the Tate Gallery? Did she know Soho Square?

One day, not expecting any sort of considered answer, I asked if she had any favourite god or goddess. This question seemed to catch her. It was as if she'd been thinking this over for some time. Her fingers stopped their work. She said she didn't have one, not really, but I could see her thinking. "Well," she said, "if you'd have me choose, it'd likely be Nephthys, not that I'd like to be her."

"Well, why's that?"

"I'm just being truthful, I suppose. That's what all the nurses would say, and the doctors too, if you asked them, if they had any idea of that sort of thing. Nephthys, you see, is the friend of the dead."

"But I'm not dead yet," I said, smiling. She finished quickly, without saying more, and went on to her next patient. She did not come back to me for some days, and when she did I asked if I'd upset her. She laughed off the suggestion and asked what I thought about the food, wasn't it approaching criminal?

Although I still could not be sure what had thrown her so badly that day, our private communications resumed, and no one knew that we grew closer, though I suspected some of the other men in the ward might have guessed what was going on between us despite Matron Simpson's admonitions to avoid fraternizing with the patients. For a few days after this disclosure, there was a lull in our conversations as she wrapped my leg. I knew she'd been shaken by her own words. Despite her change in mood, I looked forward to her visits and prepared questions in advance. But I did not question her on the gods any further.

On a Tuesday she wheeled my chair down to the river, which by early June had been reduced to a shallow brook strung with waving ribbons of algae. The willows were in full bloom now. It was a beautiful English day. She sat on the grass beside the chair. We watched the clouds don their costumes and strip them clear again. First we saw a dragon, then a tiger, then a cat, then a sheep.

The inventions were swift and effortless as the mile-high currents turned the shapes inside out.

"What will you do after the war?" she asked.

"I will do my best to forget about it, I think."

She said, "I will get very drunk and stay drunk for a week."

"That isn't very ladylike."

"But isn't it a wonderful idea?"

"I have a week's furlough coming up," I said. "I'm staying at the Union Jack in London."

"I could show you my museum."

Two weeks later, in London, she called for me at the club at half past three on the Saturday as planned. I was pleased and full of expectation. We enjoyed a short stroll around Green Park. My leg not yet entirely healed, I still walked with a limp and a cane. I wore my wound stripe, as I was obliged to do. Civilians nodded with grave admiration when they saw me. After an hour I took no more notice.

We hired a horse cab and rode between neighbourhoods. It was a wonderful escape from the hospital. We saw signs of the war—a bombed building from one of the German zeppelin raids, torn up cobble. Uniformed men were everywhere. When my eyes met another soldier's, one of us would always turn away too quickly. Was my discomfort as clear to him as his was to me? The outside world was a pleasant reminder of another life. We would remain there as long as possible. I had heard the stories of men from the Field Hospital vomiting or turning violent at the scent of a lady's perfume after months of living in the stench of blood and sewage, knocking down a well-heeled gentleman for spouting off about the war. But I felt nothing as desperate as this, only the sadness of my loss and the sharp grinding in my damaged leg.

We took a second cab to Great Russell Street and walked slowly through the museum. We stopped often to sit as my leg could carry me only a quarter of an hour at a stretch. We passed from room to room. It was lovely to leave our century, and humbling to know these great civilizations were gone—that the eyes and hands and minds were dead, and their secrets along with them.

Agnes pointed out Nephthys for me. She was drawn into a stone tablet, surrounded by lifeless bodies.

Agnes said, "You know, I don't feel right about what I said, it just seemed tasteless and insensitive, among all those injured men. I say things like that, stupid things. I feel quite ashamed of myself."

"If that's the worst of your sins you'll be okay."

Later in the afternoon, we walked over to Tottenham Court Road, where we decided to drink a pint of beer and found a dim pub. Its hard planks creaked as we walked across the floor. Weary and worn, the place smelled of old men with a faint whiff of lavatory. We took a table. A group sat at the bar drinking, exchanging sudden rough exclamations between their long silences. These usually had something to do with the war. The devils, one man said. Godless heathens. The usual sort of cursing, I will spare you. I drank two pints to the half Agnes drank. I wanted a third and was ready to ask for it but I sensed she wanted to leave. One of the men in particular was getting agitated. He said there was a wickedness attacking the heart of the British Army, a moral degeneracy that threatened to undermine morale. The pacifists and the homosexuals were proof enough that an invasion of home soil had begun and it went as high as the Foreign Office. One of the Kaiser's plots as sure as the Hun's a devil in uniform, he said. But on this subject the others were mute. He seemed a man they didn't want to bother with.

Just as I was thinking this, one of his colleagues, a large fellow, said, "Now, William, drink up and go home. Better yet, go home straight away. You shouldn't need reminding it's our boys dying for us over there." He placed his pint glass, emptied, on the bar before him.

William sipped his bitter, apparently debating his position. He finally said, "You shut your hole, I'll speak my mind if I care to."

"All right, William, all right."

"You'll not talk down to me." He shoved away his pint.

"You'd best be going home now," the bigger man said. "Or why don't you go off to war, brave William, and show us the man you are." The others, their heads hung low till now, looked up and smiled.

William glowered at him but held his tongue. He seemed to realize the man he was provoking was a good head taller and fifty pounds heavier, for he said nothing. Likely he knew he'd been made a fool of, and his only hope was to formulate some way of saving face. A sour black fog had enveloped him. I sat back in my chair waiting for a second round of insults and taunts, then looked over at Agnes. She was gazing out the small window, focused on something far off. William held himself stock-still. He didn't say anything more, simply stared at the other man.

"I'd like to leave now," Agnes said.

"All right," I said. "We'll go."

We hired a cab over to Victoria Station and waited for the Cambridge train, due to depart just after six o'clock. We watched the pigeons and the lottery sellers and the uniformed men.

"He was a drunken fool."

"Yes, he was," I said.

My leg had begun to hurt and I wanted another drink. I knew the leg would feel wooden in the morning. I was glad she was leaving. The excitement of being with her was gone. I had nothing to say and felt drained. I wanted to be alone. I walked her to her platform, where we shook hands and I helped her board the train. Then I walked back to the club.

I have thought about that day off and on over the years, and what strikes me most, I think, is the profound sadness I felt when I understood that this kindly girl could do nothing for me, despite her goodness and patience, and knew for the first time that something in my heart had been changed forever.

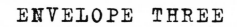

ENVELOPE THREE

Another lovely day. It has been a fine autumn here in Shansi, the air crisp and clean. Almost a month has passed since I wrote last. Please forgive me. I might say the war has detained me, which is true enough. I might plead exhaustion, which also is true. Conditions here provide few natural breaks for a man intent on looking back on his life thoroughly, as this letter is prompting me to do. Yet I will admit now that time, or its lack, is only half the problem.

The story itself, I suppose, is the other half. We've now come upon a difficult chapter in my life, and I have been hoping to avoid it. I have been circling, let's say, gathering strength. Bravery I seem to possess in abundance. Courage is something quite different.

Where, then, to begin?

The Bentley Park Hotel in December of last year.

My stay in New York coincided with some journalism that had brought Frank Pitcairn from England to New York City. I had recently finished touring with the documentary film on the unit, leaving it up in Montreal before coming down to New York to prepare for this China expedition. I tracked him down at the Bentley, wanting to thank him for the piece he'd written for the *Daily Worker*. I also wanted to take the opportunity to invite him to write a piece on our coming adventure. It was to that end that I would offer to buy him dinner and fill him with drinks and details about the cause in China. When I finally got hold of him, though, he seemed distracted. It had been months since we'd spoken. He was evasive for no reason I could understand and told me his stay in the city would be short. This was not a good time, he said. He'd already overextended himself and was working under a deadline. Yet I persisted. At length I was able to pin him down for later that night, promising a casual bite and drink, an hour or two at most.

I then proceeded by subway to the offices of the China Aid Council in the Bowery where I met with the two other members of the expedition—a Dr. Charles H. Parsons and Miss Jean Ewen, an excellent nurse, I had heard, and fluent in Chinese, who had served in Shantung for two years before the Japanese invasion began. Our meeting lasted three hours, focusing on the many details yet to be seen to. It was an optimistic meeting, I recall. I spoke of the importance of this mission, as a good unto itself and as the first wave of the internationalism we'd seen in Spain. We would be the first of many hundreds of medical teams to go over, providing the necessary inspiration. We will put China on the map over here, I said. This war will not go unaided.

Just before nine o'clock, after the meeting was dissolved, I found a telephone and dialled Pitcairn's hotel. I asked the clerk at the desk to put me through to his room, but he didn't pick up his telephone. I wrote him a note explaining the nature of the China expedition, our itinerary, departure times, members' names, et cetera, hoping he might present this to the editors of his newspaper back in London, then jumped in a cab to the Bentley. I planned to leave the note at the front desk, but I saw Pitcairn sitting in the hotel bar, hidden away in a dark corner. His face registered surprise.

I said, "I'd have mistaken you for some sort of spy, sitting over here in the shadows."

"Jesus Christ, old man," he said, standing up. He hesitated in offering his hand, and anyone watching might have thought I'd stolen his wife. "It's good to see you," he said, and in a moment he reassembled himself, but only just. It was as if he was unsure of me.

"Got you at a bad moment?" I said.

"Sit," he said. "Not at all."

*

The following Tuesday I boarded a train with Jean Ewen and Charles Parsons, bound for Seattle. From there we would cross the border up to Vancouver, where we'd depart for Hong Kong on a steamer. Charles chatted away with the other drinkers in the bar car and Jean managed to busy herself reading. I'd brought along a journalist's account of life with the Chinese Communists called *China's Red Army Marches* but found it difficult going. So distracted that concentration was very near impossible, I instead ended up watching a good bit of Indiana and Illinois roll past my window.

Three days later we arrived in Vancouver, a city hunched and brooding under a gloomy January rain. Like a vain woman, I remember thinking, it was as blessed by its natural wonders as it was cursed by its temperamental moods. The damp and the early dark cast a great pall, and the melancholy that had seized me since New York did not lighten but only increased when I found Pitcairn's telegram waiting for me at the Hotel Vancouver. I tucked it into my breast pocket and made dinner arrangements with Charles and Jean, then retired to my room, where I tore open the envelope. *Norman, the editors have rejected the China idea. Bad luck. You're on your own. Frank.*

The following morning the three of us gathered in the hotel lobby and took a cab to the port. Our luggage had gone off earlier that morning to the baggage master. I remember feeling a rush of excitement when the three great stacks of the *Empress of Asia* came into view. Gulls circled in and out of the clouds, dipping curiously like chaperones eager to glimpse the passengers they would accompany out to sea. In the excitement of the moment, the pure childlike thrill of standing before such an impressive vessel, I forgot the telegram and the succinct phrasing that so cleverly, so accurately, had let me know precisely what Pitcairn thought of me. *You're on your own.*

★

Midnight brings a faint thunder of fighting from the east. There is a cool dampness in the air. November in Chang Yu, Hopei Province. I am carried up from a shallow sleep. Just now I rose from my cot and saw dull flashes of light illuminating the far-off hills. Someone is taking it in the teeth. We won't know more for another day, maybe two. I believe my thoughts might have awakened me, if the fighting hadn't.

★

There is some pleasure as well, but mostly it is mystery and hard work that goes into the remaking of a man's life. I am finding that now. What I mean is that nothing I can say in these pages amounts to half or even a quarter of the truth as I knew it then. I'm talking about the actual experience of life. About the sound of crickets in August and the peace and wonder that fills your heart when you sit back and begin to accept the enormity of the world as it is presented to you when August comes and you feel the day and nature calling out to you. There is a full-on glory to this witnessing that only the greatest artists are able to capture. I will always believe I have seen the peasants working the great wheat harvests of Russia because I've read *Anna Karenina,* but I remind myself that Tolstoy is a once-in-a-century artist. I suppose what I'm trying to say is that the writing of a man's life at least gives you an idea of just how special it all was to him the first time around.

I recall standing on the deck of that magnificent ship, the *Empress of Asia,* and feeling the reality of what I was doing. I was leaving you. The full force of my decision came to me that morning as an almost physical pain. Much as I tried, I was unable to shake it off. But I also remember, as if possessed of two hearts, the serene joy of watching a flock of gulls darting among the ship's three funnels high above the promenade deck and thinking I had now found my freedom. More gulls fluttered just off the stern, picking heels of bread from a girl's hand. I imagined she was someone else, perhaps you, as you might appear at the age of eight or ten. She wore a blue wool coat and bonnet, and had beautiful blond curls. As she fed the birds, the woman I assumed was her mother held her by her free hand, careful not to let go as the girl leaned forward over the railing.

The child's delight was palpable. She shrieked with joy every time a gull took a piece of bread and lifted in the wind. The sun shone for most of the morning and this, too, raised my spirits somewhat. As the noon hour approached, clouds crossed over the ship, the last of the gulls folded their wings east, and it was then that remarkable columns of sunlight descended from above. This I took as a blessing upon us all, and every visible passenger seemed inspired by the spectacle of light spinning down through the clouds into the dark ocean, and by the thrill of having such a great steamer as the *Empress* underfoot, so solidly bearing us forth.

After the girl in blue waved goodbye to the last of her gulls, my colleagues and I decided to take lunch at the promenade deck's veranda café, situated at the ship's stern. We ordered a generous plate of assorted sandwiches, and Dr. Parsons, himself a surgeon, thought it a grand idea to toast the commencement of our journey with a whiskey and soda. It being quite early, Miss Ewen and I shared a small pitcher of Pimm's with lemon and cucumber. We watched the wide fan of the engine's turbines bubble and spread far below us, and before two hours had passed we'd cleared the Juan de Fuca Strait. Vancouver Island faded in the distance and then the continent itself began to slip away—her coastline, her mountains—and finally we were ringed by what seemed an eternity of water. Our conversation that afternoon was generally enjoyable and full of optimism, but inwardly I was troubled by the weight of my leaving.

I close my eyes now and recall the riches of that passage, the food, the cleanliness, the small troubles which from here seem so unimportant. What I remember is the gleam of silver tea sets, the potted palms and lilies that dotted the passageways, the pleasant light entering the tall, arched windows of the café where I took my breakfast most mornings. Now, cruelly, the aromas of the ship's kitchens appear from nowhere, waking me with the false promise of braised lamb, fresh cheese, roasted garlic. The *Empress* boasted a luxury that seems happily ludicrous. She ran more quietly than my dreams are ever able to promise, prowled as they are by the groans of dying men and mortar fire.

That first day, as we ate our lunch, I suggested to my colleagues that we indulge ourselves as best we could because the present conditions were sure not to last. The crossing to Hong Kong would take nineteen days. After that, I said, nothing was guaranteed. We should conserve our strength for the coming rigours. I planned to stay occupied during the crossing, intending to push certain gloomy thoughts aside while devoting myself to the preparations still pending. I would descend to the hold to check on our cargo, consisting of a fully equipped field hospital, complete the last of the background study I'd carried on board regarding matters of Chinese geography and politics, and send a number of telegrams ahead to Hong Kong and back to the China Aid Council in New York concerning various administrative points of interest. I also intended to seek confirmation that our man in Hong Kong would indeed meet us at the Ambassador Hotel, where we planned to stay briefly before our journey north to the mainland. As I outlined my itinerary, I noticed that Parsons had begun fidgeting. His eyes wandered. His glass was empty. He began tapping his fingers lightly on the tabletop, then raised his hand to call for the waitress.

I had calculated that my tasks might consume only a fraction of my time on board, as I had set out with a more immediate interest at hand. I had intended to sit at this typewriter (much newer then) and collect my thoughts for you, if one day you should care to read them. But the sea air failed to prove a sufficient inspiration for this first attempt, sincere though it was, for my heart felt on the point of bursting. Perhaps the sad reality of my departure tormented me more than I was aware. More than once I began this history, still unsure as to my deepest motives, for the truth comes—if at all—at its own stubborn pace. Stymied, I had no idea how to begin or what a man might say in circumstances such as mine. Where he might find the words.

What did I discover? That I was as dishonest to myself at sea as I had always been on land. Troubled, I strolled the winter decks, consumed by misgiving.

In my wandering I learned the ship's plan, a welcome distraction. Her many sections and decks were connected by a vast series of passageways, stairs and promenades, but some of these—rectilinear as any ship's plan is—were as narrow and confining as the medieval streets of a small European village. In certain sections she was quite cramped and claustrophobic, but those very same cramped passageways then opened suddenly to an airy lounge or plush dining hall or spacious reading room or bar every bit as ornate and charming as a town square in Seville or Siena. I carried my thoughts into each of these rooms and, in a state of introspection, watched the great ocean pass below. I circled her four continuous decks—shelter, upper, main and lower—all of which extended the full length of the ship, some 590 feet. I visited her cafés, restaurants and bars, her dining, reading and smoking rooms. I stood at the bow and wondered what I was headed into. At the stern I gazed back at what I'd left behind.

It is pleasurable even now to recall the luxuries of first-class passage. Delicious memories for a starved body. O the bounty we take for granted! I slept on a firm mattress smelling of cleanliness and not red clay and manure. My body ached with excess, not starvation. My cabin was a nest of pleasures situated on the upper deck, beneath the second and third funnels. I heard nothing of the ship's great engines and might as well have been camped on the shores of a remote northern lake. The cabin boasted a cherry-wood sideboard and dresser, two cavernous armchairs, a clawfoot coffee table positioned between them and an oak writing desk and chair of a type you might find in the stateliest manor in England. Unimaginable luxury compared to the cold mud, stone walls and dirt floors of these huts I now call home, with their broken windows and poorly thatched roofs.

The ship was redolent with delicious flavours. Roast beef on upper deck. Cuban cigars on shelter deck. Perfumes in the ballroom. My cabin was scented by lilies refreshed on a daily basis by a pretty Chinese lady named Mrs. Qimeia. She spoke English quite well, as did most of the Chinese stewards and stewardesses. One morning early in the voyage I introduced myself when she knocked at my door. She was modest, courteous, self-contained and efficient. As she tidied up I offered my gratitude for her fine attention to detail.

"Does this flower have a name?" I said.

"They are called stargazers, sir, a species of lily," she said. "We have a florist on board if you would like to send some."

"Perhaps I will," I said.

The lady blushed, of course. I asked if she might furnish my bed with a third pillow—a detail I dearly miss here, with not a single pillow—and wished her a good morning, then left the room in her capable hands.

I spent many hours in the lounge beneath the first and second funnels, reading and making notes on the coming expedition. It was there I tried again to begin this document, but looming demands pulled me away, or so I let myself believe. I worked as well on articles—political commentary, a paper on thoracic medicine, my specialty, another on triage procedures—and wrote letters to friends and associates. Delicate tables and chairs in the French neoclassical style gave the room a wonderful opulence. On clear days the great domed skylight overhead admitted a full warming sun.

Here I claimed a comfortable sofa facing a wide fireplace and, after a period of writing, started in on one of the books I'd carried on board. Passengers generally gathered in the lounge between eleven o'clock and noon, three and five, and then on into the evening after the dining halls emptied. Outside those hours it was a relaxing place for reading and study. The carpet was a warm russet, like the sofas, the lamp shades and curtains framing the rectangular port-facing windows.

When the lounge became too busy, I transplanted myself to the writing room, which was always quiet and ideal for study, though not so for those of us who compose on clumsy machines like this. Here I found the studious passengers, the chronic letter-writers, the poets, introverts, insomniacs and melancholics. In this room we hardly made eye contact with one another. We each stared down some far-off face, sum- moned a disembodied voice—a friend or lover waiting on the other side, perhaps even a daughter. The sea, we seemed convinced, spoke her own language: secret, coded only for the finest ear. Maybe in that room we stood a better chance of making some sense of what was to be found in its silence.

I spent many hours attempting to begin this story, but when I could bear it no longer I returned to the safety of administra- tive matters. Again I had failed. I concentrated on the China Aid Council, and on a certain crisis that was developing between myself and Parsons. Early on I was still hopeful—certain, even— that our expedition would reap great rewards. We were dedi- cated to the cause. But for the sake of complete honesty I must admit that there were signs of trouble only a few days into the voyage. Not unwelcome difficulties, at that. I was pleased to have something to distract me from the story I was struggling and failing to tell.

Charles Parsons was only slightly older, perhaps in his mid-fifties. At one time an excellent surgeon, he had in recent years been severely reduced by alcohol and by this time was well descended from the height of his powers. I don't know why he drank, exactly, but I do recall my astonishment at noticing, on our first day at sea, not the slightest pang of conscience or even *awareness* on his part when he suggested we avail ourselves of the funds we'd been entrusted with to pay for our drinks and plate of sandwiches. Quite surprised, I folded the bills back into his hand and asked the server to put the lunch on my meal chit, telling Parsons it was my pleasure. It was then that I began to harbour some doubt regarding his commitment. If left unchecked, I feared he would make a significant dent in our resources, and I resolved to keep an eye on him, though I had no intention of creeping around the ship like some sort of spy.

Of my other associate, the Canadian nurse Jean Ewen, I knew very little aside from the fact that her father was a prominent Communist back home, a highly regarded man I'd met on a number of occasions in Montreal and Winnipeg. While I saw quickly that his daughter took after him, she refused to call herself a dyed-in-the-wool Communist. She told me at our first meeting in New York that she'd never put much stock in labels, political, philosophical or otherwise. Perhaps she might call herself a pragmatist, I suggested. She lifted her eyebrows and smiled, indicating that even this might obscure the truth. She was quite young, in her late twenties, I would guess, and still quite collegial, despite her two years in China. That first day out from Vancouver she wore a black Lilly Daché cap and cape and looked set for a Sunday afternoon football game or ride through Central Park. Her dark brown eyes roamed upward to the funnels. "It's impossible to imagine that civilization can build a ship as glorious as this and still possess the mentality to wage war!" Her dark hair was cut short, just below the ear. She looked every bit the youthful adventurer that she was. Her neck, quite thin, was pale and delicate. I offered her my scarf, which she refused with a smile. She seemed nothing but a slip of a girl to me, pretty, almost dainty. "I see," I said, "you will stand up to the cold, then?" I couldn't help but wonder how she would fare under the pressures of war, and thought she might well surprise me.

I remember strolling above deck early on a splendid morning, three or four days in. I took great pleasure in filling my lungs with cold sea air as I watched the light reach up from below the horizon, as if some magical far-off land of fire and dragons were eager to catch my attention. On one level at least, I had already begun preparing myself mentally for this war on the other side of the world, bracing myself for its terrors, and that lovely thin strip of orange and yellow hovering over the sea brought a sense of calm I knew I couldn't trust. Out there the war raged; on board a different sort had just begun, and the gloomy thoughts of my leaving still turned in the back of my mind. As I walked and full morning light finally filled the sky, I saw that little girl in blue who had so caught my attention our first morning out. Today she wasn't feeding the gulls but standing alone at the railing, beside a life raft, watching the sea below. It seemed unsafe to me, a child alone at the precipice. The woman I'd taken to be her mother sat reading on a nearby bench, dressed in a red overcoat and white shawl, and taking no notice. She wore thick, black-framed sunglasses. I stopped and watched nervously as out from under her bonnet the girl's strawberry-blond hair spilled and danced about the circle of her face. She placed a foot on the bottom rung of the rail and lifted her other foot.

"Wait there," I called.

I suppose my urgent tone startled the girl. She stepped down, as if caught out, and turned with a guilty look on her face. The woman looked up from her book.

Somewhat embarrassed, I tipped my hat and stepped forward. "I'm sorry," I said. "She was climbing up. I'm not sure if you were aware of that."

"Oh, the dear thing knows no limits," she said. "I've told her a dozen times."

"Well, then."

"I suppose I'm not as fond of looking after children as I am of reading these silly poems." Vaguely she waved the book between us.

"What poems are those?"

"Do you know Wallace Stevens?" she said.

It turned out the woman was not the child's mother but her young aunt and as her temporary guardian was returning her to Hong Kong, where the girl's father held some post in the British Consulate. I presented my card, and we were soon immersed in a conversation about Stevens's poems. Her name was Gwendolyn Chambers. Two years into her doctoral thesis on eighteenth-century poetics, she'd recently fallen madly in love with the Modern Poets and was now reconsidering her studies. She was young, articulate and, not least of all, wonderfully selfless, I told her, in that she should journey such a long distance to deliver the child to her mother.

She laughed and said, "I'm not half as selfless as you might think."

As we spoke, the girl gravitated back to the life raft to look down at the water, but she did not step up onto the railing again.

⋆

I've been thinking about the possibility of my never finding you, an impossible thought that wakes me up at four in the morning. It is as if our bodies are programmed to wake up then so we can take our worries out for a stroll and exercise our darkest fears. We are at our weakest then, as if all we think we know is put aside at that hour and replaced by everything that's fearsome and terrifying. It is an intolerable thought, a full life without you, and that is why it haunts me. I could not stand that life, I promise you.

⋆

The weather was unchanged six or seven days into the Pacific crossing: cool, constant, predictable. By then I had modelled myself after it to a degree and established a daily ritual designed mostly, I believe, to prolong my self-deception. Mornings began with a brisk stroll up top, followed by a light breakfast at the veranda café. There I took a coffee and eggs with toast, juice and fruit. A fraternal atmosphere among the diners was pleasantly distracting. I sat among families, businessmen and adventurers, people who knew nothing of me or my plans for joining the Communist struggle against Japan. Most mornings I greeted the girl and her aunt, the engaging Miss Chambers, and soon we began breakfasting together. With Gwendolyn I spoke of poetry and art. I had over the years written a few poems myself—of course, none as good as Stevens's—and so had a number of ideas on the subject. I shared with her my belief that only through art could the truth of a non-shared experience be transmitted.

"Yes," she said, "I believe you're right."

"Poetry—good poetry, at least, like Stevens's—must evolve as the natural product of the subconscious mind. But here, you see, I have a bit of a problem. I believe art must be useful. It must teach us. What I'm asking for is the moral superiority of the artist. Yet if it comes from the unconscious mind, and if it must serve or educate in some positive fashion, well, then I'm asking quite a lot of the poor sod, aren't I?"

"Doesn't beauty count, Doctor?" she said. "What's to be said for beauty?"

"Beauty is an attribute of great art, I think, not the driving purpose behind it."

Later, after a pause in our weighty conversation, I turned to the niece and spoke of ornithology—she'd been enthralled by those seagulls—as well as doctoring and Vancouver's Stanley Park, where I'd been told she often played with her little friends. By then I knew the child, Alicia, was as engaging, precocious and bright as her aunt. She spoke with great excitement about seeing her parents in Hong Kong, and asked many questions about what it was like "to make someone better again." I told her it was a splendid feeling, that there was really nothing quite like it.

"I should like to become ill while on board, then," she said, "so you can cure me."

Alicia told me her father had once been gravely ill in Hong Kong, and a wonderful doctor had "cut him open" and "removed some things." I was pleased, naturally, by her regard for the profession.

★

It was on a windless morning of making my rounds that my suspicions regarding Parsons were confirmed. I had, the day before, met the ship's mascot, Baltazar, a blue and gold macaw. He was a constant fixture in the games room on the promenade deck, over which he regally presided, taking great joy in distracting serious gentlemen from their billiards with a well-timed squawk. I believe he was trying to say "bankshot" or "big shot" but "Bangkok" is also a distinct possibility. In any case he was an entertaining and intelligent bird. I watched him scramble various "parrot puzzles" with his claws. His principal keeper, a man named Mr. Wisniowski, administered the games room.

Baltazar was thirty-four years old and had made the *Empress* his home for the past fifteen years. He'd been rescued from a house of ill-repute in Manila, so the story went, when the police raided the premises and hauled his caretakers away, leaving the poor bird alone and destitute. There was a whiff of nostalgia about him, and this seemed even more pronounced when he welcomed the occasional female visitor with a nasally triumphant "*Bienvenida guapa!*" His head was a deep blue with an emerald-green crown. His neck, which Mr. Wisniowski called his "beard," though it looked nothing like it to me, was black, like his beak, and offered a striking contrast to his saffron-yellow underbelly. His primary feathers were a dark blue, his tail a somewhat softer blue. His rough cheeks looked as though he'd just endured a rather inexpert shave, though I was informed all macaws have only a thin striping of feathers there. His ice-blue eyes I found most penetrating.

His primary enjoyments seemed to be swinging on his ropes, heckling or complimenting the room's visitors, gnawing away at wooden chew toys and, of course, working on his puzzles, which Mr. Wisniowski had made, and I was invited to add to or improve if so inclined. He was remarkably agile with his sharp grey claws. He could remove the cork from a re-corked bottle in less than eight seconds, and delicately empty and refill a pack of cigarettes without shredding a single one. As if in encore he stripped a key chain of its owner's keys while hanging upside-down. He was a talented fellow, that Baltazar. Likely he had learned many of his skills from the working ladies of Manila, and no doubt they miss the old bird now, wherever they are. Despite his raucous ways— he sometimes could be quite loud—he was a treasure to visit on my rounds of the ship, and a very welcome diversion.

The day after meeting Baltazar I entered the games room only to find Parsons sitting on a bar stool in front of a snifter of brandy. "Will you have one with me, Doctor?" he asked. "Wet your whistle?" I told him it was a little early, though perhaps we could meet for a drink in a few hours' time? I thought this perfectly reasonable. I wanted to voice my concern indirectly, and thereby keep things civil between us.

"I'd be happy to invite you," I said. "Anyway, we could go down to the Steerage Bar. This one's a bit dear, I think."

"Not to worry," he answered, touching his front pocket. "Courtesy of the CAC."

I said, "Of course, you're aware that's not your money to spend."

"Now, now, one or two won't hurt, I'm sure."

"Doctor, I don't care what you do on your own time," I said, "but I'll tell you this only once: that is not your money to spend."

I had met people like Parsons over the years. In Montreal. In Madrid. I knew his sort well enough, the selfish addiction, the lying. He was the wicked and lazy servant in the Parable of the Talents who'd buried his talents in a bottle of rye.

Later, I found Jean on the promenade deck just outside the veranda café, bundled up and leaning against the railing watching the ocean. When I told her what I'd discovered, she clasped her hands over the railing and seemed justifiably concerned. I spoke in an even, hushed tone. We were shoulder to shoulder, close enough that I noticed the scent of her perfume, light, almost sweet, that came and went with the swirling wind. I suggested we come to an easy agreement as to our course of action regarding Charles, and to that end I recommended cabling New York with the demand that he be forced to provide an accounting of every last dime spent on board the *Empress of Asia*. This would definitively cut off his access to the remaining funds he carried.

Waiting for her consent, I watched the water far below us swirl and lap up against the bow like a live animal. It was deep blue, almost black.

"No," she said at last, "I will not join you in this coup."

"Please, don't let's overdramatize," I said. "This is merely a pragmatic reassignment of duties."

I went on to explain that only a directive from the China Aid Council would knock some sense into his sodden head, as he would never listen to us, certainly not to me. A strong scent of perfume came off her face then, or her neck.

"No," she said again, her answer as flat-out as it was incomprehensible. She would do no such thing. Needless to say I was taken aback. It was for the good of the cause, I insisted, keeping my voice level. I pushed her, still quietly, but with greater insistence.

"No, I will not," she said. She would give me no reason.

I wondered if her youth and inexperience prevented her from "tattling" on a colleague—an inexcusably adolescent way of looking at things, the least offensive reason available. Worse still would be a lack of commitment to the cause we were sailing into. Maybe she suffered from a fear of her own subordination, or simply an inferiority complex. Knowing Miss Ewen as I did, not well, surely, but well enough, I couldn't believe she would be so limited, so meek. I hoped above all that she'd taken this stand out of some misguided sense of compassion for a sick man. I was not afraid of ruffling feathers, I told her. Achieving our goals was of vastly greater importance than one man's suffering.

She said, still staring out to the ocean, "I know your reputation well enough, Doctor."

"Then you know I'm right," I said. To this she said nothing. "By the time we get to Hong Kong there'll be nothing left. You must reconsider. You know as well as I do how Parsons sits at that bar all day long. Good Lord, brandy for breakfast! I've seen it myself. It's astonishing. I swear I'll throw him overboard before he depletes our funds entirely. With or without your help."

This caused her to turn her head. She stared at me with those big dark young eyes of hers. She really was quite lovely, I realized then. "You will be throwing no one overboard, Doctor Bethune, today or any other day during this crossing. Not while I'm on board."

★

The evening after I confronted Jean began no differently from any other. On finishing with my writing, I was surprised to discover that it was nearing midnight. I'd been writing a paper for a medical journal, and with the intention of returning to it in the morning I set my notes aside and sought out a quiet stretch of deck up top. The ocean was calm and the air cold, a rich dampness that happily reminded me of my youth on the great Georgian Bay. I leaned against the rail and attempted to clear my thoughts. It was a wondrous thing to scatter the anxieties of the day over the ocean's wide expanse, and that is what I intended to do before retiring for the night. A glowing light was just barely visible in the west, a remnant of someone else's day, and a universe of stars sparkled overhead. I breathed deeply and conjured an image of you, my daughter, as you might be, warm, tiny, sleeping in your mother's arms.

Along the length of the deck, solemn, bundled figures leaned over the rail, caught in their own silent reveries. One of these figures, the closest to me, thirty or forty paces off, tossed a cigarette over the rail, hunched his shoulders and started for the nearest hatch, then stopped as if reconsidering. A cold wind was picking up. To me it was bracing, but for this man it might have been too much. I held my image of you a moment longer, wondering what at that precise time you were doing, when a voice interrupted my thoughts. It was Parsons. He was standing beside me.

"It's a long way down, Bethune," he said.

"Taking a break from the bar, are we?"

"Not too long a break, don't worry. Just off to the bank." He jangled the key to his cabin.

"You're a disgrace, Parsons."

"I suppose you wish we could all be a bit more like you." It was a stupid reversal. He was looking for a confrontation and past talking to, guaranteed more drunk than sober by this time of night. "You consider this your own personal cause, don't you. You think my bar tab will give the Japanese the advantage in China? That Fascism will overrun all of Asia because of a few drinks?"

"I think it best you pay your own way, Parsons," I told him, "nothing more than that. How you choose to deal with your problems is no concern of mine."

"Nor is it any concern of mine how you deal with yours. A thing like that—Madrid—stays with you, doesn't it."

I was silent, looking into his eyes.

"Yes," he said. "Madrid will be with you forever." He smiled, waiting for a fitting riposte. "Nothing to add? No righteous words from the great Bethune? Good, then I'll leave you to think this one through." And he turned casually, owning the moment, and walked away.

Clearly he thought he had something on me, but I'd been unable to ask what that might be, exactly. I suppose the violence of his emotion had silenced me. I will never argue with a drunk, not if I can help it, though I was eager to put the matter to rest.

The following morning, I planned to contact the CAC without Miss Ewen's help, even though I understood full well that only one name on the wire would be less persuasive. The telegraph room was situated just off the Captain's nest, and I was greeted there by a bright-looking young man. For a moment I was taken by the commanding perspective: below sat the entirety of the ship, bow to stern, port to starboard, while all around us the ocean stretched, peerless and indifferent. The young lad smiled and nodded. After commenting on the fine view, I explained the urgency of my telegram and directed him to send it off at the earliest convenience, and to inform me the moment my answer was received. Then I tipped my hat and left him to his work.

After a slow game of billiards with a fellow passenger I drank a lemonade in the lounge then retired to my cabin to look over some of my notes. It was a pleasant morning, unrushed yet quietly productive. I had sublimated my gloomy thoughts, and the possibility that Charles Parsons knew something more than he should have became a distant bother, not overly concerning. I caught up on some reading and later strolled the decks, learning the ship's plan more thoroughly. I enjoyed the views and, half past noon, snacked on a salmon omelette with jam and coffee at the café with a distinguished-looking Englishman who had some business with the Empress lines. As we talked, the ship's Captain greeted my companion, who then introduced us. Captain Aldridge Lawson seemed very interested in my work, as he had trained in medicine at Cambridge for a brief time before the Great War. He told me if I was free that evening he would be honoured by my presence at his table. I said he should count on it.

Later that day, as I was preparing for dinner, the knock I'd been waiting for sounded at my door. The lad from the telegraph office handed me a small envelope, barely the size of a personal calling card. I gave him a few coins and closed the door. It was not the news I'd been expecting. After reading the message, I slipped the telegram in my pocket. I have carried it with me to this day as a memento of the idiocy of bureaucrats everywhere.

DR H N BETHUNE

EMPRESS OF ASIA

COMMITTEE HAS COMPLETE FAITH IN ALL MEMBERS

OF EXPEDITION STOP WILL REQUIRE NO CHANGE OF

ACCOUNTING PRACTICES BEST OF LUCK

Despite this setback, I managed to pass a pleasant evening at dinner. Topics of discussion were as wide ranging as oceanic navigation, politics, medicine and, finally, over cognac and a cigar, the Great War. As a young man, our Captain had sailed on board HMS *Excelsior* as a petty officer with the Royal Navy. Also at the Captain's table was a terribly sententious missionary named Billingsley, out of Union College in Missouri, who showed a great interest in our expedition. He too was a fighting man, he said, but in God's army. "Bibles, not guns," he added. It turned out he was a Seventh Day Adventist. When I welcomed him to the struggle on behalf of the armed atheists and Communists of the world, he looked at me with an expression of true horror, as if he had never before laid eyes on a dirty Communist. His eyes seemed to ask how someone of obvious intelligence could support such a despicable social fantasy. Heads turned, and the other conversations at our table fell silent. The Reverend Mr. Billingsley regained his composure enough to say, "You're not *really* a Communist! Surely you see there is no future in Communism."

"On the contrary," I said, "that is precisely the future I hope will prevail. We have seen the avarice of Capitalism. Capitalism cannot care for the sick and needy. Capitalism can only enrich those still hungry for riches despite their obscene wealth."

He reached for his glass, sipped his wine and returned the glass to its place, then he folded his hands on the table and looked directly into my eyes. "We are bringing the word of God to those who hunger for it. Nothing less than the word of Jesus Christ. Spiritual hunger is what's bringing us, Doctor, and there's nothing faddish about that. Spiritual hunger is in many ways more devastating than the hunger for bread."

"My father might have said the same thing," I told him.

"Oh?" he said.

"He enjoyed a lofty career in the Presbyterian Church."

"Well, there you see. Perhaps he and I would see eye to eye."

"Perhaps you would have," I said. "He passed away some years ago."

He said, "I'm sorry to hear it."

"He had the Devil on the run his whole life."

"Isn't that what we all aspire to, Doctor Bethune, such an urgency of purpose? In one sense or another? To combat injustice, disease, war? The Devil has many names." As the white-gloved waiters appeared with a kingly looking roast of beef, I told Billingsley the story of how my family had moved from town to town in the service of the Church, and how in the end it was revealed that a pursuit of the Devil had rather little to do with it.

"Perhaps your father knew something you did not," he said. "Allow me to say that a son should not be so quick to dismiss his father's ideas."

I refrained from rolling my eyes. I only smiled, tilted my wineglass, drank and waited for an opportunity to shift the direction of our conversation. I feared that Billingsley might attempt to hatch some moral out of any story I might tell, or draw an unlikely parallel between me and my father and his desire to rout out evil wherever he should find it. For once I was not up to a heated discussion, and I didn't bother telling him that it was the people of those small Ontario towns, at first invigorated but soon threatened and finally wearied by my father's overbearing righteousness, who had sent us packing again and again.

The following morning Jean appeared at the entrance of the veranda café, wearing again the cap and cape she'd worn our first day out. I was sitting at my usual table, to port, beside a large window. It was not so uncommon, her stopping for breakfast there. We'd shared coffee and toast a number of times. I decided to cut to the point.

"Doctor Parsons is a thief *and* an outrageous drunk. I don't know for what you owe him your allegiance, but he cornered me the other night. He was talking nonsense. You wouldn't believe what he was going on about."

"Oh?" she said.

"What he said really isn't important. What's important is the quality of the man, not the nature of his lies. It is the fact of his lies that matters."

"He's willing to travel thousands of miles—"

"Look at the reality. It is the trusting nature of your youth that hopes for the best even when that's clearly unattainable."

"I think you underestimate—"

"My dear," I interrupted, "you're prone to *over*estimation. There is no alternative but to send that telegram. You will grant me that, I'm sure." I waited a moment to ensure my point had been made. She was silent. Believing all was settled, I got back to work.

Determined study has always been for me an effective tonic in the face of struggles. After taking my morning walk, I settled down quietly in the deep silence of the lounge. I felt the tension and bother of dealing with such a nuisance as Parsons fall away from me and was pleased to regain my focus. Around noon I decided, as a favour to myself, to stop off at the bar on upper deck to take something before proceeding to the café for a light meal. I felt I owed myself a treat. I'd been under a fair bit of strain and had, I thought, held up rather well. A familiar optimism was returning to me.

Just as I rounded a tall bookshelf, a man brushed against me. I was carrying a journalistic account of the China situation called *Far Eastern Front*. This young man, about thirty or thirty-five, nodded politely, glimpsed the title and said, "Snow, hell of a writer," then introduced himself. When I gave him my name, Eli Ansell said, "Ah, yes, Doctor Bethune, I was told you were on board. What a great honour."

"You're off to the war, then," I said, "or just an interested Sinologist?"

"Both," he said. "As a journalist, actually."

It took me some minutes to realize that I'd read a number of his pieces in *Voice of Action*, a Seattle-based newspaper, including an explosive article five or so years before about an innocent Negro accused of murdering a white man. The newspaper's coverage had obliged the authorities to admit the truth: that their case was racially biased and the accused totally innocent. I told him I'd followed all this as closely as I could, living at the time in Detroit. A member of the American Newspaper Guild, he was off to cover the same war I was headed into. Slim and elegant with a pencil-thin moustache, narrow fingers and a sharp, dimpled chin, he had a strong nose, thick black hair, and—I saw as our crossing continued—he was forever scribbling in a small notebook he carried with him everywhere. I asked what he expected to find in China.

"I hope to get to Nanking," he said. "What's happening there is fascinating. I understand that Tang Shengzhi's ordered a retreat to the other side of the Yangtze. The city's fallen to the Japanese. There are rumours of a street purge. I have a name to focus on— a Kraut, a Nazi, actually, called John Rabe. He's there with the Siemens China Corporation. Now he's head of the International Committee that's trying to protect whoever they can. They're setting up safety zones and getting embassies to open their doors to refugees. It's a powerful irony, a Nazi sticking his neck out like that given what they've been up to in Europe. It's a compelling story, and news is just starting to trickle out. Incredible stuff, really. The numbers are astonishing if you happen to believe them."

"The only war people care about these days," I said, "is in Spain."

"Causes don't interest me so much as stories. Characters, Doctor. Without heroes and villains a war doesn't sell papers. The man makes the story. Speaking as a journalist, that is."

"Quite the opposite in my case," I said.

"How's that?"

I thought of Spain, and then of what awaited us in China. "People don't interest me as much as the cause they fight for."

*

Earlier this evening I asked Ho to sit for me. He was uncharacteristically still, quietly reading a thin, well-thumbed book. I walked back to my hut to fetch pad and pencil. He regarded me with some curiosity, then simply resumed reading. When I finished drawing I showed him my work. I think I rather like it, but I can't tell from his reaction if he's pleased or not. I'll call it *Chinese Boy Reading.*

★

Well, the truth is, I needed to know what Parsons knew about Madrid. What did he think might frighten me? I had nothing to hide, so what blackmail could he have up his sleeve? Perhaps my conversation with Ansell about Nanking had inspired me to take matters into my own hands. Or maybe it was simply frustration. Whatever the reason, I resolved to meet Parsons head-on, since the tomfoolery between us had become time-consuming. I decided to confront him as early in the morning as possible, before the first drink touched his lips. He would, I hoped, be forthcoming, if asked directly what rumours he'd heard, from whom. Then we could have it out. For the first time in days I felt buoyant.

That morning I knocked at cabin C37 and silently stood, waiting. After a moment I knocked again. "Parsons?" I called out. "Listen, open up, it's Bethune."

There was no answer, so I tried the door and found it unlocked, then pushed it open and looked inside. The bed was unmade, with clothing strewn about, and on the ledge by the porthole sat an empty liquor bottle, beside it an overflowing ashtray. I stepped across the threshold and again called, "Parsons?" I could hear the shower running in the bathroom.

Surveying the cabin, I noticed a stack of envelopes tied with string on the dresser to the right of the bathroom door. Scattered there were a number of folders, a set of keys, a wallet, a loosely knotted necktie and an unframed photograph, curling up at the edges, of a young woman. When I turned it over and read the inscription, I felt a moment of mercy for him. Nothing in it made me think that the pretty young woman on the reverse was dead, but it was somehow obvious enough. Exhibit 1. Parsons's entire world was contained within that picture of the young woman of seventeen or eighteen—an only child, I imagined, I don't know why.

I stepped forward and examined the pile of envelopes. The third from the top, bearing the seal of the China Aid Council, contained the money in question. Minus a week's worth of drinking, it was all there. I tucked the envelope into my breast pocket and silently closed the door behind me.

Up on the promenade deck a few moments later, I found it was a chilly, bright and refreshing morning. As I rounded the bow from port to starboard, I spotted Alicia with her Aunt Gwendolyn and thought perhaps this might be an opportune time to engage them in conversation. They were taking the sun, sitting side by side in a pair of rented lounge chairs. "I wonder," I said, approaching them, "if I might make a request?"

"Anything at all, Doctor Bethune," Gwendolyn said.

I'd been mulling something over for a number of days, in fact ever since seeing Alicia feeding the seagulls that first morning. "I'm looking to make a portrait, and I'd be greatly honoured if Alicia would agree to sit for me. She is such a lovely child, as of course you know."

"Oh, yes," Alicia replied. "Please, I've never had my picture painted! Do say yes, Gwen!"

Gwendolyn smiled and said she had no objections, though I suspected she might herself have wanted a painter to fuss over her.

"You say you've never had your portrait painted?" I was still standing, slightly hunched, cupping my knees with my hands. "Well, then, what about it?"

Only slightly chilled under the weak winter sun, we met

every morning on the promenade deck. She was always there, waiting for me, as prompt and energetic as she was young and pretty, and pleased to have an adult taking her so seriously. After a casual greeting and friendly chitchat, she sat perfectly still and without complaint, wrapped in a heavy sweater, for long stretches at a time: with eyes staring out to sea; sitting, standing; lying back on her deck chair; sometimes curling a lock of hair between her fingers. Her aunt was always in the next chair, quietly reading one of her poetry books.

One morning Gwendolyn straightened her back and said, "Will you just listen to this one? It's so lovely it makes me want to throw myself into the ocean and die!"

After that day she started reading to us while I worked. Her niece listened quietly. I wondered what an eight-year-old thinks when an adult says something about throwing herself into the ocean, but it wasn't long before I saw that she understood her aunt's flights of fancy and extravagant speech. Often, when Alicia began to fidget, usually after half an hour, I recommended a break of ten or fifteen minutes. She skipped rope while Gwendolyn and I spoke about the civil war in China and the subsequent Japanese invasion, and about her interests as a student of poetry. She read the "new poetry," as she called it, because it was real and unfettered by convention or tradition. Smiling, she admitted she could only ever be an observer of genius. Perhaps, I said, but an astute observer, I'm sure. As I painted in the pale winter sunlight, chilled but comfortable enough, she read Eliot for us and Pound and William Carlos Williams and Wallace Stevens. The Pacific stretched as far as the eye could see.

We were, by then, well away from where we'd started, yet still many days from where we were headed. The colours of the ocean were muted, but it was always calm, flat and soothing, with browns and greys. Sometimes, if the light touched the surface just so, I could see a shine as of liquid mercury at the forward edge of a soft rise in the water. I painted the young girl sitting, standing, or lying while, hidden in the inner breast pocket of my light green Abercrombie & Fitch jacket, I carried the stolen money.

Time spent with Alicia and Gwendolyn was a welcome respite. I began to enjoy the company of this child and her poetry-loving aunt for their own sake, as well as for the entertainment and diversion they promised. I was appreciative of their indulgence of my painterly musings. I was not as gifted as I may have made myself out to be, though I had dabbled for many years, principally in the portraits of various friends and intimate acquaintances. Yet despite the hours spent painting Alicia, and the calming presence of the smooth ocean, the crossing was by then proving tedious.

At the end of my fourth day at the easel, I turned to glimpse an unusually dark cloud on the far eastern horizon and saw the Captain walking purposefully toward me. Could there finally be a storm on the way? I wondered. The cloud, it turned out, immense though it was, was not in our path. The Captain greeted me and, with some curiosity, regarded my painting for a moment without speaking. "You are a surprising man, indeed," he said at last.

"How so?" I asked. I didn't turn from the canvas.

"Do you play Bach and Mozart too, Doctor?"

"I have far less art in me than you think, Captain. I only entertain myself. It helps fill the time."

"I wonder if you might have heard," he said, "the news from Doctor Parsons?"

"What news is that?"

"He didn't tell you? It seems we have a thief on board."

"A thief?"

"Oh, the doctor was terribly upset. Rightly so, I should say.

A fair bit of money's gone missing." He quoted the amount in question, the precise amount hidden in my inner breast pocket. "This isn't common knowledge, of course," he said.

"Of course. But you've got established methods on board, I imagine. A protocol for this sort of situation?"

"Oh, yes, we'll get our man, Doctor Bethune. Not to worry. There are certain tricks we have for bringing a man like this forward."

"Yes, I'm sure you have," I said.

*

I walked a tightrope. I kept busy, all the while willing the ship to make land. Most mornings I met with the girl and her aunt and painted while listening to the poems of Wallace Stevens.

> Complacencies of the peignoir, and late
> Coffee and oranges in a sunny chair,
> And the green freedom of a cockatoo
> Upon a rug mingle to dissipate
> The holy hush of ancient sacrifice.

When she finished reading the poem, I said, "Did you know we have a macaw on board? An intelligent creature. I will take you both one morning to see him."

Little by little, the endless expanse of the Pacific began to shape my imagination. The ocean became a vast desert and we a minute organism crawling over its back. I immersed myself in the details of the painting as the words fell from Gwendolyn's lips. The green freedom of a cockatoo. The oranges. The light. The peignoir. When the light faded, however, I yet again set out to begin this story, and yet again failed. I was two men. Busy, engaging and visible by day. But alone in my cabin at night, solemn and introspective, my dreams troubled. The mornings were most productive. Dabbling. Listening. Dreaming as I painted portraits that gave me no end of relief.

Of course, there were options. I considered sneaking back with the money, slipping it under Parsons's door or between that stack of envelopes where I'd found it. But that brought me back to the problem of keeping Parsons sober, and long enough to hold his tongue. Plus he'd polish off another good chunk of money that would certainly have better uses in less than a month's time. One morning, as I touched my brush to a lovely daub of fresh-face pink I'd just created, the Captain rounded the corner. Had I been found out?

"Doctor," he said with a wide grin. "Good morning. I wonder if you would consider a proposition." He stopped to consider the painting. "Why, this is coming along nicely."

"A proposition?"

"I would be honoured if you would deliver an address for us. Something very informal. Unofficial. Something personal, perhaps. I understand you were quite active about Madrid, speaking to audiences on the radio and so on, and back in Canada before joining us. I've talked to a number of passengers who remember you from the wireless."

I asked him what he had in mind.

"Nothing political, of course," he said. "That wouldn't do. We shan't get into that on board here. Not quite appropriate, you understand. But something . . . more personal, I wonder? Anything, really. People are interested, Doctor. You've led an interesting life. Made a name for yourself. We have a good many important passengers on board, and I've asked a number of them. Sort of an onboard lecture series. Keeps the mind busy."

"Indeed," I said.

"Think about it, will you?"

"But I have no idea what to talk about beyond my interest in politics and medicine. This is very flattering, Captain, but personal stories? I'm not so good at that."

"Well, think about it, anyway."

Yet I was obliged to admit to myself that the idea had intrigued me. In fact I couldn't stop thinking about the offer, for a number of reasons. Was I flattered? Yes, I was. But I smelled an opportunity here, too, to advance the cause of justice in China.

★

Am feeling buoyed today, despite the cold. General Nieh has promised to secure a dynamo and a small gas engine to run it. Every bit counts, and this is more than a bit. A dynamo-electric machine is as good as gold out here. I have also requested a Chinese dictionary. My language skills are well below what they should be. Mr. Tung helps immeasurably with that, but how I would like to go the extra mile for these fine people here. They bend over backwards to make me as comfortable as possible and all I seem to do is show my impatience with them. Patience never was my strong suit, as I'm sure you've gathered, and this war's fearsome horrors are taking a toll on what little stock I started with. Every morning I remind myself that my medical staff were tilling the fields and tending livestock only nine months ago, never even having heard of such basic materials as a catheter or cotton gauze. The work is drearily repetitive and sad—so many dead and wounded, in cold relentless enough to break a healthy man—but emotionally I'm feeling better these days. Some small signs of hope, starting with the dynamo. Given all the supplies needed and twenty or thirty trained medical staff, I would be the happiest man on earth.

★

One morning on board, after a difficult night, I was stepping out to meet Alicia and her aunt for another sitting. When I opened my cabin door I was surprised to find Miss Ewen standing there. We startled one another.

"You've surprised me," she said, regaining her composure.

"You've not come calling for me?"

"I'm just walking," she said. "Learning the ship."

"I'm on my way up top. I'll walk with you." She was dressed in a cream-coloured dress and jacket suit. She was very pretty that day, I remember, with a light grey handkerchief over her hair. "I suppose it's blowing out there a bit," I said.

"Yes," she said, "it is."

As we walked the length of the corridor she asked about the supplies I carried under my arm. I told her about the portrait I was painting.

"You've fortified yourself against this monotony," she said. "Good for you. On board one has so much time to think. Perhaps a little too much."

"The mind can go in circles," I said.

We turned a corner and ascended a flight of stairs.

"I *was* coming to call, actually," she said. "You caught me in the midst of reconsidering."

"Reconsidering?"

"Yes, I'm ashamed to say. I wanted to talk to you about Charles."

"You've reconsidered my proposal?"

"I think he invented his story about someone stealing the money."

"Why do you say that?" I said. "Do you know something?"

"There is no evidence that anyone entered his quarters. I've spoken to the Captain on this matter. There's nothing to go on but his word. We already know of his drinking. That's the only thing we really do know."

"What do you suggest, then?" I asked.

"It's a terrible mess. It's all unravelling, isn't it."

We came upon a hatch leading out to the promenade deck. I pushed it open for her and touched her elbow ever so slightly as she stepped over the small rise and out into the morning sunshine. "I feel so traitorous. Villainous. The fact is, I just don't know."

"You may feel as you must, Miss Ewen, but you must also feel right about sending the telegram. I will not force you. This has to be your decision."

"It is," she said.

It was clear that Jean found it unkind and perhaps even dishonourable to go behind Parsons's back as we eventually did, and that she felt she might have crushed something in herself in turning on this "kind and helpless man." I assured her we had no other choice. She knew, finally, what she had to do. The telegram went out that same afternoon, signed by the both of us, requesting that the CAC relieve Parsons of his financial responsibilities. We stayed together a short time after that, walking slowly. I assured her that we had pursued the correct course of action. She seemed needful of assurance, so I told her that when replacement funds were eventually wired to Hong Kong, as surely they would be, every last dime would be used for the purpose intended. In that we could be proud.

What about Parsons, then, now that Jean and I had sent the telegram?

I was careful about reintroducing the money into the coffers of the expedition. It couldn't simply reappear, just like that, without raising suspicion. What I did was this: I accepted the Captain's offer to speak, on the condition that following my address, donations might be made in a discreet manner to a non-political, non-partisan humanitarian effort to benefit victims of the war in China. The Captain was delighted to comply.

When we received a telegram in response to ours two days later—which happened to be the day of my lecture—it officially discharged Parsons of all financial duties and "effected a transfer to Dr. Bethune." He might not have known before then that I'd actively set about undermining him, but he would know it now, just as I knew surely enough that not much time would pass before he came to take my measure.

During the increasing turbulence of those days I quite miraculously cobbled together some thoughts for the talk I'd promised to give. So it was, after a torturously long dinner on Friday evening, that our Captain rose, tapping his wineglass with a slender silver fork, and called the hall's attention to where I sat at the head table. Billingsley, Parsons, Jean and Gwendolyn, with pretty Alicia, were all seated about the room. The Captain cleared his throat with great force and said, "Ladies and gentlemen, tonight we have the honour . . ." and so on, and after his humbling introduction I rose, bowed as graciously as possible, and walked to the podium, which stood at the front of the hall, where a small team of busboys had assembled it as we ate. The first face I saw, of course, was that of my chief adversary.

Parsons smiled at me, and in that moment I was convinced that he'd put the Captain up to this. Invite Bethune, by all means, he would have said, he won't be able to resist. The man's vanity is unsurpassed. I returned his smile. Perhaps for a moment my mind went blank with fear. The diners were silent now. I might have blinked uncontrollably and fidgeted with my hands. Yet I remember thinking, quite clearly, too, that this was what it must

feel like to stand before your accuser—your victim, in a sense—
while observed by a jury of your peers, your every tic observed,
registered, every pause, every garbled word, every drop of pitiable
sweat as you made your case. My case, indeed. And so I began:

"Ladies and gentlemen." My eyes roamed over the audience.
I was by then a practised public speaker. I'd taken my film about
the mobile unit in Spain to over fifty cities in Canada and the
United States, and had lectured in a great many teaching hospitals. I tried to regulate my breathing. "It is an honour to share
with you some thoughts I have compiled here on the . . ."

He was waiting. Well, let him wait.

" . . . on the nature of . . . truth."

Could I be as audacious as this? I hope you will forgive me.

"The entire world," I continued, "indeed, humanity itself,
craves the basic foundation of truth, the bedrock of our existence.
Political truth. Moral truth. Social truth. Aesthetic truth."

My notes, I noticed then, were still folded in my hand. I'd not
had the presence of mind to follow what I had prepared.

"Humanity. The man to your left. The woman to your right.
We, all of us. Choose whatever avenue you care to look down, and
on a clear day you'll see what we all want in this life, no matter
where you live or whom you love. And that thing is truth. The fundamental truth of the ages, equality, purity, brotherhood. The most
profound question of existence, the question of *why,* can only be
answered thus, with an appeal to truth. That each man bears within
his soul the dignity and value of a thousand men, and each of that
thousand, each within his soul, likewise possesses the dignity and
value of that one man. Are we not here, I wonder, on board this
ship, on this earth, to seek and to find the truth as it resides within
each of us, in whatever form we may carry it? We must all have this
basis, this foundation, for the lives we lead, for without it we are

lost, loveless and bereft. Life's handiwork—our deeds—shall mark us all, individually, as seekers of truth, and it is by these markers that we know if we succeed or fail in this life.

"None of us is perfect. No science or religion or church can make that claim. But it is the perfection of our dreams that may deliver us through that great searching; and those dreams—of how the world should be, might be one day, shall be one day—fuel our hope and the fire in our breasts that we might leave this place a little better than we found it.

"This evening I stand here before you, at the invitation of our Captain and in so great a room as this, aboard such a proud vessel, to share my thoughts on the essence of *man*. For it is the men of character who enact the necessary changes that lead us, as a society, from one momentous change to the next.

"We are at just such a juncture here, at a moment of change. And it is up to us. We are the privileged generation on whom falls this greatest of responsibilities."

I sipped from my water glass and waited, but he did not rise.

"We are, most of us, strangers aboard this ship. Yet even still we are a community, a whole society of shared stories, ideals and aspirations. And it is from our experience, our shared history, that we derive these ideals and aspirations. When I think back to my own father, most certainly a wise man, to be sure, but also head-strong, prone to outburst and deeply set in his ways, I can recall mostly conflict, yes, the common conflicts of father and son, but also conflicts of a more profound nature. Yet without his example and the subsequent differences that rose between us, I would have been unable to help change my small corner of the world—and I hope my work shall continue. Why this reflection on my good father? Simply to say that there are conflicts between good men. Honest men. And when injury is sustained, let the weaker man understand that the fight was one of ideals, not personalities. Principle, not spite. My father was such a man, and though our principles clashed, our respect sustained us. Let that be true of all men as we struggle to make our way in the world."

His head was turned down. He'd picked up a spoon and was cleaning out the last of the Devonshire cream from his strawberry torte.

"I would not at this moment find myself in your midst, sailing to Asia, toward that struggle presently underway in China, without the battle that ensued between myself and my father, this clash of wills that did so much to remind me of my limitations, but also of my potential. I would urge you all to seek out the nobility that each of us holds within and to give forgiveness when it is offered, even silently, and when a man stands exposed before you to rise above your limitations, to find that fundamental truth we all share, that need for purity and justice for the one man and the thousand men. For our life and times rest in the hands of the many millions of individuals like yourselves in this world who will be brave enough to conquer first the injustice within our own hearts, and then the injustice of others."

The applause from the audience rose before me. I bowed modestly. "Thank you," I said. I smiled, bowed again, then sat down.

ENVELOPE FOUR

A lovely day, finally, here in the 1st Sub-District of Yang Chia Chuang. It is early December. We for weeks have been having rotten weather, but yesterday the cold cloud cover broke to reveal a razor-sharp, ice-blue sky. I managed a walk up the hill just north of camp and enjoyed the sound of virgin snow crunching under my boots. It is a youthful sound, and I hope you come to know it. I was able to clear my head, if only for a moment, and inhale the perfect day. Very invigorating. The respite didn't last long, of course. But it was a much-needed reminder that such moments are still possible in this mad rush to kill one another.

Perhaps it's still early enough in this story to admit to you without fear of stating the obvious that the people in my life—those who surround me now, who crowd my past—are and always have been my fuel, my inspiration, my *tabula rasa*. I cut my teeth upon their sores and injuries, illnesses and deaths. This life you hold before you is built upon the broken lives of thousands. In these dark moments I seem no more than an assemblage of their parts. In this I do not condemn myself, but there is a sadness there. Any truthful man of medicine, indeed science, will tell you the same.

But will he truly understand it, how indebted we are to misfortune, upheaval and disaster? That is another question. How, for example, an engineer benefits from the collapse of a bridge spanning the Thames, the Seine, the Ganges. Among the dead sadly bobbing in the waters below he is able to locate the structural flaw triggered by the final, unsupportable sixty-three pounds that was the nine-year-old boy accompanying his mother to school. The final straw in mangled clothes. This is the pursuit of science: the mastery and manipulation of facts revealed to us through tragedy and misfortune. Yes, mastery and manipulation. It is all but carrion for the vultures of progress such as myself. And though the test of Parsons was hardly scientific, that evening's manipulation of words aboard the *Empress* stands as an example of the dedicated scientist's will to survive to see another day.

Though I have successfully approximated the words I spoke that evening, I must confess that at the time I hardly knew what I was saying. For a time Parsons's silence was equally confusing. He said not a word. He had me as good as naked before the crowd and simply smiled. In fact he politely applauded. Of course, it is not unusual that the words of a duplicitous man be honoured. We see it everywhere with our politicians, bishops and bankers. But Parsons turned the other cheek. Could he be as big as that? Was he, with that silence, demonstrating his superiority or intellectual indifference? To these words, a shallow invention of the moment, he turned his cheek.

There's nothing like deprivation to get you thinking about who you are and what you're made of. And when you do, it registers as something of a shock that there is no easy answer. What comes instead of answers is a deep morass of images, doubts and contradictions. They applauded my words! My strength of spirit and selflessness were heralded. Perhaps we all have such shameful episodes.

So it seemed my gamble had paid off. All donations received that day went into the CAC's coffers, with an additional amount in the form of the money I'd rescued. With his reduced responsibilities and total absence of funds, Charles Parsons was silenced. An alcoholic without his comfort is like a bear without claws—at least this one was. What I didn't know was whether he'd chosen silence or it had been chosen for him. During the four days we remained on board, he seemed unable to bear the confines of his own skin. I don't know if he suffered hallucinations, but his withdrawal was a terrible thing to watch. How I admired Miss Ewen then—and strangely envied Parsons. She visited his cabin often and, I imagine, provided him with the moral support of a kind and patient soul. Did they ever talk of me or the conspiracy I'd engineered? I couldn't say. But I'm certain she felt partly responsible for his condition, though of course she hadn't separated him from the treasury that had enabled his good humour and tacit dominance over me. He no longer attended meals but ate, if at all, alone in his cabin.

*

On the nineteenth day of our crossing, the edge of Asia came into view just as a storm appeared on the western horizon. Charles, leaning over the rail, vomited, having just a moment before attempted a bit of porridge at breakfast. It was his first visit to the café since my talk. When I looked up and saw land in a thin, incandescent shimmer of blue light between sea and sky, I said, with great relief, "There it is, Charles. Have you ever seen anything like it? And those storm clouds to whip up the sea in our wake like a dragon snapping at our heels!"

He turned his head up, watched for a moment and was sick again. I left him to his misery, returning to my cabin to prepare the portmanteau in which I carried my most personal possessions, including a number of paints, brushes and small canvases. I then made arrangements with the head porter regarding the field hospital, having determined the day before that this should be sent directly to the proper holding facility once we docked. I found Mrs. Qimei, shook her hand and told her to look for a little something under the third pillow she'd provided me with our first day out. Finally I sought out Miss Ewen to inquire if she could use a hand. Around noon I returned to the forward deck. The storm was behind us, closer still. Mile-high thunderheads cast a shadow over the ship, but we were outside its immediate influence, and Hong Kong was clearly visible ahead, sparkling in bright sunlight. It looked, from the bow, even from the distance of a hundred miles, perhaps, a busy and optimistic town. It was a sign of hope, a beacon pulling us in. We would beat the storm and complete the crossing without seasickness. As I stood admiring the view, the Captain approached.

"The case will stay open, naturally," he said, after I inquired. "There are still procedures. Lines of inquiry."

"Could this be a crime with no criminal? Is that possible?"

"We have beaten the weather by only a few hours," he said. "Our man may think he's gotten away with something too, I suspect." We shook. "Perhaps we will meet again," he said.

"I should like that."

Mid-afternoon, after walking about the ship to bid farewell to passengers, such as the journalist Ansell, with whom I'd shared a drink and conversation, we entered Victoria Harbour. We disembarked with great excitement, and after passing through Customs and collecting our things from the baggage master we entered a waiting throng. Gwendolyn and the girl were greeted by a young woman—Alicia's mother, no doubt—and I decided not to interrupt their happy reunion.

I was just then thinking that our adventure was now truly begun, when Parsons turned to me, quite recovered from his sickness that morning. In fact he was defiant.

"What is it?" I said.

He put his finger in my face. "Bethune, you're a son of a bitch."

"Let's just get on with it, shall we?" I said. "We've got bigger fish to fry, don't you think?"

His face turned red. He looked as if he were about to explode. "You're a manipulative scheming son of a bitch. And you," he said, turning to Jean, "you were part of this. But I'll give you some advice. He found you useful. No more than that. How much longer before he sticks a knife in your back? He's not here for the reasons he says. Ask him about Madrid. Go on, ask him."

"Charles," she said.

"Jesus Christ, woman!"

The poor girl simply shook her head, flummoxed.

He cursed, turned and pushed through the crowd. When I lost sight of him I said, "Should we follow him?"

"He has every right to detest us for what we've done," she said.

The rest of that first day in Hong Kong she wouldn't speak to me. For a time that afternoon I believed I'd soon be on my own. Without a word, she cut through the crowd to begin arranging our transportation to the hotel. Rather foolishly, like an imp of a husband suffering the vile moods of a temperamental wife, I meekly soldiered on. But before long, I shook off this constricting fantasy by quickly running through the facts as they stood. If she didn't grasp the basic assumptions of war, sacrifice and adaptability, well, she would have to learn.

Our cabs were rickshaws piloted by coolies, whom we found among a large group of labourers gathered at the port's entrance. Our man loaded our luggage in the small compartment at the back of the contraption, helped Jean up and off we went. We rode in silence but for the quick breaths of the fellow ahead of us, his rapid pedalling and the general buzz of the city. It was a refreshing tour in that it provided much diversion. After the sombre blues and greys of the winter-bleak Pacific, we saw here a wild feast of smells and sounds and colours. Kabob and fruit vendors filled the air with their delicious offerings. Even now, I recall the joyful clatter of the busy streets, the racket the coolies made calling after one another in their flat nasal tongue, the local merchants rubbing elbows with the fashionably dressed Brits shuffling between appointments. It was a land where nationalities and races met, I saw immediately, and nothing like Europe. There was too much to absorb and too much at stake for the petty concerns of a young nurse to interfere. It was already passing as I watched this glorious city unfold before my eyes. I had made it. And if the topic of Madrid happened to surface between us, well, that would be dismissed as the raving of a detoxifying alcoholic.

We were delivered to the Ambassador Hotel, in the Wan Chai district of shops and restaurants, but found no communication waiting from our contact or any indication that he might make himself known. By now it was quite clear that Jean would spend the rest of the afternoon digesting the fact of Parsons's defection. I would use the time to ponder alternative plans. "What do you say we meet down here in the morning?"

She agreed without a word, just a nod, and left me. After unpacking in my room I sat and considered our circumstances. First, she was only sulking. Second, I must compose a note to our contact, which I left at the front desk in a sealed envelope. In it I indicated that we'd arrived and were eager to commence the next leg of our journey to the mainland.

I used the remainder of the afternoon to go over the final edit of my paper for *The Journal of Thoracic Medicine*. I typed out a clean copy and left it at the front desk to be posted. It was by now past six o'clock. I decided a brisk walk to stretch my legs was in order, then asked the concierge for the most recent English-language newspapers. He produced a three-day-old edition of the *South China Morning Post* and a *Manchester Guardian* dated January 8. I thanked the man, tucked the papers under my arm and set out to find a well-lit bar and catch up on what was happening in the world. The evening sky was clear and cold. It was dark now. I wandered through the neighbourhood for close to half an hour before dipping into a small pub named The Goose's Lantern. You might have thought you were in Soho or Piccadilly. I found a quiet corner, ordered a double brandy and flipped through the *Guardian* first. I wasn't merely surprised by what I found, I was overjoyed. After reading the article through twice, I tore it out and put it in my pocket.

MADRID

The rebel military commander at Teruel, Colonel Rey Dancourt, has surrendered with 1,500 men, it is claimed. The Colonel is reported to have said that only a small group of rebels, with whom he had been out of touch, remained in the Convent of Santa Clara. His surrender would seem to indicate that no more than a handful of rebels are now putting up resistance there.

Outside the city, however, the battle still continues with unabated fury. The rebels are daily massing new troops in order to recapture Teruel. These troops are being withdrawn from other fronts.

The Republican Command declares that the rebels today employed the famous Italian 'Black Arrows' for the first time on this front.

Yesterday, which saw the fiercest fighting since the rebel counter-offensive began, they made repeated attacks from Concud, the village to the northwest. Preceded by intense artillery and aviation bombardments, these attacks were supported by tanks and armoured cars. The Republican infantry, it is claimed, not only maintained their positions but forced the attackers to retire with heavy losses.

In the Muela de Teruel sector the Republicans took the offensive and occupied several positions, which they held under fire, on the Villastar–Teruel road.

The rebel army is considered here a spent and weary force. During the last eight days it has suffered several setbacks and enormous casualties. It is felt that the rebels' determination to recover Teruel is dictated by the knowledge that its presence in the hands of the Government must completely upset plans for any offensive on other fronts.

It was a major victory, as you can see. Delighted, I ordered another drink. After savouring this news a moment longer I turned to the *Post* and found nothing about the war in Spain, only a small article about the situation in Nanking, where Ansell was heading to look for his good Nazi. This wasn't such a joyous bit of news. The story itself concerned not the fall of the city but an article published only a few days before in an Osaka newspaper. *The Mainichi Shinbun* reportage had been about morale-boosting among the troops, and two officers said to have engaged in a "killing competition" on December 24, tallying over a hundred Chinese civilians each; final score, it said, was 106 to 105. These murders had been sanctioned by Japanese command in order to provide inspiration for a patriotic song about their valiant warriors' shining swords of steel. Curiously, the *Post* presented this story without editorial comment, its blasé manner making an odd and terrible story even more disturbing. I'd seen men killed in Belgium, France and Spain. They'd always fallen on the battlefield. This type of systematic, barbaric slaughter had nothing to do with war. It was a new brand of Fascism, a nihilism even more absolute and hideous than what I'd witnessed in Spain.

I remember reading through both papers, and when finished I watched the street fill with nighttime revellers. I ordered another brandy, bought a package of cigarettes and smoked, pondering the recent developments near Madrid. Certainly they would reduce the likelihood of a renewed offensive against the capital, open the Madrid–Barcelona corridor and generally swing the war's momentum in favour of the Republic.

When I returned to the hotel, just before midnight, I found that our contact had not yet presented himself to the front desk. It now seemed he would not show, and that we would be denied the support promised by the Ba lu Jun, the anti-Japanese network based in Hong Kong that had organized the second leg of our journey. As the head of the unit, Parsons had likely been informed where to find them, but we had not. From this point on, we'd be responsible for arranging everything on our own. Annoyed and dismayed, I decided then and there to make alternative plans. With medical supplies that were urgently needed, I could not abide any avoidable delays.

The following afternoon, after meeting Jean for breakfast— at which we spoke politely, though she still seemed somewhat distant—I went out for a better look at the town, believing she only needed a bit more time to herself. I walked at a brisk pace but was often stopped in my tracks by the faces I encountered. Though temporarily trapped on this small island, already I felt the lure of a giant continent looming in the mist only forty miles to the west. Energy, excitement and mystery dripped from the air like the juices of a mango. Here were banks and streetcars, pharmacies, jewellers, groceries and fishmongers, pubs, currency exchangers, beggars and churches—all things I'd always known, but here angled differently, tinged in new and exciting colours that filled me with uncontained wonder. Everything that made a city modern. Yet I was also confronted by its historic self, shadows and myths shining in the eyes of a people, beautiful, diminutive and deferential. All around me I saw the undeniable hues of the ancient in the bony chests and wiry arms of the rickshaw coolies who plied these streets with the bountiful spirit of children, men who I now know might work a lifetime without ever owning the rickshaw they wheel about.

I awoke refreshed the next morning and breakfasted at the cafeteria on the ground floor. Jean joined me not long after I ordered, seemingly recovered from her mood. I told her I was glad this debacle was at last behind us. We spoke, finally, of the business at hand and decided we couldn't afford to wait on the caprice of an anonymous contact. Our man had failed us, so we resolved to take advantage of a contact of Jean's. She had, you'll remember, lived and worked in Shantung in the early 1930s. She had a number of connections, all foreign nationals, including the American journalist Agnes Smedley, whose book *China's Red Army Marches* I'd attempted to read on the train from New York to Seattle and finished on board the *Empress*. It offered a riveting account of Mao's famous Long March in 1935. Of course, I knew about this epic event before picking up the book. It was, without doubt, the most significant turning point to date in the Chinese civil war, as it had guaranteed the survival of the Communist Army. Mao Tse-tung had led tens of thousands of men from certain death at the hands of the Kuomintang, Chiang Kai-shek's Nationalist army, by breaking through their lines in southern China, at Kiangsi Province, and delivering them over a three-year, five-thousand-mile ordeal into the hard, desolate hills of Shensi Province, where they were able to reorganize and swell their fighting force by perhaps a hundredfold. Smedley grasped the enormity of this achievement perhaps better than any other journalist I was aware of. It would do well to make her acquaintance. Clearly she wasn't hampered by journalistic neutrality.

Jean got a cable off to Miss Smedley within the hour, and before noon we had received her reply, urging us to join her in Hankou, some seven hundred miles north, on the mainland.

★

Our arrangements with the China National Aviation Corporation were made that very day, and the following morning, close to nine o'clock, we climbed aboard our plane and bade farewell to Hong Kong. The DC-2 bounced around somewhat as she lifted into the air, and the noise of her twin engines rang through her thin silver plating with a vibrating scream that continued through the anxious length of the flight. The first hours over the mainland were spent seeking cloud cover, as all Chinese aviation, including civilian traffic, was considered legal prey by the Japanese fighters that regularly patrolled the skies west of the colony. One expected at any minute to see a pair of Ki-27s come racing out of the clouds, machine guns blazing, to send us to our deaths. I'll admit here feeling quite helpless, like a sitting duck, but Jean seemed perfectly calm. We touched down a few hours later on a grassy strip near Wuchow. Here our aircraft was refuelled as a dozen men, forming a human conveyor belt, passed hand to hand fifty or sixty five-gallon canisters of fuel, beginning at a small wood shed on the bank of the river and ending up in the fuselage of the plane, a process that took a good half hour. During this time all passengers—travellers of various nationalities and ethnicities—were invited to disembark and stretch their legs. This was also a safety precaution, as enemy fighters would find a fat, refuelling DC-2 an irresistible target for strafing or bombing.

I left Jean standing with the other passengers fifty yards upwind of the stench of gasoline, huddling together against the chill air, and wandered over to the river. My ears still ringing loudly from the noise of the engines, I passed over a dozen patches in the airstrip where bomb craters had been filled with sand and gravel—repairs so recent as to be soft under the heel. I bent down to leave my mark, put my handprint into the Chinese earth, and then continued on to the river. Finally, the flight attendant ushered us back aboard and the aircraft lifted off again. We inched northwest over the vast expanse of China toward Hankou, where Chiang Kai-shek had moved his government after the fall of Nanking.

As we flew farther west the threat of Japanese fighters diminished. They had by then taken only the coastal cities of Peking, Shanghai and, farther inland, Nanking, and had not come as far as this middle territory between the south and north. The Hupeh plains opened below us, a snowy vastness as mesmerizing as the Canadian prairies at mid-winter.

Finally, nearing five o'clock that afternoon, we began our final descent at Hankou, situated at the confluence of the great snow-fattened Han and Yangtze rivers. The city, a sprawling smudge of grey and black, rose from the banks, and half a mile north of the airfield a racetrack became visible—two specks on the face of that vast stretching landscape—as well as a number of small road-ways, outbuildings and vehicles. Jean leaned into me to watch the scene open up below us, and the scent she wore brought to mind the first days of our crossing.

"A bit bumpy," I said.

"At least we didn't see the enemy."

"Soon enough."

The landing strip was slick with melted snow and, unlike the strip at Wuchow, paved. As we taxied in I noticed more recently filled in bomb craters, as if we'd flown out of reach of one arm of the enemy and directly into the other. We parked alongside four DC-2s belonging to the same airline and a lone biplane. Once we stopped on the tarmac, a ground attendant led us toward two rather antiquated buildings on the north end of the runway. A stiff wind was blowing. On the roofs of these two buildings three chimneys sticking up from among the red-and-white radio antennas billowed smoke. The attendant ushered us into the first building.

Here, as we waited for our luggage to appear, a western woman about my age entered through the main doors wearing a black velvet cloche hat, heavy cloth coat, thick dress and winter boots. She studied the newly arrived passengers and started in our direction. She was a remarkable-looking woman, beautiful in the extreme, I thought, with lustrous dark eyes and skin that brought to mind the Gypsies of southern Europe.

This, of course, was Agnes Smedley.

A life-long Socialist, by all accounts she was uniquely devoted to the advancement of women's and workers' rights. I knew she'd been charged in 1917 under something called the Espionage Act for speaking out against America's entry into the Great War. She had also spent time in prison for distributing educational literature on birth control.

When she saw Jean and me, in a Midwest accent she said, "I see you've brought a man this time!"

They embraced affectionately. I stood back for a moment, then introduced myself.

"Well, Doctor Bethune," she said, "you'll have to tell me all about Spain one day. I've heard about the work you were doing over there. Simply brilliant. I'd like to know more. But let's get something to eat now, shall we? I've arranged a little something for you."

Her face glowed with delight at the prospect of acting as our guide in this dreary, bleak waste. Then a high-pitched wailing erupted. My ears were still ringing from the noisy flight, and for a moment I didn't know what was happening, but the ground crew and guards and welcoming parties all seemed to recognize this as the wail of air-raid sirens. All at once the war was upon us—not inappropriately, I thought, as thus far we'd enjoyed too easy a time of it. Now the enemy was reminding us where we were.

"Blasted bloody Japs," Agnes Smedley said, "every time I'm here. Off they go with their damn bombs!"

She led us quickly out the door she'd just entered and across a field, opposite the airstrip, to an underground shelter that wasn't much more than a pit covered with timber and sandbags. The ground attendant rushed the remainder of the passengers and their receiving parties down into the hole, and the forty or fifty of us huddled together listening to the enemy come in low over the airfield.

She cocked an ear. "Mitsubishi two-seaters. Three of them."

"Where are they coming from?"

"Off Shanghai," she said. "They pay us regular visits every time I come out here, but they don't seem too interested in anything more than getting rid of their bombs. As if they just want to get back to where they started from. They hardly ever hit anything, just pester us. Mind you, they have a way of getting on your nerves."

"And can we count on any Chinese attack planes?"

"What planes would those be?" Miss Smedley said, dryly.

A male voice, the class clown most likely, called, "Welcome to Hankou," for which he got a few nervous twitters. Miss Smedley and I began chatting again, but every time the Japanese planes rounded and swooped low over the field a silent, collectively drawn breath was felt in the shelter. And when explosions were finally heard in the distance and the planes sped off, a palpable shared sigh issued before the chatter started up again. This happened five or six times, with at least one or two explosions on each pass, but the raid lasted no more than fifteen minutes.

When the all-clear siren sounded Jean and I decided to hang back in case we were needed. Two bombs had damaged the main building, and soldiers and the ground crew led us through the destruction, looking for casualties, with Agnes close behind offering rhetorical advice and direction. "Oh yes, move that beam. Yes, look under there. Well done." She was well-intentioned, at least.

The attack could have been much worse. Five other bombs

had landed somewhere in the fields, far off their mark. But the acrid smell of cordite, a smell I knew so well, lingered in the air.

We found no casualties in the main building, and gathered our things together before proceeding to Miss Smedley's automobile, a green 1930-model Citroën. Then we heard a man calling as he ran toward us from the west. His clothes were lightly burned but he seemed none the worse for wear. When he caught up to us he spoke rapidly, not stopping to catch his breath, and kept pointing behind him. Naturally, I had no idea what he was saying. When Jean translated the gist of his message, we drove to the racetrack we'd flown over on our descent and found sixteen of his twenty horses had been killed outright by the Japanese bombs. He was their groomer. The stables had sustained a direct hit and the smell of burning horse flesh filled the air. Using an old pistol produced from Smedley's automobile, we euthanized the remaining four.

"Yes, welcome to Hankou," Smedley said bitterly, then walked out into the field and vomited.

Somewhat deflated, we climbed back in the car and drove for thirty minutes to a quiet, snowy street on the western edge of town, a few blocks up from the river. Here we found, behind clusters of poplars and birch, the modest home of Bishop Roots, an American Episcopalian convert to all things Chinese.

Opening his door to us, the Bishop gave a brief bow and boomed, "Well, the Japanese welcoming committee didn't put an end to you after all. You've survived your first day in Hankou. Well done. Please, enter," and waved us in.

As generous as he was bald, erudite and long-thinking, he and Agnes had organized a small reception of some twenty or twenty-five local VIPs. He'd been in China for over forty years, and knew everyone worth knowing. It was an impressive showing. Over the course of the evening we were presented to military officials mostly, but also journalists, artists, missionaries, professors and even a well-known actor from the Chinese stage, whose name escapes me now. The Bishop smiled broadly and nodded when introducing. His sense of destiny and assuredness reminded me of my father, in that he harboured no doubt whatsoever regarding the rightness of the struggle.

"Don't think of this war, Doctor Bethune, as you might of Spain, or any other," he said, leading me about by the elbow. "This is a Chinese war, and like all things Chinese it is unlike anything else. Imagine the struggle in Spain expanded a thousandfold, with a third prong, the full brunt of the Nazis, marching on Madrid. That third prong here, the Japanese, will fail, ultimately. But that will take time, in which the Communists will do most of the fighting. What's certain is that Chiang Kai-shek has already shown himself to be a coward. Only his kidnapping last year brought his Nationalists into the United Front in the first place. If the Communists hadn't turned him around, he'd still be a coward and an appeaser. Even his generals know this. They were behind his kidnapping, you know. Chang Hsue-liang and Yang Hu-ch'eng. This miraculous conversion. Suddenly he stopped talking about eradicating the Communists and turned his attention to the Japs. The lord of the house had permitted the infestation of rats in his basement, on the promise that they wouldn't raid the larder! Men like Chiang, you see, are very brave with the lives of others; with their own, the matter is quite different."

I asked the Bishop if he thought the United Front would hold.

"My daughter has just returned from Shensi Province, where Mao's forces are based. She reports wonderful things. An animated, galvanized people. This is more than a gathering movement. It's a revolution, and I believe it will hold long enough for the Maoists to defeat the Japanese in the north and extend their influence southward toward Nationalist territory. Their support spreads by the day. Chiang's willingness to tolerate the Japanese presence is mocked there on a daily basis by the common people. The United Front will last, but only as long as the Communists need it to."

He wasn't as interested in specifics, only the larger picture. He was impatient with talk of shifting front lines, supply routes and international aid—all subjects I was deeply interested in. He was perfectly avuncular, though, and in so being could not have been less condescending or superior. His contempt for Generalissimo Chiang, the Chinese Franco, was refreshing.

"Of course," he said, "the important thing is that the Japanese be repelled. A most barbarous enemy, I believe. There is talk of rape houses they call Consolation Houses. No, we'll accept the meagre Nationalist support until we drive these devils out. And if Chiang can stomach the alliance long enough, we'll use his resources. Land for time, that is what they're saying these days. China has enough terrain to kill an enemy twice or three times as powerful as the Japanese."

"Land for time?" asked Jean.

"Ceding land so the Chinese forces can regroup—buying time, as it were, acre by acre, in order to put something of a resistance together and establish factories in the west of the country."

"The farther away from the ports," I said, "the harder it is for the Japanese."

"The Japs have a superior air force, but yes, you're right. The existing industries are on the coast. The farther they have to extend themselves, the better for Mao."

"High-stakes poker," I said. "How much do you give? How long do you wait?"

"It's the only game the Communists can win at this point. You've seen what the enemy is capable of doing. Peking, Shanghai, Nanking, all cities within a hundred miles of the coast. They can control city blocks and government buildings in Shanghai, but let's see if they can control the Chinese countryside, five million square miles."

The Bishop introduced us to a Dr. R. K. S. Lim, head of the Chinese Red Cross. The small man bowed politely before me, expertly balancing a cup of tea as he did so. I bowed in return, and the Bishop acted as our interpreter. Lim, noting that my reputation preceded me, said he was eager to have me and my assistant join his organization. "They're in the thick of things, really," said the Bishop, "but since the Red Cross is a non-aligned organization, your safety is quite assured. But then, anything can happen."

"Please tell the doctor that we are not concerned for ourselves but for the men offering their lives in the fight against Fascism."

"May I wish you all the best," Dr. Lim said, and withdrew.

We were next introduced to Lieutenant Chin Po-ku, the Coordinator of Medical Supplies for the Communist Eighth Route Army, presently engaging the Japanese, and under the military command of General Chu Teh.

"It is an honour, sir, to meet the great war surgeon Bethune," he said. His hair was parted down the middle, Western style. "The Chinese people have observed your struggle against European Fascism."

"As we take inspiration from this nation's fighting will."

"An exceedingly polite race, really," said the Bishop, smiling. "You'll find that."

"Tell him I'm eager to put into practice here what we learned in Spain. Tell him that with the right supplies and support, I'll establish units like the one established in that country, where our survival rate on the front lines was close to 90 per cent. Tell him the new medical techniques I bring to the guerrilla war in China will be a shining example to the world, and that I'm eager to get to the front as soon as possible. Please tell him that the first order of business is to arrange for our transport to the Eighth Route Army's base."

The Bishop obliged, yet despite my expertise and enthusiasm, I was told that issuing a pass ensuring transit north would take some time, since the Nationalist government held that swath of territory. Meanwhile Hankou, as the de facto capital since the fall of Nanking, was sure to provide a stimulating sojourn. It was, the Lieutenant added, full of entertainments and internationals, including spies, British naval officers, black-marketeers and prostitutes.

"And sometimes they're not so easy to tell apart," said the Bishop, smiling.

Growing impatient, I said, "Tell him I'm here to work. And the sooner the better. I don't care to socialize with expats. Ask him how long we might expect to be delayed."

"Impossible to say," said the Lieutenant.

"Days?" I asked.

The Bishop smiled yet again and didn't bother translating the question. "You would do well, Doctor Bethune, to think of this war as an old mule labouring up a mountain trail. Nothing about it moves very swiftly. Nor should it, my good man. History such as this must be savoured." And with that he took my arm, and Jean's, and delivered us to a small table set with tea and cakes, where we found Agnes Smedley, bottle of gin in hand, holding court with a Finnish industrialist and a short, unshaven Italian journalist.

*

It has occurred to me that I have not spoken much about your mother's family, but sadly I know little of her life before we met. I wish I could tell you some things about her childhood and your maternal grandparents, but the simple fact is I cannot. I know only what she told me. I suppose your mother left me with so little in that regard because we never really understood how precious the time we had together truly was. That it would be taken so quickly. We believed Spain was only the beginning, I suppose. What she told me was that her carpenter father had gone to America in search of work at the age of twenty-eight, never to return. As so many men did in his day, he crossed the Atlantic to find a new life and prepare the way for the rest of the family. After three months he would send for them. With a pack on his back, he climbed aboard the SS *Numidian,* sailing from Stockholm. He promptly found a steady job at a lumberyard in Chicago, on the north side of the river, but also what he hadn't bargained for and couldn't possibly fight against. Enraptured by the dream of new beginnings, he found a life there before his family was able to join him. A fresh start, he heard everyone saying, is the meaning of America. So he fell in love with the pretty German maid who worked at his rooming house in the Swedish neighbourhood of Armour Square. He believed a young German wife was what young America had intended for him. "So there, you see," your mother told me, "we were left behind, Mother and I. But I always thought of him. I always wondered. Always prayed that the letter telling us to come would arrive the next day, or the next. I still live like that, always expecting something to change in my life. But it never does. Maybe that's why I came here. War changes everything."

"It changes a person," I said.

"But I'm still waiting for something."

"Then I'll take you to America. That will change you. It turns you into something you can't know. There you can never rest, never appreciate. You only aspire. It's like a war."

"I don't know how we managed," she said, "to live without a man in the house. I think my mother forgave him, but his absence was always painful. Then one day a solicitor came to say he was sorry to inform us that my father had died. It was a great loss, he said."

"What happened then?" I asked.

"He'd left money behind, enough that my mother didn't have to work any longer. We moved to the seaside, and when his body didn't come home we had our own services there. My mother prayed that I would have the strength to forgive my father, and I prayed as well. We stood in the sea and prayed and then went up to our cabin and prepared a meal together." She paused. "When I got older I began to see what my mother had been forced into when we had nothing. I saw that it was not our failure but the failure and shame of living without the protection of a man in a man's world. I began to understand my mother's degradation." She looked at me. "Does that shock you?"

"I'm sorry," I said, feeling embarrassed. It is a shameful thing to say. Sometimes we're embarrassed by our silences, if not by our inability to care about things we should have known all along. "This is what brought you here?"

She said, "Prostitution is a form of nihilism, wouldn't you say?"

It is easy to judge those you don't know, but often difficult to accept the ways of those whom you do.

I have wrestled with this thought now for some time. I wish I'd had the chance to meet your grandmother, to stand in the sea and listen to that prayer.

★

It became clear soon enough that the Bishop knew all too well
what he was talking about. The transit passes proved a major
stumbling block that held us back no less than three weeks. But I
decided that I would not spend this time idly, as a tourist samples
the local foods and takes in the sights. Everywhere I looked those
first days in Hankou, on all the faces I encountered, I saw tales of
the greater struggle waiting just beyond our reach. The Bishop
was again correct. As the seat of the Nationalist government, the
city was lively, bristling with military attachés, British officers, and
American privateers (the Flying Tigers were making something of
a name for themselves there), diplomats and businessmen, as well
as the artistic and society types, the "war tourists," as your mother
called them, that feed off the glamorous danger of a besieged and
transitional capital. I was told, I think by Smedley, that the British authors Auden and Isherwood had passed through Hankou
only days before, looking for their next book. I knew they'd been
in Spain, with the Republicans, and wished them well, but also
hoped they were truly interested in the cause.

China was now the only story. Here one saw the many refugees flowing down from the north, the simple villagers and farmers mercilessly ripped from their land and now hapless in a city
unprepared for their arrival. But they were not a story. They were
a fact. Meanwhile, the international problem was growing. Mixed
in with the Tartars, Manchus and Mongols, I discovered around
this time the small but very noticeable community of white Russians, blurry-eyed and violent, that favoured certain teahouses
and bars in the seedier neighbourhoods. Their daytime melancholy often rose to a peak of drunken violence by nightfall. Early
on during my stay, I saw a group of them walking unsteadily
down the wet, snowy street, clearly drunk. It was a cold Tuesday

evening. One man produced a bottle from his heavy coat—Russian vodka, probably—took a long drink and unceremoniously broke it over a companion's head. That man fell to the ground, stunned, and for a moment remained on all fours, like a beaten dog, blood emerging from his long shaggy hair. I was about to intervene when suddenly he rose and lunged at his friend. They set upon one another in a rage, then just as quickly, and without a word, collapsed into each other's arms in hilarity.

War tourism, so agreeable to some, was obviously not for me. I could not stand by, simply observing. After three days, and at my insistence, Jean and I were given a temporary assignment at the Presbyterian Mission Hospital in Han-yang, a quarter of an hour west of Hankou, until such time as we would be provided with our transit papers north.

We found the hospital in a sadly primitive state, barely limping into the twentieth century. It was in desperate need of supplies and equipment, overrun with TB and typhus, its staff undertrained and overworked. Temporary though we might be, its management would certainly benefit from the expertise of two experienced staff. The director, an ebullient Englishman named Morrissey who enjoyed drinking rice wine and telling stories of his youth in Manchester, was a good doctor, an island of iron will and professional conduct in a country torn apart by internal conflict and a foreign invader. He simply could do no more. Grateful for our help, on more than one occasion he very nearly begged us to reconsider our plans for heading north.

Morrissey, having been in China some twenty years, turned out to be a great and prolific gossip. He knew all the latest, it seemed. He spoke with great relish of an odd romantic entanglement between a Portuguese consular official and a German general's wife; he was very good with a German accent and, for some reason, quite ruthless toward the Portuguese. I think gossiping, along with the rice wine, was his preferred method of saving himself from overpowering anxieties. Occasionally we dined together, Jean sometimes joining us. He seemed to long for English-speaking company and took every opportunity to take me aside for a chat. He had a pretty wife from Hankou and a grown child now studying in England. He was very obviously homesick, despite his deep roots here, and quite despondent when finally our transit passes were issued.

During the almost daily bombing sorties over the city, our orderly descent into the cellars beneath the hospital was uneventful and routine. We treated a variety of wounds, primarily lower-body trauma, as most wounds above the waist prove fatal within twenty-four hours. We moved those patients we could, others remained in their wards. One day, preparing a leg for amputation, I was thinking how grateful I was to be back at work after close to two months away from it, when the sirens sounded. I looked up, and Jean was waiting for my order. This poor man, like so many others, had been subjected to unimaginable horrors over his long journey to my table—on average, over ninety hours—from the nearest front. I walked quickly to the window and watched the Japanese planes on their approach. By then I knew my aircraft. The three planes coming in were the Ki-15 Mitsubishi, a light attack bomber. I turned back to the man, who was still conscious. Just before the sirens started up, he'd attempted to thank me with a salute for doing him the service of cutting off his leg. When I turned to face him from the window, he smiled and mustered what strength he had left to raise his right hand and shoo me away to the basement shelter.

"You go," I told Jean. "I'll stay with this man."

As I said, there had been raids almost every day, but the

bombs usually fell miles away, toward the middle of the city or harmlessly into the river. In lighter moments we'd even begun calling the bombs "fish killers." What Smedley had said was true, for the most part: the Japanese pilots seemed eager to get rid of their bombs as quickly as they could, before coming into range of the feeble air defences. People died in Hankou and Han-yang, yes, but more often as a result of bad luck than precise bombing.

In a moment, however, we heard the radial engines screaming toward us. These pilots, for whatever reason, were not of the jittery type we'd grown used to. The anti-aircraft guns started up, but the planes didn't veer off and they came in low over the city. Then came the sound of a bomb whistling through the air, and another, and another, followed by a series of explosions. I laid my body over the patient, a slow, deliberate act, almost as if I were covering him with a blanket. Jean ducked close in to the exterior wall and hugged her knees as the entire hospital shook with the force of an earthquake. The window just above her was blown out, filling the room with shards of glass. A powerful fist of air filled the room and turned our guts and shook loose plaster and debris, raising a cloud of dust so thick that I could see nothing before me but a dull haze.

I lay atop the man for many minutes, protecting his wound. When the sound of the planes began to recede, the rescue teams began to fill the yard and hallways, the dust began to clear and the all-clear sirens sounded, I pulled myself up to find the man grinning from ear to ear. Jean got back up onto her feet, unhurt, and dusted herself off as if she'd just slid in to home base. She smiled.

"Jesus Christ," I said, "show a little fear at least."

The patient said something to me.

"What's he saying?" I asked her.

"He says his ancestors are grateful and he's thanking you."

★

It was here, in Hankou and Han-yang, and with Dr. Morrissey's help, that my introduction to the Chinese way of being and thinking began. Every day I was surprised by something I learned. He answered an endless number of questions and was very helpful on the most basic issues of manners, custom and diet. He shared his ideas and provided me with volumes of reading, which unfortunately I was only able to skim, for my time, as you can imagine, was stretched quite thin. Where it was our natural tendency to treat the world as an entity distinct from ourselves and our interests, he said, the Chinese held that the individual was intricately connected to a greater, older, wider world and could not exist without it. There was a certain indebtedness and responsibility that they were always aware of. He described the Chinese spirit as hierarchical, based on age and wisdom, and much more reverent of the past than the Western mind. This brought to mind the selflessness of the man who'd bidden me to retreat to the air-raid shelter at the expense of his own safety, and his unusual gratitude when I had chosen not to.

"He thanked me on behalf of his ancestors," I said. "It was an unusual sort of thank-you."

Morrissey leaned in and said, "Norman, that's it, right there. You've got it. If you want to understand the Chinese, remember that moment." We were sitting in his cramped office overlooking a lovely park, its cherry trees covered with a light dusting of snow.

"Have I?"

"Well, you see, it's faith for us in the West, isn't it? Faith in God. Faith in a cause. Whatever you believe in, it's faith, this self-imposed engine that, rightly or wrongly, permits us to hold on to our beliefs. Are you a religious man, Doctor?"

"No," I said. Not like my father, I thought.

"I didn't suspect so. For the Chinese, faith is nothing. What they have in place of it is duty. You see it in the real religion here. Buddhism? Confucianism? That's horses——t. This civilization's been around for thousands of years, and those ideas only for a few hundred. The real religion here is ancestor worship. In every house, every cave, every room you'll find a shrine, a candle, something that represents the dearly departed, and not just granny or your favourite dead aunt. And any people whose principal religion is situated in a pure devotion to duty," he said, leaning back in his chair and crossing his hands over his lap, "will never, not in a thousand years, lose a war."

It was during one of our conversations that Morrissey began to ask questions about Spain. He was cut off here and desperate for news. I told him what I could, attempting to provide an overview of the political realities there and a frank assessment of our chances for victory. I mentioned the victory at Teruel, the one I'd read about in the *Guardian,* but didn't have any news more recent than that. I described in some detail the mobile blood-transfusion unit and the documentary Karpathi and Kline had made. He listened with great attention, and pursued a line of questioning consistent with a medical man's interests. After we had exhausted the topic, he suggested I might be interested in visiting Hankou's Changchun Studios, the most famous of the film studios in the country, where the Hungarian Robert Capa was spending a couple of days, preparing some groundwork for a documentary.

I asked him if he knew Capa. Though I'd never met him while in Spain, I knew his most famous pictures, particularly the "moment of death" photograph that had garnered him, and the Spanish War, such attention. Morrissey told me that he did not, but had been informed of his arrival in Hankou—from Spain via

London and Hong Kong—only two or three days before. He knew everything that happened in Hankou, this Morrissey, especially if it involved well-known foreigners.

★

You know what I thought the other day? In this Godless army I imagined myself a chaplain administering last rites. Can you imagine? At least playing tricks with myself gives me an occasional chuckle.

★

I have just now recalled something. I wrote recently that your mother had talked to me only of her father's journey to America and the difficult times that resulted. Well, I have remembered something else that you might be interested in hearing about. She told me that her favourite place on earth was her mother's kitchen. She didn't even have to think about it. We were playing a silly game to help pass the time, waiting for Kajsa's blood to fill the bottle sitting next to her. We both added to the blood supply as often as we could, usually after hours when the clinic was closed to the donating public. "Where would you be if you could be any place on earth?" I said, and she said, "In your arms," and I said, "Seriously," and she said, "Sitting on the counter in my mother's kitchen waiting for the apple-nut strip to come out of the oven." I said, "That sounds perfect," and slipped the cannula from the vein. When I applied the gauze and told her to bend her arm she said, "Light as a feather. Can I go now, Doctor?"

★

The following Saturday in Hankou, stealing a moment away from the hospital, we hired a rickshaw to deliver us to the studio, located in an industrial corner of the city, with the Yangtze at its eastern edge. The lot covered twelve acres and was a busy hive of men and women, all eagerly serving the war effort. My first five minutes there I was obliged to remind myself that the wounded I saw walking about laughing, with their heads bandaged, bleeding from gaping wounds, were in fact actors in costume. The set we visited was a perfect replica of the interior of a city apartment, with its walls blown out and windows smashed. The resources were vastly superior to those we'd had at our disposal in Madrid. We did not find Capa but spent an interesting hour watching them shoot a propaganda film that would be completed and ready for the screen within two months.

Two days later, another rickshaw brought me to the offices of Chiang Kai-shek's confidant and publicity chief, Hollington Tong. He was a severe-looking man with square shoulders and a hard, impatient gaze. Every afternoon he stared down a gathering of jaundiced American and British correspondents who, unimpressed, slouched in their chairs, doodling, daydreaming or otherwise waiting for the true story to come their way. At the conclusion of each press conference, these men reconvened at The Blond Dutchman, a bar frequented by white Russians and voyeuristic Americans, where they caught up on the real news from the front. This, at least, according to Agnes Smedley. I was very eager for the latest word on the war, both official and unofficial, and this, she told me, was where you could hear it. At the press conference, the government told you what it wanted you to know; for everything else you went to the Dutchman.

I arrived early, under a cold grey sky, and was ushered into a small room by an unassuming clerk. Uncomfortable wooden stools had been placed before a large oak desk, from which I presumed the daily press release would be read. Posters on the walls declared the rightness of the Generalissimo and Madam Chiang's New Life Movement. This was Chiang's thinly disguised attempt to fill the vacuum left in the hearts and lives of people who have been denied the inspiration of Communism. In place of a true social ethic, Chiang's movement calls for a ban on spitting, smoking in public places, and the fraternization of men and women in the street. There is even said to exist on file the proper length of sleeve of a chaste woman's frock—one inch longer or shorter and her virtue will be questioned. In its highly rigid code of conduct, you find nothing directed to the inspiration of the spirit, only a schoolmarm's list of rules.

Other posters consisted of colourful drawings of a group of Chinese tanks, a squadron of I-15bis fighter planes and troops rolling forward to the Sea of Japan. There was no mention here of the Red Army or Mao's heroic trek north to Shensi or the tens of millions of peasants who'd taken up arms in his name. This was the sanitized face of two Chinas, united for the time being against the Japanese. I sat at the back of the office and was wondering if I'd come to the right place when Eli Ansell, the journalist I'd met on board the *Empress of Asia,* stepped inside and smiled. "Good to see you again, Doctor Bethune," he said. "They told me you were in town. Have you met this degenerate? We've been looking everywhere for you."

The degenerate to Ansell's left was in fact a very handsome man with a wide grin. I recognized him immediately as Robert Capa, his likeness having accompanied some of his magazine work. His dark wavy hair was slicked back, Valentino-like. The man deserved a harem. You might be forgiven for imagining you were in the presence of a motion-picture celebrity or high-living Continental but for his reputation as a recklessly brave and superbly talented photographer. He was barely in his mid-twenties, I think. After we were introduced he asked what had drawn me from Madrid.

"Wouldn't it be the rightness of it?"

"Convincing enough answer," he said. "Madrid was right, too, though, wouldn't you say?"

"What about you, Ansell, did you get to Nanking?" I asked. "Did you meet your good Nazi? What was the name?"

"Yes. I tracked him down. John Rabe. I found him at the German Consulate smoking a large cigar. He's saved more lives than a whole fleet of surgeons. Incredible, really. But still a loathsome sort. A wonderful study in contrasts."

"I trust you'll do something with it," I said.

"Likely. But I've got this degenerate on my hands, and all he wants to do is take pictures of beautiful girls and get drunk."

"I prefer the Spanish face," Capa said.

"Isn't that scandalous? You've no shame, do you, Capa? You should be congratulated for your candour, then shot for your vanity."

Soon three other correspondents arrived to complete our small gathering, two Brits and an American. We chatted briefly, then sat down on our uncomfortable little stools. Mr. Tong entered the room, followed by a small man wearing glasses. This second man was Mr. T. T. Li. Mr. Tong began the press conference by rapping his knuckles on the surface of the table where he sat, clearing his throat and welcoming us to Hankou on behalf of General Chiang. His presentation lasted perhaps three minutes. He spoke in unadorned English of the United Front's triumphs, studiously avoiding any mention of its setbacks. He received no questions from the gallery, whereupon he vacated his seat for Mr. Li, who then read the day's official press release. Afterwards, we all made for the Dutchman.

"I saw you in Kline's documentary," Capa said. "I'm here to make one myself."

He explained that he wanted to find a mobile unit of the Eighth Route Army and follow a child soldier around to see if that could be turned into a documentary. "You know, a child's face in war."

"There are lots of those," I said.

The Dutchman was underground, cavern-like, with arched brick ceilings and deep recesses like the vestibules I'd seen under Madrid. We sat at a wooden table in one of these recesses. The bar was loud. A man at the far end of the room was playing a piano, his long, scrawny back hunched over the keys, swaying slightly. The air was thick with tobacco smoke. I saw no Chinese.

"Your friend here believes you should be shot," I said.

"The Hungarian is to be shot at dawn," Capa said. "Do you know what Capa means, Doctor? It is not my real name. My old name is Friedmann, you know. But Capa—*capa*, that's 'shark' in Hungarian. Shark. Do you know who Robert Capa is? He is my invention. It's true. I am an invention. He who sits before you is an invention. At this precise moment a drunken invention. If I cease what I'm doing I no longer exist. I know I will die soon."

"That's lovely," I said.

"But you are not an invention, I can see that. You are a serious man, Doctor. You are a scientist. A pragmatist and a realist."

"I think the Shark is drunk," I said, turning to Ansell.

"Have you ever brought a dead man back to life, Doctor?"

"I suppose *you* have?" I said.

"You think I'm drunk but I have. More than once. My falling soldier's alive, you see. He is alive. He lives on in *VU* magazine, September 23, 1936. And *LIFE* magazine, July 12, 1937. I have given him life. He is resurrected. This is the power of art. Such a man didn't have a fighting chance before he died, if you see what I mean. Perhaps he was a noble fellow. Perhaps he loved his wife. Perhaps he had children and a glass of wine after work. But now he is immortalized."

Ansell was sitting in the corner, his back against the brick wall. "We need more to drink," he said. "I think the Shark's falling asleep."

Capa said, with his eyes closed, "I think I'll go find the war tomorrow."

★

It occurred to me yesterday that this landscape in northern China is a tremendous demonstration of God's great will and design. Isn't that a funny thing to admit? Or something my father might have said? How pleased he would be to know that, but in truth I'm almost inclined to agree with him on this point. It is really quite stunning out here, these hills so perfectly formed. Can nature be so geometrical, so studied? They say the Russian steppe is quite similar. But beyond this mathematical precision, what befalls you here is a sense of tranquility. Is this only my yearning for some order among all this raging chaos? Could this be the same reason my father aspired to his God? The irony is not lost on me that this landscape is busy with death. But let us remember, it is not this good earth's fault that so many murderous armies should prowl over her fine skin!

★

I would not wish upon my worst enemy a journey as difficult and circuitous as ours was to reach the Eighth Route Army in Shensi Province. Thousands of uprooted peasants swelled the railcars, and the lines we travelled on and the various towns and villages we passed through repeatedly fell under attack. It was an ordeal I would like to forget. Rivers ran swollen, slowing our progress. We stopped often to treat the wounded, and this too slowed our progress. The Eighth Route Army was in retreat, and eventually we were forced to fall into retreat with them. At Tung-kuan, our first stop, a Canadian Red Cross worker advised us to turn back. It was advice we decided to ignore, instead waiting a number of days until we were finally able to find a train heading north to Linfen. Upon our arrival, the city was in a frenzy of motor vehicles, horse-drawn wagons and civilians on foot, carrying with them what few personal belongings they had, streaming south to Tung-kuan, where we'd just come from. The state of confusion was so great that we weren't able to report to the local military commander, for whom we might have done some good. After painful deliberation we decided we had no option but to return to Tung-kuan.

We found room in a railcar loaded with an irreplaceable cargo of government-issue rice, perhaps four hundred bags in all, stacked right to the ceiling. Approximately three hours into our journey, however, in the middle of the night, I was awakened by an all-encompassing silence. We were no longer moving. Wondering if the track had been sabotaged or blockaded, or if at any moment we'd fall under attack, I leaned my head out the window into the darkness. Crickets were all I could hear. I looked ahead and saw that the locomotive had left us behind on the siding of some backwater station, in a village called Goasi, if I was to believe the sign posted on the wall. Ours was the only car left behind.

I woke Jean up and said, "It's time we made some new plans." After I explained our situation, we stepped down from the railcar.

"How far behind do you think the Japanese are?" she asked.

"Far enough not to worry. I'll find the quartermaster."

It was a clear night, the stars shining overhead. It seemed all of China was asleep. The quartermaster, the major who'd granted us permission to ride back to Tung-kuan, was already off the train and organizing the nearby villages for the evacuation of his precious rice.

By first light the following day he had arranged, in the name of the United Front, for the purchase of every mule in the village, totalling forty-two, along with a cart for each beast onto which volunteers would transfer the load. After three or four hours of lifting, sometime near mid-morning, I discovered that almost all my personal possessions, trunk and portmanteau, were gone. I was down to my kitbag, as was Jean, though she didn't seem the least bit concerned.

It was near noon by the time we'd transferred the last of the rice sacks. The quartermaster informed us that instead of going on to Tung-kuan, he and his guard, approximately fifty men and boys carrying only five rifles among them, would make the three-hundred-mile trek to Yan'an, back in the direction we'd just travelled. We were left with no alternative but to accompany them, for otherwise, with no transportation whatever, we'd have been abandoned in that village.

The first ten miles, despite the circumstances, made for an almost pleasant outing. The air was clear and the sun shining. Over my shoulder was slung only my kitbag. My boots were still in a decent state of repair. I was not yet skin and bone. It seemed this leg of the journey might provide some temporary respite from the chaos we'd witnessed at Tung-kuan. I might even have smiled out there on that dusty track, for the peace that descended over me, moving as we did at our snail's pace over that seemingly endless expanse, might almost have been described as "trance-like."

A few miles on, however, the reality of the war returned to me. In quick succession we encountered three walled villages whose inhabitants had fled or were unwilling to show themselves. The terror that was sweeping the land could not have been made more clear. Or so I thought, until my melancholy was replaced with fear by the sound of approaching aircraft. Two Japanese bombers appeared on the horizon as two missiles. Their drone grew louder, and then ferocious as they screamed overhead. We scattered, leaving the mules and cargo helplessly exposed. As the two aircraft roared past, the lead bomber dipped its wings to and fro to indicate to the second plane the decision to attack. Cutting a wide arc against the blue sky, they came around again to begin the hunt. The animals waiting below were easy prey, still locked to their carts.

What followed was a vicious display.

When the planes retreated Jean and I tended to the four wounded men, none of them critical, and then helped to clear the mule carcasses, which we heaped at the side of the road like mounds of red and grey sacking.

It was a miserable night of walking. Our spirits were battered by the attack, and matters were made worse by the damp cold that stung to the bone. We walked in silence. The night sky beckoned; the hard dirt road battered the feet.

Before first light we reached the Fen River, where we rested at an inn while waiting for an opportunity to cross over to Chiang-chou. As the barges that were finally provided for our animals and cargo were loaded, I studied the river and the far bank and the profile of Chiang-chou as it sat upon a low hill. I pulled my coat collar up against a biting wind. The Fen was swift and dangerous-looking, and when, mid-morning, I finally stepped onto the far bank and entered the town, newly chilled but grateful we'd made it that far, I discovered that it was largely abandoned, like those walled villages behind us. The Japanese cavalry was said to be only a half day's ride to the east. Mostly the old and the infirm remained. We treated as many of them as we could through the day and into the night before nodding off in a small room of the rectory provided for us by the two Dutch Franciscan priests who presided over this dying town.

Shortly after the noon hour on the following day we resumed our journey. A cold wind rushed at our backs and whipped up the tails of the animals before us. Our immediate objective being Ho-chin, some thirty miles distant and set on the banks of the Fen, we followed the river's southwest flow. We encountered dozens of wounded, all of whom we tended to with our ever-diminishing cache of supplies. As we walked, our ranks were joined by hundreds of refugees: desperate, lost souls who seemed much relieved to fall in with our ragged column. We were a river swollen by many dozens of human tributaries, and on March 3, still barely twelve hours ahead of the Japanese, we entered Ho-chin.

That grim town had fallen into a riot of misrule. Officers had lost the trust and discipline of their retreating soldiers. There was no organization among them. Desperate men roamed the neighbourhoods kicking at the black, long-eared pigs that snorted through the refuse piles heaped and stinking at every turn. Our numbers dispersed into the muddy streets for the night, and the following morning, anxious to leave that place, we made for the promise of the Yellow River. On the other side lay Shensi Province, our promised sanctuary. We would put the river between us and the enemy.

We collected in a deep gorge on the banks of the Yellow River, our party and many thousands of pitiful refugees and armed fighters, a full day's march from Ho-chin. It was an interminable night we passed on that cold, rough ground. The river pulsed and splashed out there in the dark, and in the dim light of the hundreds of campfires scattered along the riverbank crouched our expanse of miserable humanity. I walked among these people and offered what cursory medical attention I could. Infants, toddlers, young mothers. The aged. As I tended to the wounded and the infirm I read the fear of the unknown in their faces. How much had the enemy gained on us? Would we even survive the night?

In the morning Jean and I were among the first to cross, along with many wounded and precious supplies. Snow fell heavily from a charcoal sky to further engorge the river, which was, I now saw in the dim light, treacherous with jagged ice floes. There were only four junks in service at this crossing point, each with a capacity of approximately one hundred passengers. It would be slow going to clear the east bank, I remember thinking, and easy hunting for the enemy should the evacuation stall.

The first night on the other side, we set up a makeshift triage unit in a nearby village, which we then transferred to a cave closer to the river when the Japanese artillery barrage began the following afternoon. There in that cave, some forty feet underground, Jean performed with a consummate and unwavering professionalism. If she felt fear during the attack, I couldn't see it in her eyes or her actions. Committed to caring for the wounded, she showed no thought for her personal safety and repeatedly forswore the security of the cave to greet the stretcher-bearers, without regard for the constant shelling.

She also proved to be a useful interpreter of language and customs. On the second day of the bombardment I remember a wounded boy was delivered to me. The barge that had carried him across the river had received a direct hit. Dozens of women and children had been killed outright or drowned. This boy's mother, a woman of no more than twenty, had survived the attack and somehow managed to pull him to shore. Wet and shivering, she stood before us and begged us to save her son. Jean told her that we would do all we could, and then an orderly led her out. Not much later we heard a strange, primitive howl echoing down into the depths of the cave.

When asked what was happening, Jean said, "The boy's mother is calling his soul back. She thinks it's lost out there, wandering in the hills."

It took four days to evacuate the east shore of the Yellow River. On the morning of our departure the day broke sunny and clear. As we emerged from that cave for the last time I wondered about the many souls that would be left behind there, including that boy's, trapped between the steep walls of that valley.

I asked Jean if she believed any of that business about scattered souls. A contemplative mood had seized me. She shrugged and looked down across the river into occupied China and said, "I don't know what I believe any more."

At Han-ch'eng, after a full day's walk, we slept in a village house, provided for us by the military council of the region, on beds of wood and straw that were at least dry if not warm and comfortable. Sheets of stiff white paper served as windowpanes. Our only source of light was a single candle propped up in a wine bottle. The label, though mostly obscured by wax, looked impressive.

"Where would you find a bottle of wine like that in the middle of this war?" I said, wishing it were still waiting to be drunk. "It's French."

"It's probably been empty for twenty years," Jean said.

Some minutes of silence passed between us.

"You're still young," I said. "You have something to look forward to when you get back."

"That seems very far off."

A light wind rattled the paper window.

"Yes, it does," I said. "What will you do when you get home?"

"Who says I'm going home?"

Outside there was no noise to indicate fighting in the area, only the sounds of the nighttime village. Doors closing. Distant calling. A dog.

I said, "You like it here that much?"

"I think I do," she said.

"Tell me something about Shantung. Why there? Why not somewhere else?"

"Where would you have me go?"

"That's up to you," I said.

She looked at me, her eyes glowing in the candlelight. "I've been thinking about what Charles said that day."

"What was that?" I asked.

"Something about Madrid."

"Parsons wasn't *in* Madrid," I said. "Madrid is long gone."

*

Here I am, Christmas in China. Not a soul around here has heard of it. It came and went yesterday without a peep, and truthfully I wasn't bothered. It was possibly the most peaceful Christmas I have ever experienced, though likely the coldest one, too. Some things are best kept to oneself out here. That's what I decided. I sat with my memories for as long as I could stay awake, watching my small fire, and that was enough. Maybe I'm getting used to it out here. Perish the thought!

*

We were stalled in Han-ch'eng for a week, waiting for transport to be sent down from Sian. The two-hundred-mile journey took another two days, and when we arrived we were presented to Chu Teh, Commander-in-Chief of the Eighth Route Army. It was a great relief to see with our own eyes the capable intelligence of this man after so many days of chaos and retreat. My confidence in the ultimate success of this struggle had not been dashed, but it had been severely tested under those trying conditions. Here was a man who inspired those around him.

At the conclusion of our meeting, the Commander promised to augment the field hospital that I thought was still waiting for us back in Hong Kong with any supplies presently at his disposal. When I told him of my concern for our field hospital, and how it would be safely transferred over that great distance, he informed me that it was already on its way under military escort.

*

Weary but excited as we set out, I pondered the vast fields of wheat that reached to the horizon, up some inches already, and their graceful dance beneath the endless sky. We were nearing the end of our journey; it was already late March 1938. We were among a caravan of supply trucks moving north to Yan'an that would reach that city after three days of slow, steady driving. When we passed over the loess plateau of Chin-kang K'u, where pale-yellow silt, like fine gold dust, collected along ridges to form terraces of astonishing geometrical precision, I imagined a painter's delight in the face of such beauty, and remembered the paleness of your mother's skin, and my failed attempts at capturing her likeness. It seemed already that a lifetime had passed.

We were greeted in Yan'an by a group of children who crowded up singing a happy greeting I was unable to understand. I embraced the smallest of them, who seemed no more than twelve or thirteen years old, and he held on to me as a son would a father. The frozen town had heard of our impending arrival. There was excitement afoot. It was known a man had crossed an ocean in his efforts to join them. But my journey had spawned rumours. This man had been killed—not native here, he was sadly untested on the treacherous footing—first by rock slide, then machine-gun fire, mortar barrage, dysentery and diphtheria. They said, too, that he'd died of starvation, his leg pinned beneath a shifting boulder.

So it was as if a ghost or a minor god appeared before these people on that cold March afternoon sixteen months ago, bearing what supplies a small fleet of trucks—guarded by fifty soldiers—could carry. At my side was Jean Ewen, by then more exhausted from our journey and my relentless ideals than I was able to tell. My brave Florence Nightingale. Many of these children had never seen white people with their own eyes, apart from an American doctor named George Hatem who'd lived among them for more than a year. Here he was known as Ma Hai-te, and he now stepped through the gathering crowd.

"You've made it, Doctor, wonderful," he said.

We eagerly shook hands. "The excellent nurse, Miss Jean Ewen," I said.

"I'm honoured," he said.

"This is a wonderful welcoming party," Jean said. "Thank you."

"Entirely spontaneous, believe me. It's not every day we get visitors from the outside. You coming up here is a real morale-booster. It's a sign that the world is listening."

"I wish it were true," I said, "but we shall change that, the three of us."

As Dr. Hatem led us around the centre of the town, the crowd of children followed, sniggering and laughing whenever we spoke. When we turned our attention to them, rubbing heads and embracing them, they swarmed even closer, as if eager to be touched by the mysterious foreigners. It was a wonderful moment for us, our grand arrival. But it was also a sad reminder of the war surrounding us. Despite their high spirits, we saw immediately the malnourishment in their eyes and skin. It was a starving population. When I touched one boy's head, he took my hand and held it tightly, then began pulling me. It was, it seemed, an offer to lead me around town. We laughed. "You've found your guide," Dr. Hatem said. "Hang on to him, you'll need a boy."

He was a delicate child, his face terribly thin. I wondered whether he would even survive the last of the winter snows. But his smile was radiant.

"Ask him his name," I said.

"Ho Tzu-hsin," Dr. Hatem told me.

"And how old is he?"

He and Jean spoke with the boy, and then Jean said, "He's sixteen. He says he has no one left. His parents were killed at the start of the war."

I was surprised that he was as old as that. To my eyes he looked only twelve or thirteen. He could not have weighed a hundred pounds. I placed my fur cap on his head and put my arm around him.

"All right," I said, "tell the boy he's hired."

The good doctor did so, and directed him to deliver our things to the Yan'an Guest House. This is where all visitors stayed their first days here. We walked ahead, through the narrow winding streets, and found our lodging at the base of a small hill on the edge of town. It was an ancient wooden building in what looked to be the signature architecture of ancient China.

"The Han Dynasty," our host corrected me.

Its soffits ran sloping off its clay roof like a curling moustache. Its doors were heavy as trees and painted a bright red. In the reception room, small carved dragons licked out at passersby from the door frames. Near the end of the tour, we were shown our rooms, and the boy appeared to await my instruction. I gestured for him to enter, and to place my bags on the floor. After he did, I thanked him in Chinese. He nodded and smiled, then withdrew.

★

Yan'an is a dry, dusty city; it is completely treeless, in fact, and so you might imagine it as a rather hard, cheerless place. Nothing could be further from the truth. What it lacks on the one hand is more than compensated for by the revolutionary hopes of all those who flock there. It is a city whose inspiration and ideals are not for a moment contained by the ancient walls that run around its perimeter.

It was there that Mao Tse-tung's Long March ended in triumph only three years ago, and there the Great Leader still resides. It claims its own university and military college and functions as the operational centre of the war against Japan. In those three short years its population has swollen from less than ten thousand to perhaps three hundred thousand, due to the influx of Chinese and internationalists, workers and intellectuals, eager to take up the anti-Fascist struggle. As a protection against aerial bombardment, student collectives dig their own dwellings into the gritty loam of the hills that surround this town, and there they live and study, wholly devoted to the improvement of self and society. There is not an idle hand to be seen there. Not once did I witness the inhumane degradation of beggar or vagrant, for all are swept up in the greater cause.

After a very brief tour of the hospital, Dr. Hatem took us to a co-operative noodle house busy with diners, women and men alike dressed in bulky uniforms of grey cotton that looked very warm and well suited to the harsh conditions of rural life. They all seemed exceptionally lively, despite appalling dietary realities. Over our meal of wheat noodles, Dr. Hatem explained that each man in Yan'an was provided with four cents a day for basic foodstuffs, and students or soldiers double that. As five hundred grams of meat cost forty cents, one's daily intake was dangerously lacking in certain proteins and fat-soluble vitamins. Added to these concerns, the extreme cold and overcrowding in the caves produced ideal conditions for TB. He had already treated dozens of cases this month.

After dinner the doctor showed us the cave in which he lived. It had the dimensions of a large living room, going back into the hill some twenty-five or thirty feet, with rounded ceilings that, like the walls, were painted white. It was heated by a charcoal-burning stove. By the light of a kerosene lamp he prepared coffee captured, he explained, along with a Japanese officer. We took our cups and sat on low wooden benches. Outside the temperature was no higher than minus ten degrees centigrade, but inside it was considerably warmer. Even before the war, Dr. Hatem told us, people preferred these caves to the houses in the town, which often were much more difficult to heat. He then said he'd heard that our team included three medical personnel, or had he heard wrong?

"No, you didn't," Jean said. "We started as three."

"What happened?"

"There was some trouble during the crossing. The man was an alcoholic. A sad case, really. He drank and, to continue his drinking, stole money. The money he was holding for us. I put an end to it."

Jean looked up at me sharply when I said that.

"Good for you, Doctor," he said. "Shameless S.O.B., it sounds like."

"Shameless enough, yes," I said. "We turned him around at Hong Kong. We won't be hearing from him any more."

We were walking back to the guest house, just the two of us, when Jean said, "You weren't talking about the telegram, were you, when you said that about putting an end to it? You took the money, didn't you."

I didn't deny it.

"Of course you did," she said. "I don't know why I didn't see that right away."

"You knew just as well as I did that someone had to get that money back. I wasn't going to wait two weeks for a telegram."

"And you led me to believe—"

"I led you to believe nothing you didn't already choose to believe. I only wish I'd taken it sooner."

"And Charles? You cared nothing for him. You helped him believe he was a criminal. I think he actually believed you in the end."

"Was I supposed to care for him?" I asked. "He believed what his conscience told him to believe. At least he had that, a conscience. I myself didn't make him believe anything." We were standing face to face.

"Forget about that. It's over. Look where we are now. Look there," I said, pointing to the hundreds of cave dwellings. Each door, painted white, shone like a pearl against the dark cliff. It was a beautiful, cold night, and our breath was steam at our mouths. "Behind each of those doors up there, do you know what you have? You have the heart of the revolution waiting for our help. This is the centre of it all. Don't waste the opportunity with point-less moralizing over Charles."

"At any expense?" she said.

"Expense? I committed no crime at all. Don't you under-stand that? It wasn't his money. It belonged to these people here, and it's because of me they'll have access to it now. I can save dozens of lives with the money I retrieved."

She turned and strode angrily up the hill to the guest house. I followed along, but I was in no rush. If my point hadn't been clearly made here, once and for all, it never would be. There was nothing more to say. I was relieved to be turning in for the night, and relieved to be rid of her. Her temperament was begin-ning to wear on me. Naturally, she was troubled by the business with the money. But did she now believe she couldn't trust me? It seemed some kernel of doubt would never go away. She was tender, even immature. I wondered if perhaps I'd misjudged her preparedness for what was to come, because what we'd seen and done to this point was scarcely the tip of the iceberg. She had, thus far, been very brave indeed, but in a short time we would see hardships much greater than these brief clashes and occa-sional aerial bombings.

The day had been exhausting, and perhaps the long journey had exacerbated her reaction upon finding out what had really happened on board the *Empress*. In any case there was not much I could do now. Once in my room, I stripped down and rolled into bed. But then, too excited to sleep, I got up and stood at the win-dow, looking at the surrounding caves and hills and the ancient pagoda bathed in moonlight under the great dark sky of China.

I have arrived, I thought. I am finally here.

I must have just dozed off when a knock sounded at my door. For a moment I supposed it was Jean, though I could think of no reason why she'd be calling so late. And when I opened the door, a slight young man was standing before me. He spoke softly, and while understanding nothing of what he said I could guess from his manner that he was sorry for the late disruption. He indicated that I should follow him, waving me forward. I dressed quickly, stepped across the hall and knocked on Jean's door. "We are being summoned," I said. It took her only a few moments to ready herself. I could hear her moving about in her room, and when she joined me it was without a word.

The man led us to a cave on the north cliff. It was a steep climb. He didn't speak. Naturally, I presumed we were being called to a medical emergency and hoped all the supplies we might need would already be there, wherever we were going. He knocked once at a white door that bore no marking or insignia. No guards were stationed there, nothing out of the ordinary. As we waited I watched the town below, in its mountain cup of darkness. A ringed moon seemed only moments away from dipping behind the walls of the ancient city. I turned when the door was opened, and we were ushered in. Halfway toward the back of the cave I saw a tall man standing in the light of a single candle. He turned to us casually, as if surprised by our presence, his face still shrouded in shadow. He was dressed in a blue uniform no different from any other I'd seen in the village. He was, though, unusually tall.

The man stepped toward us out of the darkness. His high, pronounced cheekbones lengthened an already gaunt face. His thick head of hair, parted down the middle, was unkempt and much longer than you usually saw on men in this country. His appearance was rumpled and dishevelled, his large bright eyes were radiant in the half-light. It was immediately clear that we stood in a commanding presence. All these things I noticed as he stepped closer and gripped my two hands. He grinned widely as the interpreter, who'd just then emerged from the shadows, translated his first words to me. "A compote?" he asked.

I will never be able to transmit to you fully the mixture of confusion and pride I felt that night as I sat in the cave of the Chairman of the Central Soviet Government, Mao Tse-tung. But had he brought me there in the middle of the night to share his dessert? Mao was already a legend, as he surely is as you read this, perhaps decades from now—a man whose tactical brilliance had engineered the salvation of thirty thousand men and women from the Generalissimo Chiang's noose in Kiangsi; a man whose vision, expressed through the "Rules of Discipline and Points of Attention," acknowledged that a people's revolution would earn their respect and support through education, not terror; a man whose will was a force to be used for the people, not against them. How, then, could this inspired revolutionary be summoning us to his cave after midnight for *dessert*?

"He's saying he'd like to share his compote with us," Jean told me.

"Please tell the Chairman I do not understand."

Through his interpreter, he said, "There is no mistake, Doctor. We have lovely local sour plums."

Still not convinced, I merely nodded. The translator walked to the back of the cave and returned a moment later with a small tray.

"He's offering plums," Jean said.

His aide placed the dessert on a small table set against the rock wall to my right and said, "Please, sit." Mao Tse-tung gestured with his hand, as if bidding us to begin.

I dipped a wooden spoon into the bowl of plums before me, nodded and tasted the fruit. I smiled. "Yes. Tell him it's very good. It's lovely, thank you."

The interpreter spoke. Mao listened, then smiled. I had imagined, were I ever to meet such a great man as this, weighty pronouncements on political economics, dialectical materialism and the social sciences. Yet what I saw here was a simple man, generous, almost light-hearted. We ate in silence for a few minutes, and he cleaned his bowl with the thorough attention of a thirsty cat at its milk dish. He dipped his head with quiet enthusiasm, indicating his satisfaction, and said through his interpreter, "Well, Doctor Bethune. Welcome."

"It's an honour," I said. "My companion has travelled with me from America. She is an excellent nurse. Miss Jean Ewen."

He welcomed us both, and when she said something in Chinese, his face lit up. Delighted, he slapped the table with his palm. After a short exchange he turned to me again.

"There is medical work here for you," he said. "Our doctors will learn from you. This, and not the lovely plums," he said, smiling, "is the reason you have been brought to me in the middle of the night."

"We would like to begin immediately," I said.

"There is time. Tomorrow you may begin. Tonight we will discuss your ideas on improving medical care at the front. You will have your perspective. I know something about your work in Spain. You will have ideas. It is not every day a celebrated battle surgeon comes to us from the West." He nodded. *Begin,* he seemed to say.

"My ideas are simple," I said. "Their implementation is not."

"What are these simple ideas?"

"Front-line medical care. A mobile blood-transfusion unit."

As I outlined the logistics of getting the idea off the ground—training staff, procuring equipment and funding—a different side of the man began to emerge. He was an eager student, a brilliant strategist who asked many questions. Cool and analytical in his thinking, he sometimes paused for long moments to consider something that had been said. I watched his mind working, his dark eyes moving between me and Jean and the depths of the cave. His questions were the very ones I'd asked myself when first setting up the unit in Spain, and even some I had not. His hands, folded before him on the table, remained perfectly still. "We must take cultural realities into consideration," he said, "when talking of blood donations." His head nodded slowly. "Such a thing is a very foreign concept for people here. Perhaps not so for Europeans. Here it is bordering on witchery."

"Your army will follow your instructions," I said, then I quoted from his First Rule of Discipline. "'A soldier must without hesitation carry out all orders issued to him.'"

Again, he nodded. "Very good, but he must first understand the necessity of the order. He must be educated."

Our interview lasted long into the night. Jean helped greatly with the interpreting and added much to the conversation. Mao listened respectfully, nodding, and thanked her for her thoughts each time she finished speaking.

He said, "And who now leads the people in Spain? I have heard of a man named Durruti."

I reported that he'd been dead for two years. There was no true representative, I said. It was a weakness for the Spanish people. There was suspicion and ill will among the parties. I told him of Largo Caballero, leader of the Popular Front. They called him the Spanish Lenin. I said, "He has united the Communists and Socialists and the Republican Union Party. But the anarchists are outside this union."

Near the end of our meeting I informed Mao Tse-tung of the supplies we had brought with us from America, and the additional supplies that had been promised by Chu Teh, Commander-in-Chief of the Eighth Route Army. Our field hospital would pass through Nationalist-held territory on its journey here from the south. It was my argument that the Yan'an Border Region Hospital, consisting of nothing more than a vast series of cold damp caves, would be the safest destination. Of primary concern was the fact that the Nationalists had stipulated that our supplies, in order to pass through their territory, must be utilized only on the civilian population, not the Communist Army. The danger of the Nationalists closing their territory to future shipments was indeed high, I insisted, and that would doom any mobile blood unit in Shensi Province to failure.

"Chiang Kai-shek," said Mao, "will manufacture other reasons to close the supply routes when he learns of our successes." He rose then and crossed the narrow room to a desk on which sat a candle and writing paper and pens, returning with two small booklets. "You may find time for this. Perhaps the lady will translate this for you, Doctor Bethune. Do you read Chinese characters, *mademoiselle*? Your Chinese is very good."

"Not many," she said.

They shared a brief exchange in Chinese, and then the Chairman said, through his assistant, "Well, then, Doctor, you will have to find another translator for these writings."

I saluted. Chairman Mao extended his hand to us and said, "Your day has now begun. Welcome to Yan'an."

We accepted his gift, shook his hand, saluted and were then led out by the assistant. When the cave door opened, fresh, cold morning air rushed over us and the bright sunlight startled our eyes. Blinking, and refreshed by the sharp air in our lungs, we started down the narrow rocky path toward the guest house.

"What was that last bit about?" I said.

"He said if I weren't such a talented nurse, I might be used as a translator. It's a rarity, foreign Chinese-speakers."

"We all have a part in this," I said, "whichever role you choose to play."

As we walked down the pebbled hill a curious sense of freedom enveloped me, and I felt more purposeful than I'd ever been. It was as if on this glorious morning of hope I had been absolved of all frailty and self-interest. I would devote myself exclusively to the fight ahead. It was a duty now, purer than religion or blood. Seeing only a Chinese future, I yearned to immerse myself in the conflict that surrounded us. The great man's passion had taken hold of me.

ENVELOPE FIVE

We are at the front near Ho Chien, Hopei Province, with the 120th. No sleep tonight. Just listening to the silence. I've always loved that, generally. I would love to share a silent night like this with you, sitting on some front step somewhere, or in a garden, just listening. How I loved hearing spring rain splashing against the new leaves. Do you know that sound? The guns will start again, soon enough. Can I put them out of mind, if only for an evening?

You will suspect by now that there must be a reason, apart from the war itself, that in my fiftieth year, I find life here so essential. Naturally I'm not referring to the abundant lilies and the wild beauty of this landscape. Certainly I refer to neither the food, so inadequate and unvaried, nor the conversations, for I stand alone, isolated in this language but for the help of my interpreter, the good Mr. Tung. What, then, could the attraction be, other than the denial and sacrifice that surround me? I can almost fool myself into believing the rumbling of my stomach is a soft purr of content-ment, not the cry of hunger. Or that the pain in my head and the deafness in my left ear are the welcome reminders of greater agon-ies I have eluded. This is not a question of half empty or half full. The world here, to arrest any misconception, is almost entirely used up, broken, lost. There is no joy. No pleasure. Nonetheless, I cannot help but feel that beyond all the obvious destruction, something else is off kilter, that something—perhaps disguised in the noble drapery of self-sacrifice, yet there in my own deepest reaches—is in full downward spiral. My beliefs, I assure you, are sound. What's troublesome, as Parsons was so eager to point out, are my motivations.

I do have my work, and isn't that enough? If not loved by the daughter I've never met, at least I have a place where I'm necessary—and, more than most, I know the importance of belonging. My life has never seemed so crucial. To date I have performed more than seven hundred operations and examined well over a thousand who were sick, injured or wounded. I have written three textbooks to be used for medical training. Last year in these rough lands I travelled some three thousand miles, every step of which heightened my com-mitment and quickened my blood. But still I regret the bias and greed of this world, its blind eyes, its false pretenses, its first and second and third conditions layered one atop the other like a teetering Pisa of compromised ideals. I resent the deceptions of Madrid—or, to be clear, the lies—that have reduced this country to little more than the second, desperate chance of an embattled man.

*

I have been thinking to ask Mr. Tung to deliver these pages to George Hatem in case anything happens to me. I believe he'd prove a reliable courier. What a great and useless abstraction all this typing would be if chucked in the incinerator with some dead doctor's bloody smock!

★

In Yan'an last year, I lay awake at night, turning, those weeks we spent waiting for our travel status to be clarified. We worked sixteen hours a day but made little progress. The war seemed eager to demonstrate that it would not so quickly recognize my efforts, or even my presence. Its appetites were astonishing. And the conditions of the cave hospital were like nothing I had ever seen. April rains muddied the world around us, reminding me of the nightmare of Belgium. Anxieties only worsened when word came that our supplies had been stalled in Sian. After a few days I decided Jean should return there in order to speed their safe delivery to Yan'an. With her command of the language, she was the obvious and logical choice. She departed on April 25.

You are correct. She did not return.

Three days later, the supplies arrived. It was a great surprise when Ho appeared and began tugging at my sleeve. He kept injecting my arm with a make-believe needle and holding his head in his hands. After the confusion—followed by handshakes and back-slaps—I sent word to Jean that she was to return immediately. Twenty-four hours passed with no word of confirmation, so perhaps she was already en route. I waited another day and sent a second telegram, gruffly worded, perhaps. I wonder if she ever did get it.

On the fourth day I set out for the front without her.

Some small part of me was still hopeful, though. My desire to see her again perhaps had to do with the fact that I felt I needed to berate her for a failure of conscience, or soft ideals. A doctor finds his students' weaknesses and turns them into strengths, and a delicate stomach should be trained to tolerate all manner of bile. Of course, I wondered where she'd gone, and why. Somehow appalled by me, or still moping about Parsons, or caught up in a situation more demanding than she'd expected?

In early May I completed the final stage of my long journey to the Border Regions with Richard Brown, an Anglican doctor I'd met in Sian. We were just six miles west of the Yellow River, some seventy miles south of the Great Wall. Dr. Brown had arrived in Yan'an sometime mid-April, on loan from the Mission Hospital in Sian. I'd found him a quiet and patient man, admirably handy and self-reliant. Such was his dedication to the cause that he had decided to devote his two months' leave to our work in Shensi Province. I imagined his colleagues bemoaning his absence hourly. We didn't speak of Jean, though I suspected he felt my mood. I was surly, agitated, short. Neither did I let him know of my admiration for him, but it was refreshing to watch his talents and abilities display themselves as our journey continued. When a lorry broke down, he tended to it. He would walk fifty yards off the road, disappear for ten minutes, then return with a hare in each hand. He read the stars for directions, spoke the language and commanded the respect of our escorts on a personal level that seemed unimaginable to me. That he showed no interest in my moods seemed even more impressive.

I began to suspect he knew what had happened, for it was no secret that I'd been travelling with a nurse who'd failed to return to duty as instructed. Could this be of a personal nature? A lovers' spat? It would do no good that a pretty young nurse had affected the great doctor so thoroughly, causing him to behave so unprofessionally.

One night we encamped on the pebbled bank of a small stream. Our escort of twelve fighters, two guides, two orderlies and a cook were already pulling out their woollen sleeping bags. Dr. Brown and I stayed by the fire. As the stream crackled and splashed in the dark, I said, "If she showed up now I'd have her shot as a deserter." He looked at me but said nothing.

The following day's drive was slow, impeded by rain and mud. The roads of Spain were racetracks compared to these of packed dirt, ungraded and often washed out and treacherous. We followed the Yen River upstream before our road veered off into the Loess Hills. We crossed tributaries of the Yen at three points, and each time the wheels of the big trucks spun wildly in the silt as if suspended in mid-air. The first night we spent in a hamlet not far off the road and gratefully accepted the offerings of what little food the locals possessed. Before departing in the early morning we treated a case of pneumonia, a leg wound, a bloody abscess and two influenzas. The second night, after a full day of slow driving, we reached an isolated village of perhaps a thousand souls, many of whom hadn't tasted meat in months. A diet so lacking in protein had left its mark on this small population—gaunt, pale, some of them suffering from advanced malnutrition. I wondered for the first time, driving into the heart of the war, how a people so generally undernourished, so weakened by famine and these incredibly harsh surroundings, could defeat an adversary as efficient and ruthless as the Japanese.

It was there, that very evening, this puzzle was solved. Dr. Brown and I were told about a young child who'd been trapped in a collapsed building, far above ground level, pinned by rubble too precarious and heavy for anyone to help her.

"How long has she been up there?" I asked.

"Twelve days."

The woman led us to her daughter, whose head was clearly visible beneath a large rock five times her size. She was unconscious. The village had studied the problem, we were told, and after a week had determined, mercilessly, that the girl would die there. Early on a crowd had gathered every morning, but no onlookers remained. Retreating out of guilt and helplessness, people had returned to their own misery. Alone, the mother had used brick and wood planking harvested from the fallen building to fashion a platform rising to the height of her daughter's ordeal. She now lived with her up there, twenty feet above the village. All night she spoke and sang to the girl, caressing her hair and promising her she'd be freed from that prison, and during the day she brought her water and whatever herbal medicines she could scrounge that might help her sleep.

She led us through a narrow dirt lane to the building, whose north side was collapsed but for a single exterior wall. I saw the girl halfway up, pinned by an enormous slab of rock and mortar. Only the top of her head was visible. Her mother wasn't crying. She was concentrating as she called out to her that, as Dr. Brown translated, the foreign doctors had come. Foreign doctors. Imagine. Special men from the West.

There was no response. I believed the girl was unconscious.

There was only enough room on the platform for one person. First the mother climbed up, held her daughter's head for a moment and whispered in her ear. When she came down she spoke with Dr. Brown, who then went up and examined the child as best he could. When he came down he told me her breathing was shallow. He saw no trauma to the head but could tell nothing of her internal injuries, and there was likely severe damage to the body. She might last another few days in there, no more, nor was there any way of extracting her.

The mother said something I couldn't understand, and Dr. Brown told me, "She's saying we have to help her."

The woman didn't speak after he explained there was nothing we could do. She stopped insisting and bowed deeply. Then she climbed back up onto her platform and sat quietly with the child. It was heartbreaking.

The moon was full when I returned to the building later that night, unable to sleep. It was well past midnight, and a silence surrounded the village. The girl's mother stirred and looked down as I climbed up the rickety ladder. There wasn't enough room for both of us, so I sat on a large stone in the broken wall. The girl's head was perhaps two feet below me, facing down. In the bright moonlight I could see the individual strands of dark hair, lovingly brushed. She wasn't moving. Once I was up there, her mother paid me no more attention. It was as if she again were alone with her daughter. I opened my coat pocket and offered her the syringe I'd prepared. She clearly understood its purpose, but would not take it. I sat with her a while longer, then climbed down and walked unhappily back to my bed.

Next morning, we continued north through terrain empty of tree or bush. We crossed eight rivers in one day without seeing a single bridge. The next five nights we stayed in villages and treated the ill and dying before sleeping in borrowed rooms on mud floors, but never again did I see anything as terrible as that child trapped in the building. Her image haunted me as I lay staring up at some dark ceiling while Ho slept the sleep of the innocent and untroubled.

Conditions at the Eighth Route Army Base Hospital in Ho-chia Chuang were even more horrifying than those at Yan'an. Hungry cats were permitted to sit unmolested upon windowsills and under chairs waiting for discarded bandages to be dropped to the soiled floor, while men were starved of medicine and care. The entire hospital smelled of death and decay. The doctors and nurses were visibly exhausted, scandalously undertrained and thoroughly demoralized. After we treated the most urgent cases (which took five full days), the sorry staff was assembled before me. "This will not stand," I said. "Mr. Tung? Tell them, in the strongest terms possible, that I have had the dishonour of teaching undergraduate medical students with a more solid foundation in medicine and anatomy." I was, perhaps, overly harsh. But is that even relevant? This is not the real world here, after all, if by that one means a world interested in the delicate egos and moods of the faint-hearted. This is no hospital ward where we punch a clock and entertain notions of seniority, union dues and advancement. This is an alternate world, an unreal world. It is a world of man's blackest construction.

Shall I tell you what was in that syringe I left for the mother? You will know. It was enough. That is all I can say. I held it to my arm to demonstrate the procedure. I pretended to stick myself, then indicated where the thumb compresses the pump. I did it again, holding it out and miming the steps. She watched, silently. Then I handed it to her and climbed down the ladder.

The mother might have left it there, or thrown it into the rubble below, or sold the unused needle in the local black market. Or perhaps she slipped it into her daughter's arm, then into her own.

Please do not judge me. The world cannot be cleaved into two convenient halves of right and wrong. War and peace, black and white. Lovely notions but terribly flawed. I hope you will understand that these words and actions stand only for my own thoughts and deeds and are meant to represent no one else and no other place or thing. I saw a situation and acted as best I knew how. I claim no privileged domain over right and wrong, not as it applies to individual behaviour. I have seen too much of the world to trick myself into believing that. You will have your own sense of how things should be, and that is as it should be.

*

Ho sits on an upturned trunk beside the window, looking through my recent drawings. What does he learn from them? Perhaps he's not a poet after all but an artist or surgeon intent on overtaking the great Bethune at his own game. How pleased I should be! Perhaps he will be my student one day. I have put tea on for us. When it's ready, I will flip open the Chinese dictionary and ask if he takes sugar. I might see him smile.

*

It was at Ho-chia Chuang, a border town of perhaps ten thousand situated between Shansi and Shensi provinces, that I cemented my reputation as a feared presence. Eyes turned down at my approach. I was a feared officer by then, a man of legendary temper. How I shudder now at the thought. People shrank from my presence. Conversations ceased, and in silence they gave the open-palmed salute to the forehead. I understood the dead, so the living and their small concerns did not interest me. It was as though I saved my compassion for the dying. For anyone else I had no patience, and this I regret. The near-dead, curled and silent or clawing the air in their pathetic contortions, were my only concern. So what if my students, those would-be doctors, nurses, orderlies and aides, could not stomach the arrogance of a stranger, even if he happened to be the pinnacle of their aspirations? Well, then, they were dressed down, shamed for their selfishness and told to leave.

Upon my arrival I made myself available for queries and then, when no one spoke, their eyes downcast, I ordered each man and woman to formulate a question. "Make it a good one," I said. I demanded that they learn, and fast. "Those of you with strength and character will change the direction of this war, and will stay on here. The others will find postings elsewhere," I said. "Nothing matters here at all except the comfort and dignity of our patients." With each question posed, if I sensed weakness I'd remind the speaker of his profound ignorance; when he returned the next day, I'd heap praise upon him. Nothing but exactitude, dedication and order would suffice. I told them it was my duty to rid the hospital of anyone whose natural inclination was to drop bloody gauze on the floor, ignore the pain of his patients or dream about the end of his shift before it had scarcely begun. That person was useless to us. At times now I cringe when recalling my tone, but I made a hospital out of that chaos. That is our triumph, and it must be remembered.

After those few days it became clear enough that no one but I could achieve a similar success throughout the entire Border Region. I was the most experienced and most capable. For the Director of Medical Services of the Eighth Route Army, Dr. Chiang Chi-tsien, I prepared a written report concentrating on the lack of sanitary conditions and proper medical training, the frequently incorrect use of medicines and an overall and alarming absence of supplies and discipline. I conducted a thorough investigation, interviewed the entire staff, ran through all the procedures. This facility had failed utterly, and I had no reason to believe it was different from any other in the region. The underlying problem, I concluded, was the Eighth Army's woeful lack of adequate training. I had begun to remedy this situation, I said, and detailed my preliminary efforts.

After I spoke with Dr. Chiang, it was decided that I would prepare a manual outlining basic measures regarding sanitation, wound cleaning and dressing that could be printed as a booklet and distributed to clinics and field hospitals throughout the province and beyond.

In order to continue this work I departed on a tour of the front near the end of May. I was accompanied by Mr. Tung and Ho, my boy, two student surgeons, a Mr. Ping and a Mr. Sun, a nurse and an armed escort of three soldiers. For over six weeks we travelled from village to village like a Gypsy caravan. Instead of bottled herbs and ancient recipes we carried as much spotty evidence of the twentieth century as could be loaded onto our sweaty, half-starved, overworked animals, as if we aimed to deliver the healing powers of modern medicine and technique over the limitless reaches of an undiscovered empire.

*

We were still without a permanent base we could return to. By mid-July Dr. Brown was obliged to return to the Mission Hospital from which he'd been given leave. Now I was alone for the first time since meeting Jean in New York fifteen months before, and the only trained doctor in over 100,000 square miles. As a distraction from the reality of these overwhelming odds, I threw myself into my work with even greater vigour and spent my days reorganizing all medical procedures at Sung-yen K'ou. Of course, there was nothing so grand as a hospital there, only a series of huts and shacks that had been appropriated from the villagers, a breeding ground for untold infection, in which wounded men lay, largely unattended in their filth, stretched out on their hard mattresses with not so much as a blanket or change of clothes.

In order to begin the process of correcting the lamentable conditions there, I saw to the construction of an operating room, a sterilizer, one hundred leg and arm splints, standardized dressing trays, urinals, bedpans, stretcher racks and an incinerator.

To instill routine and improve procedure, I drew up operational checklists defining nursing responsibilities, began holding one-hour tutorials on basic aspects of anatomy and physiology, making much use of a blackboard, and convened a weekly conference at which questions and concerns might be raised. I was aided in this respect by the indefatigable interpreter, Mr. Tung, who had proven himself more than useful in getting across not only my words but also my displeasure, disgust and rage at the frequent incompetence.

It was here at Sung-yen K'ou, in sight of the Great Wall some ten miles distant, that we built our hospital in the shell of an abandoned Buddhist temple. Beside this structure, I was provided an office in a small house that had belonged to a large farming family who had perished in the war. Given seed money of two thousand dollars over a period of two months, carpenters and stonemasons transformed the temple into the Demonstration Hospital, whose thirty beds would serve as a training centre for all medical matters. Every morning, sometimes as early as six, I was awakened by the sound of hammers, saws and axes. It was with the pride and humility of a beneficent ruler that I walked among the rising walls of this great cathedral, encouraging the workers with a cheer or double handshake, bowing deeply under the hot sun to praise their efforts.

My hospital opened three months later, on September 15, 1938. It was indeed a proud day, and one that I wish I had been able to share with your dear mother. How her face would have glowed with joy. But I did not stay long to bask in the glory, the Japanese made sure of that. We struck out for Hopei Province, where there were new reports of a gathering threat. Throughout the remainder of that month and well into October we travelled by horse and by foot, with three tethered mules bearing the burden of our equipment and supplies, visiting one village after another. Ho and Mr. Tung were always at my side; the latter now, in addition to bridging the linguistic divide between me and the world, served as my anaesthetist. We moved from skirmish to skirmish operating and, when time permitted, instructing those men and women who were able to learn.

One night, shortly after the evening meal, a young man approached me and Mr. Tung. When he saluted me, I rose.

"What is it?" I asked.

His face was visibly upset. Not unlike Ho, he was very young.

Mr. Tung listened to him and then turned to me. "There has been an attack," he said, "on Sung-yen K'ou. The Japanese have overrun the town. Nothing is left."

"The hospital?" I said.

"Destroyed," he said.

Ho appeared then. He had not yet heard the news. He leaned across the table. I suppose now he was going to remove my plate. Perhaps it was the expression I wore on my face, the rage he saw there, but before he was able to withdraw his hand, I grabbed his wrist and raised it to my face, examining it as if for some abrasion or proof of . . . I don't know what. I knew I had terrified him, though, and I had no business doing that. From the corner of my eye I could see the fear on his face as he glanced at Mr. Tung. His limp hand offered no resistance. I threw it down in disgust and walked out into the dark.

I walked through the village and out into the country. I don't know precisely where. But there are hours I cannot account for. The Japanese knew perfectly well how to strike at the morale of the Eighth, how to cut its heart out perfectly. I had been warned

that the hospital might prove an irresistible target, yet my persua-
siveness and vanity had won that argument. And as if to shame
myself further still I had assaulted the person as loyal to me as
if he were my own son. Children are the heritage of the Lord, I
heard myself say.

The following morning I awoke in my tent. My limbs ached.
My stomach was empty. I dressed and slipped out from under
the tent flap. Light was just breaking over the hills. Ho sat alone
by the cooking fire. He rose and saluted, still afraid of me. When
I motioned with a hand to my mouth, he turned to the fire and
began preparing my meal. Watching him, I wondered: Had I
become my father?

★

I have been thinking a fair bit about mortality lately. You might
suppose I've always done this, but you would be wrong. You might
lose your shirt on that one. I have spent a lifetime in the presence
of death. I have watched it, touched it, regretted it, bereaved it
and done my best to dodge it for these last forty-nine years, but it
strikes me as odd that I have not really pondered it. I am not one
to duck philosophical issues, nor am I easily frightened. Could
there be in the inner reaches of my heart some residual Christian
belief that I draw upon in moments of need? It surprises me even
to think this.

It has been a difficult stretch, lately. We are all worn out.
I'm often too tired to write and yet find myself wandering in
thought more than is usual, even for the dreamer I am. I've
been recalling the surgery I underwent to collapse my tuber-
cular lung so many years ago, in October of 1927. Why should
this occur to me now? I remember walking lost among the
great dark trees along the shores at Saranac Lake the day before

the procedure, in my mind running through the operation I'd chosen to subject myself to, when I saw my old mother quietly standing beside a large pine, watching me. I hadn't known she was coming. I had informed her as to the state of my health, of course, and the date of my surgery. Even so, her presence there surprised me. It was as if she'd felt her own life's blood at the edge of extinction.

We walked together quietly. A light breeze drifted over the lake. It was an odd reversal, I thought, the mother walking slowly for the son, who in turn resembled an old man shuffling off to his own funeral.

"I know what I'm saying," she told me. "I know you'll be fine. There is still much in this world for you to do, Norman."

"The world needs a fair bit of correcting, I'll grant you that, but I'm not so sure I am the one to do it."

She took my hand in hers. "You are a special man. You're on this earth for a reason. The Lord will see that you understand that reason."

I said, "That I can offer myself as a guinea pig?"

She said, sternly, "Don't mock His ways."

"What, then, is this great plan of His? The Kaiser? Sixteen million dead of the bloody Spanish influenza? Is that His great plan? Forgive me if I don't drop down on my knees."

"Will you pray with me?"

I looked at her. "You know I almost killed a man? Only three weeks ago. Frances's lover. Did the war do that to me—the faithless, jealous husband?"

She didn't say anything. We were stopped, standing on a pebbled shore. Out before us the lake was a sheet of unbroken glass, reflecting the sky. Here was all Heaven and Earth spread before us and I could think only of mocking the beliefs that had formed me and defined the one woman who had always loved me, unconditionally, perfectly.

I said, "What do you think of God's plan now, Mother? A murderer if I'd shown half the bravery I like to think I have."

She turned and walked back up the shore. I'd hurt her gravely, saying that. I thought I'd driven her away for good. To my shame, I was glad to have her gone.

That night we ate in silence. She had reserved a guest cabin. We sat on her porch, our chairs positioned to face the lake.

"I want to apologize," I said. "I haven't been thinking straight."

"I know. A mother knows."

I said, "He couldn't come?"

"Your father gave it a fair bit of considering. He fears his congregation would be lost without him. I told him it was the other way around. 'You should think about that,' I said. He didn't appreciate my saying that and went upstairs for the rest of the night. At breakfast he gave me a letter. He went out without touching a thing."

She got up and went into the cabin. The screen door slammed. The sound carried over the lake. She returned a moment later and placed the sealed envelope before me. I didn't move to pick it up.

"He's a good man, Norman," she said.

"I'll read it later."

That letter remained unopened, tucked into the pages of a medical text, for the rest of my stay at the sanatorium. When I left, the book was packed among others and shipped, after the house where Frances and I had lived in Detroit was closed down, to Montreal, where it remained sealed, forgotten, until Father died in 1932. The evening I learned of his death, I opened the letter.

I poured myself a strong brandy, sat at the kitchen table of my small apartment and inserted a knife into a slit at the corner of the envelope, pulling the blade along the crease. I took the page out and read it, then folded and returned it to its envelope.

I found it again on an October morning, four years later, as I packed up my things for Spain. It was a poignant reminder of the end of things, a good life frustrated by silence and shame. Without thinking much about it, I slipped the letter into one of the books I'd set aside for the journey and resumed my packing. But I have kept it with me ever since, and want you to read it now.

Toronto
Oct 22, 1927

Dear Norman,

You have by now spoken with Mother, and perhaps she is at this very moment sitting before you, watching you read this letter from your absent father. Perhaps you are alone in that little cabin you have written to us about, I hope in swift and complete recovery following your operation. Either way I regret the fact that I have been unable to visit with you at Saranac Lake. I am told by a congregant—James McGovern, Jacob's son, do you remember him?—that it is a lovely place of trees and hills and peaceful dark lakes. Much like Muskoka, he says, where you spent your early years. In any case, I am hopeful that this peace James referred to fills your heart now at this trying time.

As a father getting on in years I see that my life's regrets are not few. Principal among them is the reality that for many

*years now I have been somewhat estranged from you, my son,
and yet not in any absolute sense, for our relations are commonly respectful, as you will likely agree. But it is clear enough
that there has remained between us an enmity the root of
which I cannot but fail to explain or grasp. We are, it often
seems at familial gatherings, reserved and suspicious strangers obliged to share a taxicab during a spot of summer rain.
A mean characterization, but do you agree? It has been this
way for as long as I can remember, and it is a terrible thing to
admit, as I write this, so late (though God will show us that
it is never too late) on the eve of this serious medical predica-
ment you now face. Perhaps I have been too hard, too distant,
too demanding a father? I am willing to assume what guilt I
must in order that we together root out this hardness that you
harbour toward me, for in my heart I feel much pride and love
for you, as any father could toward his son. It is my great and
sincere wish that you soften your thoughts toward your aging
father, and that from this medical treatment you will emerge
healthy and strong.*

*You must know you are not alone at this time. "After these
things the word of the LORD came unto Abram in a vision, saying, 'Fear not, Abram: I am thy shield, and thy exceeding great
reward.'" Genesis 15:1*

Please remember these words, Norman.

*Your brother, Malcolm, and sister, Janet, send their love, as
your dear Mother will have told you.*

Your Father

★

I am proud to say I have pulled together a regular unit to accompany me on some short inspection tours throughout northern Shansi and Hopei. It is a good group, consisting of the two surgical students, Mr. Pin and Mr. Sun, as well as Ho and Mr. Tung. We are usually accompanied by a military escort of between two and twelve men, depending on the distance and area we are to cover. Behind enemy lines we usually take only two, as a larger group is more easily detected.

Recently we went up to Chia Kuan, a small grey town serving as a temporary base for soldiers of the 359th Brigade, and overrun with lice, chickens and more coughing black pigs. There we were greeted by Dr. Ku, Chief of Sanitary Service, and a Mr. Yuan, Political Commissar, both of that same brigade. It might once have been a picturesque village, Chia Kuan, whose mud streets were then dusted like Christmas brownies by dancing snow, but it had been transformed into a wasteland of sickly poultry eagerly pecking at one another's startled eyes. Among the wounded men of the 359th, gangrene and the insidious bubbling abscesses caused by indifferent medical attention were chief among our concerns. In one day we treated seventeen patients, operating on five, one of whom, only eighteen or nineteen years of age, had lost the lower half of his face. What was so remarkable in this boy was that his eyes, only a breath above his disfigurement, had retained a soulful, almost angelic innocence. He seemed to watch patiently as I went about my work. That is not possible, I know, but those eyes led me to believe that in his mind—his mouth having vanished—he was, perhaps for an instant, smiling at me. Still a child not long absent from his mother's arms, despite this mortal wound he was capable of hope. His eyes had not lost their belief that this world he knew, so harsh and uncaring, might yet yield goodness. They were the beautiful eyes of youth, and then, two hours later, he was dead.

We continued west to Chuan Lin Kiou, where we established another base for treating men from the 359th. Thirty-five more were delivered to us from Lia Yuan, a three-day trek over unforgiving road. The day after arriving there I was presented to Brigade Commander Wang Chen. He was tall for a Chinese, elegant and very serious, with the hands of a musician and the fine features of a leading man in the cinema. He received me in a large stone house at the edge of the village that had been given over to Company Command, its walls festooned with maps. He rose from his desk, saluted and welcomed me to Chuan Lin Kiou, then asked my opinion of the medical conditions in the military district. Again, Mr. Tung translated.

"They are very poor," I told him.

"And here in Chuan Lin Kiou?"

"Also very poor," I said. "The care your men have received is bordering on outright neglect."

He tilted his head back and stared at me, as raven-eyed and fearsome as a wronged protagonist in some Cantonese opera who was poised to take the head off an old adversary. He rose and leaned over his desk on his clenched fists. I believed at the very least that Mr. Tung and I were about to be ejected.

A half minute passed, but I didn't once remove my eyes from his. "Tell him again, Mr. Tung, that his men are dying needlessly."

"Do you think this is Hong Kong?" was his response, after my words were translated. "Do you suppose the world is at your disposal? We are surrounded by the enemy and bound by hundreds of thousands of square miles with few roads and no rail line. Paris does not care about us, Doctor. London does not care.

Nor does Washington. Surely you know this. We have nothing here but our will to defeat the enemy."

"The world is coming," I told him. "I am an example of that."

"And when they bring us supplies you shall have all you ask for. But not until then."

"I ask only to know in advance when your troops will next attack."

He looked amused. "What will this achieve?"

"Beyond saving lives? Is there more?"

"Yes, you can prepare their graves in advance." With a rueful smile he sat down.

The high mortality rate of the 359th, I explained, was due to infection and gangrene, and this might be severely reduced if a mobile medical unit were deployed within two miles of combat. Such a unit would require notification of an impending action in order to establish an aid station and administer treatment within five or ten hours instead of the usual forty or more. If wounds were treated faster, infection rates would fall. "That is what is killing your men now. Infection. Sepsis."

He thanked me, then rose and saluted.

I believed my appeal had fallen on deaf ears. The fact that I was a foreign national, I thought, had not gone in my favour. I'd met many such men here, angered by the world's indifference to their suffering, and I could hardly say I blamed him. But that evening I saw Commander Chen enter our operating theatre like a man retaking the stage to reconsider his conscience. He stood at the front of the room and said nothing as my two students performed an amputation. He stood silently while I searched inside a man's abdomen for fragments of the bayonet shattered inside him. Small bubbles of gas escaping from his crusted wound told me the infection was deep, and I withdrew the shards of hard metal and dropped them into the tin cup at my side.

He stayed with us through the night and the following day, observing us at our work. In the afternoon I was summoned again to the room lined with maps and informed that my mobile unit should be readied to operate behind any future engagements with the Japanese.

Three days later, on the evening of the 26th, I was summoned from my tent and informed that three regiments of the Eighth Route Army were preparing an assault on a Japanese line north of Lin Chu, some forty miles northwest. The logistics were detailed in the extreme. Delighted to begin preparations, I instructed Ho to gather my non-medical essentials—cold weather clothing, sleeping gear and so forth—before nightfall. We arrived at our base, Tsai Chia Yu, in the early morning. There we were provided a guide to deliver us to Hei Ssu, a village of perhaps two dozen homes set beside a narrow mountain stream. I was pleased to see that a small aid station had been prepared in advance, even though it was housed in a primitive stone dwelling whose four rough walls were covered only by flat shale laid atop heavy branches. Only one glassless window looked west over a breathtaking landscape of wind-blown scrub rising gently to the world's snowy heights. We had over seven hours before the Eighth Regiment's wounded began arriving late that afternoon. I rested for an hour. Retrieving a notebook from my pack, I recorded some observations for my monthly report and then took the booklet Mao had given me and studied its mysterious characters, imagining what wisdom they held, before closing my eyes and waiting for the casualties to arrive.

*

I'm thinking about your mother now more than ever. The farther I move away in time, the more often she returns to me, and it sometimes feels to me that we're two pencil points in a slowly closing circle. One day we will touch hands and the circle will be closed, I'm almost sure.

It's dark now, and quiet, which makes remembering an easy thing.

Today my memory is of a walk in the hills we took together. Earlier that day I'd told her about the blue, shimmering sea, and watching helplessly as the planes came in over a harbour in the south of the country. I'd seen a boy of five or six years stare up in awe, with a child's absolute wonder, as they swooped in low, as if he expected the pilot to wave to him from that sleek, speeding air-ship. Even when the crowd began to scatter, he stood fixed in place, enraptured, as the bomb was released. It wobbled awkwardly like a stick swinging through the air, and exploded far enough away that the concussive force didn't knock him over. But an eye-blink later, his head jerked suddenly back, his knees gave and he collapsed, and died as the harbour rose up in horror and flames.

I told your mother this two weeks after she'd taken those photographs of the tank column heading for the Guadalajara front.

A Catalan surgeon named Frederick Duran Jordá asked me to talk to his team in the sierra north of Madrid about my transfusion unit. He was hoping to start up something similar in Barcelona. I had returned from the southeast only three days before, and the news of the attack on the Almería–Málaga road had beaten me back to Madrid.

That evening in the sierra, in a large stone house on the edge of a village, I came to discover that the conference wasn't what

I had been led to believe. A car had come down to Madrid for us and, an hour later, dropped us at the gate of a large walled property. Here we were met by two men dressed in green and brown corduroy coats and pants. They wore berets and well-worn mountain boots and each carried a rifle. One of them accompanied us through a garden, past an empty swimming pool and into the house, where we were introduced to Captain Weber, from Syracuse, New York, a Spanish captain named Aroca and El Viti, the leader of a partisan group based near Segovia, a large, fit man who didn't smile and continually bit the inside of his mouth. The American asked if Kajsa would please wait outside.

"This is my assistant," I said, which by then was my custom.

"That's fine," he said. "Would your assistant mind waiting outside?"

I walked her out to the garden. When I returned Weber explained that a man of my expertise was needed in the hills near Segovia. My specific knowledge was required, he said. He was not able to go into detail.

"Once you have arrived," he said, "you will be told what you're needed for. Not before then." He nodded at the partisan. "This man will guide you, El Viti. He knows only where he's to take you." Aroca listened carefully, his eyes moving back and forth between the two foreigners.

"I can be ready in twenty-four hours," I said.

"Tonight," Weber said. "It must be tonight."

"Can I see your orders?"

From his breast pocket, the Spaniard withdrew a document. It was stamped and signed by General José Miaja.

"You're opening another front at Segovia?"

He ignored the question. "This man will take you. It must be tonight."

"The girl?"

"No," he said.

In the late afternoon, as I waited for nightfall, your mother and I walked over the rocky fields at the edge of the town. We were just under an hour north of Madrid, and another hour from Segovia. I didn't know where this man with dark emotionless eyes was taking me, but it couldn't be as bad as Almería. The hills rose up into low mountains in the distance, and all around us grassy tussocks seemed like small islands among paths carved by generations of wandering goats.

We climbed over a stone wall covered in bramble and black raspberry. I was distracted. My thoughts had been in Almería and the small boy I'd seen fold over on his knees, but now my imagination was up in the hills, over the Guadarrama Pass. Their coming up into this territory meant that they were planning on opening a new front at Segovia, and this entailed medical reconnaissance. I wondered when the assault would commence.

Kajsa was unusually quiet, and I supposed she was troubled by the incident at the house.

"Do you ever want to have children?" she said after a while.

"Not after what I saw down south."

A driver and I had taken a new Renault down to Málaga, which was already emptying itself out, a whole city of refugees heading east on the coastal road to Almería. A hundred thousand people glutted this thin artery running parallel to the sea. We drove headlong into a catastrophe of women and children, twenty miles of sick and broken people and animals dying at the side of the road. Occasionally, without hurry, a Heinkel dipped from the clouds for a strafing. We began ferrying whoever we could the seventy miles to Almería. And then the bombers came. We saved hundreds from the jaws of death only to deliver them into the belly of the beast.

Walking, we came to a shallow gully. I stepped over, then leaned back to offer my hand. She took it, and stepped across.

"Not even eventually?" she said. "After all this?"

"I can't imagine a time when all this is over."

We walked along the gravel road to the village.

The village sat on a hill looking down over a greening valley studded with grey stone fencing, goat trails and, far below, the road and rail leading back to Madrid. We walked along the high street, where most of the shops were closed and soon only the bars would be open. We wandered the smaller streets that reached up the hillside and ended at rock walls or abandoned buildings looking for somewhere smaller and quieter to have a drink, but nothing was open up there.

We went back down to the bar beside the fruit-seller, who was just then pulling the steel grate down over his storefront. He didn't look at us as we walked by him into the bar, which was crowded with men and their families. It was the hour of the aperitif, close to eight o'clock. The air was thick with black tobacco smoke and loud talk.

An empty table at the back of the bar overlooked the valley, where the evening sun cast a low golden light that left a lake of shadow below us but turned the eastern slope of the valley a resplendent, fiery green. We sat down with our drinks and watched two men playing chess at the table next to ours. One of them, much older, was being beaten badly and had only a few pieces left. The other man, who I realized was his son, was showing no mercy as he took one piece after another. Both father and son had short, stubby fingers. They were both labourers. The father didn't look up as his son brusquely knocked pawns, knights and rooks off the board with his own pieces.

I gazed down at the road. "Madrid's only thirty or forty miles away, full of terrified mothers."

"It doesn't look as if there's a war on from here. From here it just looks like Spain."

I said, "I don't know what Spain looks like without a war going on."

I turned to the chess game. The son was smiling widely, pleased that his old father was two or three moves away from losing his king. He called the waiter over, ordered another anis and lit a cigarette. He smoked *Ideales*, the labourer's brand. Apparently, his elderly opponent didn't merit another anis.

"Where is that American captain taking you?"

"Up into the hills."

"What's happening there?"

"I don't know," I said.

The son was now standing over his father. The old man's king was on the floor by their feet, and he sat without moving, his hands resting on his thighs. His head bobbed slightly, then was still. His son was talking to him, but he didn't answer. Puzzled, he laid a hand on his father's shoulder.

I stood and stepped over, touched the old man's hand and neck, then turned to your mother.

"Tell him his father is dead."

We returned to the villa, both of us quite unsettled, and two guards led us down a series of winding streets to a small plaza on the other side of the village with a cathedral on one side and a small bar on the other. The partisan was standing there smoking a cigarette. He snorted, smiled and spat.

"A drink before we leave," he told us.

We followed him into the bar, whose ceiling was something to behold. Legs of ham hung from the beams, each with a small cup piercing the bottom to catch the drippings of grease. Kajsa had been quiet for a long time.

"The girl?" said El Viti.

"My assistant comes with me."

He shrugged.

When the barman began mopping the floor, we carried our drinks and a white plate of olives out to the sidewalk and enjoyed the last of the day's sun on our faces. He began spitting again, slowly and delicately, turning his back to us. I mentioned that I'd been told that from the Guadarrama Mountains, over the hill from this village, you could see all the way to Old Castile. He said the view toward the north was of strategic importance, and for this reason small outposts and pillboxes had been constructed along this range and staffed by men from the villages on the south side. I gazed up at the cathedral, opposite us, crowned with empty storks' nests.

"Those old monuments are good for something at least." He snorted and spat.

"The observation posts on the mountain?" I asked.

He speared an olive, ate it and threw his toothpick to the sidewalk. "No," he said, "I mean this *puta* church and the old *puta* buzzards up there sh——ting on the priest's head all through the day. Everyone s——ts on the priests these days, even the *puta* storks. I s——t on the milk. It is not so pleasant to be a priest now, my son," he said, smiling.

I suspected he was in favour of shooting every last priest in Spain. We'd all heard stories of summary executions.

"It's a lovely birdhouse," I said.

He smiled again, then said to Kajsa, "The men up there—they haven't seen a woman in weeks. They'll tear you to pieces with their eyes. Going up there is not something you want to do."

"I go with the Doctor," she said.

"How far are we going?" I said.

"We shall arrive in the morning, at first light," he said. "How are your legs?"

"My legs are fine," I said.

"And the lady?"

"The lady's legs are fine," she said.

He told his barkeep friend to leave his mop and prepare food for us. We drank another vermouth while talking about the war. Kajsa was sipping a brandy.

"What about those bunkers?" I said. "How often do those men come down here?"

"Whenever they feel like it. Everyone here is for the Republic. On this side of the mountain there is no trouble." A whistle sounded from inside the bar. He went inside and returned with a large rucksack.

"Food?" I said.

"Ours and the lunches of the others. We do not go up empty-handed."

We finished our drinks and I went inside to pay, but the man waved me away with his big hand. *"Viva la República,"* he said. I answered in kind, thanked him, and the three of us set off along cool narrow streets where old ladies stood in their doorways and rabbits and *botas* hung in shop windows. Beside the town post box we met up with the two guards and another man, all carrying carbines. They did not speak.

We took the dirt road leading out to the main highway, also dirt, and walked for a quarter of an hour until we turned on a secondary road and followed it into the foothills where a yellow gate marked the trail that would lead us up to the old partisans who sat watching, day and night, for movement in the valley below. I wondered if there was a man of importance up there whose wounds needed tending, a man who couldn't be moved. That wasn't likely, though I no longer cared to ask. El Viti would say nothing. His English was good, but we spoke little as we walked. He cleared his throat of phlegm and set a steady pace up a dry streambed gouged deep into the rock. Large boulders that had been washed loose and fallen fir and pine trees slowed our progress considerably. Through the trees I could see horses on the side of the mountain. Branches overhead obscured the last of the day's light, and the air was cold. The three men accompanying us did not speak.

Occasionally we discovered small pools of water, and I asked if there were any fish.

"Farther down," the guide said, "below the town. If they've not all been blown up. You know, Doctor, that a Spaniard has no sport. He uses a stick of dynamite."

One of the other men said something, and he translated. "He says if we used our ordnance on the enemy and not on the trout we might kill more Fascists."

One of the men quietly began to sing, and a moment later the others joined him. It was a song I'd heard before, but in the dark it sounded remorseful.

Nearing midnight we approached an observation post at the ridge overlooking the northern slope. We came from the west and stopped two hundred yards off, and one of the men disappeared into the darkness. Fifteen minutes later he returned and led us to the clearing where the sentry stood waiting, his carbine over his shoulder. Wisps of snow blew over his boots, and a bright moon lit his gaunt, grey face. An old man, he tried to smile but looked tired, as if he'd just been woken up or this war had been going on his entire life.

"It is quiet here," he said. "What have you brought me to eat?"

He talked with the others while El Viti showed me the stone building the man occupied. Constructed of native stone and thus invisible as a man-made structure, it wasn't much more than a cave with a firepit and viewing window and a log for a bench, but it was positioned so that everything below was visible for fifty miles. That sparkle of lights was Segovia, and, our guide said, you could see dust or flashing glass or metal from any convoy of more than three trucks at a distance of twenty miles.

We left the man his food and a bottle of wine, and continuing west along the ridge we met more such men, all over sixty. Each time, one of our guards went forward to warn the sentry of our approach. The fingers of the last man were clawed with rheumatism, and the snow there covered the path. I wondered how he managed so high up. After giving him the food and wine, we walked on.

Over his shoulder, El Viti said, "We shall eat something when we get to the top, higher up along the ridge. *Señora*, how are these old men, are they as bad as I said?"

"They're happier to see the wine than they are to see a woman," she said. "And it's '*señorita.*' I belong to no one."

He looked at me, then at her, and smiled.

I saw him wondering what the correction implied. *I am with no one.* To a mountain man like this, it meant, *Even if I am with the doctor, he has no claim over me.* We continued up the path. It was very cold now, and the footing on snow-covered rocks was treacherous. Yet the men carrying the guns moved easily, their breathing untroubled, whereas my lungs burned. Perhaps they knew these trails from boyhood. The path soon disappeared, dropping into a bend. One of the men walked ahead. Then me, then Kajsa. I followed it down a slight incline and then up and up until I could see the end of the treeline. It would be light in a few hours.

I assumed the men somehow knew what had transpired. I felt their superior grins. An important doctor who can't keep a rein on his woman, they would be thinking. Perhaps this is how foreigners are, with all their grand talk, nothing more than cuckolds. I loosened the straps of my rucksack and continued on, wanting to send them all to the devil.

Then I heard your mother cry out, a short shriek that filled the night air completely. I ran back along the trail and found her buckled over on her knees and holding her stomach. She looked up and she dropped her hands to the ground.

"I am all right," she said. "Keep those men away."

"You have to rest."

"I'll be fine," she said. "Just keep those men away."

Before long, she regained her strength and we took her back down to the last observation post. I left her there with the old man with the clawed fingers, then started off again up the mountain.

★

Five days later, back in Madrid, I met her at the Crystal Palace in the Retiro Park, where we'd emerged from the tunnels into daylight almost two months before.

"I'm sorry about all that," she said.

Her cheeks were flushed. In fact she looked as healthy as I'd ever seen her, as though she carried a light within her, and I told her so. She turned and watched the ducks nibbling the underwater weed of the pond. The sun shone. It was late April.

"I have something for you," I said. The perfume was wrapped in brown paper, and the small envelope held a card on which I'd written a poem. She read it, and then I asked, "Do you have time tonight? You could wear this."

"I'm not sure I want to," she said.

On the opposite shore the towering statue of Alfonso XII, overdressed in his cautious suit of sandbags, looked south over the city.

We walked up to the boating lake and sat at the busy outdoor café and drank coffees with anis. It was a nice break from the war, I remember thinking.

★

I regret the delay in getting on with this narrative, but I have come to Yang Chia Chuang to begin work on establishing a training school. I have little time for anything other than this important project. There is still much work to be done, Lord knows, but the first hurdle, and perhaps the highest, has been cleared: I have persuaded Dr. Chiang Chi-tsien, Director of Medical Services for the Eighth Route Army, and a number of his fellow colleagues, that within months such a school will begin to ease the chronic shortage of medical care at the front, and that I'm the only person available to make the school a reality. It is my hope that in the first six months we will prepare hundreds of mobile medical units. My efforts on the ground have not been enough, as I cannot win this war fracture by fracture, heart by heart. I understand, now, that my time is best spent educating a new generation of doctors and nurses.

I have completed the medical text I began some months ago. Despite overwork and exhaustion this has been a time of great energy and optimism. I envision each regiment of the Red Army equipped with its own field unit, and with this school, and possibly others, we might achieve that goal. I might spend a day in the operating theatre and save perhaps ten lives. What a wonderful day that is. But now, with this program, I might save a thousand.

★

What is the qualitative difference between the deed done for its own sake and one accomplished for purely selfish reasons, though resulting in the same benefit? Is there one? Does it matter? I was unable to consider this question during those months in Madrid. But now that I am asking it of myself here in the thin air of this mountain night, I am forced to pause and look about me.

What do these people do but give every ounce of sweat to the labours of survival and an improved lot for the future? Not a single man or woman, not even a child, Ho would assure me, places himself or herself above this cause. And can I say the same? I wonder how much of my life has become a drama in which I daily costume myself in gown and mask. How much of my life has taken its own course, in spite of me? I will give of myself to the last breath, of that I have no doubt. But has the actor been outwitted by the grand tragedy he serves?

Shortly after the New Year, thirty qualified candidates chosen from all corners of the Border Regions arrived to Yang Chia Chuang to immerse themselves in the three-week course I had prepared. There they would learn the essentials of front-line medical care. By then I was under no illusion. I was not teaching the art of surgery, but my students were learning the basic skills so vitally required and so often lacking at aid stations throughout the territories. Graduates would return to their precincts with that vital knowledge and continue the process of education. It was a far cry from the actual surgical training truly required, but it met an urgent need.

Within four weeks I was confident that the school was capable
of operating without my stewardship. I was eager to return to
the field. It was an unhappy addiction, these frequent forays, but
of pre-eminent importance. Through that hard winter and into
the spring my eighteen-member team sought out field hospitals,
medical units and guerrilla fighters. We were strafed, bombed
and sniped, pursued by the Japanese, and we very nearly froze
to death almost every night before March brought its first thaw.
Always we came upon wounded who were holed up, entrenched,
and dying all manners of death—from trauma, sepsis, starvation,
TB. Great numbers or simply one man, abandoned to his fate.
We were received as angels of mercy. So far gone were the hopes
of the men we encountered that any help at all, even if only to
help them die faster, was welcomed. Under enemy fire we cut and
stitched, stabilizing peasants and partisans and regular soldiers so
they might be delivered out of harm's way.

For some time I had been riding a horse captured from the
Japanese. One day, while returning from an inspection tour, I got
to wondering what might have become of its previous owner.
Lost in thought, I rode on, only slightly behind our lead guide.
Perhaps I'd been partially hypnotized by the slow clomp of the
beast beneath me, exhausted as I was, and by the thin air of that
mountain altitude. Where was he? I wondered. Who had he been?
Perhaps not so unlike me. Was he somewhere behind us, like so
many of his comrades, eyeless, their dirt-filled mouths crying out
mutely for a solemn return to the homeland? Yes, your horse is
alive, I wanted to say, alive, if miserable in its new calling, and you
are not. The beast outlives its master.

I wondered if perhaps it would be appropriate to shoot it once
I arrived at the Base Hospital, as if in respect for its fallen owner,
but it had proven too useful for that. Spurring it on, I pondered if

it was better to be a beast of burden or, say, a little monk nibbling away at time as a mouse does cheese? A horse has a use, at least, and a quiet dignity in its labours. A monk is utterly useless and without consequence. I forgave the animal its origins and urged it to climb higher. It was early morning. The light was faint, almost blue, the sun not fully over the ridge to the west.

Near midday we came across a man alone and left for dead. The Japanese hadn't done such a thorough job on him. Perhaps they'd left him like this for a reason, or else had become bored with their torture, impatient to move on to better things. I asked Mr. Tung to come forward. The other men kept away. I dismounted and with Mr. Tung walked over to the man. The landscape was barren. The wind, carrying small flakes now, prowled in upward dancing surges. Snow snaked between the rocks as if scurrying from itself.

He was lying there, watching as we approached. He made no gesture, no movement, but his eyes were full of life and terror. His severed hands lay beside him, gripped in comradely greeting. When I kneeled down, his gaze shifted to his hands and made a strange face. It was as if he were trying to make them respond. His legs were broken and splayed out, bent and distorted from beneath him, his knees snapped backwards. He would be dead in a matter of minutes.

There was a wound in his chest I could fit my hand into, and his lungs were filling. There was no use for Mr. Tung since the man couldn't talk. He tried to smile at me, it was an apologetic smile, then he looked at his hands again. They were just out of reach. He seemed more aware than I had ever been in my entire life. Of all the eternity of moments that had been lived and were yet to be lived, this one in this timeless place, and with us as bystanders, had been fully dedicated to this simple man. This was the centre-point of his life. This was the fire, the flame moving underground. It was perhaps all he would amount to. Whether the precious facts of his life were in any respect complete or significant, it didn't matter now. This was the most important moment in his life, the exact moment of consciousness he'd wondered about while sleeping in caves and on the rocks of this mountain, freezing, sweating, eating gruel and starving, listening to his friends' stories of home, he himself dreaming of his life and always trying to imagine what death would be like when it came. And now, as I'd seen hundreds of times before in the faces of other men, he was sitting patiently, resignedly, staring down over the retreating landscape.

He sat before his entire life and waited to die as I sat beside him. Perhaps he'd raised his hands in supplication to his murderers, beseeching them, and then the *katana*, in a swift arc of reply, had cut through the air.

After he died, I crossed his arms over his chest and placed his hands there, curled, still clasped. Then we mounted our animals and started off once more.

*

Ho has joined me now. I do not usually write during daylight hours. There's never enough time. But today I have completed my rounds and performed three surgeries and managed to eat a bite and still there's light in the sky. I sat down and was just about to begin when Ho came to my door. Seeing my typewriter he retreated deferentially, but I got up and pulled him inside and asked him to sit. So here he sits, watching and waiting.

Last night I dreamed you came to me here. You were a child. "Go," I said. "The war will be over soon, and I will come for you." You looked at me and your smile revealed you were missing two teeth. You knew nothing of the horrors of this world, only its perfect beauty. I took you in my arms and carried you outside to a pasture with a stream and a bright light falling from the blue heavens and majestic oaks thrumming in the breeze. I set you down in the grass and went back inside.

Ho is a patient lad to sit here like this. Why do I invite him in here? Is it that I, too, am alone?

To keep him occupied I handed him a sheaf of pencil drawings I've been working on, with no words but the title. The most recent is "Burn Injury of the Left Arm with Surgical Amputation." He nods enthusiastically.

*

I've been thinking lately about matrimony—mine, to be precise. A strange preoccupation in the middle of a war. I have been thinking about you finding happiness with a good and patient man. Does that mark me as sentimental? Well, so be it. Perhaps he's leaning over your shoulder as you read this. I find that thought comforting. No union in life is as dear as marriage, and though I may have been more susceptible than most to the frailties of the heart, I still believe it. None of us is so different in that regard. We all harbour an abiding belief that even after failure there can be hope for the future. That is our greatest resource, I think, eternal hope. Some basic truths bear repeating, and this is one of them. I can tell you that the mystery of our loves is the deepest mystery we have, the most beautiful and ennobling, too, and the most deserving of our ceaseless energies and wonder. I imagine you will know by the time you read this that a first love is not often successful. I discovered this when I was younger, that one failure might strengthen you for another. The name of the woman who helped me to become that better man your mother fell in love with was Frances Penney. She became my wife, and two times I left her, walking back into my lonely life.

The Great War had ended and I had begun writing and painting again. I had found employment at Number 23 Great Ormond Street, London, working with children. One evening, in the fall of 1920, I met with an Australian friend, Clifford Ellington, at a pub in Soho. We were talking over a number of my poems and having a glass of beer when a group of four young women entered the pub. One was glamorous-looking, very beautiful. Her large eyes darted around the bar, and she produced a cigarette from her purse. She made much of this simple act. It was very much worthy of the pictures, I remember thinking.

Her dark hair was cut short, bobbed, as all the girls were wearing it then. She crossed her legs under her chair, then leaned into the middle of the table and remarked upon something that made her friends laugh. The four of them looked inelegantly in our direction as they did so. "A flock of parakeets mocking the baboons," Ellington said. The server spoke with the young ladies and returned behind the bar, where we were standing. She busied herself with polishing a glass while the barman prepared their drinks. My left elbow was damp from leaning on the bar where someone had spilt a beer. My heart thumping, I asked the server "Would you please mop this up for me?"

We returned to our discussion, Ellington arguing that I should refrain from sending my poems out. He held the sheaf of poems in his hand, waving them as he spoke. They were, he said, childish and morbid, vain and self-important. Very nearly offended, I suggested he didn't have an ounce of creative or critical blood in his veins. "Bethune, this is not poetry," he said, or something along those lines. He was an intelligent man and a very good doctor, and I enjoyed his company immensely. But I found it difficult to take his criticism seriously, though foolishly I'd asked for it. I never really liked his poems, greatly inspired by a fashionable Australian poet of the day who for good reason had yet to be discovered anywhere else in the English-speaking world.

"Norman, you're a charming drunk and a gifted doctor," Ellington said, "but I would advise you to hold off with these. They make you seem a bit pathetic, really."

I was pleased to change the subject. "For the sake of keeping the peace, let's concentrate on the parakeets over there."

"I don't know why you wouldn't write about that. You know women almost as well as you understand the lower intestine."

"You are vaguely pathetic yourself, aren't you."

"After you," he said.

"No, after you," I said, but we didn't move.

"I suppose we'll be bachelors the rest of our lives," Ellington concluded.

Well, those girls took the initiative and soon we were shaking hands all around, drinking and having a grand time. Later, after we'd visited a number of pubs, I stopped dead in my tracks. I had left the sheaf of poems somewhere. Perhaps Ellington was right about them being a bit vain, for I was less a gifted poet than a confessional one. They served as a journal, a diary in verse, so to speak, and without them I was lost. Abruptly I excused myself and left the party. Ellington saluted drunkenly, not the least bit concerned. Why would he be? I retraced our footsteps and in each locale my mood grew darker. I was stricken. I'd neglected to make carbons of the pages, and they were such long poems that I'd committed only a few of them to memory.

I was perhaps even more despondent the next day. On my way home from the hospital I stopped in at the Pig & Clover, where Ellington and I had started the previous evening. The pub was filling up but I was in no mood for socializing. I noticed a pretty young woman reading at the other end of the bar, a half-pint of Guinness before her. I couldn't help but smile when she glanced up. I saw something romantic about a pretty woman reading alone in a bar. I was not so different from her, I thought, craving solitude and seeking company in a book. This spoke of the sort of quiet desperation I often felt, and which most others chose to conceal.

When she turned the page I saw what she was reading was held in a sheaf. I rose quickly. "Excuse me," I said, "that belongs to me."

"You wrote these?"

I closed the booklet.

"I'm sorry. I thought it was a menu. I saw it here," she said, pointing, "wedged up against the wall. I think they're quite beautiful." She glanced at the cover. "H. Norman Bethune?"

"Yes."

"Frances Penney," she said, offering her hand. "Will you publish these?"

"One day, I'm hoping."

"I liked the one about the British Museum. It was very sad, somehow. You won't mind my asking who Agnes is?"

"I made her up."

"May I?" she said, reaching for the sheaf. I eased off my hand. She flipped through and found the page. She read the poem aloud.

I have carried it with me in memory all this time.

Nurse Agnes of Cambridge Visits the British
Museum with Limping Soldier

He had never considered the souls
buried within the clay and gold,

the distant stone and iron brow
that held their long gaze
found so properly housed
in the greatest museums of the age;

They were just masks, he'd thought,
pretty things set out for display
on any afternoon of
any given day.

What are they though, she said that
afternoon, but reminders that you shall see
that same look of death looking
back at thee?

In a future exhibit entitled Post
Post Byzantium of the Long Lost Apocalypse
entry 5 shillings
the one expression we least of all deserved
will represent our age
and all its men
forever preserved.

Save your money, sir, and take a walk instead;
any good nurse will tell you more
about Nephthys of Egypt
than the old curators of the dead.

Her soft Scottish voice stayed quietly between us. Frances was,
I decided right then, a remarkable beauty. When she finished reading she did not lift her eyes. She stayed like that, leaning slightly

forward into the page. She might have been reading through the poem again, looking for some key to slip into a lock I had fashioned without any conscious intention. She might have been stalling, searching for kind things to say. I was ready to pounce on any interpretation she might offer, as I'd been the night before when Ellington had offered his thoughts. At most I'd thank her for recovering my poems, then leave. I waited, growing more uncomfortable by the second. She seemed so entirely lost in the page and unaware of me that I was free, nervous though I was, to let my eyes roam over her. She wore her striking dark hair cut short and parted on the left side, the tips of it curling in to her face just below her ear. Her eyes gleamed as they moved back and forth in the dirty half-light of the pub.

"But did you love her?" she finally asked, looking up at me. The question came as a surprise. "It's make-believe," I said.

"But you can't invent emotions."

"Not if they're genuine, I suppose."

"Did the young man love her, then?"

"I'm not sure," I said.

★

I saw her again the following week. That is when she first called me her Poet-Doctor. I didn't mind. In fact I was thrilled. She brought me books of poetry: Donne, Shelley, Byron. While I had read most of them, I happily accepted these gifts inscribed with lovely notes. We nosed about the old bookshops on Charing Cross Road, and naturally I took her to the British Museum. I introduced her to Ellington, as she did me to her girlfriends, Norma, a pretty secretary at one of the larger law firms in the city, and Eunice, a student at Chelsea College. At the time I was a solitary creature, riddled by my own romantic impulses and irked by crowds. In solitude I was safe, but not happy. Frances cured that in me.

As a young doctor I was used to sharing myself with the sick and the dying, perhaps because their solitude and complete dependence on me made it all but impossible that I might be slighted or denied. There is comfort to be taken in the fact that a brash young doctor is never pushed away, for he brings hope in times when it is most precious. Young love is a different matter entirely. At first what I felt for Frances was confusing, often painful and always difficult. As I said, I was solitary by nature, and no single individual could change that. Frances, of course, devoured the company of others. She encouraged me to share my dreams and emotions. I painted portraits of my young love and praised her in my poems. Though cautious, I was an idealist, I can see that now, for those oblique paintings and colourless poems were at least a young man's attempt to understand and glorify this new world he'd recently entered. But soon enough those efforts revealed my deficiencies. We didn't talk about the war. We shared our food and friends. With me she shared her money, for she'd been left a fair bit by her wealthy father, and with her I shared my ambition and hunger for the world.

I will admit to being a bit of a dandy in those days. You would probably laugh if you could see how I went about town wearing a wing collar, black tie, gloves and homburg, smoking a Dunhill pipe with an aristocratic French-turned bowl and carrying in my right hand a silver-tipped cane. I must have looked ridiculous, though it was all in keeping with the finer tastes and fashions of the day. I recall with some amusement now that I was asked to attend a number of dinners and parties at the great houses of many famous people, to whom I was introduced as one of London's most promising medical men. Some of these individuals were recognized as pioneers in their chosen fields—whether fellow physicians, business tycoons or professors—while others were famous only for the company they kept. I was not easily swayed or impressed by these social functions, though they were, as I say, an entertaining and pleasant diversion from the demands of establishing one's practice. In October 1923 I became the house surgeon at Great Ormond Street and gave myself over completely to my duties at the hospital. I withdrew almost entirely from the exciting if shallow demands of "society." Of course, Frances and I were in greater demand as a result of my heightened prospects, but I was happily consumed by my work at the hospital and Frances herself had little time for socializing.

We were a pair to behold in those days. We shared our money with the old antique dealers of Portobello, the young painters of Soho and whoever else sparked our appetites, from the bohemians of Marble Arch and Brick Lane to the fine restaurateurs of Covent Garden and Piccadilly. In the hospital at Great Ormond Street I didn't think much about Frances, but once returned to our parallel world, I shared with her a grand opulence in our decision to marry, and then with the men who drove our horse cabs through Paris and Rome on our honeymoon we continued to share what money we carried, and with the waiters and barmen in Vienna, too. We shared first-class cabins with American tourists and stopped with them in somnolent French villages and at the boisterous Italian seasides. We amused ourselves with these travelling strangers until it was time to resume our own journey, always with names and addresses scribbled into dime-store novels and on train-ticket envelopes. This wealth and freedom provided us with a world of friends that soon, as in all romantic comedies they must, trickled to nothing when shortly after our return, our inheritance and optimism fell flat. Once the old man's money was used up we waited in London for a change for the better. Surely it would come.

We sojourned on Sunday mornings and drank champagne, trying in vain to recapture that sense of effortless motion, and the following year we made the decision so many were making then. North America was heaped before us like an unclaimed ante, and we would avail ourselves of it.

On the ship over, we took a modest cabin. We were a handsome couple, still finely dressed in cashmere and silk, now relegated to steerage. Much of the crossing we spent reading and playing cards. I might have written a poem or two. In the windowless cafeteria that served our class, we supped on bread and lentils, watched the old men at their dominoes, and waited.

The winter snows were heavy on the ground when we made port at Montreal. From there we journeyed to the small town of Stratford, Ontario, a sad forgery of the inspired original, where my sister had lived since marrying. We did not linger there. After a dreary car ride into Quebec scuppered the idea of settling in that small European outpost, we felt stranded in a wilderness bigger than France itself, and it became clear that the marriage would not last in this Precambrian waste.

We drove southwest and crossed the border into Michigan. We found an apartment at 411 Seldon Street, near the ravenous centre of Detroit. There, where I believed I would earn my fortune, I gained my first true understanding of the underclass—Southern Negroes, Hungarians, Italians, Yugoslavs, Poles, Russians, migrant workers from Mexico, all second-class citizens lured there by the promise of opportunity, as I had been, so few of whom would ever rise out of their impoverished and diseased neighbourhoods. What did I do? Still bewitched by the dream, I opened my practice to the richest of that city, determined to make my name and become rich myself. But it was to the needs of the poor that my heart began to be pulled.

On the fringes of this wealthy city lived people whose only means of survival was luck, guile, criminality or some combination of the three. Detroit soon seemed to me a Petri dish for the doomed experiment of Capitalism. I remember well the night I spent at the railyard, working to save a Mexican labourer's baby. The families gathered outside the boxcar in the dark waiting for word about the mother and her newborn. The small fires they'd built along the edge of the tracks glowed and flickered. The men slowly passed a bottle among themselves. I told the husband to close the boxcar door, and then he knelt again beside his wife and began muttering his prayers. I knew this man, who cleaned the office building across from the Seldon Street apartment. The baby was in the breech position. When I delicately attempted to turn the baby around, the mother fainted from the pain. Her husband kept praying. *"Dios,"* he said again and again. Perhaps he was praying for the American Dream to shine down on his family and rescue their child, or maybe for enough money so his wife could deliver his child in a regular hospital, like the white people whose offices he cleaned. Filled with sleeping bags, utensils, paper bags and backpacks, the boxcar was home to the families waiting outside in the switching yard. He spoke some English, and I told him, "Do not watch this." I removed a blade from my bag. "Do not watch this." I cut the woman's abdomen, down through the skin and fat and muscle and into the membrane of the uterus, then scooped their baby boy out of his mother's suffocating womb like a blind blue fawn.

★

Today is my birthday. March 4. Somehow Ho found out about it and attempted to make something special. Well, his resources are limited, as you know. At the evening meal he produced a rice cake with a small candle stuck into it. He sprinkled a half-spoonful of sugar over it and presented me with it while Mr. Tung and a number of others gathered round and attempted an uneven if not unrecognizable rendition of "Happy Birthday." It was the best present I could have asked for. After a bit of light-hearted banter we got back to work.

Now I am alone, thinking through the day. It's past midnight.

I have been thinking about how there's a point in your life when a birthday becomes a sad marker of time passed rather than a pleasant survey of times to come. Do you know what I mean? We get closer to death with each passing year, and it affects people. But not me. I'm glad Ho found that silly candle and helped celebrate the day. I suppose I'm still amazed by the rapturous wonder of being alive. I hope you will understand the gift that being alive is, even in the hardest times.

There are so many moments in your life I have missed already. Your first tooth. Your first step. I never even got to hold you. But I'm thinking about that now, and I want you to know that I understand what I have missed in your life, and in mine. This is something I regret very deeply. I have delivered a number of babies in my day and birth has always seemed a miracle beyond any sane man's comprehension, but I don't think I ever truly understood the pure ecstatic wonder of birth simply because those beautiful babies I helped into the world were not mine.

Now I close my eyes and think of you running through swells of field grass whooping and hollering with all the power of your young lungs, muscular and celestial. Though you are yet an infant, as I write this I see you moving through the fields—an image that gives me great joy. And tonight I will sleep with you in my arms.

★

We were quarrelling over money. How clearly I recall it! We quarrelled over every aspect of our life together, over the tilt of my hat and the shine on my shoes. Something had to give, I suppose. Now, in retrospect, I'm glad it did. Frances went off to Nova Scotia to visit a girlfriend from Scotland, and from there she journeyed to California to conspire with her brother, or so I thought, in the land of sunshine and freedom.

How I envied her! It was an extended holiday away from her husband, and from grim, desolate Detroit. While she was away I wrote artful letters of contrition, blame, compromise and reconciliation. I wrote what I thought love was, what it was that bound us together. I sent only the graceful ones. I have no doubt she was sincere in her original premise—simply some time away, nothing more. What spouse doesn't dream of such escapes? Perhaps you will know this yourself one day, and realize that longings don't necessarily foreshadow the end of love but perhaps invite a new beginning for a tired and hurt love. But by then she'd felt entitled to call me overbearing more than once. Perhaps time away was not a sufficient cure. I was not an easy man. We hoped to close this chapter of our life and resume our love affair, as a reader returns to a difficult book after a restful sleep, refreshed and eager to see its hero through to the end. I wrote often. I needed her, I said, but also needed some time alone before I could love her again. My letters, you see, were an elegant batch of contradictions.

I remember one evening, not long after she returned, sitting at the kitchen table working over some lecture notes. Frances was sitting in a deep chair by the living room window. I'd heard her turning the pages of a novel. After working for quite some time, I rose to stretch my legs. When I entered the living room she looked up. I remember her closing the book, slowly, over her finger, and smiling. In her I saw a woman who just then, as if in a moment of revelation, had given herself over to her husband, completely and absolutely.

"Do you have something to tell me?" I said.

"Silly man. Like what?"

What she wanted was to live as a good wife should. The metamorphosis was startling. It was as if she'd been seized by the American Dream. This is what I always wanted, she seemed to say, and with the man I always wanted. To be together, here, in this place, or any place. There was in this emotional embrace all I feared and hated in the world. Instead of a loving wife content to live in the misery of this grey existence, I saw a total, unabashed surrender. I saw pity, falsehood, the embrace of second best. And eventually I came to see a spirited woman willing, finally, to submit to me. How had I destroyed her? That restlessness that burned within her—and within both of us—along with a refusal to submit was suddenly replaced by a smiling, pathetic contentment.

"But I'm so happy," she said, "with what we have. I realize that now."

I stood frozen. Here, in the squalor of our life, in one of the few truly benign and peaceful moments she'd ever offered me, I had the desire to obliterate her from my sinful heart. I would have preferred saucers and plates shattering against the dingy wallpaper to her coquettish smile. But there she sat, her face framed by a dark-paned window, smiling that lovely smile. I thought her more beautiful than ever. She leaned slightly back into her chair, then stood, and I strode across the room to take her in my arms. I didn't know if this was love or a selfish act that was a kind of revenge. Afterwards, I realized how desperately I did not want her in my life. The invented domesticity of home-life suddenly sickened me. The entire world awaited me: that was one truth I was sure of. She spoke to me softly, questioningly, while I watched the ceiling of our bedroom, and soon I returned to my lecture notes.

Was that the evening our life changed? Was it then, as my fingers touched her, that she saw the hard, distant man she'd married? The brilliant facade crumbles as eventually it must. I had used my gifts against her—I know this now—as an adversary might, to deceive a woman who was willing to believe in me.

The next morning, as she prepared breakfast, I said, "I didn't tell you last night." I was sitting at the table.

"That you love me? I noticed."

"I've been feeling poorly," I said. I shifted in my seat. "Fatigued. I had it checked while you were away."

"Why didn't you tell me sooner? What? What is it?"

"There is tuberculosis in my left lung."

She sat in a chair across from me and took my hand.

"We might be able to do something about it."

"How advanced is it? How long—?"

"A man at the College, a Doctor Amberson, speaks highly of a sanatorium in the Adirondacks. I might be able to get a place there. There's a chance."

"You see? Yes, a few months of bedrest," she said, caressing my face. "That's all you'll need."

"Please don't cry."

"You've been working too hard," she said.

"Yes."

"A few months and you'll come back better."

"Yes," I said.

"And then there'll be babies and everything will be all right."

"Please don't cry," I said again.

I didn't know how long I had to live. It might have been six months. The TB spiders, as I thought of them, had already firmly housed themselves in my left lung. It was likely they would take up residence in the right one, too, if I weren't admitted somewhere quickly.

The Trudeau Sanatorium had been founded in 1884 by a doctor from New York named Edward Livingstone Trudeau and quickly recognized as one of the best of its kind. Trudeau had been drawn from New York to the Adirondacks by the promise of clear air and untouched forests. These, he thought, were the ideal climatic conditions to help heal the afflicted lungs of a TB patient. In October I went there alone to place my name on the wait list, then headed north over the border to pass my days at the Calydor Sanatorium in Gravenhurst, Ontario. At the time I was unable to sidestep the grim irony of returning to the sawdust town of my birth with the distinct possibility of dying there. My life, bookended by the narrow prospects of that sleepy, insular place, would prove deadeningly, pathetically inconsequential. I lay there confined to a bed, writing letters to Frances while waiting for a space to open at the Trudeau, never sure that I would go out into the world again. It was a misery, but the pained romantic and brooding poet in me relished the solitude.

The time spent away from Frances acted as a balm. Remembering only the happiness we'd shared, I grew optimistic. When I recovered, that sad chapter in our lives would close and we could return to our love affair. I needed her, I wrote, but in order for me to love her again, as she deserved to be loved, some part of me first had to die, and it would die here in the place of my birth. This return to my hometown was, of course, heavy with symbolic meanings not lost on me. I hoped for a rebirth, if you'll permit the poetic licence. I wrote poems and confessional letters. I bared my soul. There were, I wrote, certain things about myself that could stand second consideration. I was contrite. But here was an opportunity. I was committed to returning as a new man, I said, in body and in spirit. I would look afresh into my heart, and find in this dreary isolation a new optimism.

Not long after I returned to Frances, only a month later, our marriage stumbled again. We were both back into the thick of it. The optimistic words about our future had meant nothing. It was as if we'd never been apart. We finally agreed upon an official separation. Then, in the middle of December, the wait list for the Trudeau cleared.

Deep in the heart of the Adirondacks, I bunked with a young physician named John Barnwell and was restricted to bedrest. It was customary to be given passes to leave the grounds just three times a month, but I resisted all attempts to constrain me. Anxiety over Frances, and the financial status of my practice now floundering back in Detroit, only added to my desperation. Sick as I was, I was also deeply resistant to the idea of someone exerting control over my life after I'd already given up what little freedom it offered. I was restless and eager to declare myself however I could.

As a remedy for the monotony, Barnwell and I soon took to visiting Brook's Tavern, a small establishment on the road leading into the town of Saranac, its walls covered with fishing and hunting memorabilia, stuffed trout and deer and wolf heads and antique hunting rifles and colourful pheasants and photographs of proud men standing beside poles sagging under the weight of snow hares, wild turkeys and grouse. The log building contained a bar and a small dining room, with an outfitters' shack butted up against the west end where you might purchase hunting and fishing gear, camping supplies, tobacco, stamps, magazines and newspapers.

Pickerel, trout, perch, whitefish and venison were offered on the menu, though we never arrived before the kitchen had closed. It was only at night we came here, after the sanatorium had closed down for the evening. As patients we were not permitted to drink or smoke, and so as a consequence of this most reasonable policy our little establishment became a welcome oasis of liquor and tobacco in an abstemious sea of lake, rock and pine. The owner came to know us well. He was a sympathetic New Yorker who'd lost his leg at the Battle of Manila Bay in the Philippines. He limped around behind the bar on his prosthesis, pulling draft beers and pouring single-ounce shots for the foresters, travellers and locals who collected there after everything else had shut.

During the day I recall reading widely, making full use of the sanatorium's library. I also delivered a series of lectures on human anatomy to the nursing students at the school connected with the sanatorium. In order to further distract myself I laid out a scheme to establish a university on the grounds, since I'd noticed how many highly specialized patients, myself included, had been attracted there. To provide much needed status, and to fill out faculty requirements, I decided my new university should be affiliated with NYU and McGill University in Montreal. It was a wonder no one had thought before of a highly specialized teaching hospital at the foot of the Adirondacks. I took my plans to the Trudeau board and explained in the greatest detail the need for just such an institution, but my hopes were dashed by a table of wooden, conservative men who saw little value and no practicality in this enterprise. That night, in my familiar oasis, I listened to stories of the Battle of Manila Bay.

Around this time, I arranged for the sale of my private practice, then sinking into a morass of unpaid bills and shrinking patient lists. These negotiations briefly kept me busy and lifted the tedium off my shoulders. A young doctor by the name of Wruble paid me $5,000, a small triumph that did little to assuage my financial anxieties. Toward that end I returned to Detroit and resumed my teaching at the Detroit College of Medicine and Surgery.

Things between me and Frances had not improved, and on a grey Sunday afternoon in April, I said the inevitable words: "I want you to do me a favour, Frances. I want you to divorce me. It will do you a world of good to get away from me. You're miserable, you must admit that. We've tried long enough. You want to go home. You want to be happy. You want a family. I can give you none of those things."

She stared at me silently, expressionless. And so, without another word, after only three short years of marriage, that was that.

*

My health took a turn for the worse shortly afterward. I checked into the Trudeau again in June of that year, 1927, but my return was cloaked in dread. It was now clear to me that my TB was no less than a death sentence. My friend Barnwell had died over the winter, and I would surely die there too. The odds were highly stacked against me. The slightest physical task was now practically unendurable, and walking fifty paces soon became intolerable. At my insistence, Frances had retained a lawyer, and our separation would become legally binding by the end of the summer. I was alone, as I'd wanted to be, though I know now this solitude stemmed not from purely selfless motives, as I'd led Frances to believe, but from a selfish and destructive anger.

I can tell you now that I did very little in those days to be proud of. Ill health is a terrible thing, however you choose to look at it. But for some people the thought of death is a first step toward redemption. To getting his affairs in order. To setting things right between himself and those he may have wronged. After a last hushed conversation and a handshake, he makes his peace. There is a beauty there that I marvel at whenever I see it.

It shames me to admit that I sought neither peace nor redemption. Instead, my anger and frustration grew to the point that I decided to take my own life. I stared up at the ceiling of my cabin, the pressure and pain in my chest increasing by the hour, running through the most efficient manners of suicide. For days I lay motionless in my bed, summoning the courage.

It is not easy for me to tell you this. I have always wished, if and when the time ever came, that I would be able to offer my life up to you as a shining example of the wisdom and the glories that accrue as you grow old. But I was simply ungrateful, consumed with resentment for the hand I'd been dealt. I know now that each single day is a wonder and privilege to behold, yet during those difficult months, held in the grip of that illness, the opposite thought became stronger as my body grew weaker. The lake was only a hundred yards away, no more, and in the mornings I'd walk there slowly, resting when necessary, to stand on the shore and imagine sinking into the water.

In the infirmary I slipped the first 50 cc ampoule of morphine into my pocket. As a doctor, I knew what was needed. At night, sleepless, I imagined myself floating out onto Saranac Lake under a ringed moon, wearied, heavy with that diseased lung, yet warmed by the late hour's peacefulness and the soft summer breeze shifting the water's glassy surface. These last few moments alone in a rowboat would prove to be the focus of my life, the narrow end of a funnel that had collected and directed all experience to this one last perfect moment of distillation. Somehow the night would know this and show both gratitude and a proper respect. It was there in the ringed moon, in the dirge of the loons crying for the end of me, in the moonlight on the water, in the harmony of midnight. I knew a man could never know a greater solitude than the one he sees as he peers into his soul and prepares for his death. Having seen it in other men, I now saw it in myself.

Yet as I lay on my bed on those nights, I remembered all the damage I had done to others. None of my triumphs sparkled there, only my failures and the sentence of death that was the heaviness in my lung. I imagined the warmth of the drug streaming through my veins, the euphoria that would rise up within me as I disappeared into the lake.

I needed only one last ampoule. One sunny morning I sat quietly on the front step of the infirmary, gaunt, frail and grey, yet filled with resolve. I knew this trial would soon be over. As I gathered my strength to continue on, a young woman from the main desk approached to tell me that Mrs. Bethune was calling on the telephone. She then helped me inside, my elbow in her tender grasp as if I were an eighty-year-old pensioner, to where the receiver of the telephone sat on a handsome edition of *Walden Pond*. I picked it up and heard Frances's voice. She was in tears.

"Please, Norman, promise me only this."

I waited.

"Promise you'll do nothing," she said. "It was my fault. I was foolish."

"What happened?" I said. I'd heard of her new companion, a pioneer in children's speech therapy at Johns Hopkins who was, according to a letter she'd sent some weeks before, a kind and elegant man.

She'd spent the weekend with him in Pittsburgh, she said, where he'd gone for a conference. She'd humiliated herself, following him around like a puppy until he sent her away.

I imagined their time together, the humiliation. It was a reflection of my own callousness. "Did he do anything else?" I said. "Did he touch you?" I was overwhelmed by jealousy and rage.

This is a shameful episode in my life that pains me now to recount, especially to you. I was not the man I am today, please understand that. I was seized by an insanity I'd never known before and have not known since. But this abject, perverse insanity shaped me for the better, which is why I include the episode here. Through adversity we reach the stars, I've always enjoyed that thought. Since then I've attempted to live up to it in my own way, by pursuing the work I do. Back then it directed me away from the darkness of self-destruction and allowed me to see what awaited me.

What did I do? I dragged myself across two states with a mind to wreak revenge on a man I'd never met. The man who'd taken my place at my wife's side. Through the window of my train compartment I watched the flickering lights of sleeping villages and desolate whistle-stops. The world was indifferent to my passage and the murderous hate I carried.

It was early morning when my train pulled in at Pennsylvania Station. Commuters ran for their connections; young boys waved newspapers in the air that tomorrow would feature the face of the murderer I would become. Weakened further by my journey, I was jostled and bumped as I made my way out onto Liberty Avenue and hailed a cab. Frances had named the hotel where the man I was looking for could be found. It was a respectable establishment only four blocks from the station. I took a room there, rested for the balance of the morning, then journeyed down into the street.

I purchased a pistol, left a note for the speech therapist at the front desk and waited for evening.

I held the pistol in my right hand. A surgeon's hand. I sat in wait by the window of my room, watching the street, listening for footsteps just beyond my door. My fingers felt every bit as dead as that cold steel. Was it my destiny to be the first Bethune to kill not in war but in a last, defiant act of love? Could this be so wrong? Would I not be vindicated? I knew the man hadn't touched her, but he had abused her nonetheless. He had led her to believe that he could replace me and had failed to do so. He had dashed her hopes, as I had so often done.

The pistol grew slippery with my nerves. I paced. I was sick to my stomach. The afternoon and evening wore on. I stared at the gun, barely able to believe that I was there, about to commit this crime, but also convinced that this was, in some bleak narrative, a merciful end to my story. I was no more than an embodiment of gloom: not a dime to my name, my wife gone, my health destroyed. I had seen death so often that another would make little difference either way.

When the knock came I raised my eyes from the pistol to the door, more fearful than I'd ever been. Trembling, I rose and placed the gun under the bed pillow, then walked over and opened the door. Standing before me was a short man, already undone by life, it seemed, around forty years old. He wore a grey suit and shoes of tired leather.

He tipped his hat. "Doctor Bethune?"

When he entered, I closed the door and crossed the floor to stand by the window. "Drink?" I said.

"No," he said.

I stared at him.

"You've come all this way to speak with me?" he asked. "I understand you're ill."

"It's none of your concern how far I've come."

He stood awkwardly, hat in both hands.

I picked up my glass. "I've lost my wife to you, so there probably isn't much left to say. Should I talk to you? Should I ask how things are going between you? Should I express an interest in your affair?"

"No," he said.

"We agree on at least one thing, then," I said.

He was standing in front of the closed door. I poured a glass of whiskey, then turned and walked it over to him. My hand brushed against his when he took the drink. He didn't raise the glass, just stood there watching me.

"I understand you are separating, legally separating," he said. "I would not come between a man and his wife."

"What about a dying man and his wife?" I said, reaching under the pillow. "What about that?" Then I hit him across the face with the butt-end of the pistol. "Would you come between them?"

His head jerked back again and again as I kept hitting him. A wound opened on the left side of his face. I didn't stop until he fell to the floor.

It was then that I looked into his eyes. Then I knelt beside him and wept, begging his forgiveness.

I tended to his wounds and sat with him in silence. When he was able to walk I delivered him to the hospital, then rode the train back to the Adirondacks and strode firmly, as morning broke across the hills, into my second life.

★

I hope Ho will do me the kindness of never writing a poem about me. He would find only confusion and contradiction. He might even imagine horns sprouting out of my head. I would tell him as much, if I could. But if he chose to look, to really look, what would he discover in a man like me? Ho is an observant fellow, after all, and just might, one day, take after the Chinese poet whose work he has committed to memory. His eyes hang a moment longer than they would otherwise, collecting a last glimpse, a delicate wrinkle. Isn't this the modus operandi of the poet? He is one for details unobserved by others. He notices habits, tics, hidden joys and fears. Who knows? When I am here, watching, he is so deferential as to be almost invisible. He glances at a certain cherished likeness set here, to my right, angled just so to catch the light. It has not moved in weeks, despite the fact that he often takes it up in his hand and looks for my likeness in the soft features. It is a painting. But no, the portrait isn't what it seems, I want to tell him. Despite the likeness. It is not who I would like it to be. Despite the thrill of possibility, despite this deepest wish.

Ho has learned the peculiarities of a stranger. No doubt he thinks this need for pure undeniable order is common to all foreigners, strange incomprehensible devils that we are. But he cannot always be right, perceptive though he is. He will tell his friends that I devote all my writing efforts to medical and administrative matters, offering this as another example of my commitment to this cause. He would not be far off in thinking that. I have devoted a great deal of time of late to the last of my three textbooks, as well as the ongoing struggle to keep up with the monthly medical reports I'm responsible for. The light in my window signals the sleeplessness of a devoted man. But he knows nothing of this secret text, yours and mine. Here you have the re-imagining of a life in all its crepuscular beauty. Perhaps he would, if he knew, revere the efforts of this exploration.

But despite his poet's soul these words would make as much sense to him as a Shakespearean sonnet or a Catholic mass. You see, I have been here long enough that he cannot imagine me having a past anywhere else. And can I blame him? As far as he's concerned I have stepped out from the clouds. I'm only as good as his best poem, perfectly internalized and subjective. Not entirely real, in any case, and conjured from the mists. Any life outside these mountainous walls, though richly imagined, can be no more real than the promise of Belgian chocolate or American tobacco.

I see him out in the night, a small dark figure set against the towering rock of the Jui Li San Mountain and hear him talking with the other boys as they smoke their local tobacco. The rancid plumes disappear in a laugh. Quiet talk of the war, girls, food, the things boys like to talk about—but certainly also about the man at the edge of the village hunched obsessively over his trusty Remington. The mad white doctor, they might say, the bloody terror, the saviour, the half-deaf surgeon who fell from the sky. The man who in a rage yells and throws dull scalpels at terrified nurses. What must they think of me? What sort of poem do you shape in the image of a stick of a man who moves like a machine between patients without rest for three and four days at a time? In the absence of sleep I dunk my head in buckets of freezing water. My raging is easily enough explained away. It might even be understandable. In any case, they do not judge, and bless them for that.

*

Another clear evening. I have been studying the moon from my window. Do you know the Shelley poem?

Art thou pale for weariness
Of climbing heaven and gazing on the earth
Wandering companionless
Among the stars that have a different birth.

It is my honour to share Shelley's moon with you tonight.

*

Last night Ho came to strip off the ribbon as he usually does. I lay still, too anxious and distracted to sleep. He worked silently, first rewinding, then releasing the small wheel from its housing. His hunched silhouette at my desk, a young, slight Bethune, I thought. He rose, then slipped out the door.

*

Man's absurdity survives like diamonds in this peasant land, and we are reminded of this with depressing regularity. I recall not too long ago we were lacking blood of a certain type, namely B positive. There was nothing unusual in this, since blood supply is as constantly uncertain as the air is thin up here. Countless times I have used my own veins to demonstrate the donor procedure to these peasants, but an infuriating mystery and fear still surrounds this basic operation. One afternoon, a dying man was admitted to my care. We checked all the patients' charts and found that we had a compatible donor only a few beds down. I called on him and, through an interpreter, informed him of the situation. Perhaps the expression on my face registered my disbelief and disgust when he refused. He shook his head from side to side like a child standing at the edge of a lake, afraid to take his first swimming lesson. He put his hands over his eyes.

I said, "Tell him he is a brave man."

My interpreter did so.

I said, "Tell him he kills the Fascists to save his comrades-in-arms."

My interpreter did so.

I said, "Tell him it is strange that he is willing to die for his brothers, yet refuses to give them his blood."

My interpreter did so.

I said, "Tell him this is a feather tickling your arm compared to a bullet."

My interpreter did so.

I offered to demonstrate the procedure myself. The man shook his head in terror. I held the cannula for him to see. I said, "This is not a bullet. This is a pinprick."

He pushed my hand away.

He smelled of the mountains he'd spent the last two years fighting in. Even after several days with us he carried the scent of the soil and horses and the ragged clothes he'd worn for months and of the men he'd killed and seen killed. These smells had soaked into his skin. He was fearful not of the small prick in his arm but of the modern wonder of science. It didn't involve pain or sacrifice or death, only the elementary truths of his world. I might have remembered that, but I didn't care to.

I ordered him restrained, and he whimpered as the cannula entered his arm. I both hated and pitied him. After his blood was introduced to the patient, I stood in the cool sunlight and watched the distant peaks shining in the north, at the edge of Mongolia.

Tonight the lilies in their clay pot outside this window look as though they've turned to charcoal. It is as if my staring at them all week has bled the lustre from their stems and leaves. The failed light has robbed them of their colours. Maybe I likewise have been robbed of my own certainty.

But isn't that the point? A certain man is a lazy man. Here I am, committed as never before, yet robed in doubt. If only my father had known the feeling.

I never looked at that man again. It shames me to say I passed in front of his bed half a dozen times afterwards and didn't once even glance at him.

*

Another month gone. We are with the Third Regiment Sanitary Service at Shin Pei, West Hopei. A warm glorious spring rain spilled over the countryside this afternoon. Now I see moonlight sparkling in the puddles outside my window. The moon insists that we take note, all of us, even those too timid to look up.

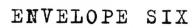
ENVELOPE SIX

I left Madrid in springtime, gathered my few things together and retreated. I told my associates my work was done, that I was needed elsewhere. They pretended to be sorry. Was there not enough work here? What could be so urgent as to force me to abandon Madrid?

The documentary was finished, I explained, and I would take it to America to raise money for the Republic. I would report stories of our progress here to the outside world. Your mother understood. I told her the night I finished her portrait.

"Go," she said. "I'll be all right."

Months later I was sitting at a table at the Bentley Park Hotel in New York struggling with that feeling of unease I was telling you about. The feeling I described to you of thinking Pitcairn was hiding something from me. Do you remember me telling you that?

It was not him hiding the truth. Months ago, when I recalled that conversation for you, I was not strong enough to relive it truthfully. Now, perhaps, I am.

"You're a slippery fish tonight," I said.

"Nerves, I suppose."

"Let's have a drink, then," I said, summoning the waitress.

I remember thinking that he was trying to rediscover the camaraderie we'd shared in Madrid not that long ago, eight or nine months. Certainly not long enough to explain his discomfort. Men generally are changed by too much living, I thought, too much adventure, too much ducking into bomb shelters. I saw it in myself. Perhaps this was why he'd come to America.

Hoping to put him at ease, I said, "Isn't it true that when you're out there, all you want is to come home? You're sitting in some dingy cellar wondering why the hell you're there, wishing it all away. Then, poof—you're suddenly home and safe in your comfortable bed and you still can't help thinking: why am I here?" I said, "People like us, Frank, with the *choice* to come or go, we're the difficult ones, aren't we."

He didn't say anything.

"War's a bloody beautiful sport," I said, "until you see what it's done to you. Sometimes I think it's a lot safer not to leave it at all."

He said, "I'm not even sure you know about it."

"What would you have me know that I don't know already?" Of course, I took this as a knock against me. I looked him in the eye, ready for a more serious challenge.

I realized then that he wanted to talk about your mother.

Was he going to tell me that she'd gone back to Sweden, or come to America in search of her father's legacy? Or was he going to tell me she was up in Chicago retracing his footsteps, that she'd simply quit the war and wasn't the person I'd thought her to be?

The drinks came, and he took a long swallow.

"Well, why the face?" I said. "You look like you're going to be sick on me."

"They took her in a second time, right after you left. I don't know if you heard that. Madrid was full of cutthroats and informers. You know how it was. Calebras was a f——ing jingoistic fraud. You know as well as I do."

"Yes."

"Kajsa was convinced he'd teamed up with Sorensen and Sise. They wanted to humiliate you. They each had their own reasons. But that didn't matter. Calebras wanted the mobile unit under his name. They wanted the glory to go to the Spanish. The others just wanted to get you out. They thought you were cracking up. Sise thought you had a death wish. He always said you were a reckless son of a bitch. Sorensen didn't like your grandstanding, your chasing after reporters all the time. He said your claim that it was all for the good of the unit was horses——t. Your fundraising, too. It was all about your vanity, he said. You were more important than the wounded, the cause, the war."

He shook his head. "I met with Kajsa once a couple of months after you left. She said it was Sorensen who'd alerted the authorities about all the foreigners coming around to the clinic. And the maps, the photographs. If he believed it, I don't know. But it worked. He got their attention. You saw how they swooped down. That was the first real strike against you."

"They drummed me out," I said. "You think I don't know that? I'm glad I had the film to fall on. Better than a sword."

"The next step was to bring her into it. She was the perfect humiliation. She worked with the Mujeres Libres, a branch of the anarchist FAI. The anarchists scared the s——t out of the Popular Front alliance. You know how it went in Madrid. If they wanted to take you out of the picture, discredit you completely, the easiest way was to set Kajsa up as an anarchist, even a spy."

"That's absurd," I said.

"I know it is."

"Where is she now?"

"After you left she told me she was worried about getting taken in again. She said you were the only person who could protect her. I told her it was dangerous even talking. I'd never seen her like that. 'Just get out,' I said. 'Get up to France.'"

He picked up his glass and swished the liquid, but didn't drink.

"Where is she now?" I said.

★

I was greeted by three men at the entrance to the clinic the morning after meeting your mother at the Retiro Park. I recognized one of them from that encounter my first morning in Madrid the previous November, when I was detained on account of my suit and moustache. I couldn't tell if he recognized me. It was just luck, and bad luck at that, for our paths to cross again. He and his two colleagues were accompanied by four armed guards, two down below in the street, the other two standing beside the lift on the third floor. My assistant, who hurried to the door when I appeared, was told firmly to return to her business. We by then had a staff of no less than twenty-five, and in full view I was led into my office. The door was closed behind us. The leader, whom I'd never seen before, motioned to a man carrying a briefcase to flip it open, and he produced the bottle of perfume and the card I'd given Kajsa the day before. In English he said, "Please sit down." He paused, as if considering something from a number of different angles. "Yes, you see, this is interesting. Here I see you have written some words about love. You are a man of many talents, Doctor." He held up the card. "These are your words?"

"What is this?" I asked.

"What is this? You will tell me now." His English was clear but heavily accented. "I can ask the same. What am I looking at?"

"Perfume," I said. "A gift. A token."

"And this?" he said, holding up a series of photographs.

"Where did you get them?"

"Of course you know where," he said.

"Pictures. Bridges and roads."

"And tank columns. A doctor interested in tanks?"

"That photograph is incidental."

"And to whom do you pass these photographs? Only the Swede?"

"They are for our purposes. They are for study. To minimize travel time."

"Whose travel time?"

"The travel time of this unit."

"We know this work you do, Doctor. The Spanish people thank you. Yes. But it is something else to distribute these photographs, considering this company the Doctor keeps." He lifted his eyebrows. "What can we think of this situation?"

He pointed at the perfume and card, which he'd set on the desk. "It's a wonderful thing to be loved. To have a woman. But we do things for women, too often stupid things. We cheat for them, we lie for them, we commit criminal, illegal acts for them. We betray our friends for them. For what? Only to be with the Swede? Two times more. Ten times more." He repeated this in Spanish for the benefit of his colleagues, and I recognized a vulgar word. "When you have so many nice Spanish girls to go with, you go with the Swede, and then you talk to her about bridges and tanks?"

★

The village is quiet. Nighttime in Shin Pei.

They are shooting dogs up in the high villages and eating them with what little rice and millet the peasants left behind, spilled from pockets and hastily packed bags. At least the enemy is starving too, that is our one consolation. When it is known they are near, the last of the peasants move off into the night toward the next village, some fifteen or twenty miles away. Then, when that village falls a day later, those who looked upon the fleeing souls with pity now scoop up what can be carried and join the exodus, and so grows the wave of refugees washing down from the mountain villages of north China. Soon Wu-t'ai and all of Shensi and Hopei provinces will be empty but for the partisans and remaining dogs and the invading Japanese. The lucky peasants will find the Peiping–Hankou rail line, eighty miles to the east, and travel down along it to wait out the war in the south, in Sian and Louyang.

To the west and east it is no different. It is rumoured that the southern corridor that connects us to the rest of China will close by late summer. The war is all around us. It is a noose. But here, in the quiet of this mud-brick house, I am in an untouched oasis. When I'm not leaning over a casualty in one of our makeshift surgical huts, I can close my eyes and wonder what the air would taste like if unspoiled by the smell of suppurative wounds and camphor and cordite. What would this world be like if I were with you back in Spain or Montreal, or wherever they took you?

★

First, imagine a mountain stream at midnight, carrying with it one living man and one dead. The living man is your father; the other, his guide. I hear the stream that we rode down the mountain on only four days ago. Its splashing still echoes in my head. I hear it through the night, in the still air. How impossible the war seems on nights like these. It is as quiet as a conversation with the dead.

We'd been waiting for our guide at an assigned meeting point for less than an hour when he stepped out of the dark like some ragged phantom, a thin wisp of a boy, very near starving. He didn't look relieved to see us, only troubled. We welcomed him and gave him tea and rice. The medical unit consisted of Ho, Mr. Tung, two student surgeons and two armed escorts. We watched the boy eat and drink and waited for the night to deepen. Clouds crossed over a bright moon. It was prudent to travel in this part of the country only after dark. The boy was troubled because he knew well enough that it was much more difficult to lead a troop of seven up into the mountains than it was to come down alone from there. He finished his meal, and when he sat back, one of the student surgeons offered him some tobacco and he rolled a cigarette in his thin fingers and smoked it until the ember died. We waited another twenty minutes until the darkness was almost complete. The boy spoke to Mr. Tung, who then asked me if I was ready, and we set out in single file, the guide and an armed escort first, then me, then Ho and Mr. Tung, then the two student surgeons, each member of my team leading an animal, and finally the second escort. Up we started into the Wu-t'ai Mountains.

We walked at a steady pace for two hours without stopping to rest, pausing only when the boy slipped into the darkness ahead to make certain that the area was clear for us. Ten minutes later he would reappear and indicate the way and off again we would walk, a silent column of men and beasts moving into the deepening darkness of the mountains. The night was warm. There was very little breeze and the air was comfortable and smelled of sage and wild mint. The boy held us up with only a single word to

Tung, who would look at me, and the rest of the column would halt as the boy slipped out again and left us waiting there. This occurred seven times. On the eighth, the boy did not return. It was past midnight.

"Mr. Tung?" I whispered.

"I don't know," he said.

"Ten more minutes. Then you will lead the others back to where we started. I'll wait here for the boy."

After half an hour I told Tung to go, instructing him to remain at the camp below until daylight and then return to Chin-kang K'u.

"And you?" he said.

"I will find you in the morning."

I watched their faces as Tung translated my orders. Ho would not show his face to me, as he expected I'd think less of him if I saw terror or tears or both in his eyes. I handed him the reins to my animal and he walked the horse back down the trail.

After they left I sat quietly in the dark and watched the moon move through the high clouds. When they parted there was light enough to see by. The guide would know where to find me if he was still alive and he hadn't abandoned us. It was now past two o'clock. I believed I was the last man fighting this war. The last man in China. So immense was the quiet and solitude that I might as well have been the last man on earth. The enormity of the sky felt larger than the vastness of all oceans and all memory. The stars were infinite, and below them the silence was suddenly broken by a sound that might have been the boy returning from his reconnaissance. I didn't move, just sat looking up into the infinite sky and listened and waited for a sign. I waited ten minutes. My heart raced. The sound did not come again. I waited another half hour and the boy did not appear.

I dozed off and it was nearly morning when I awoke. I stood up and moved about. It felt good to stretch my legs. With my pack I moved slowly outward in the direction the boy had gone. I heard another sound. This time it was closer, and it wasn't the sound of a footfall or a dull thud but the human sound of a sob or groan. I moved toward it, despite telling myself this was a baited trap, remembering the night I'd carried Robert Pearce on my back. But as I moved forward now the sound came again with more clarity, and I stopped in order to place it. I walked another fifty yards into the darkness, low to the ground, and there I found it. I practically stepped on it.

This boy was no older than our guide. His Japanese uniform was in rags. He was sitting up against a rock, his right hand pressed against his neck, eyes bulging with pain and dehydration. The stab wound was just above the collarbone. Blood dripped onto his chest and pooled in his lap. He watched me approach without making a sound. He was unarmed. Then I saw the body of our guide, lying not far from the soldier. The bayonet had pierced his chest, and it seemed incredible that he'd been able to turn and slash the man who'd stabbed him before he died. The rifle and bayonet lay on the ground beside him. I positioned the boy face up, crossed his hands over his chest and rolled his eyes shut, then returned to the Japanese and examined the wound. He did not resist as I pulled open his shirt.

"You will die very soon," I said, "like the boy you killed. I know you don't understand me." I pointed to the boy lying beside the rifle and bayonet. "Like him."

It seemed his slight nod was meant to offer acknowledgment or agreement or resignation. He didn't say a word.

I sat beside him while he died. It took only a few minutes. He whispered softly, and I touched his face and said, "There you go."

I hoisted our guide over my shoulder and started down the hill. It was easy going at first. He was so slight that I barely noticed him. Returning to the stream where we'd begun our expedition the evening before, I walked over the hard, uneven ground, and soon began to feel his weight in my knees, then as a pain in my shoulders. I laid the boy on the ground and sat down for a minute, breathing heavily. I didn't know how much farther I had to go before I would find Tung and the others in my party. I was wondering about the odds of my survival, alone and unarmed, with very little food and water, when again I thought of that nighttime journey through the mud-fields of Belgium a full lifetime ago. Was it my turn to die now? Why had I survived these extra twenty years when others had been in the ground all this time? Why, in my third war, was I still alive?

I pulled the boy back up onto my opposite shoulder and started walking again, as fast as I could, no longer certain that I wasn't moving deeper into the occupied north. The dead boy's head was bumping against my midsection, legs kicking against my back. The rhythmical bouncing of his knees and feet began to play on me and I started hearing his voice echoing up through my body. He didn't like being held upside-down for such a long period of time, he said. I should stop so we both could rest. I did not listen to him. I kept on, and he kept asking to be put down. I said my first words to the boy. "Shut up," I said. "You're no longer living and have no right to speak. Just stay as you are, and I'll get you back so they can do what must be done. But just stop talking so much, someone's going to hear us."

He fell silent for a time. I tried to walk with less of a bounce to keep him quiet. But the path grew difficult and again his feet pounded into me and his voice rang into my gut and up into my inner ear.

"No," I said, "I believe I have every right to be here. No, I shouldn't have died twenty years ago. No, it's not just that others died and I lived. Of course not. There's no plan out there. There is no fairness. You step into a roomful of Spanish flu and come out with not so much as a cough. Some people get out without a scratch. It's not about being deserving or skillful or even lucky because luck implies something too. It's only about random chance. It's a roulette wheel, this world."

He didn't answer, and I just kept walking. I came to what I believed was the stream where we'd met this boy the night before. I didn't know if he was still talking. I'd stopped listening. I stood on the bank, wondering if my remaining strength would allow me to ford the stream. I stepped in and began the crossing. The stream was rocky and swift but not deep. In the middle I stopped, exhausted, and sat down in the water. I leaned back on the boy to end his talking for good. His mouth filled with water, and then I fell asleep, my face turned up to the sky.

In the morning I dug his grave beside the stream with the five members of his band who'd discovered me bobbing in the shallow water, still hoisted up on his body. They shook my hand to thank me for returning their comrade to them. They knew of me, the White One Who Comes. It was their camp we'd been destined for, fifteen miles west of where they found me. I examined each of the men after we put the boy in the ground. They suffered from malnutrition, two of them from abscesses in the teeth, one from an improperly dressed flesh wound on the hand. I administered what care I could with the few supplies I carried. Then we sat and fed ourselves, not far from the fresh grave. I kept looking over at it, wondering if he was listening to his friends' conversation. In the daylight it all seemed ludicrous, and I dismissed the night as an eventful hallucination. I had been close to an exhausted collapse for two weeks. The partisans took me to Chin-kang K'u, eight miles downstream, transferred me to the care of a medical team I'd recently inspected there and bade me farewell.

I have not thought of that boy's words until now, tonight. The dead do not have words. I know that. Only the dying have words, and those who are still to come.

★

No sleep again tonight. It is past two in the morning. Today I operated for seventeen hours. How strange it is that the mind controls the body so, even when the body can barely hold itself upright. But I am thinking, of course, always thinking.

I can see your mother now as she would have awoken on the morning of my interrogation. The thugs were coming.

She sat up when the door was thrown open. The men occupied the room with a borrowed authority. The questions began immediately, from a bespectacled, leather-coated man who bobbed on his toes as he waited for the preferred response. He leaned into her face, smiling and threatening as he looked into the eyes of a woman who, before the war, he would have approached—if he'd dared to at all—like a timorous boy. Who would have caused him more fear than outrage. The war is a lucky place for some, as he might have known, a field of opportunity. What delightful turns of fortune we find in these times. A woman alone in her room.

His associate, a shorter, uglier man, sifted through her possessions. Her clothing, books and toiletries came alive most pleasurably in his hands. When he picked up Kajsa's hairbrush from beside a half-full glass of water, he noticed on the pale pine desk by the bathroom door a book that held the envelope containing the photographs.

★

I have been thinking much about how value is ascribed to one's life after the act of living is done. Not deeds or accomplishments. What I mean is that a part of me will live on in you even though I will not have had the privilege and responsibility of being part of your life, at least not fully. Even if I live to meet you there will always be this gulf, which is why I need to write this history for you. That is a failure of the first order. You see, there are so many things I will miss telling you, as a father would, through the years as you grow into adulthood. The small and inconsequential things and moments that make up the great quilt of your existence. What would we have learned from each other had we shared but one walk through an August rainstorm? What infinitesimal yet lasting truth would you have taken with you and remembered over my grave had we tossed a baseball back and forth on a Sunday afternoon? Well, what do you have now? You have none of that. Only the dry touch of these pages.

★

I found out about your mother at the hotel bar in New York. I've been trying to think of a better way of telling you about this, but have not been able to, and I'm sorry that I have to tell you now. I think I've been trying to protect you. Though you have every right to know the circumstances, it seems I have only been picking away at subtleties, stalling, hoping to wake up and find all of this nothing more than a terrible dream. It is proper and respectful, then, at this point, to be as forthright as possible. All my life revolves in a mysterious circle. At the beginning and the end and in the centre is the story that begins now.

I recall distinctly how my arms and fingers began to tingle and the room shifted slightly forward when I learned of your mother's death. As a boy I used to love walking through grass tall enough to reach over my head. It was the sensation of being hidden from the world, yet so thoroughly immersed in it. No one for miles around could see me, even from a high point on a hill or rooftop, so connected was I to the earth and its elements. That's something like the sensation of losing someone. You are never in your life so alive, and so aware of being alive, yet so isolated and abandoned, as when a loved one is taken from you. The planet will move right through you like wind through stalks of grass.

*

There are so many unexplored shadows.

In New York, Pitcairn leaned into the table and said, "Get in touch with the FAI, with the Mujeres Libres, Norman. The war won't go on forever. Wait till the war is over, then go back there. Go to the orphanage where Kajsa got work for those street girls." He paused. "They waited."

I said, "For what?"

"They waited until your daughter was born."

*

Today I remembered Genesis. I stood in the footprints of Abraham and understood the brutality of the world. It is man's first and last state. "And he looked toward Sodom and Gomorrah, and toward all the land of the plain, and beheld, and lo, the smoke of the country went up as the smoke of a furnace." Say what you will, they knew what they were talking about. I marvel sometimes at how spot-on the Good Book really is. The only instinct that rivals our urge to scour this planet with its own blood is this urge to weep.

★

We, too, are eating dog now. I suppose enemies in all the wars of all the ages have shared one another's basic miseries. It tastes the same in my mouth as it does in theirs. Certainly more binds us together than separates us, isn't that the point? Isn't it a fact that it's only the strength of ideas that wrenches us worlds apart? Yet how strange it is that we're willing to kill for ideas. In peacetime an idea can be bought and sold with money, argument, dismissal. It can be ignored outright and no one bats an eye. Not in war. How undervalued life becomes out here, and how precious the idea.

Ho has just now presented himself and sits on the upturned trunk, waiting. I have pulled out a couple of new drawings. He seems impressed.

You know, I think he's beginning to learn something from these drawings. This pleases me.

I am pleased, too, when the peasant farmer turned training nurse learns quickly and asks intelligent questions. Such are my accomplishments now. I am pleased when Ho sits with me, watching me write or flipping through these drawings of mine. I am pleased when only one arm and not two must be amputated, when there are only three deaths and not sixteen. Beyond my most basic needs, I enjoy little physical comfort. I don't mind this so much, though I am lonely. It seems I have been in training for this life for a long time.

★

It strikes me with brutal force that I don't know myself nearly as well as a man my age should, especially considering how close I am to death on any given day. I'm forty-nine years old. Isn't that old enough? How long is a man supposed to wait before he knows for certain that no ray of light will shine from above, that no eternal rest or emptiness will come, that his life was well spent or wasted?

I can say with confidence that my life here is spent well. At least I know that. But on balance? What about everything that preceded my work here? Can one good year make up for so much lost time? I am happy. Is that good enough? I am happy and lonely and not convinced either that I will return to you or that I will not.

Will I have the strength to see that you receive this story?

My physical presence has been diminished somewhat. If you'd known the before and after versions of your father you would be quite shocked, I am sure. I'm very near skeletal and half-deaf and always chilled. These clothes I have brought from home, I noticed just this morning, are now baggy beyond recognition. My teeth ache, my energy's low and I've been battling a deep, persistent cough. Yet on occasion I feel a sense of destiny waiting for me here, though I cannot account for it. If I have time in the mornings I go walking. I enjoy watching the sun come up, and when its orange and yellow light touches the mountains I feel as blessed with purpose as this planet is with beauty. Make some good use of your life, I was told. Well, here I am. In these moments I'm confident that this is what I was born to do, to stand here at the edge of existence in the light of a new day and heal with these hands those who can be healed and commit to the unknown those who cannot. It is as if it's no longer up to me. My mother, in the end, was probably right. These talents of mine are only on loan.

I think you know Spain was my great disappointment, the death of my idealism and of part of me. But I can assure you there will be no second failure. I have learned my lesson. There are rumours that things again are teetering on the edge in Europe. Will there soon be a time when only the dead enjoy their peace, when one war will follow another, with another after that, and so on, with no end in sight? War might be for your generation as it was for mine, but I certainly hope that is not the case.

Please do not misunderstand. Does it sound as if I've given up? I have not. Remember what I said: We do not go down without a fight, we Bethunes. What I see here gives me reason to hope. I am not planning on dying a martyr's death in China or anywhere else. I'm deeply committed to this struggle, nothing more. I would give my life for it, and might end up doing just that, but I will take no joy in it. I am, I think, too in love with all this Creation out here.

Despite the lice and hunger and the ignorance and poverty and withering solitude, I confess to a devotion stronger than anything I've ever known. I even feel privileged for it. I hope you understand what I'm trying to say. Perhaps you think less of me for this life I have taken on. Surely you will feel some resentment. But you can see the good in it, too, can't you? There isn't a bone of common sense left unbroken in my body; you'd be right on the money about that, if it's crossed your mind. But do you remember what I said to your mother that day, that common sense and ideals don't often go hand in hand? Well, I think that just about sums up my life.

*

This morning Ho came to me with my favourite breakfast. He has finally perfected the boiled egg! The poor boy, how I ride him. How he wants to please me! And the abuse I dole out in return! I made such a fuss when I saw that egg. I suppose I was trying to make it up to him. He was very proud. After a hundred attempts here it was. For six months he has, when in possession of an egg, slaughtered it, so to speak, with his overzealous ways. Perhaps he

is a poet, after all. Hapless in the domestic arena, prone to episodes of daydream, lost in those hot-water bubbles.

We commemorated the occasion with a photograph. Before
the doorway of my mud-brick house we set up a small knee-high
table and my straw-backed chair. I sat and leaned into my egg like
a king over his banquet. Ho stood to my left, holding a magazine
that had been sitting on the chair I now occupied. Why he picked
up a year-old English-language magazine I cannot say. Perhaps
this was some small bridge into my life. Perhaps there was more
relief on his face than pride.

"This is a memento," I said. "There, translate. Please tell
him this is a perfect egg." The man with the camera, Mr. Tung,
addressed the boy holding the magazine.

I said, "Tell him I'm leaving. Tell him I'm leaving but that I'll
be back. I'll be back in six months."

"Will he go with you?" he said.

"He will not," I said. "He stays. Let him go back to his village
if he likes."

*

September. I have taken some time off from writing. You will
forgive me, I hope. Over the last month we have toured the aid
stations in the surrounding villages and instructed the local
staff. We travelled by horse and mule, and there was a fair bit of
walking, too. My old Japanese animal came in handy, though his
torn and battered hooves have seen better days. The poor beast
isn't quite cut out for this terrain of mountain trail and rock
slides, and I almost think a lowly burro might be better suited
for my purposes.

Yes, of late I have been occupied, mind, spirit and body. There
is no rest to be had here. Along with my travels I have also just

completed the final draft of a book that will not, alas, provoke literary controversy. It's called *Organization and Technique for Division Field Hospitals in Guerrilla Warfare,* and the good Mr. Tung is now working on the translation full bore. When he's finished it will be printed and widely distributed in under a month by the Regional Government. So you see, busy in body and mind. There simply hasn't been time. My writing, my surgeries, my teaching at the hospital that was once, not so long ago, the Buddhist temple of this polite and desecrated village, threatened to consume me entirely. (We have displaced a large number of hapless monks, by the way—obsequious, soft and annoying men who are certainly not lacking in time, a remarkably aimless lot.)

But now there is at least a break in my routine, and I can return to these pages. Here I sit in this small grey mud-and-brick town of Shin Pei, so similar to the other villages I've occupied over these last twelve or fourteen months, again back at this account of life, war and memory. Patience, please. But the war, the deprivation, the heat, these are factors that send my imagination in all directions. I would be a different man strolling along the Champs-Elysées, with bowler hat and cane. Or bathing at Sunnyside Beach in Toronto. Or boating on that small lake in the Retiro Park. Perhaps one day you will jump into the great Lake Ontario from your father's shoulders. You, a pink little thing, shrieking with all the world's delight. How my heart explodes at the thought! The month is September, somewhere around the sixteenth or seventeenth, I think. With the completion of that witless textbook, basic illustrations included, a space now opens before me at this typewriter, a space I may now fill with thoughts of you, and all I can think about is going home, of meeting you, holding your wiggling body up to the sun.

What is happening back there? I am desperate for news. All I see are San Francisco papers and magazines, a year or two old, used by merchants as wrapping for sugar, tea and cakes. And not even political pages but reviews of Frances Farmer and Cary Grant in *The Toast of New York* and the new Terraplane Coupe automobile. Perhaps one day we shall have such an automobile, you and I, and I shall spirit you about grandly, blowing the horn to the wind.

★

Tonight the world is consumed by these ravenous mountains. So many are waiting to die. The Japanese noose tightens. Colours drain from the courtyard, from these flowers in their clay pots. The night in her mercy erases all evidence of men. Only voices carry through the dark, but now, hushed, they seem more animal than human. Staring at this page, lost in thought, it's as if I'm looking through my one last window to the world.

★

Last night, Mr. Tung appeared at my door and said, "If you release the boy from your service he will die."

I stood. "Why do you think that?"

"If he returns to his village, he will die there. Do you know what a House of Consolation is?"

"No," I said. "Not precisely."

"One of these places was set up in his town after the Japanese came. The rest of his family was captured, his mother and two sisters. He lived in the hills outside his town for months, waiting for the Japanese to leave, but sneaked back in at night. He knew it well. It was not so difficult. The Japanese soldiers were easy to fool. He knew enough not to venture out under a moonlit sky. By then the enemy believed they owned the town and had grown complacent. Often the boy went to his house. His father was dead, taken away by the Nationalists years before. He never saw any sign that his mother and sisters had been there looking for him, as he was looking for them, but he left notes in case they came, saying that he was safe and not to worry.

"One night he slipped past a store where an old man had sold goods from faraway cities like Shanghai and Sian. Teas and herbs and medicines. But the storefront had been altered. It had been taken over by the Japanese, like everything else in the village. He did not know its purpose. The sign, in Chinese, said: HALL FOR JAPAN–CHINA FRIENDSHIP. He told me he looked in the window. It was very late at night, almost morning, in fact. But if the hall required guards, none were stationed here. He imagined it could not be such an important place. And why would a Friendship Hall require guards? He climbed through a window.

"At first he heard nothing. Then the sound of weeping drew him through two rooms to a large warehouse without windows where the old man was said to have stored a car, but the boy had never seen it. It was very dark in the warehouse and he waited for his eyes to adjust. Before long he could see many women tied to their beds, simple boards covered in straw. The women stretched out on them were of different ages, but mostly young, some younger than the boy. There were twenty-two women in all. The boy's mother and two sisters occupied the last three beds to the right. He ran to them and kneeled at his mother's bedside. 'I am here, I can take you away,' he said, 'all of you.' His mother kissed him and began to weep. She told her son to leave. 'They will come soon, at first light,' she said. 'Any minute now. Go quickly.' The men would come with red ticket stubs, she told her son, checked for each visit, allowing them to enter here and choose any one of them. 'Go, please. You cannot see this.'"

Mr. Tung paused.

"He tried to free her. He struggled with the ropes lashing her wrists, but it was no use. He was too frightened and so young. He was fifteen years old. His younger sister began to cry. His mother shushed her. The other women were quiet. They were straining their heads, watching to see what the boy would do. His mother said, 'Listen to me. Go now. Go as far away from this war as you can. Do not return for us. They will capture you. They will think nothing of killing you. Go away from this place.'

"He heard the first men enter the front room of the old man's store. Everyone's head turned. Their loud boots stomped against the wooden floor. Their two voices were businesslike and unrushed. These were the military keepers of the Friendship Hall preparing for a new day. Soon after the morning meal the soldiers bearing their red tickets would stroll over and strip down to their loincloths and wait patiently for the administrators to take their tickets, check the small box that indicated another visit had been made and then admit them through the last door into the ware-house of women.

"The boy begged his mother to let him help her and his sisters, but she said, 'You cannot help us. We are already dead.'

"The sound of soldiers walking and talking began to fill the streets. The occupied town was awake now. The loud voices of the men approached. As the door to the warehouse opened, the boy slipped under his mother's bed and the men began their selection. He remained frozen under his mother's bed until night fell."

We sat quietly for some time. Afterward, I let Mr. Tung out the door, then lay down on my cot and stared out into the night.

I will come to you. You shall see.

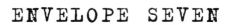
ENVELOPE SEVEN

I have just now been studying my hands, which scarcely resemble the ones I started this journey with. They are more skilled, yes, and as steady as they have always been. Determined, yes. But even if they've aged into the claws of a monster, how could they send this boy back to certain death?

I am exhausted. Sick. My teeth rotten. My eyesight blurred and uncertain. I'm skin and bone, my ribs showing through as clearly as if in an anatomical drawing. If the left ear isn't ringing with the sound of distant artillery, it is completely silent.

I have been thinking about the boy.

Why am I going back? To find out what is happening. To investigate the dithering and procrastinating ways of spineless bureaucrats in New York and Toronto. To rip off some heads, if I must. I was promised funding that is nowhere to be seen. I have received no word from the China Aid Council or the American

League for Peace and Democracy. Resolutely, I am off to whip up some trouble and give them a piece of my mind. Despite my bony chest I am ready for a fight. In response to my repeated requests for updates on the absent funding I have received not a word, not a postcard, not a kiss blown to the wind. So I mean to go and find out myself. I shall cross to the other side of Shensi and go down on foot to Yan'an, some five hundred miles. I estimate it will take six weeks; then I'll go on to Chungking and Yunan by way of French Indochina, jump a boat for Hong Kong and buy my way onto a freighter laden with tea and rice bound for Hawaii, the land of my father's timid embrace. Two weeks later, sometime in late February 1940, I will make landfall in San Francisco. A triumphant return. A walk along the beach, perhaps, a bottle and a pretty girl. All innocent, nothing untoward. That is the least they can afford me, an hour or two to gaze back over the bay at sunset. Perhaps I'll become drunk on champagne and sleep till noon in clean sheets up to my chin, smothered by a harem of pillows, and enjoy a three o'clock luncheon at the bar in the near presence of beautiful women and their enterprising young men.

I have already made preparations. I am leaving within two to three weeks. Of course, it will be difficult to abandon this place. And to abandon him, my faithful servant. I am his best hope for surviving this war. I know it and he knows it. But his vulnerability cannot dictate the arc of history. Without me they will likely put a rifle in his hands. The partisans will take him; he'll go of his own accord. A hundred-pound soldier off to protect the Motherland. Last month we celebrated his eighteenth birthday. He is a man now. You wouldn't know it to look at him, but his voice cracked long ago and is oddly deep, even in this nasal language—and so much more incongruous issued from that weak chest. He puffed himself up and recited a poem composed for the occasion. I clapped when everyone else did, then Mr. Tung whispered into my ear, "It tells of the Great Bethune's struggle."

Clever boy, I thought. But which struggle? What would he think of the Great Bethune if he knew of my excitement about returning to America, and without him? Am I allowed such thoughts? Since making my decision I am rejuvenated, helium-inflated, drunk with joy. But is this joy purely for the good work I shall do there? My aim is to raise for this war effort $1,000 per month in gold, and yet the promise of clean sheets, hot roast beef and French wine crowd my heart. What do you think of that, poor Ho? Have I deceived you? What he does not know of me! Yes, a starved man must replenish himself. But there is more. Of course there is. More than anything else, what awaits is you. And it is to you I shall pass this irregular, green-typed stack of petroleum- and lavender-scented archaeology, so that you will have the truth in your hands, come what may. This is my great optimism. This is the calm silence that now greets these eager peasants as I attempt to impart to them the basic laws and practice of sanitation, physiology and biology. This is the joy that fills me as I walk silently to my brick-and-mud shack after sixteen hours of surgery, rest my aching elbows on this desk and roll another sheet into the machine—the first clack, the ringing imprint upon the refreshed ribbon, like a small stinging bullet. Is life so good that I am to be provided a second chance? Will I find you? Will you love me as a child loves her father? Can I love you, an unknown existence so close to my own? Does a family await, after all? I must finish this story before I can know.

★

But now, you ask, am I too happy dreaming of a homecoming and champagne to remember the festering wounds and lice and horror of this place? Am I too enamoured of thunderous, admiring applause to step back into the lion's jaws? No. With my joy comes renewed energies. I step back into it. You see, you power my heart. You enliven me. By now, what is it I have left to prove?

We returned to the front, at Hua Ta, on the banks of the T'ang River, and there set up shop, our workhouse of small miracles, in an old farmhouse that had been cleared out and prepared for our arrival on the orders of an intellectual-looking regimental commander by the name of Jao. He was a small man who wore a pair of round black-rimmed glasses on his small nose and walked with an untidy rolling limp in his left leg, making it seem as if he'd been caught in an invisible surge of water that pulled forever to the left. When I received word of an impending attack I decided that this would be the last of my daredevil overland crossings before setting out for the other side of Shensi and Yunan and my glorious homecoming.

When our team arrived, poor Ho by then dragging his feet, I conducted an inspection of the building and surrounding facilities, then presented myself to the hobbled commander to pass along a list of our requirements. He read through the list, the good man, and handed it to his assistant with instructions that I be provided with all we needed. He then informed me to expect casualties within six hours. I returned to the farmhouse–aid station to oversee the preparations and quickly ate a bowl of rice provided by Ho, along with a pot of tea. On the stone wall of the house, sitting over my emptied plate, I studied the formal portrait of the family that had once lived here, or so I supposed. They were a hungry-looking lot, a mother and father and three small children smiling with rehearsed conviction and dressed in their Sunday village best. I wondered what foods they could have put in their mouths for the price of that professional photograph and those crisply pleated fabrics. They were, unfortunately, nowhere to be seen in the village. Like so many others they had been pushed from their home and now, very likely, were more skeletal than ever.

When the wounded began to arrive I believed the flow might never stop. It was a large assault consisting of three regiments. For three days we did not rest, the wounded coming in a steady torrent. We ate standing as the next casualty was laid before us. The sharp autumn air, this high up, tingled on my fingertips. My nose, ever active, always alert to the morbid fecal smells of a nicked bowel, rejoiced in the mountain breeze that lifted the curtain of that refugee family's home. We worked. We ate. We slept in ten-minute intervals. As time moved forward it began, too, to move backward. I stumbled. I began to dream. In these waking dreams I imagined this family. When I saw a small girl's head encased in the stone wall, unconscious though smiling, a syringe held like a rose in her teeth, I put my own head in a bucket of ice water.

On the second day, treating a badly broken leg, I was using a chisel that had been taken from a farmhouse near Chi Huei two or three months back. Imagine the creator of, among other instruments, the Bethune Rib Shears humbling himself with a lowly carpenter's chisel. But I—always adapting, innovating—had discovered certain properties in its construction that proved beneficial for my work. It was nicely weighted and its hardwood handle could withstand long and frequent bouts of boiling, for disinfecting. Primarily, though, it was the tempered steel, forged in Belgium, that made it so useful in cutting through and shaving off bone. How this tool had travelled so far I couldn't say, but I am glad it did. When I get out of this war you will not find it in my black bag of doctor's instruments, yet it has proved highly useful over the months. On that particular day, however, this chisel that had sat so comfortably in my hand for so long jumped off the splintered femur of the unconscious man beneath me and dug into the middle finger of my left hand.

One of the nurses quickly disinfected and wrapped the cut. Hindered, but not grievously so, I tidied up the amputation, put my head in a refreshed bucket of cold water and then, an hour later, had a second nurse re-dress the wound. As she did so I sent Ho for a candle and had him melt it down. He presented the melted wax to me in a rice bowl which, oddly enough, bore a small illustration of a flamingo, and I bathed the wrapped finger in the wax so as to seal it against infection. Another inspiration, really. Luxury of luxuries. This was as close as I'd come to wearing rubber gloves in longer than I could remember. Bandaged like a lollipop, the waxed finger was awkward and heavy, and for the rest of the day I might as well have worked with only the right hand. The following day, after three hours' rest, when I examined my wound, the cut looked fine. But halfway through the morning I decided I couldn't continue like this. I peeled the wax off the finger and got back to work.

★

This morning I awoke from a dream. It was of the morning the *Empress* set sail. From the height of the promenade deck, Jean and Charles had been enjoying the view of the dockyards and the city beyond, leaning over the rails, I suppose pretending they had their own send-off party down there, smiling and waving. I attempted to push myself forward into the excitement of the moment but I felt a weight on my chest. After a minute or two I excused myself and went below decks to find my cabin. But when I inserted my key and pushed the door open, the room was occupied.

Your mother, in the form of the painting I'd made of her at the Santander, was sitting on the bed. In it her shoulders were covered by a blanket, and she smiled.

I touched my hand to the painting. When I did, her face began to disappear, the paint coming off like dust under my hand until only the canvas remained.

★

When I awoke in the pre-dawn morning of the fourth day, only two days ago, Ho looked at me with concern. My body was trembling from lack of sleep. He himself looked unwell in the struggling light of the small stove-fire he'd set in the far corner of that one-room house to warm my tea. Then Mr. Tung stepped inside.

"What news have you heard?" I asked. Ho handed me my tea. I sat sipping, both hands shaking.

"Only that they're near," Mr. Tung said.

"How near?" The tea spilled. "Another cup, Ho."

"They will be here soon," Mr. Tung said. "Before midday. We are falling back."

The limp-footed regimental commander summoned me to his quarters and said the line had collapsed. He praised our work, thanking me personally, and then ordered our return to the Base Hospital at Yang Chia Chuang. He saluted, turned and parted, that leftward tide pulling at his body more strongly than ever. Straight-backed, I returned along the dirt path to the farmhouse–aid station. As the rose-coloured sunlight began to warm the western face of the distant Mo-t'ien Mountains, I felt an unusual buoyancy take hold. I felt almost euphoric. Then, entering the building I again saw, and for the last time, the strange face of that dead child framed by the perfect construction of fallen stone that contained her. I stopped to study her. She made a lovely picture. But now she was dead. What Capa might have done with her! I thought. What lasting images he could have produced, those hardened veins reanimated with silver nitrate and mercury, bathed in his alchemist's bath and introduced to the world as another anthemic tribute to the horror of war. Yes, he was a famous man. Relentless. Driven by the beauty of conviction. "You," I said. "Yes, you."

The dead girl opened her eyes. "Me?" she said.

Visions of children bricked into standing walls notwithstanding, I am well. Do you doubt my sanity? These spells shall pass. It is overwork, my dear. Physical exhaustion, nothing more. So what do I do in the meantime, as I wait out these small hallucinations? They are no more than a dizzy inconvenience. What do I do? I wonder about you. I wonder what might have been. I wonder what you will make of this history. Will you permit me the idea, the fantasy, that one day, as an older woman perhaps, you will turn these pages with forgiving sighs? The very name, the Border Regions, for all its portent, for all its distant mystery, connotes ambiguity, possibility, breadth. Will I benefit in this undeclared realm? Where certainty fades can there be rejuvenation? Does forgiveness live here in this unknowable terrain? Yet this wide landscape is really only the one small chair that holds me, this one small house. This could be anywhere. Can you see the bejewelled monster that crawls into my dreams as I sleep? Do you share the same monsters? Mornings aboard the *Empress,* those distant brief mornings with small Alicia, that lovely child, and the poems her aunt read to us while I painted return to me often:

> Among twenty snowy mountains,
> The only moving thing
> Was the eye of the blackbird.

I wonder now if there could be a more desolate poem, or a quieter life, than that of a poet who brings silence down so absolutely upon an entire mountain range with fourteen simple words. Perhaps this is why I find it comforting, this illusion of company that writing to you now affords me. These words, though hacked and banged out on this old machine, though so crude compared to those of an artist, bring you here to these Border Regions, where I no longer own my past but instead offer it to you. You see, these words mark you as present. With them I can place, see and touch you. You are whole. And in some ways, as I write this I, too, am whole. I find wonder and warmth, and if this world I now occupy lacks anything it is those two dreams of wonder and warmth. You are my last opportunity; you are the moving eye of the blackbird.

Will I place this package in your young hand and say, "Wait till you are older"?

The question is this: When will you be old enough to understand me, yet still young enough to forgive?

*

The war exists. It is a raven hanging in the clouds over Tu Ping Ti and over the whole of this magnificent land. It picks at holes in the stomach and strips of unclaimed flesh. Tired, I ask myself what difference one man can make. On a beautiful autumn night. I wonder how I ever got it into my head that I might hold down every man who refuses to offer his blood. Can I teach the world how things should be done? Can I change the ways of these people, so backward and noble? Yet those questions pose another: Could I bear to be away from this place? The answer is no. Of course not. But that isn't good enough. There is no real answer.

I pick at the truth like some weakened bird of prey.

With each page I can't help but think I reduce myself yet another degree in your estimation. Why? Perhaps I can't stop myself now. Will you hang on long enough? Have I nothing left to recommend me? Perhaps I know in my heart of hearts that you will never lay eyes on your father's words. Has this solitude led me so wide from my original path that I'm afraid to say what I set out to do? Which was what—to sway you? Elicit forgiveness? Embolden myself? Record the facts? Now none of this matters. The enemy encircles us, bearing down from the north, east, south and west. Their hungry machines eat away at this small oasis with each passing day. The noose closes.

Yet here I am. More important is my desire to surround myself with the thick blanket of these memories. Only that. I wait for these hours of escape. It warms me, this simple act of memory and reconstruction. I am sustained. I have a voice in this silent land. I return to this darkened house chilled and hungry but almost peaceful. Every night it's the same. A lonely man's imagined dialogue with the portraits of you and your mother. On occasions when the war becomes everything, I can hear myself and the anger in my voice, the exhausted frustration. Then I stop writing, alarmed that I'm talking only to myself. Is the great Bethune talking to himself? Is this what I have become? Does Ho listen? Does he scurry off to find Mr. Tung to aid in his eavesdropping? I go days without uttering anything but barked commands and threats of discipline. I send people from my sight like an enraged schoolmaster. Even my own voice sounds strange to me now, as do the things that bring me pleasure. Steamed potatoes mixed with eggs and sugar, for example. This is Ho's current specialty, which he brings to me wearing the proud face of a master chef. He really is something. This morning, though, I thought

I detected a smirk of recognition not very well camouflaged by a smile. The nerve! I think. The little bastard. The servant poisons his king. Is that what these dizzy spells amount to? What secret does he throw into this hash?

*

I imagined the terror that would have plagued your mother as she bore down upon that struggling mass within her, knowing that once her body had completed its birthing she would be wheeled out and placed against a wall, or shot there in her bed, still with the warmth of your exit burning on her flesh. It was unimaginable. I could imagine nothing else. It possessed my thoughts. I stood at my hotel window and watched New York City below, wandering in my mind through the maze of possibilities. It was a world of indifference I saw below me, both to the death of your mother and to the war that claimed her. It was one and the same, a tragic absurdity that these people simply didn't matter. If the death was not in your house, you didn't bother with it; if death was busy elsewhere, all the better. I could not tolerate these images flooding over me. I imagined the agony of your birth, which your mother knew would signal her own death.

I know now how unjust were my first thoughts toward you, the result of a madness that took hold of my vile heart.

How can I even write them now? Only with the belief that you will never see this. Only with the comforting thought that I will fail in this task and my secrets will remain.

When a child is born we offer expressions of joy, hearty handshakes, even the odd cigar. Here is evidence of nature's generosity, this simple miracle providing an opportunity to live one's life over again and to correct one's errors and to embrace what one failed to cherish the first time around. These are thoughts a man might possess in normal times, but I felt only the terror of your mother's last days. For me, this was the embodiment of that betrayal of Spain.

I could not drive these thoughts away. For months they tormented me. From New York to Seattle, to Vancouver, then on board the *Empress* and finally into the vastness of this land, I was a man haunted by the terrible fact that I could feel rage against the innocent child whom I'd left behind.

I imagined it again and again. Your mother glancing over her shoulder as the door swung open. This at the Alemana, at our table. Were these the men who would take her away that last time while I carried my film between Montreal and Toronto?

Was I staring up at that documentary and thinking of your dear mother when they pulled you from her womb?

*

This is how I see it. The murderers released her after that first detention, allowing her back out into the world to lead her tormentors into a buzzing hive of plotters.

The Alemana tavern was busy by nine o'clock. The pale-yellow plaster walls were trimmed with dark oak and hung with cinema and bullfight posters. The zinc bar ran perpendicular to the street, with white dishes of cheese, sardines and olives, baskets of bread covered by a damp cloth.

By now the news of Bethune's ouster is old news. Pitcairn knows of the embarrassment. And he knows well enough, too, that his association with the woman sitting before him might facilitate his own speedy repatriation. Perhaps he'll go to New York, where his press credentials won't be revoked for talking with a Swedish national of dubious allegiances. I imagine his kind mouth twisting as he listens.

"I'm tired," she says, "I'm always tired now."

This perhaps is when she first mentions the tenacious pregnancy, the one believed at first to have been terminated as a consequence of a vigorous pace up a steep mountain trail.

His eyes narrow, the first question marked by the entrance of another trio of drinkers. "Does he know?"

"No. And he won't. He thinks the child—"

"I'm leaving for England next week. If I could get word to him—"

"He knows as much as he needs to know. If anything happens to me—"

"Nothing will happen. Go to France. Leave tonight."

"If anything happens—"

"Nothing will happen if you leave."

"If it does, take the baby. They won't hurt the baby."

She pushes her chair back. Its wooden paws drag loudly over the stone and sawdust floor. Heads turn. Beside them sits a young couple, infinitely less complicated, innocent as birds, really, silenced by this start. She rises and walks across the room. She might just be showing now, but hiding it cleverly under a loose sweater. Her friend, the newly appointed guardian, wonders if it could possibly come to that, a woman as formidable as this embarrassed by an unwelcome pregnancy.

Then, two months later, another round-up. Did she lead them to anyone? Those men, the same bunch who'd picked me up, by now would have grown bored. Were they surprised to see the growth in her belly? The little spy Bethune had left behind. The Communist's son or daughter. What negotiations would have ensued? We will spare your child, just tell us some names. Your child shall be looked after. Only some names for the sake of the child, no? We will wait for the child to come.

Your child buys you three, maybe four weeks of life. The child of a miracle-worker, a good Communist. But you, we're not so sure of. Only a few names and perhaps it will see its father one day. Together they will remember you. Your legacy in exchange for a few names.

*

I knew nothing of this. I thought you'd died in the hills above Segovia. I knew only my anger. I'd been pushed out of Spain. I made do with what remained.

With that propaganda under my arm, I toured North America like some tweed-suited evangelist, eloquent, righteous, unforgiving—the very picture of my father. It was my rage that carried me. I didn't know what was happening back there. I had no contact with anyone. I had no idea where your mother had gone. The letters I wrote her in care of the Santander disappeared, swallowed by the war.

I presented that film in auditoriums, union halls, arenas, churches and theatres across Canada and America, and then, exhausted by my own righteousness, slipped back to brood quietly in the dark and watch how those scenes, so familiar, so devastating, played before the eyes of enraged Montreal, shocked Toronto, indignant New York, sympathetic Chicago. I was a huckster of ideals, nothing more, a travelling one-man circus, an itinerant used-car salesman. This was how I attempted to ease the anguish after my humiliating defeat. By working. By fighting harder.

Every night for four months I stared up at images of the opportunity that had been denied me, the place where I could do the most good, the war that so quickly became the symbol of my infamy, considering this black-and-white testimony the lasting document of my shame. And after the lights came up I would again rise to address the audience in the practised preacher's tones that could barely contain the anger mistaken every night for my seething hatred of Fascism and a passion for democracy.

Every day I arrived in or departed from a new town. Every presentation was as draining as if it were my last, me gasping as if I breathed with only one lung. I was a husk. I wrote nothing but pained letters to your mother. Painted nothing. I stayed half drunk. Thought of nothing but the treachery that had befallen me, of the Brutuses who'd slain me with their lies and conspiracies. I brooded, how I brooded. But was the focus of the hatred that had united Sise and Sorensen in cowardice to denounce me to the Party simply that they didn't like my methods? Imagine being surrounded by fallen neighbourhoods and screaming, dying children while your peers, these petty bureaucrats, are satisfied with nothing more than a gentle demeanour, a soft touch, the obsequiousness of an apprentice waiter. You will not find that here, I guarantee it, not in China!

There were occasions, I believed, when the audience sensed this moral panic, when, judging from the empty shine of the collection plates, I felt they'd seized upon my collapse—after the last drop of blood had been drained from my body, my lungs crushed with the effort and passion of my speech—by making donations that were nothing less than an insult to every man, woman and child in Spain and, above all, to me. And so here it was in Sudbury, northern Ontario, so close to the fields of my youth, that I was roundly snubbed, ignored and belittled by a crowd of seven hundred whose generosity totalled $22.40. $22.40! Did they know the true nature of my raging? Had the rumours already begun? I paced nervously backstage as these blackguards mingled, surely sniggering at my public shame.

What does a man do in this circumstance? Or when he's trapped in the mud with a wounded comrade? He fights back. He lifts the man upon his shoulder and returns him to safety. He does not accept his fate. He argues for it. He fights. He walks stiffly back to the podium and berates the hundreds who remain for their petty selfishness, their adipose greed, their Fascist sympathies. Yes, this is what I did—that man I barely recognize now, whose breathless audacity shocks me still. He retakes centre stage and announces to the departing crowd's embarrassment that Spain is nothing if not the staging ground for the gathering war in Europe that shall consume the lives of our sons and daughters. The insult of $22.40 shall forever be connected to this miserable village! Spain is not simply a war of principle to suit your caprices, and it shall not be denigrated with the small change of a panhandler. This war is being waged deeply within each of us, and for each of us the enemy—in case you weren't listening the first time—is our darker nature, our selfishness, our comfortable denials. This is a struggle to restore man to his noble self! And on I went before that fearful, shocked crowd, ranting feverishly, and perhaps half drunk, I don't recall. But up the ante I did.

Ship. Plane. Automobile. Each journey was the same, yet each destination offered the slightest glimmer of hope. Would it be in Quebec, or the Maritimes, in Chicago, or in the towns and cities of California, on the Prairies, or in British Columbia that the film would speak in a new voice and transform itself into a kind of love story—to set the record straight and right the wrong? I waited and each time listened to the opening, always crushingly the same and, as I was myself, unable to be transformed into something more.

Your mother appears once in the documentary, a beautiful face caught for a moment, laughing in joyous union with the

fighting men and women of Castile. Is it a party? A victory celebration? Was your mother giddy with love?

And then the painting, like a man on a stretcher, being
evacuated from the Prado.

The delusional rage left me, for a time, in Toronto. Here
I was the returning hero, a god fallen from the clouds but still
god-like as he walks through the crowds and is lifted upon
strong backs in triumphal celebration. How lovely it was, and
how schizophrenic. Upon my arrival at Toronto's Union Station I was greeted by a sea of five thousand working men and
women who waved me on as our car motored up Yonge Street to
Queen's Park, where I mounted a makeshift stage and delivered
my pronouncements from Europe. But a week later it was back
to the same pleading anger, the same thinly disguised passions,
the same pathetic wanderings.

And then, in January, I sat down in a hotel bar in New York
with Pitcairn.

He told me of you and how I'd find you.

*

The evening casts magic over my village, this fairy-tale idyll of
Asia—a spell of coppery light. The stream in the valley below
rushes blindly on, its slashing music slipping up to the ears of
the child soldiers who sit perched on the moist rock, its current
cleansing the blood from these mountains.

Will the passage of time likewise wash the thought of you
from my memories? Will the advancing months reduce these
passions to shadows?

A surgeon in a theatre of war, I am accustomed to failure
and the numbing effects of relentless slaughter. This cannot be
overstated. Once upon a time, I walked through the night reciting

favourite poems, in hopes of unburdening myself of a drudgery I could barely survive but which only hinted at the terror to come. Now I sit here content, polishing these fragments of memory in an attempt to make something of a life pitted by failure, abandonment and war. This is the one perfection remaining for me after a lifetime of compromise and fallen ideals. No, these musings shall not diminish that which is lost. You cannot fail in memory as you can, so horribly, in the operating theatre.

★

One hundred and four degrees at 6:45 a.m. I am with the Tenth Regiment. I don't know the name of this village but do not think it matters. The bustle of men is all around. Their calls to attention have awakened me, the cocking of rifles, the march of purposeful boots. We have been travelling for some time now, two or three days, I think, from village to village, with me largely unconscious, I am told, like a warm corpse upon its restless catafalque. Even when conscious I have been too ill to admire this vast kingdom. Perhaps I should let China take care of me for a change. A charming thought, being pampered. This is a situation I should learn from. It might help me become a better doctor. At least I can derive something from these wasted days. Illness is not anything I have ever been resigned to. Its pathetic, wheezing ways suit some, but not me.

How poorly I take instruction. I already knew that. It is not so comfortable here as it was at the Trudeau Sanatorium so many years ago, drinking and smoking and riding boats on the lake. Sickness as holiday—how good that seems now in the light of memory. We sat out on the porch gazing at the dark pines every night, remembering our freedom and health, if we weren't leaning against the bar at Brook's Tavern. I was tended to by admiring nurses. In my frailty, as the TB spiders nested in my lung, I organized lectures and prepared to take on the world. To think of that now. How sweet that sickness, how luxurious.

*

I am told five days have passed now since our return from that farmhouse–aid station. How I miss my typewriter. The ribbon's completely dry. Ho is unable to work his magic out here. We will have to wait for that. I miss the green letters and the scent of your mother's perfume. In the meantime, I hope you can make out this chicken-scratch. Ho has found me this stub of pencil and a small stack of writing paper, stolen from some functionary's desk, I suppose. Always scrounging, if not one thing then another. Now he stands at the entrance of the tent.

*

I have instructed the supervising medical officer to inform me if any abdominal or skull cases arrive. Even in this state, weakened but alert, I am the only one qualified. Perhaps I will drip this fever onto the hearts of my wounded comrades. The poetry is dire, I know, but there is something to it, you see, this suffering shared by comrades-at-arms. Blood and sweat. We shall rise again. This is not the first finger I have cut open during a surgery. I have sliced the heart out of the truth.

I am off soon to America with this badge of courage, and with my signed confession for you. If a lack of courage forces me to send this package in care of Frank Pitcairn, you will at least have it, long after I've retreated again from your life. I will defend myself no longer. The story speaks for itself. I already abandoned you once. And the first time is always the most difficult.

The absurd intrudes upon the absurd. Yes, acts of bravery there are. Every day for close to two years I have closed the eyes of men who performed such acts, perhaps despite themselves, and paid with their lives. I only wish my hands had been clean enough to leave unmarked the last touch of dignity on their faces, not smearing them with blood or worse. But no man is brave, not really. No sane or wise man. He is only running.

I did not tell you. When we returned from our latest tour I found the door to my house standing ajar. Sitting at my desk was the famous photographer Mr. Friedmann—Mr. Capa, otherwise known as the Shark. "Don't look so surprised," he said. "You're not that difficult to track down in this oversized country. How was it out there? It looks like you took a thrashing. The Japs get hold of you or something?"

"You've come to bring the dead back to life, have you?"

He said, "You look bloody awful. You'd better sit." He got up, but I didn't move. He shrugged, as if to put me at ease, and motioned to the half-finished portrait on my desk. "You're a bit of an artist, I see," he said. "Will wonders never cease?"

"What do you want?"

"We're not so different, really," he said.

"I'm not so sure that's true."

"You don't feel like a vulture sometimes?"

I said, "The death of high standards. You started with a good dose of it yourself. But neither of us is here for the reason you might expect. You can't really fight a war for the right reason. There never is a right reason. There's always something else—a lover, a death, revenge. Look at Ansell's man, the Nazi who saved five thousand Chinese. Life for life. A noble man, you'd think, right?"

I sat down on the floor.

"I'll come back. You look bloody awful, old man. But I'll bet you saved a dozen lives today." He helped me up and put me in my bed. "I inquired in Hankou," he said. "They say you're leaving."

"Soon."

"What is it?"

"I'll be better tomorrow," I said.

"Afterwards you won't need your boy, right?"

"He stays. When I go, he stays."

"I told you about my idea, didn't I?"

I said, "Ho Tzu-hsin is not a child soldier. He is a valet. A servant boy. He cooks and cleans."

"You know he'll become a soldier when you leave. I will follow him. My idea is complete in this way. An entire journey is a beautiful idea."

"I am not his father," I said. "He does as he likes."

"And that's why you can leave. He could live at least a while longer. Likely he'd already be dead if it weren't for you. You gave him a year, a year and a half. That's more than most of them get up here."

I said, "You will put your camera on him and wait for him to die."

"I'm filming this war. If that is the case, then I will film it."

"You're interested in watching a boy die. The instant of death, and then you go."

"He may survive. We can't be so certain."

"Go back to Spain, Capa."

He said, "That war is dead for me. Sooner or later all good causes die."

"At least we have that in common."

"Stay here, Bethune," he said, "for as long as you can. As long as something is left here for you."

"There is nothing."

"Isn't the boy something?"

"Take him," I said. "Make your film."

He walked to the door. "Maybe you should get some rest, old man."

★

Travelling these last days with the Third Regiment Sanitary Service on stretcher and mule-back, I'm bounced over this rocky Chinese landscape like a bucket of snails.

This morning I again saw him, the boy studying one of my drawings. I was shivering in my cot, soaked by my feverish chills, and he, standing in the grey light, shining like some lucent dream-creature.

It shall be only days now before I am working again. I'm feeling better this morning, bright and alert. I have sent Ho off for another handful of Aspirin and a pot of coffee to help thin my blood. This should speed my recovery. Also he carries another message to the staff that I must be informed of any abdominal or skull cases. When I'm recovered I will catch up with Capa, wherever he's gone, snapping photographs to send out to the world, to tell him he cannot have the boy. The boy is mine. I have decided he will come with me to America. The face of Chinese youth. The innocence, the purity. He will be worth more to the cause there, in Bethune's Travelling Circus, than here. You shall meet the boy, my dear. You'll see what a noble youth he is. Perhaps he'll hold you in his arms. Perhaps he'll recite a poem for you. You will love him, surely. The abandoned children united. You see, we all have this in common. Behold this child, for you are he. Forgotten by all who loved him, then taken up in the great fraternal arms of this noble cause. How pleased the poster boy of the Chinese Revolution will be.

I have decided to talk with him. I will warn him that he must not be immortalized like one of his poems, by that photographer. I'll tell him to keep close to Mr. Tung until I'm well.

What could Capa do with little Ho? He prefers the Spanish face, after all, and I have never seen a more Chinese face! Under my arm and protection Ho will be an inspiration to future generations. Do you want to be worth more to the cause dead than alive? Your life's worth far more than that. You shall come to America! America awaits! The youth of the West shall learn from your example.

But not before I have an opportunity to ask some questions of him. Of course, my questions. I saw him studying my drawings again, last night after I finally blew out my lamp.

I must be informed of skull and abdominal cases.

★

I have been working on your portrait as I while away this sick time. I am inspired, electrified. How my energy has returned to me, for brief moments, at least. You are my tonic, my hope. Does that sound desperate? It is the truth. Now I shall go back in time and cross out all these odd ramblings that have escaped my feverish mind. I do not want to present a bad first impression. It seems I have been off my head these last few days. An elegant diagnosis, I know. But I am pleased to say I'm feeling better on this, the sixth day of this difficult stretch. The uncontrolled vomiting has left me weakened. But I am bright now, more than ever, and alert. The night was an improvement, and today the temperature, 102 degrees, is down somewhat.

This morning I asked after Capa. "Mr. Tung," I said, "where has he gone?" Mr. Tung was leaning over me, cooling my forehead with a wet towel. I waved him away. "Will you answer?"

At length, the delicate Mr. Tung said, "There is no photographer here, Doctor. We are alone."

"Has he taken the boy?"

Mr. Tung left my bedside. Without another word he left me.

When I awoke hours later I found this machine here, placed on a small stool beside the bed. I have been typing for some time now, perhaps hours, recounting what has transpired over these last few days. Did Mr. Tung bring it to me? Was this an apology for his rudeness? Or was it Ho, atoning for his strange behaviour? They will not answer my questions, but neither will they silence me. I shall not be silenced. Not here. Not in America. My ribbon is refreshed, though the ink is slightly off. Closer to blue than green now. You can see it. Yes, it must have been him. Blue is fine, I shall tell him. Don't be so cagey, boy!

I have rallied and I am sitting upright. Look, that wasn't so difficult. This thing sits comfortably on my skinny thighs. I feel the pop-pop of the keys resonate down into the femur. Writing on the bone. What a lovely metaphor to think about.

When I get to America I will show you my paintings and drawings, long after all this is done with. They are much better than these small doodles.

You know, I finished your mother's portrait the day I departed from Madrid. Did I tell you that? I wish you could have seen it. It was taken, along with my other belongings, from that stalled train in Goasi. Perhaps it will be returned to me one day, and you will see how beautiful she is. Of course, you can see that in my documentary, too. But film cannot capture the love of an artist. You will see how much I loved her.

How different it will be once we have won this war! I will show you more than the sketches buried under these green ramblings. Might something good come out of America after this? Has the war in Europe begun? Are you now safely growing to girlhood in a Stockholm neighbourhood? Or still in Madrid where Pitcairn told me I'd find you? Isn't that war finished?

I will have Ho help with my paintings and drawings. Where is he? He'll pack them up for me. And Mr. Tung, when he finishes with his translations. Perhaps I shall bring some along and leave them for you to look over when you are older, when Europe and America have come to help the war here. These mountains will only be a memory by then. I will know you. Perhaps I can visit you often. You'll be as beautiful as your mother. Wouldn't it be grand to see your mother and father together? We could walk along a riverbank holding hands. You'd enjoy that. *For if they fall, the one will lift up his fellow: but woe to him that is alone when he falleth; for he hath not another to help him up.* I have to leave my bed to find the boy, so will leave off here. Does he mean for the failing doctor to come crawling? Well, then, so be it. I will get up and march onwards. But I am tired. The doctor is tired. I will lie down here for a moment. I can get back to this soon enough. Perhaps I will tell Ho to soak this ribbon in the meantime. I see it's beginning to fade already. Where is he? Has he already started off to America? Those hills are too much for just one boy. I can take him on my shoulders. Are there any abdominal cases? I will stroll past the hospital for a look before we set off.

I hear the boy coming now. I know that lively step. I'll bet he's saying one of those old poems. A poem for you, perhaps.

How these hands tremble. There is still so much more to tell. As I write this I'm imperishable. I am completely here. Please know that. It pains me to leave these pages now. But I have to rest. How I am looking forward to completing this history. As you read this I'm radiant. We will be radiant together. Something tells me this can be a beautiful story after all. But first I will rest.

19 Dec 1939
Yan'an, Shensi Province

Comrade Mao Tse-tung
Chairman of the Central Soviet Government

Esteemed Chairman,

While the writings contained herein represent personal histories that may be of interest to certain
family members of Doctor Bethune, this committee has found that they cannot be used to serve the
People in their struggle against the Japanese Imper-
ialist invaders or the Nationalist Kuomintang Army.
It must be stressed that, although the Doctor's
personal efforts in the Border Regions of Shensi
and Hopei provinces were exemplary and highly beneficial to the Communist cause, it is also clear that
certain of his actions and beliefs can be viewed as
less than exemplary of and likely harmful to the
Communist ideal, as it is so clearly and inspir-
ingly detailed in the Chairman's own
political writings. It is the considered opinion
of this committee, consisting of the undersigned,
that Doctor Bethune's value as a symbol of the
rightness of this struggle would be significantly
reduced if these writings came to light. It is
recommended, therefore, that these seven envelopes
remain untranslated from the original and sealed
for the interim and that they be reopened and
considered for translation only at the conclusion

of a Communist victory, at such time as Doctor
Bethune's importance as an international symbol
of China's Marxist-Leninist Revolution is past and
the historical and personal value of this memoir
becomes its primary interest.

The various belongings of Doctor Bethune also
recovered—including personal articles such as toiletries, the memoir herein recorded, and clothing,
thirteen books and pamphlets, one painting of a
girl (perhaps the seagull-child) and numerous drawings, one Remington 5 portable typewriter, seven
maps (personally annotated) and various other medical and political pamphlets and treatises—may be
examined by a separate committee regarding their
propagandistic and/or historical value. It is
recommended that if no appropriate committee can be
formed at this time all articles be kept for
a later date.

In conclusion, the committee finds that only with
significant editing and rewriting will the Bethune
memoir be suitable for translation and printing for
wide-scale distribution. It is advisable that these
documents remain sealed until that time. However,
given the revolutionary and international importance
of Doctor Bethune's life, a brief, more idealized
biography or political eulogy of the subject might
prove extremely beneficial to the present war effort,
and find continuity in the larger canon of the Chairman's political and philosophical writings.

With comradely salutations,

Lu Ting-yi,
Director of the Propaganda Department of the
 Central Committee of the Chinese Communist
 Party, Yan'an

Major Szu Ping Ti,
translator, Propaganda Department, CCP

Lieutenant Tung Yueh-ch'ien,
interpreter for Dr. Bethune, Eighth Route Army

Zhou Erfu,
Lu Hsun Academy of Literature and Arts

Jean Ewen,
surgical nurse, Fung Yiu King Hospital,
 Hong Kong

ACKNOWLEDGEMENTS

While the central character in this novel is based on the Canadian doctor who served in Spain and China in the 1930s, the aesthetic concerns of storytelling often outweighed the more standard historical versions of the Bethune story. The same must be said of the other characters in this novel. They are based only loosely on actual characters who passed through Bethune's life or, in some cases, are completely imagined. The character of Kajsa von Rothman, however, is not my invention. Very little is known of her but for the suspicions that she inspired in Republican wartime Madrid. A 1937 government report makes it clear that von Rothman was officially suspect, and that her intimate relationship with Bethune, a high-profile Communist, was cause for concern. On January 4, 1937, all members of Bethune's staff at the Vergara Street address, including Bethune himself, were taken into custody for questioning. One of these men, an Austrian by the name of Harturg, is said to have been executed. Bethune and von Rothman were both released. Despite his great accomplishments in Spain, Bethune left that country under a dark cloud. Von Rothman's fate is not known.

ACKNOWLEDGEMENTS

In particular I am indebted to Larry Hannant's *The Politics of Passion: Norman Bethune's Writing and Art,* for bringing this history to my attention; Roderick Stewart's *Bethune,* for the outline of Bethune's life and the chronology of his travels in China; Mary Larratt Smith's *Prologue to Norman: The Canadian Bethunes,* for the family genealogy; Dave Love's *The Second Battle of Ypres, April 1915;* and W. H. Auden and Christopher Isherwood's *Journey to a War,* for their first-hand look at China at war.

I would also like to acknowledge the support of the Canada Council and the Ontario Arts Council, the staff at the Toronto Reference Library and the generosity of Beatrice Monti della Corte of the Santa Maddalena Foundation.

Lines from "Sunday Morning" and "Thirteen Ways of Looking at a Blackbird" are reprinted from *The Collected Poems of Wallace Stevens* by permission of Alfred A. Knopf, Inc., a Division of Random House.

The newspaper clipping describing the re-taking of Teruel is as reported in *The Manchester Guardian,* January 8, 1938.

LAW MAKING, LAW FINDING AND LAW
SHAPING: THE DIVERSE INFLUENCES

LAW MAKING, LAW FINDING AND LAW SHAPING: THE DIVERSE INFLUENCES

The Clifford Chance Lectures

Volume Two

Edited and with an Introduction
By

BASIL S. MARKESINIS

With a Foreword
By

THE RT. HON. THE LORD BINGHAM OF CORNHILL

OXFORD UNIVERSITY PRESS
1997

Oxford University Press, Great Clarendon Street, Oxford OX2 6DP

Oxford New York

Athens Auckland Bangkok Bogota Bombay
Buenos Aires Calcutta Cape Town Dar es Salaam
Delhi Florence Hong Kong Istanbul Karachi
Kuala Lumpur Madras Madrid Melbourne
Mexico City Nairobi Paris Singapore
Taipei Tokyo Toronto
and associated companies in
Berlin Ibadan

Oxford is a trade mark of Oxford University Press

Published in the United States
by Oxford University Press Inc., New York

A catalogue record for this book is available from the British Library

Library of Congress Cataloging in Publication Data

Law making, law finding, and law shaping: the diverse influences /
edited and with an introduction by Basil S. Markesinis; with a
foreword by the Rt. Hon. the Lord Bingham of Cornhill.
p. cm. — (Clifford Chance lectures)
Includes bibliographical references.
1. Judicial Process. 2. Law—Methodolgy. 3. Law—Decision
making. I. Markesinis, B. S. II. Series.
K552.L39 1997
347'.012–dc21 97–28132
ISBN 0–19–826497–6

Typeset by Vera A. Keep, Cheltenham
Printed in Great Britain
on acid-free paper by
Bookcraft Ltd., Midsomer Norton, Somerset

Foreword

It seems to have become the practice for hosts at public dinners to offer prospective guests an opportunity to indicate any special dietary requirements they may have.

Such a practice has not, I think, invaded the realm of scholarship. But if the editor and publishers of this book were to follow this practice they would be obliged, in good faith, to make clear that there are certain dietary requirements which the papers collected here, for all the richness of the banquet which they offer, cannot claim to meet.

The book offers no sustenance to the insular and introspective English lawyer whose legal world is bounded by the Tweed to the north, the Channel to the south and the North and Irish Seas to east and west. It sends empty away the chauvinist English practitioner who believes we have nothing to learn from sources beyond our shores, and least of all from those bred in the European civil law traditions. There is nothing here to titillate the palate of those who believe that isolation is splendid, or who believe that between the professional practice and the academic study of the law there is a great gulf fixed, such that none may pass from one to the other. This is a book for those with open, receptive minds, prepared to profit from the learning and experience of others, willing to judge arguments on their rational strength and conformity with principle, not on their source or country of origin.

Those who enjoyed Volume One of the Clifford Chance Lectures will welcome the appearance of Volume Two. But there is a difference. The papers in Volume One were delivered under the auspices of the Institute of Anglo-American Law at Leyden, and accordingly had an Anglo-American focus. These papers, delivered under the auspices of the Centre for the Advanced Study of European and Comparative Law at Oxford, have a broader, more comparative, more international canvas. This is in keeping with the far-flung international pratice which Clifford Chance conduct, and which has made their name familiar throughout most of the developed world. Readers will be grateful to them, not only for sponsoring the conference at which these papers were given, but also for their generous and sustained support of the Centre, in the most practical way possible, during its formative early years. The phenomenal growth of the Centre is a matter of record; as it strides confidently into the new millennium the importance of its work will become ever more obvious.

The Rt Hon Lord Bingham of Cornhill
Lord Chief Justice of England

Royal Courts of Justice
The Strand
LONDON WC2 2LL

Table of Contents

List of Contributors

The Rt. Hon. The Lord Bingham of Cornhill is the Lord Chief Justice of England and Wales and the Visitor of Balliol College, Oxford.

Professor Peter Birks, QC, is the Regius Professor of Civil Law at the University of Oxford and a Fellow of the British Academy.

Professor Paul Craig is a Fellow of Worcester College, Oxford.

Mr. Roger Errera is Conseiller at the Conseil d'Etat of France.

The Rt. Hon. The Lord Goff of Chieveley is Lord of Appeal in Ordinary, a Fellow of the British Academy, and the Lord High Steward of the University of Oxford.

Professor Arthur Hartkamp is Advocate General at the Dutch Supreme Court and a Fellow of the Royal Netherands Academy and the Royal Academy of Belgium.

Mr. Timothy Herrington is a Partner at Clifford Chance.

Mr. Thijmen Koopmans is Advocate General at the Dutch Supreme Court and a Fellow of the Royal Netherlands Academy.

The Hon. Mr. Justice Gerard V. La Forest is a Justice at the Supreme Court of Canada.

Professor Dr. Jutta Limbach is President of the German Constitutional Court.

Professor Basil S. Markesinis is Clifford Chance Professor of European Law at the University of Oxford and a Fellow of the British Academy, the Academy of Athens and the Royal Belgian and Netherlands Academies.

The Rt. Hon. Sir Brian Neill was, until September 1996, a Lord Justice in the Court of Appeal.

Professor Walter van Gerven is Professor at the University of Leuven and a former Advocate General at the Court of the European Communities. He is a Fellow of the Royal Belgian and Netherlands Academies.

I

Introduction

by *Professor Basil Markesinis*

Three years ago the highly respected multi-national firm of Clifford Chance took the decision to endow a chair in European Law at the University of Oxford. This act of generosity was not unique since Oxford (and other Universities) have often in the past benefitted from the support of the legal profession. But if the gift was not unique, the aims behind it were. For the donation was part of a strategy to promote closer cooperation between the various branches of the legal profession — judges, academics, and practitioners — and to do so in the context of current 'European' developments. For though the political climate towards Europe has, in recent years, been confused if not sceptical, the intellectual attitudes were never more open and imaginative. Oxford shared these intellectual aims; and was anxious to use this chair as the starting point for the creation of a Centre which not only would be involved in the teaching and research of European law (both in the sense of Community law and comparative private and public law) but which would also have a truly European character and composition. Clearly, what it was not to be — and should not be — was an Oxford-based research unit with European interests. Three years later the Centre, which since its inception has been entrusted to my care, has seen its staff grow from zero to eighteen, a figure which includes four Germans, three French, two Italian, one Dutch and one American. The rest, as the saying goes, is history.[1]

Our pre-occupation now is with the future. And nothing brings more to the fore these combined aims for the future than the Clifford Chance Lectures which are fast becoming part of the European legal landscape. For this is the second volume to be

---

[1] Readers interested in the Centre, its precise aims, and its achievements can obtain a copy of the *Director's Second Annual Report* by writing to The Centre for the Advanced Study of European and Comparative Law, St Cross Road, Oxford OX1 3UL.

published by the Oxford University Press; and, we hope, a third will follow soon. And as with the first volume, which appeared under the title 'Bridging the Channel', this second volume brought together judges, academics, practitioners, and law students from many European countries and, in this instance, Canada. The richness of views offered by the key-note speakers will not escape the reader of this book; but he will have to imagine how much richer the discussion was, as over one hundred participants[2] for two days responded to, disagreed with, or elaborated on the themes of the twelve speakers whose essays are reproduced in this volume. Incidentally, the title of the conference was 'Judges and Legislators, Academics and Regulators: Are They Getting their Act Together?'—the purpose being not only to look at the work of some of the modern agents who make, discover, and shape law, but also to discuss how coordinated (or not) their efforts are.[3] For the purposes of a book, a shorter title was deemed more appropriate; but, we hope, the one chosen still captures our main theme: the diversity of the various influences which come together and 'make' modern law.

The question how coordinated these agencies are is another matter. Our conclusions and, to some extent the essays published here, were not unanimous. Moreover, they revealed another dimension to this problem of lack of coordination and disharmony. For, at the international level, a further important discrepancy becomes apparent namely, the difference between pious political pronouncements about European cooperation and integration and the continuing realities of state protectionism and regulation in its various guises. Mr. Herrington's essay is a technical piece which will appeal particularly to the kind of 'business' players who typically seek the benefit of his professional expertise; but it can also lead those who are more oriented towards political speculation to ask what would have happened if the Single European

---

[2] For a list of participants see Appendix.

[3] On the national level this has been done several times. Examples abound, but two taken from the law of obligations, will suffice. The first is the almost simultaneous but un-coordinated attempt to deal with the problems of negligent misrepresentations, by the House of Lords in *Hedley Byrne & Co. Ltd.* v. *Heller & Partners Ltd.* [1964] AC 465 and the legislator in the Misrepresentation Act 1967; the other, designed to address the liability of negligent builders and developers, can be seen in *Dutton* v. *Bognor Regis Urban District Council* [1972] 1 QB 373, and The Defective Premises Act 1972.

Act had really been put into effect ten years before 'Maastricht' managed to get us into some of our present predicaments. We shall return to this problem later on when we add some further remarks on Professor van Gerven's piece which also addresses this problem, albeit from a different perspective.

The varied essays included in this book can be looked at in different ways.

One notes, for instance, that our general theme was approached from different angles. Thus, three speakers (Craig, Limbach and Koopmans) chose to focus on the relationship between the legislator and the judiciary[4] while three others (Birks, Goff, and La Forest) paid special attention to the potential role that academics can play in what, for lack of a better expression, one might call the background shaping of the law though one of them (Koopmans) boldly and, it seems correctly, maintains that in the area of community law 'academic writing [has] followed the Court's case law, rather than paved the way for it'. Yet another of our speakers (Hartkamp), showed us how all four agents in law making and law shaping (legislators, judges, academics, and administrators) combined in a rather unique and, on the whole, harmonious way to shape the admirable new Dutch Civil Code.[5] Another of our keynote speakers (van Gerven) brought his formidable experience of the European scene to bear on the thorny relationship between the national and supra-national legislator. The last two speakers (Errera, Neill) refreshingly opted out of the fields of legislation, adminstration, and commerce and chose, instead, to show us how the transplantability of ideas is shaping another, delicate area of the law: that involving diverse personality rights. Professor Errera's essay is an elegant cry for greater legislative sensitivity in a country which has not always been a model of tolerance towards its immigrant races.

Any attempt to summarise the individual theses contained in these essays would not only be crass but also useless. The reader of this volume does not need its editor to undertake such a task for him. Yet an editor of a book of a learned collection of essays might

---

[4] Though Professor Koopmans is, rightly one might add, anxious to warn the reader not to jump too quickly to comparisons between national legal systems and the institutional system of the Community.

[5] Though he fails to remind us that this collaborative effort required forty-three years of gestation before it produced an offspring!

be permitted to highlight some points and invite readers to agree or disagree with his own synthesis while making their own. Those who know my work will not be surprised to see me restate my conviction that behind the diversity of the individual themes or approaches also lies a certain degree of unity which is discernable, at any rate to those who are willing to look for it.

Take, for instance, those of our contributors who chose to discuss the modern ambit of judicial review. All, in their individual ways, stress that both legislators and courts must behave responsibly and with mutual respect for each other's legitimate role; that the demarcation line between their respective roles and duties is not easily drawn; that it is not for the courts to substitute their judgment on matters of merit for that of the legislator or the administrator; that notwithstanding the above, the intensity of the review is growing, especially when certain matters are deemed, by their very nature, to warrant such extra sensitivity—the protection of basic human rights being the obvious example. The notable exception here from this cry for 'compromise' appears to be Professor Koopmans, who first proceeds to explain (and justify?) why and how the European Court has acquired a dominant position within the European Community and then considers with undisguised apprehension the growing national reactions against such increased powers. (For once, it is not only Britain who is 'in the dock'.) His conclusion suggests that the judicial toga has taken precedence over the academic gown; and that in his case both suspect the politician. Thus, Professor Koopmans concludes his essay with the bold peroration that 'the European Union is too important to be left to diplomats and politicians'.[6] Vintage Koopmans here for those who have had the pleasure of knowing (and admiring) over the years his lively and mischievous intellect; but also provocatively incomplete in so far, at least, as he leaves us guessing why he is 'prepared' to allow what are often essentially political issues to be shaped by un-elected judges, some of whom cannot boast the richness of his own, multiple careers as a civil servant, a law Professor, and a senior judge.[7]

[6] Ironically, the peroration owes much to the celebrated aphorism of a famous statesman's (Georges Clemanceau) that 'War is too important a matter to be left to the generals.'

[7] The differences in the professional backgrounds of the judges, especially of the Court of Human Rights, makes their ability to act as judges a topic worthy of further research.

One finds other common threads which are discernible in most of these papers and which are worthy of some note. For it is certainly legitimate to stress the fact that, secreted in footnotes (which few read carefully) are references which show how our systems are influencing each other. Ideas are thus travelling;[8] and again, if one is to judge from the content of the footnotes, academic writing is as much responsible for this cross-pollination as are judicial decisions. We see this most clearly in a number of pieces, even where they did not choose to focus on the role of the academic (For instance, Limbach, Errera); and Mr. Justice La Forest makes this point with an abundance of references taken from his native Canada. Thus, no one reading this volume can be left in any doubt of the fact that the highest judges of many of the highest courts are nowadays consulting academic literature more than ever before, even if their judgments (for reasons of tradition or otherwise) may not always make this obvious to all.[9]

The European idea is also obvious in most of the essays; and, again, not only in essays such as those by Koopmans, van Gerven, and Hartkamp who have openly adopted it as one of their central themes. Thus, the case law of the Court of Human Rights finds favour with the Court of the European Communities. Often, its ideas are shaped out of national material. These raw elements are common in more than one system, even though their wide prevalence on the European Continent is often concealed by different terminology. The raw material is re-formulated by these European courts, turned into 'European Law', and then re-exported to the member countries where a further 'mixture' is taking place with ideas coming from across the Atlantic, mainly the United States Supreme Court. This happens even in England; and it is happening more and more despite the fact that our judges—but not only *our* judges—like to pretend that our system is not influenced by European law since its own armoury is as good as that of its

---

[8] As John Milton, among others, had wished when he wrote 'As wine and oyl are Imported to us from abroad: so must ripe Understanding, and many civil Virtues, be imported into our minds from Foreign Writings, and examples of best Ages, we shall else miscarry still, and come short in the attempts of great Enterprise.' The Character of the Long Parliament (1641) in *The Works of John Milton*, vol XVIII, (New York, 1938), 248, 254.

[9] This concealment of the academic influence has, in England at least, become the subject of some criticism. Thus, see Birks, 'Adjudication and Interpretation in the Common Law: A Century of Change' in *Bridging the Channel, The Clifford Chance Lectures*, (1996), vol I (B. S. Markesinis, ed.), 135, 150 ff.

neighbours.[10] In recent times, we witnessed such claims most clearly in the areas of defamation and free speech, though how convincing they are is, it is submitted, another matter. In the same cases we also note a greater tendency to be influenced by American decisions rather than by European. This is an interesting tendency which can only be noted in passing (though Sir Brian Neill's thoughtful piece provides an excellent starting point for such speculation). For my part, I am content to add here that it would, I think, be too facile to explain this predilection for the American material solely by reference to the fact that our judges can understand the American texts more easily than the French or German. I say this for two reasons. First, because I take the view that one must not readily admit to the transplantability of the American material given important differences in the constitutional structures of the two countries.[11] Secondly, because I believe (more controversially, I suppose) that on a number of issues our English sense of values may lie closer to the European than to the American.[12] Once again, however, these are themes which, though found to a greater or lesser extent in many of our essays, others will have to develop further in the years to come. Collections of Essays are not meant to be used as text-books are,

[10] Recently, Professor Guido Alpa of the University of Rome gave a public lecture in Oxford about the Italian law of privacy. In it he told his audience how this part of the law was developed, partly under the influence of Anglo-American ideas and partly as a result of the European Convention of Human Rights. In later years, however, the Italian Courts have chosen to base their pro-privacy decisions on the Italian Constitution and disclaimed the influence of the European Convention. Thus see his excellent 'The Protection of Privacy in Italian Law' published in 1997 by the Oxford Centre for the Advanced Study of European and Comparative Law. The parallel here with the attitudes of the Court of Appeal and the House of Lords in *Derbyshire County Council* v. *The Times Newspapers Ltd.* [1992] QB 770 and [1993] AC 53 is obvious.

[11] The theme of an important monograph by Professor John Fleming entitled *The American Tort Process*, paperback ed. (Oxford, Oxford University Press, 1990).

[12] The theology of the First Amendment (often criticised by important American specialists such as, for instance, Professor Fred Schauer) would never, I believe, find on this side of the Atlantic the devout followers that it has in its own environment. I first advanced this theory (but have yet to develop it fully) in my 'Some Comparative Reflections on the Right of Privacy of Public Figures in Public Places' in *Privacy and Loyalty* (ed. P. B. H. Birks) (1997), 111 ff. Since then, I believe the idea has found some support in Professor Reinhard Zimmermann's erudite 'Savigny's Legacy. Legal History, Comparative Law and the Emergence of a European Legal Science' in 112 (1996) *LQR* 576, 584. But, as stated, this thesis awaits further elaboration.

as a source of information but as a source of ideas; and, I submit, there are plenty of ideas in this volume!

The constant changes in the political, economic, and legal environment are undeniable. Not expressly considered in our essays, they nevertheless stand behind many of the ideas found in them. It is these changes which account for the convergence of our systems; and it is these changes which account for the growing interest in European law which nowadays one finds in British Universities, my own included.

One may doubt, however, whether this convergence is accompanied by sufficient awareness that it has been facilitated by our common heritage, which post-19th century ideas about 'sovereignty'—a vague notion at best—have encouraged us to forget. Though this has been a favourite theme among some eminent modern European (especially German) scholars,[13] it was not pursued at this conference except in passing. But warnings were voiced about this re-discovered 'unity' and about its dangers if we tolerate its growth in a manner that invokes Llewellyn's marvellous image of the bramble bush. Birks thus makes the plea for a rationalised taxonomy of law (found, one must stress in Gaius, but not in the classical Roman law[14]) which is no less appealing for having been pleaded by him in the past; and all who attended the conference and recall the gusto with which the message was delivered will acknowledge that the infectiousness of his enthusiasm adds to the rationality of the message. It is, again, for the reader to pick up these threads, found here and in the citations given in the notes, and bring them together as he thinks best. Here we should only single out another, related, but unwelcome side effect of this unsystematic growth: the de-harmonisation which 'harmonisation' is bringing in its wake.

This contradiction in terms is, arguably, the central theme of van Gerven's multi-faceted essay; and it has a 'negative' aspect as well as a 'positive' one. The negative one is, as he puts it, that 'harmonisation measures undertaken by the Community are . . . far from coherent. Moreover, they do not achieve unification

---

[13] Notably, German law Professors such as Reinhard Zimmermann and Reiner Schulze and others. The tradition is, of course, a long one and goes back to the works of Koschacker, Wieacker, and Coing.

[14] The topic was recently considered by Professor Peter Stein in his Maccabean Lecture in the British Academy, entitled 'The Quest for a Systematic Civil Law', *Proceedings of the British Academy* (1996), 147–64.

amongst national laws, especially not when they are contained in directives . . . [t]he consequences of all this is a substantial amount of incoherence and inconsistencies.' This part of his thought-provoking essay deserves particular attention, for like Herrington's piece, it points out how big the gap still remains between proclaimed goals and reality. But van Gerven's message also has its 'positive' side. It lies in his belief that judges, practitioners, and academics can play an important part in restoring the desired degree of harmonisation which is often eluding the legislator and the regulator. He thus skilfully introduces into his essay all the 'players' who figure in the title of the conference; and as far as academics are concerned, he achieves a subtle compromise with the Koopmans thesis. For, if as already stated, in the Koopmans cosmology academics play a minimal part in the creation of the new order, in the van Gerven scheme of things, they have a crucial role to play in tidying up the debris which remains after the 'Chaos' has given way to the 'Cosmos'. To put it differently, no one ever pretended that the creation of the new European order and the working out of its relationship with the national systems was ever going to be quick, easy, or painless. The creation of a workable model will, clearly, require the co-operation of all the agencies here examined, accompanied by a good measure of that most rare of human qualities: imagination.

Given my own interests in foreign law and comparative methodology I hope the reader will excuse me if I devote the remaining paragraphs of this short introduction to Lord Goff's essay. Read together with his recent Wilberforce lecture[15] it contains some thought-provoking ideas about foreign law and the future of the Common law. Lord Goff is not only one of our most erudite judges; he is also the one who, in his Child lecture[16] in Oxford over ten years ago, launched the contemporary debate about the utility of the comparative method. What he has to say on these topics is always listened to with the greatest respect; and it must not be brushed aside by the insularity of our gut reactions. But before we turn to his views, we ought to look briefly at those of Mr. Justice La Forest.

[15] 'The Future of the Common Law', to be published in the Autumn 1997 issue of the *ICLQ*.

[16] 'Judge, Jurist and Legislature', *Denning L J* 2 (1988), 79. See, also, his 'The Search for Principle' Maccabean Lecture in Jurisprudence, *Proceedings of the British Academy* 69 (1983), 169.

The decisions of this learned Justice have won much acclaim over the years. In his paper he tells us about the kind of influence academics had on him and his Canadian colleagues and provides meticulous evidence for his assertions. There are many reasons why his ideas deserve careful reflection.

La Forest begins by telling us that until just after the Second World War the Canadian Courts displayed the kind of indifference towards academic views that ours have done until even more recently (some might even argue they still do!). The same indifference existed towards foreign law, though obviously the French influence in Quebec was always present. The reasons for the cosmopolitan shift of late are multiple: emancipation from the Privy Council; recruitment of academics as judges; the use of clerks; the coming into force in 1982 of the Canadian Charter of Rights and Freedoms. Some might reject the relevance of these factors for the English scene. For instance, the prospect of academics on the (English) Bench must be extremely remote (though one must stress the fact that Canada and Australia have not done badly by harnessing such talent). Practitioners would certainly dislike it. Likewise, many (though I do not think all) British judges remain doubtful about the utility of clerks. (Some have even admitted to me in private that they would not know how to use them!) But the last of the learned Justice's points—the catalyst effect which the adoption of the Canadian Charter had on this point—might be repeatable in our system as well. After all, the chances of the European Convention of Human Rights coming into our law in some form or another seem to be growing by the minute; and if, or rather, when this happens it is bound to encourage new ways of thinking,[17] the use of more international material, and even mandate different judicial approaches. In this context, academic and comparative material will find a new role, and this whether the conservative Bar likes it or not. One may thus not find it easy to dismiss as irrelevant to the English scene Mr. Justice La Forest's statement that 'today, all my [Canadian] colleagues routinely use academic, international and comparative material. *And because we do, counsel cite them.*'[18] So, to Lord Goff's brief but thought-provoking comments about how comparative law can assist English judges in their task.

[17] See, for instance, Lyon, 'The Charter as a Mandate for New Ways of Thinking About Law' (1984) 9 *Queen's LJ* 241.   [18] Infra, p. 75. Emphasis added.

First, an important distinction must be made between judges (and practising barristers) who are not willing to learn from another system and those who are but may at times find it difficult to do so. Lord Goff does not deal with the first category. He clearly belongs to the second category; and to an open mind such as his, the fact that there may be lawyers who are willing to remain insular seems almost inconceivable. Yet, with a minimum of ingenuity, this first category can be seen lurking behind a conversation he reports (in his paper) as having had with 'a young English Queen's Counsel' which, apparently, left him speechless.

One reason for this concern must, surely, be the volume of material which both counsel and judge have to sift through before they reach if not the right decision, a decision. But I have said elsewhere,[19] and was delighted to see Lord Steyn adopt the same stance in *White* v. *Jones*[20] that 'it is arguments that influence decisions rather than the reading of pages upon pages from judgments'. Approached in this way, the question becomes not a matter of volume of material but of selection of relevant material. After all, is not this what (good) law faculties are meant to teach their students? And if they can do it, why can't our judges do it also!

Lord Goff then wonders whether there will be another case like *White* v. *Jones*.[21] To be sure, it is typical of the English Common law to take one step back the moment it has taken two steps forward. This pattern of Hegelian dialectics can be seen most clearly in the *Anns*,[22] *Junior Books*,[23] *Peabody*,[24] and *Murphy*[25] type of cases to which, interestingly enough, Lord Goff alludes. For in *Anns* a forward step by a great judge (Lord Wilberforce) was, in a subsequent case (*Junior Books*), taken one step further (by unnecessarily broad dicta) and triggered off the antithesis which

---

[19] Markesinis and Deakin, 'The Random Element of Their Lordships' Infallible Judgment. An Economic and Comparative Analysis of the Tort of Negligence from *Anns* to *Murphy*' (1992) 55 *MLR*, 619 ff.

[20] [1993] 3 All ER 481, 500.

[21] [1995] 2 WLR 187. For a fuller comparative discussion of this case see: Markesinis, 'Five Days in the House of Lords: Some Comparative reflections on *White* v. *Jones*' 3 *Torts Law Journal* (1995), 169 ff; Zimmermann, 'Erbfolge und Scadensersatz bei Anwaltsverschulden' 1996 *ZEuP* 672 ff..

[22] *Anns* v. *Merton London Borough Council* [1978] 1 AC 728.

[23] *Junior Books Co. Ltd.* v. *Veitchi Co. Ltd.* [1983] 1 AC 520.

[24] *Peabody Donation Fund* v. *Sir Lindsay Parkinson & Co. Ltd* [1984] 3 All ER 529.

[25] *Murphy* v. *Brentwood District Council* [1991] 1 AC 398.

came in *Peabody* and was consolidated in *Murphy*—a decision
which, I venture to suggest, will not mark the last step of the
evolution in this part of our law as it has not in other parts of
the Commonwealth. Yet, strangely, this antithesis of *Peabody*
was foreshadowed by two decisions of the German Federal Court
a good twenty years earlier;[26] and any one who reads the (English version) of the texts[27] can easily see that the reasoning was
transplantable. Indeed, what we have in Lord Keith's judgment in
Peabody is another example of what Lord Goff tells us happened
to him in *The Aliakmon*:[28] reaching the same result which the
Germans did much earlier but through independent inspiration.
But if this can happen spontaneously, why cannot it be the result
of planned and studied action? Why, in other words, must we start
from the premise that there is nothing that the Germans or the
French can teach us? Or that there is never any time to delve into
these materials in search of gold nuggets? For important causes we
can make time; and in real life, it is undeniable that it is always the
busiest people who find time to do more things. In my opinion any
one who takes such introverted views is guilty not just of insularity
but of supreme intellectual arrogance. The real question, therefore, is not whether we can learn from (or teach) the 'Europeans'
but: (a) whether we have intellectually inquisitive judges willing to
borrow from others, *especially when the law on a particular point is
uncertain or unformed*[29] and (b) how we, the academics, can help
such judges satisfy that curiosity and put it to good use. I am
confident that if we do the right thing, the judges will oblige; and
counsel will be dragged along, willingly or not. Lord Justice La
Forest said as much; and other examples can be found across the
entire Commonwealth and the Americas to support his views.

One last point needs to be stressed from Lord Goff's brief
but stimulating paper; his interest in procedure. This is as pronounced—he returns, for instance, to this theme in his Wilberforce
lecture[30]—as it is novel since not that long ago some of the great

---

[26] BGHZ 39, 358 = NJW 1963,1821; BGHZ 39, 366 = NJW 1963, 1827.

[27] Markesinis. *The German Law of Obligations*, vol II, *The German Law of Torts* (1997) 581-5 ff.

[28] *Leigh and Sillavan Ltd.* v. *The Aliakmon Shipping Co. Ltd.* [1985] QB 350.

[29] *Darbyshire* was a case that fell into this category; other examples abound.

[30] 'The Future of the Common Law', The Wilberforce Lecture 1997, to be published in the Autumn issue of the *ICLQ*.

masters of comparative law used to tell us that procedure stood outside the ground which could be usefully tilled by comparative lawyers.[31] Yet, how right Lord Goff is; and how important (though not necessarily acknowledged) this (foreign) influence has been when one looks at Lord Woolf's recent Report[32], probably the most important set of reform proposals for the Common law this century. Conscious or unconscious, the *rapprochement* with Germanic ideas is important; and in my view shows that those Common lawyers who wish to go on plying their trade the way they were taught it thirty or forty years ago and ignore the 'European' factor will contribute to making England the Louisiana of the new Europe. A controversial prediction; but why not prepare the reader of this volume to be shocked and to think? After all, this is one of the roles which the study of foreign and comparative law is meant to perform; and, I believe, this book does it admirably.

[31] Thus, for instance, Professor Harry Lawson in 'The Field of Comparative Law' reproduced in *The Comparison, Selected Essays,* Vol II (1977), Chapter one *passim*, and, more emphatically, Kahn-Freund, 'On Uses and Misuses of Comparative Law' 37 *MLR* (1974) 1, 20.

[32] *Access to Justice, Final Report to the Lord Chancellor on the Civil Justice System in England and Wales,* (HMSO, 1996).

2

Community and national legislators, regulators, judges, academics and practitioners: living together apart?

Professor Walter van Gerven

'Living apart together' is the expression which is used these days to refer to partners living under different roofs but being tied to each other by close links of 'togetherness'. On the level of states such kind of togetherness refers to an intergovernmental relationship. Member states of the European Union, on the contrary, have chosen to live together under the same roof at least in certain respects. One may wonder, however, whether such togetherness does not hide a substantial amount of 'separateness' between national and Community institutions which naturally reflects upon the ways in which they put their act together. Hence: the title of this chapter: 'living together apart'?[1]

I. THE ECJ'S PAFITIS JUDGMENT: NATIONAL REGULATORS LEFT IN THE COLD?

On 12 March 1996 the European Court of Justice (hereinafter the ECJ or the Court) rendered a judgment in Mr. Pafitis'[2] case which concerned the interpretation of Articles 25 and 29 of the Second Company Law Directive.[3] In earlier judgments[4] the ECJ

---

[1] I would like to thank Jan Wouters for his comments on an earlier draft.
[2] Case C-441/93, *Panagis Pafitis and Others* v. *Trapeza Kentrikis Ellados EA and others*, [1996] ECR I-1347.
[3] Directive 77/91/EEC of 13 December 1976 on coordination of safeguards which, for the protection of the interests of members and others, are required by Member States of companies within the meaning of the second paragraph of Article 58 of the Treaty, in respect of the formation of public limited liability companies and the maintenance and alteration of their capital with a view to making such safeguards equivalent, *OJ* 1977 L 26, 1.
[4] Cited below in notes 10 and 14.

has already dealt with those articles and said that they can be relied on by individuals vis-à-vis public authorities before national courts to derive rights therefrom. The *Pafitis* judgment is taken herein as a starting point to illustrate the problems which will be discussed in this essay. In preliminary questions submitted to it, the ECJ was asked whether banks coping with severe financial difficulties could be held not to be subjected to the requirements of Articles 25 and 29 because of the necessity to protect the interests of small depositors as well as the solidity of the banking system as a whole. It was argued before the Court that the protection of these interests requires national banking supervisory authorities to be able, without much ado, to mobilize additional capital resources from new shareholders when a bank is in difficulties.

1.1 The legal context

Panagis Pafitis was one of the old shareholders of Trapeza Kentrikis Ellados AE, a commercial bank having the form of a public limited liability company (hereinafter 'TKE Bank'). Together with other shareholders he brought suit in the court of First Instance of Athens to challenge increases in the capital of the bank which were effected by decision of the Governor of the Bank of Greece and the temporary administrator of TKE Bank. Those authorities were acting in the stead of the company's general meeting of shareholders pursuant to a decision of the Bank of Greece which had placed TKE Bank under the supervision of a temporary administrator. The Bank of Greece was authorized to do so on the basis of a special law according to which, where a bank is unable, or refuses, to increase its capital, its license to trade may be withdrawn, and the bank be put into liquidation, or a temporary administrator may be appointed in which case all the powers and competences of the organs of the bank are to lapse automatically and are to be vested, together with the management of the bank, in the administrator.[5]

In proceedings against TKE Bank and others, Mr. Pafitis and his colleagues objected before the national court to the amendment to the statutes of TKE Bank increasing the capital from 670 to

---

[5] For a fuller account, see para. 2 et seq. of the ECJ Court's judgment, cited supra in n. 2.

1,700 million DR. They founded their action mainly on the ground that such amendment gave effect to a decision taken by the temporary administrator without the general meeting of share-holders having been convened to decide upon any increase of capital, and to allotment of the shares to the new shareholders of the bank following the increase of capital.[6] They also sought annulment of the decisions concerning three subsequent increases of capital, and the corresponding amendments to the statutes taken by the general meeting of shareholders in which the new shareholders had participated and voted, arguing that the plain-tiffs had not validly acquired the status of shareholders.[7]

The national court decided to submit three preliminary ques-tions to the ECJ concerning the interpretation of the Second Com-pany Law Directive and in particular Articles 25 and 29 thereof. According to Article 25(1), first sentence of the Directive, '(A)ny increase of capital must be decided upon by the general meeting' whilst, according to Article 29(1): 'Whenever the capital is in-creased by alteration in cash the shares must be offered on a pre-emptive basis to shareholders in proportion to the capital represented by their shares'. In the case of *Pafitis* the temporary administrator—and not the general meeting—had decided the first increase. However, by notice published in the political and financial press, he had invited the existing shareholders of TKE Bank, to exercise their pre-emptive rights within a period of 30 days. It was only after the plaintiffs had failed to exercise their rights by the end of that period, that the new shares were allotted to third parties.[9]

1.2 The judgments preceding *Pafitis*

Pafitis was not the first (Greek) case coming before the ECJ. In the earlier *Karella* case[10] the Court had already examined, at the

---

[6] The appointment of a temporary administrator to manage TKE Bank and the measure by which the latter ordered the allotment of the new shares to the new shareholders were ratified by Article 24(2) of Greek Law No 1682/1987: see para. 10 of the judgment.   [7] See further para. 11 of the judgment.

[8] According to Article 29(3) of the Second Company Law Directive the offer for subscription had to be made by publication in the national gazette or, if all the shares are registered, in writing. That provision was the object of the third preliminary question.   [9] Para. 9 of the judgment.

[10] Judgment of 30 May 1991, Joined Cases C–19/90 and C–20/90, *Marina Karella* v. *Minister of Industry et al.* and *Nicolaos Karellas* v. *Minister of Industry et al.*, [1991] ECR I-2691.

request of the Greek Council of State, whether Article 25(1) of the Second Company Law Directive was applicable with regard to public rules which govern undertakings of particular economic and social importance for society and are undergoing serious financial difficulties. In that case two shareholders challenged the validity of capital increases in a public limited liability company in which they held shares. Those increases had been decided upon by OAE and approved by the State Secretary for Industry, Energy and Technology. OAE is a Business Reconstruction Organization set up under Greek law to contribute to the economic and social development of the country through, amongst other measures, the financial rejuvenation of undertakings and the establishment and operation of nationalized or mixed economy undertakings. However, the Minister for the National Economy may decide to apply the same rules to undertakings, such as the company of which the plaintiffs were shareholders, which undergo serious financial difficulties. On the basis of these rules the competent Minister had transferred the provisional administration of the company involved to OAE which decided to increase the company's capital, provided that the original shareholders would have an unlimited pre-emptive right which they had to exercise within one month of the publication of the decision. Instead of exercising their pre-emptive right Karella and Karellas requested the Council of State to annul the ministerial decree approving the increase of capital on the ground of unconstitutionality (which plea the Council regarded as unfounded) and of incompatibility with the Second Company Law Directive.

In reply to preliminary questions submitted by the Council of State the ECJ decided (i) that Article 25(1) of the Second Company Law Directive has (vertical) direct effect, that is, may be relied upon by individuals against the public authorities before national courts; and (ii) that Article 25 in conjunction with Article 41(1) — which article provides for an exception 'to encourage the participation of employees . . . in the capital of undertakings' — precludes national rules which, in order to ensure the survival of undertakings of particular economic and social importance, provide for the adoption by administrative act of a decision to increase the company capital.[11]

---

[11] See the ECJ's dictum in *Karella*.

As to the latter point the ECJ emphasized that such an increase by administrative act 'would have the effect either of obliging the original shareholders to increase their contributions to the capital or of imposing on them the addition of new shareholders, thus reducing their involvement in the decision taking power of the company'.[12] The Court continued to say that the safeguard which the directive intends to ensure for members' and third parties' rights must, in order to be effective 'be secured for *members* as long as the company continues to exist with its own structures. Whilst the directive does not preclude the taking of execution measures and, in particular, liquidation measures placing the company under compulsory administration in the interests of safeguarding *creditor's rights*, it nevertheless continues to apply as long as the company's shareholders and normal bodies have not been divested of their powers'[13] (emphasis added).

Before *Pafitis* the ECJ has confirmed *Karella* in two later judgments, *Syndesmos* and *Kerafina* which raised almost identical problems of Community law and related to the same type of companies (and thus not banks).[14] In *Syndesmos* the Court said that also Article 29(1) of the Directive has direct effect against public authorities.

1.3 *Pafitis* not distinguished from *Karella*

The main question of interpretation to be decided by the ECJ in *Pafitis* was whether Article 25 of the Second Company Law Directive applies to measures for the re-organization (such as, it was alleged, the increases in capital at issue) of banks which are in financial difficulties. But first the Court had to answer the question whether the directive applies *as a matter of principle* to all public limited liability companies, including banks having taken that form.[15] To answer that question in the affirmative the Court relied on the title and the text of the directive which indicate that the

---

[12] Para. 26 of the *Karella* judgment.

[13] Para. 30. The directive provisions remain applicable, the Court added, where there is only a 'rejuvenation measure' involved.

[14] Judgment of 24 March 1992, Case C-381/89, *Syndesmos Melon* [1992] ECR I-2111 and Judgment of 12 November 1992, Joined Cases C-134/91 and C-135/91, *Kerafina* [1992] ECR I-3699.

[15] As stated above, in n. 8, the third question concerned the interpretation of Article 29(3), requiring a special form for the publication of an offer of subscription

decisive criterion to define the scope of the directive, is the legal
form of the company, irrespective of its business.[16] The Court
found moreover that, although various articles of the directive
expressly take account of the particular features of banking in
order to allow exceptions to certain of its provisions,[17] the directive does not contain such a derogation with respect to Articles 25
and 29.

As to the second (and main) question, two lines of reasoning
were put forward to convince the Court that rules on the reorganization of credit institutions are of such a special nature that they
should be regarded as falling outside the scope of Article 25 of the
Second Company Law Directive. The first line of arguments[18]
relates to the alleged necessity of special provisions for credit
institutions. That necessity is also recognized at Community level,
as is shown by the numerous legislative measures adopted or
envisaged by the Community with respect to the reorganization
and the winding-up of credit institutions and to deposit guarantee
schemes,[19] and with respect to the functioning of financial institutions generally. The special nature of financial institutions was
poignantly underlined by the Portuguese government in terms
summarized in para 34 of the judgment as follows:

The Portuguese Government also considers that, in the event of a financial
crisis, the situation of a bank differs fundamentally from that of a public
limited liability company in general in that, first, the liabilities of banks are
essentially represented by their depositors' funds and, secondly, the care
and management of public savings are an essential function of banks.
When a bank is in financial crisis, it is necessary both to protect the
interests of its depositors by taking all possible action to make certain that
their assets will be returned to them and to ensure that the depositors are
not seized by panic, which would spread to the public at large, precipitating
widespread withdrawals of funds throughout the banking system.[20]

---

law: see para. 67 et seq. of the judgment, where the Court—while stating it to be
unnecessary to rule on that question since it had not been submitted to the Court—
nevertheless gives some indications as to how it should be answered.

[16] Para. 19.   [17] Reference is made to Articles 20(1)(c), 23(2) and 24(2).
[18] Paras. 27–33.
[19] Reference is specifically made by the defendants to the amended proposal for a
Council Directive concerning the reorganization and the winding-up of credit institutions published in *OJ* 1988 C 36, 1 (which is not yet adopted at this moment). On the
subject of deposit guarantee schemes, Council Directive 94/19/EC has been adopted
in the meantime: see below n. 31.   [20] Para. 34.

That special nature of financial institutions is more specifically acknowledged by the Second Banking Directive, and more in particular Article 10(1) and (5) thereof, with respect to the own funds of such institutions.[21]

The ECJ rejects these arguments emphasizing mainly, as it had done in its earlier judgments, and particularly in *Karella*, that the Second Company Law Directive 'seeks to ensure a minimum level for protection for shareholders in all the Member States' (para. 38) whereby the Court attaches little importance to the fact (to the point of only mentioning it) that Article 54(3) (g) EC Treaty on which the directive is based, requires Member States to provide safeguards for the protection of not only members but also of others (by which creditors are meant in the first place). That is even more surprising in the special context of financial institutions where the creditors to be protected are most frequently small depositors which very often outnumber shareholders (even in the case of a bank whose shares are quoted at the Stock Exchange).[22] Moreover, as underlined by the Portuguese Government, there is always the risk, in the case of a bank in difficulties, of widespread withdrawals not only nationally but also internationally if depositors are seized by panic.[23] That risk is at the origin of the cogent need to protect the solidity of the banking system as a whole, which is certainly an imperative reason of general interest.[24] Since it is most unlikely in such situations to find the old shareholders ready

---

[21] Council Directive 89/646/EEC of 15 December 1989, on the coordination of laws, regulations and administrative provisions relating to the taking up and pursuit of the business of credit institutions and amending Directive 77/80/EEC, *OJ* 1989, 386, 1. See paras. 36–7 of the judgment.

[22] In its more recent judgment of 19 November 1996 in Case C-42/95 *Siemens* v. *Nold*, [1996] ECR I.6017, para. 13, the Court takes a more balanced view of the Second Company Law Directive's objectives by holding that 'the Second Directive is therefore intended to ensure minimum equivalent protection for *both shareholders and creditors* of public limited liability companies' (emphasis added). In para. 19 of that judgment, the Court considers 'ensuring more effective protection for shareholders' as 'one of the aims of the Second Directive'.

[23] Because of huge interbank deposits within the global banking system, such panic may affect the solidity of the banking system even worldwide when a large financial institution is involved (see below note 24). The risk of panic cannot be eliminated, but only temporarily prevented, by national guarantee schemes which will never be substantial enough to stem the tide (but see para. 53 of the judgment).

[24] Precisely the particular sensitivity and specificities of the banking system have led the Commission to a cautious and well-balanced application of the EC Treaty rules on State aids to the banking sector. Cf. the Commission's *XXVth Report on competition policy 1995* (Brussels-Luxembourg, 1996), 74, para. 197: 'This sector

to decide, and subscribe to, increases in capital, the banking supervisory authorities will need to attract new shareholders who have the expertise to help the bank out of its difficulties and who are ready to take the risk of important capital investments. In such a situation, compliance with the requirements of Article 25 (1) and 29 (1) and (3) of the Second Company Law Directive may prove to be counterproductive.

The Court also rejected the second line of reasoning put forward to limit the scope of application of the Second Company Law Directive with respect to capital increases for banks in difficulties, cutting short any discussion founded on arguments pointing to economic and financial realities.[25] That second line of reasoning is based on the fact that supervisory rules in the banking sector are provisions dictated by the public interest which constitute a closed and coherent system of provisions designed, first, to protect the financial structure and preserve public confidence in it, and, secondly, to protect depositors.[26] Measures facilitating increases in the bank's capital by new shareholders acting at the initiative (if not under pressure) of the public authorities and against the will of the old shareholders who do not wish to subscribe themselves by exercising their pre-emptive rights, are an essential part of such a closed system of (national and Community) provisions. The Court did not uphold that line of reasoning even although it has accepted in other judgments, and more in particular in its *Bachmann* judgment, that there may be exceptional circumstances

---

has particular characteristics that are chiefly social and statutory (protection of savers), macroeconomic and financial (necessary stability of the sector, smooth operation of the payments system), political and international (possible repercussions in the form of 'panic' in other establishments in the same country or other countries due to the considerable interdependence existing in this sector, especially in the event of a major institution failing).' See already, with regard to the Spanish authorities' rescue plan for the Spanish bank Banesto, the Commission's *XXIVth Report on competition policy 1994* (Brussels-Luxembourg, 1995), 188–9, para. 378. The Commission fully elaborated its subtle approach on State aids for credit institutions in difficulties in its decision 95/547/EC of 26 July 1995 giving conditional approval to the aid granted by France to the bank Crédit Lyonnais (*OJ* 1995 L 308, 92).

[25] See paras. 49–53. Also with respect to the question dealt with in paras. 57–9 as to whether the appointment of a temporary administrator should be regarded as a liquidation measure (of which the Court has said, of its own right, in *Karella* and in *Syndesmos Melon—supra*, n. 10 and 14—that they are not precluded by the Second Company Law Directive) the Court uses purely legal arguments. See also *infra*.

[26] Para.46.

under which the cohesion of such a closed system (in that case of tax rules) may justify the non-application of Community law prohibitions.[27]

2. THE SHORTCOMINGS OF HARMONIZATION

Harmonization of national laws is most certainly needed in fields of the law, such as in the field of company laws and banking laws, where the establishment and the functioning of the internal market, and the inherent freedoms, are hindered by differences in national legislation. However, since the harmonization process is, by necessity as we will see, of a limited and specific nature, it does have its shortcomings.[28] These are, on the one hand, that the separate directives are often not supported, not even when they relate to the same field of the law, by a coherent and comprehensive view at the level of the Community and, on the other hand that, although directives do achieve some harmonization between the national laws of the Member States, they are at the same time responsible for growing disparities within the legal system of each Member State, between national rules affected by Community law, and those relating to similar issues which are not affected by Community law.

2.1 The limited and piecemeal nature of the Legislative Harmonization Process

The Community legislature is not free in determining whether it wants to harmonize national rules (or policies). For it to do so, it

[27] Judgment of 28 January 1992, case C-204/90, *Bachmann* v. *Belgium*, [1992] ECR I-249. Also judgment of the same date in case C-300/90, *Commission* v. *Belgium*, [1992] ECR I-305. However, in later judgments, amongst which *Pafitis*, the Court has consistently denied reliance on that argumentation. See Case C-279/93 *Schumacker* [1995] ECR I-225, Case C-80/94 *Wielockx* [1995] ECR I-2493, Case C-484/93 *Svensson* [1995] ECR I-3955, Case C-107/94 *Asscher*, [1996] ECR I-3089. See J. Wouters, *Het Europese vestigingsrecht voor ondernemingen herbekeken*, Ph.D. thesis, University of Leuven, 1996, at 505–10. See also with regard to the restrictive application of the fiscal cohesion defense in the *Schumacker* and *Wielockx* cases, P. J. Wattel, 'The EC Court's attempts to reconcile the Treaty freedoms with international tax law', *CMLRev*, 1996, 223, at 238.

[28] See also P. C. Müller-Graff, 'Private Law Unification by means other than of Codification' in Hartkamp et al. (ed.), *Towards a European Civil Code*, 1994, at 19 ff.

must be able to rely on competences which have been conferred upon it (explicitly or implicitly), or objectives assigned to it (art. 3 b EC). With respect to the harmonization of national rules, there are in the first place specific competences, such as the ones referred to in, amongst others, Articles 54 and 57 EC relating to free movement of persons and services, or in Article 118a EC relating to improvements in the working environment.[29] Whereas the harmonization of company laws has taken place on the basis of Article 54 (3) (g)[30] the harmonization of the banking directives has been based on Article 57(2) EC, first and third sentences.[31] Besides these specific competences, a general competence to effect harmonization is provided for in Article 100 EC regarding national rules which directly affect the establishment or functioning of the common market, and in Article 100 a(1) EC concerning national rules which have as their object the establishment and functioning of the internal market. Since Article 100a constitutes a *lex specialis*, Article 100 applies in areas which Article 100 a(2) excludes explicitly from the scope of application of Article 100 a(1). Those are: fiscal provisions, provisions relating to the free movement of persons and provisions relating to the rights and

---

[29] That is the Article at issue in the recent (and by the UK government badly received) judgment of the Court of 12 November 1996 in Case C-84/94, *United Kingdom* v. *Council*, [1996] ECR I-5755, relating to Council Directive 93/104/EC concerning certain aspects of the organization of working time.

[30] First Council Directive 68/151/EEC (nullity grounds, etc.) of 9 March 1968, *OJ* 1968 L 65, 8; Second Council Directive 77/91/EEC (formation and capital) of 13 December 1976, *OJ* 1977 L 26, 1; Third Council Directive 78/855/EEC (mergers) of 9 October 1978, *OJ* 1978 L 295, 36; Fourth Council Directive 78/660/EEC (annual accounts) of 25 July 1978, *OJ* 1978, L 222, 11; Sixth Council Directive 82/891 EEC (division of companies) of 17 December 1982, *OJ* 1982 L 378, 47; Seventh Council Directive 83/349/EEC (consolidated accounts) of 13 June 1983, *OJ* 1983 L 193, 1; Eighth Council Directive 84/253/EEC (statutory auditors) of 10 April 1984, *OJ* 1984 L 126, 20; Eleventh Council Directive 89/666/EEC (disclosure requirements for branches) of 21 December 1989, *OJ* 1989 L 395, 36; Twelfth Council Directive 89/667/EEC (single member limited companies) of 21 December 1989, *OJ* 1989 L 395, 40.

[31] Thus, a.o., First Council Directive 77/780/EEC of 12 December 1977, *OJ* 1977 L 322, 30; Second Council Directive 89/646/EEC of 15 December 1989, *OJ* 1989 L 386, 1; Council Directive 89/299/EEC (own funds) of 17 April 1989, *OJ* 1989 L 124, 16; Council Directive 89/647/EEC (solvency ratio) of 18 December 1989, *OJ* 1989 L 386, 14; Council Directive 92/30/EEC (supervision on consolidated basis) of 6 April 1992, *OJ* 1992, L 110, 52; Council Directive 92/121/EEC (large exposures) of 21 December 1992, *OJ* 1992, L 29, 1; Council Directive 94/19/EC (deposit-guarantee schemes) of 30 May 1994, *OJ* 1994, L 135, 5. Compare with, e.g., Council Directive 91/308/EEC of 10 June 1991 on money laundering, *OJ* 1991, L 166/77 which is based on both Article 57(2) and Article 100a EC.

interests of employed persons. When no legal basis can be found in the provisions granting specific or general powers for harmonization to the Community, there is still the implementing legal ground of Article 235 EC allowing the Community to take the appropriate measures to attain, in the course of the operation of the common market, one of the objectives of the Community, if the EC Treaty has not provided the necessary powers therefor, and the possibility for Member States to conclude agreements within the framework of Article 220 EC, or outside that framework, but then without any obligation for the Member States to enter into negotiations.

Obviously, the necessity to find a legal basis for every harmonization effort on the part of the Community unavoidably leads to the promulgation of measures, very often directives,[32] which aim to attain very precise objectives.[33] The preciseness of the objective, and the lack of jurisdiction of the Community in related areas falling outside that objective, lead necessarily to a lack of coherence both at Community and at national level. At the level of the Community, because the limited jurisdiction makes it impossible for the Community Institutions to legislate for a whole sector (for example to lay down rules governing contractual or tort liability in general). At the national level because Community measures being of a limited nature (for example the directives on unfair terms in consumer contracts[34] or concerning liability for defective products[35]) cut through, and therefore de-harmonize, more comprehensive national laws (in the examples given, the laws on unfair contract terms, or the laws on liability for products, in general). The lack of coherence at the level of the Community is further enhanced by the existence of substantial differences in procedures of decision-taking.[36] Those differences have for effect

[32] In some cases the Treaty allows the Community Institutions to use all kinds of measures which the Treaty provides, in other cases only directives may be used as an instrument.

[33] It also leads to a considerable amount of litigation before the Court, between Member States and Community Institutions, or between Community Institutions, to determine whether a specific Community measure has been taken on the correct legal basis, and therefore according to the correct procedure of decision-taking. Thus e.g. the Court's judgment referred to in n. 28 between the UK and the Council.

[34] Council Directive 93/13/EEC of 5 April 1993, *OJ* 1993, L 95, 29.

[35] Council Directive 85/374 EEC of 25 July 1985, *OJ* 1985, L 210, 29.

[36] For a general overview, see the description of the Community legislative process, and the six basic types of procedure, in P. Craig and G. de Burca, *EC law, Text, cases and materials*, (1995), at 119 et seq. and 120 et seq.

that related matters (for example harmonizing working environment conditions as opposed to social *policy* matters[37]) are to be
dealt with in separate Community measures and that different
institutions, and advisory committees, intervene in the legislative
process, each with its own preferences and sensitivities, which in
turn account for differences in approach or emphasis.[38] They also
account for different degrees of flexibility to amend Community
rules once they have been adopted, in order, for example, to make
them more consistent amongst each other. Further inconsistencies
at Community level are due to the peculiar traditions and mental-
ities of Directorate-Generals which do not always agree with
each other, even not on basic issues and, perhaps even more so, to
the point in time on which they were enacted (see hereafter, under
2.2).

2.2. The inconsistencies to which the harmonization process gives rise in the field of company and banking directives

It is generally recognized that the harmonization of national company laws, which is required by Article 54(3) (g) EC, is not based
on a coherent vision of European company law. The Company
directives, of which nine have been adopted so far, relate to a
variety of subjects, such as nullities, representation, acting *ultra
vires*, capital, public issues, financial accounts, mergers and division of companies. They have not been the object of a systematic
reflection on how to reform company law in general but are rather
the exponent of an *ad hoc* approach.[39] One of the reasons for this

[37] See again the Court's recent judgment in *UK* v. *Council*, cited in n. 29, at para.
26 et seq.

[38] In the fields of company and banking law where directives are based, respectively, on Article 54(2) and (3)(g), and on Article 57, differences are not that important because of the application in both instances of the procedure referred to in Article
189 b. Some differences exist, however. On the one hand Article 54(2) prescribes the
consultation of the Economic and Social Committee whereas Article 57 does not
provide this and, on the other hand, Article 57(2), second sentence provides in a
special procedure derogating from the Article 189 b procedure, in the event of the
amendment in at least one Member State of 'principles laid down by law governing
the professions with respect to training and conditions of access for natural persons'
(a situation which will normally not arise in the case of banks).

[39] One has to admit that in the sixties and early seventies the Commission followed
a more or less systematic approach with regard to company law harmonization,
which can be found in the *Berkhouwer report* of 1966 (*Parlement européen. Documents delséance*, 1966–67, 9 May 1966, doc. 53) and in the *Colonna memorandum* of
1970 (*Bull. EC*, Supp. 4/70). The 'grand design' of EC company law has, however,

is, as explained above, because the Company directives have for their purpose to facilitate the freedom of establishment and of rendering services for companies engaged in interstate commerce within the common market—which is why they are limited to the types of companies most active on a own-border basis, namely, limited liability companies (and in some cases, like the Second Directive, only public limited liability companies—in view whereof safeguards 'for the protection of the interests of members and others' have to be made equivalent. Matters which cannot be related to that legal purpose fall outside the parameter of harmonization (of at least Article 54 (3) (g)) even although they may be closely related to matters which come within that parameter. Another reason is that some draft directives have so far not been adopted for lack of agreement between the Member States, although they constitute an important element of the harmonization process.[40]

On the other hand the harmonization of national banking laws— that is the other subject dealt with in *Pafitis*—which was carried out on the basis of Article 57 EC, has been inspired by a more systematic view, as reflected in the Second Banking Directive. This Directive and the amendments which it made to the First Banking Directive, are based on three principles: minimal harmonization of national rules concerning access to, and exercise of, banking activities (for example with respect to the granting of a compulsory authorization), mutual recognition in principle of national legal rules, and the principle of home country control.[41] Here also the harmonization is aimed, according to Article 57 (1) and (2) EC, at making 'it easier for persons to take up and pursue activities as self-employed persons' (including companies or firms in the sense of Article 58) who wish to use their freedom of establishment or to render services within the common market. The approach of the harmonization in the banking directives is,

vanished with the years and has more and more become, as C. W. A. Timmermans has put it pointedly, a process of 'muddling through' in C. W. A. Timmermans, 'Methods and Tools for Integration', in *European Business Law. Legal and Economic Analyses on Integration and Harmonization*, R. Buxbaum, G. Hertig, A. Hirsh and K. J. Hopt (eds.) (Berlin–New York, De Gruyter, 1991), 129. Cf. J. Wouters, *op. cit.* n. 27, at 235–40.

[40] That is the case of the proposed Fifth Council Directive (structure of public limited companies and powers and obligations of their organs) *OJ* 1983 C 240, 2, amendments in *OJ* 1991, C 7, 4 and C 321, 9.

[41] See B. Sousi-Roubi, *Droit bancaire européen*, 1995, 97 et seq.

however, far different from the harmonization attained by the company law directives, because their aim is not so much to directly protect the creditors of the bank individually (unlike in the case of company directives where the protection of individual shareholders and creditors is looked after) but to provide for the indirect protection of mainly creditors by setting up a satisfactory supervisory system, and enacting rules for safeguarding the solidity and capital adequacy of credit institutions.

Because of the factors described above, the harmonization measures undertaken by the Community are, already at the level of the Community, far from coherent. Moreover, they do not achieve unification amongst the national laws, especially not when they are contained in directives, which leave some rule-making (and decisional) powers to the national legislators and regulators.[42] How much depends, in the first place, on whether the directive (if that is the instrument used) intends to regulate the (limited) subject matter in an exhaustive way, that is without allowing the Member States to go beyond the measures contained in the directive. It depends in the second place on whether and to what extent the directive leaves, within its own regulatory framework, more or less discretion to the Member States by providing a larger or smaller number of exceptions or derogations, or by using wide concepts such as the notion of general good in the Second Banking Directive which may cover a variety of national measures pursuing the protection of users of financial services, such as depositors, investors, insured persons, etc.[43] It depends, in the third place, on whether the directives, such as many Company law directives, were taken when the Commission was still relying on a concept of detailed harmonization[44] or, whether they were

[42] In the exercise of their rule-making (and decisional) powers, as left to them by a Community measure, national authorities, including national legislators, are of course bound to respect all rules of primary or secondary Community law. National measures constituting an infringement of (directly effective) Community law must therefore be set aside by national courts and may, eventually, when they intend to give rights to individuals, give rise to compensation of injury which the infringement has caused.

[43] See Draft Commission Communication on Freedom to Provide Services and the Interest of the General Good in the Second Banking Directive, *OJ* 1995 C 291, 7.

[44] Times have meanwhile also changed for company law harmonization: see the Commission's redrafted proposal for a Thirteenth European Parliament and Council Directive on company law concerning takeover bids (*OJ* 1996 C 162, 5), in which the Commission claims to provide a demonstration of its pragmatic approach to ensuring respect for subsidiarity (Commission's press-release IP/96/120 of 7 February 1996, 'Streamlined Proposal for Takeovers Directive').

taken, as in the case of most of the Banking Directives, when the Council and the Commission had already expressed their preference for the concept of mutual recognition.[45]

The consequence of all this is a substantial amount of incoherencies and inconsistencies (of which the *Pafitis* judgment is no more than an illustration). Those are: (i) inconsistencies between Community rules and policies in fields such as company and banking laws, which, although different, may be closely related, that is, where the former are applied to banks having taken the form of a public limited liability company. The *Pafitis* judgment shows how the absence of a coherent approach may create significant problems of interpretation where, as in the case of a bank in difficulties, important conflicts of interest between shareholders and creditors are involved; (ii) inconsistencies at national level because of the impossibility for national legislators and regulators — whose legislative powers may be considerably reduced in fields covered by Community law — to develop, or maintain, a coherent and global approach of their own accord. Such impossibility arises because of the fact that, for matters which do not fall under a specific measure of Community law, and for persons not affected thereby (thus in the case of *Pafitis*, banks which have not taken the form of a public limited liability company), national authorities retain full powers whereas for similar matters which come within the Community measure, and for persons affected thereby, the national authorities are left with limited powers; and (iii) incoherences due to the fact that national administrations, to which the application and enforcement of existing legislation is entrusted, are not always succesful in managing a dual system of rules in a sufficiently harmonious and efficient manner.

The latter two incoherences can only be eliminated if and when the national legislators decide to harmonize national rules affected by Community legislation and those not affected by it, that is if they decide, by virtue of a principle of efficient or good governance inherent in their national law (and thus not pursuant

---

[45] In the banking field, the idea of mutual recognition was already spelled out, at least as regards branches, in the tenth recital of the preamble of the First Banking Directive, *supra* n. 31. It was, together with the principles of home country control and minimum harmonization, strongly promoted by the Commission in its White Paper: Commission, *Completing the Internal Market. White Paper from the Commission to the European Council* (Milan, 28–29 June 1985), COM (85) 310, paras. 102–4.

to a principle of Community law), to adopt the solutions contained in Community rules also for purely national issues ('spill-over' effect of Community law), thus for example in the area of competition rules.[46]

3. HOW TO COPE WITH THESE SHORTCOMINGS?

The foregoing may suffice to demonstrate how the harmonization process and the division of work which it entails between, on the one hand, Community legislators and regulators and, on the other hand, national legislators and regulators, unavoidably account for incoherences and inconsistencies at the Community as well as the national level. Incoherences and inconsistencies which are far greater than the imperfections which are 'normally' inherent in the legislative process in the national legal orders. Obviously, under such circumstances the burden of preserving efficiency falling on the other legal actors—who are requested, and sometimes forced, to remedy the incapacity of the legislators and regulators—will also be heavier. Those other actors are: judges, practitioners and academics.

3.1. The issue of 'Judicial Activism'

In a study published in August 1995[47] Sir Patrick Neill QC, Warden of All Souls College, Oxford examined various leading ECJ judgments such as those rendered in *Van Gend en Loos, Costa* v. *ENEL, Van Duyn, Francovich, Defrenne II, 'Les Verts', Chernobyl, Sevince, Zwartveld, Foto-Frost, Marleasing*. After a thorough examination of these and other cases, he came to the conclusion that '(T)he cases discussed above provide many examples of judicial activism. The methods of interpretation adopted by the ECJ appear to have liberated the Court from the customarily accepted discipline of endeavouring by textual analysis to

[46] See under Belgian law where the national competition rules have incorporated the basic provisions for Community law. See also, on the new draft of Dutch competition law, K. J. M. Mortelmans, 'De aansluiting van de ontwerp-mededingingswet bij het EG-mededingingsrecht: symbiose en osmose' in Eylander, et al. (ed.), *Markt en Wet*, 1996.

[47] 'The European Court of Justice. A case study in Judicial Activism' in House of Lords Select Committee on the European Communities, *1996 Intergovernmental Conference*, Minutes of Evidence, House of Lords Session 1994–1995, 18th Report, 1995.

ascertain the meaning of the language of the relevant provision . . .' (at 47). Most of the judgments examined by Sir Patrick refer to the issue of legal protection of rights which individuals, or institutions, derive from Community law, and to the remedies which Community law and domestic laws should, according to the ECJ, make available for such individuals or institutions. It is undoubtedly true that the Court has been very imaginative in the field of legal protection through judicial remedies. It has done so by interpreting provisions in the Community Treaties broadly and boldly, and by looking for general principles—of which the funda-mental rights embodied in the European Convention on Human Rights are an integral part.

It may also be true that the Court has gone very far in certain cases, too far according to some. However, one should keep in mind that the ECJ's so-called 'activism' relates to matters which belong to the hard core of any judicial activity, that is when it matters to protect the rights of individuals, and to grant them legal remedies, against infringements of 'the law' (Article 164 EC) by Community and national authorities alike. It would seem that, from a viewpoint of comparative law, there are examples of instances to be found in any national legal system, and particularly in the case-law of the national supreme courts, where the courts have ensured individuals a maximum of judicial protection when their rights were infringed. The post-*Factortame* decision of the House of Lords in *M.* v. *Home Office* offers a most interesting example. In that case the rule of immunity of the Crown was set aside also in purely national law matters, as Lord Woolf observed, that it would be 'an unhappy situation' if the rights of individuals risk being less protected in pure national law than in areas affected by Community law.[48] The House of Lords came to that conclusion by re-interpreting section 31 of the Supreme Court Act 1981.[49] The creative way in which the ECJ interprets Community law when it comes to ensure the requirement of efficient legal protec-tion, is in stark contrast with the ECJ's overcautious attitude

---

[48] [1993] 3 WLR 433, [1993] 3 All ER 537. See also the HL's earlier decision in *Woolwich Building Society* v. *Inland Revenue Commissioners* where Lord Goff re-marked in respect of the remedy of restitution that it would be strange if the right of the citizen to recover overpaid charges were to be more restricted under domestic law than it is under Community law.

[49] Re-interpreting national law in light of a new development in Community law is what the ECJ also did in *Marleasing*, a judgment which is severely criticized by Sir Patrick in his paper cited in n. 47.

where it has to review the legality of acts of the Council or of the Commission taken in the exercise of powers of wide discretion (for example in the field of commercial policy towards non-associated, third countries), *or* with the Court's cautious attitude when it has to interpret specific provisions in directives, as was the case in *Pafitis* or, for that matter, in *Marleasing* in so far as that judgment related to the interpretation of Article 11 of the First Company Law Directive. In cases of interpretation of directive provisions—with the exception of directive provisions which are the prolongation of basic provisions of the Treaty (such as the directives on equal treatment of men and women)—the Court chooses indeed to apply very orthodox interpretation methods.[50] The same holds true when the Court has to review the legal basis for acts of the Council (or of the Commission) and to interpret, in view thereof, Treaty provisions in addition to secondary law provisions.[51]

3.2. The Court's 'non-teleological' interpretation in *Pafitis*

As indicated above, *Pafitis* concerned the interpretation of Articles 25 and 29 of the Second Company Law Directive.[52] These questions were submitted to the ECJ in a national litigation initiated by shareholders who wanted their pre-emptive rights to be affirmed with respect to capital increases which had been decided by the Greek banking supervisory authorities to save a bank in difficulty and thus to protect the bank's creditors. As

[50] See further my article 'The ECJ case-law as a means of unification of private law?', to be published in the second edition of *Towards a European Civil Code*. For an example of a broad interpretation of a directive provision implementing a basic provision of the Treaty, see Case C-13/94, P.V.S and Cornwall County Council, [1996] ECR I.2143.

[51] That was also the case in the ECJ's judgment in *UK* v. *Council* cited in n. 29 where the Court, to use the words which Bingham J. pronounced on another occasion—see following note—was 'laboriously extracting the meaning from words used' in the EC Treaty and the Directive involved.

[52] Sir Patrick distinguishes in the concluding part of his presentation the interpretative methods of the ECJ with those of English courts, referring to Lord Diplock who said that the ECJ applies 'teleological rather than historical methods... sometimes indeed... to the exclusion of the latter' and to Bingham J. (as he then was) who said that '(T)he interpretation of Community instruments involves very often not the process familiar to common lawyers of laboriously extracting the meaning from words used but the more creative process of supplying flesh to a spare and loosely constructed skeleton'.

already recalled, the first question submitted to the Court was to know whether a bank constituted in the form of a public limited liability company falls within the scope of the directive, to which it answered that 'it is clear from the title and Article 1 of the Second Directive that . . . (T)he criterion adopted by the Community legislature to define the scope of the (directive) is . . . that of the legal form of the company, irrespective of its business'[53] The question may be asked whether one could imagine a more orthodox method of interpretation.

Also the second question which was to know whether measures for the re-organization of banks taking the form of an increase in capital had to be decided upon by the general meeting, as prescribed by Article 25 (1) of the Directive, and whether existing shareholders must be allowed to exercise their pre-emptive right, as required by Article 29(1), was answered by the ECJ on the basis of a very orthodox legal reasoning. The Court gave an affirmative answer by referring to the wording of Article 54(3) (g) of the EC Treaty, to precedents in its own case-law—in which it had confirmed the strict application of that Article aiming at the protection of the shareholders even in the case of companies of particular importance to the national economy when they are in financial difficulties—and to the wording of Article 25 which does not make an exception for credit institutions.

The Court could have followed a different path, for example, by emphasizing that Article 54 (3) (g) EC asks not only for the protection of shareholders but also for the protection of creditors of the company, and by interpreting the wording of Articles 25 and 29 of the Directive so as to restrict the shareholders' rights provided therein for the sake of the creditors. It could have done so by bringing the decision taken by the Greek Central Bank, and the temporary administrator appointed by it, under the exception which the Court, in its earlier case-law, had read in the directive, namely that it does not preclude 'liquidation measures placing the company under compulsory administration with a view to safeguarding the rights of creditors' as opposed to 'ordinary reorganisation measures . . . taken in order to ensure the survival of the company . . .'.[54] Emphasizing the special circumstances of the

---

[53] Paras. 18–19.
[54] Para. 57 of the *Pafitis* judgment referring to the *Karella* and *Syndesmos Melon* judgments cited in n. 13.

insolvency of a bank and the adverse consequences thereof (the assessment of which the Court could have left to the national judge) the Court might have re-interpreted that exception to encompass measures, such as those decided by the Bank of Greece, crucial to the protection of public savings and to the solidity of the financial system as a whole. The Court choose, instead, to apply strictly legal arguments assimilating the appointment of a temporary administrator—even although all powers of the organs of the company were transferred to him—with an ordinary reorganisation measure[55] for a normal company, that is a company not exposed to the risk of panic and the ensuing withdrawal of deposits.

I do not wish to say, or even to suggest, that the Court should have followed the latter line of reasoning, but only point out that the Court could have done so, if it had wanted to apply a 'teleological', rather than an 'analytical', method of interpretation.

3.3. Practitioners: learning to cope with differences. Academics: bringing the common legal heritage to the fore

Lack of consistency between legislative measures at Community level and, as a result of a limited harmonization of the laws of the Member States, growing disparities within the national legal systems between areas of national law which are affected by Community law and areas of national law dealing with similar issues which are not so affected: those are the major insufficiencies which under normal (that is ideal but rarely prevailing) circumstances must be solved, if not avoided, by legislators and regulators, and of which one cannot expect that they will be solved by (Community or national) judges. The question remains whether academics and practitioners (apart from judges) can do something to make the harmonization process work more smoothly.

It was a wise decision on the part of the Community taken in the mid-eighties (that is long before the subsidiarity principle became popular) to choose that harmonization of national laws should be kept to a minimum and to emphasize, instead, the principle of mutual recognition of national laws.[56] As a matter of fact such an approach is fully in line with the nature of directives through which

---

[55] Para. 58 of *Pafitis*.   [56] Cf. supra, n. 45.

the harmonization is frequently carried out, which 'shall be binding, as to the result to be achieved, upon each Member State to
which (they are) addressed, but shall leave to the national authorities the choice of forms and methods' (Article. 189, para. 3 EC).
That formulation gives expression, *avant la lettre* so to speak, to
the principle of subsidiarity.[57] However, the principles of minimal
harmonization and mutual recognition of national differences will
only work properly when practitioners of all kinds (solicitors,
barristers, tax and social security advisors, banks and financial
service consultants, patent agents, auditors, accountants, etc.) are
educated to cope with differences. The reason why undertakings
from the US were the first in the early sixties to take advantage of
the common market is because their law firms, and other service
suppliers, were used to work with differences.

Coping with differences constitutes, to a certain extent, a valid
alternative for a time-and-energy consuming harmonization process. That is why the objective of making the (consultancy) service
industry truly competitive across national frontiers must be a top
priority for the Community. That is also why it was right for the
ECJ to read in Article 59 EC a broad prohibition on restrictions of
the freedom to provide services within the Community.[58]

Also academics have a role to play in making the harmonization
process work. Their role is, however, of a different sort. It consists
in uncovering and strengthening the characteristics which the
legal systems of the Member States have in common. Or to say it
in the words of Article 128 (1) EC on cultural diversity (with which
the legal diversity is closely related) 'while respecting . . . national
and regional diversity . . . the common cultural heritage (should be
brought) to the fore'. Bringing the common legal heritage to the
fore means in the first place that general principles are to be found
which, as Article 215 (2) EC states with respect to tort liability of

[57] The practice of making very detailed and precise directives, which was adopted
by the Community legislator at an early stage, is in fact contrary to Art. 189, para. 3,
EC. One might even think that the fact that the ECJ could grant direct effect to
directive provisions because they are sufficiently precise and unconditional, amounts
almost to a *contradictio in terminis* when account is taken of the definition of a
directive in Art. 189, para. 3.

[58] As in *Säger* with respect to an English patent agent wanting to do business in
Germany: Case C-76/90, *Säger* v. *Dennemeyer* [1991] ECR I-4229. See further W.
van Gerven and J. Wouters, 'Free Movement of financial services and the European
Contracts Convention' in M. Andenas and S. Kenyon-Slate (eds.) in *EC Financial
Market Regulation and Community Law and Company Law* (1993), at 48 et seq.

Community Institutions, are 'common to the laws of the Member States'. Only by developing a core of common rules, and solutions, will it be possible to strengthen the 'centripetal' forces that keep the legal orders of the Community and of the Member States together in spite of the growing inconsistencies, disparities and distortions to which the co-existence of various legal orders and the efforts of harmonization may lead.[59]

Academics should in the second place assist the courts, and more in particular the Community courts, in finding solutions which are acceptable to the legal orders of the Member States for the problems which those courts are confronted with. In that respect, the *Pafitis* judgment may, once more, serve as an example. The incorrect application by the Greek authorities, in that case the Greek Central Bank, of Articles 25 and 29(1) of the Second Company Law Directive, as ascertained in the Court's judgment, may give rise to claims for reparation on the part of individuals under the ECJ's case law (which is now well established after *Brasserie, British Telecom* and *Dillenkofer*[60]) regarding the extra-contractual liability of Member States for breaches of Community law. In the case of a directive which is not, or wrongly, implemented in a way amounting to a sufficiently serious breach,[61] such liability will, however, only arise if the infringed directive provision intended to give a right to the plaintiff. As yet, it is unclear what the expression 'granting a right' exactly means. In the cases which came before the ECJ and in which the Court accepted, or seemed ready to accept, that the infringed directive provision intended to grant a right, *specific* rights (in the

---

[59] I am convinced that such common legal principles may be found in the statute and case law of the national legal systems. That is why I am engaged, with the help of many, in a project *Casebooks for a common law of Europe*, on which I have reported in a short article published in 4 *Eur. Rev. Priv. Law* (1996), at 67 et seq.

[60] Joined cases C-46/93 and C-48/93 *Brasserie and Factortame* [1996] ECR I-1029; Case C-392/93 *British Telecommunications* [1996] ECR I-1631; Joined cases C-178/94, C-179/94, C-188/94, C-189/94 and C-190/94 *Dillenkofer* [1996] ECR I-4845. See also my article 'Bridging the unbridgeable: Community and national tort laws after Francovich and Brasserie' in *ICLQ*, 1996, at 507 et seq.

[61] The ECJ does accept, as is shown by the BT judgment cited above, that no such breach is committed when the Member State involved has acted in good faith. See also Joined cases C-283/94, C-291/94 and C-292/94 *Denkavit* [1996] ECR I-4845. It also appears from both judgments that the Court will first address the question of the existence of a 'sufficiently serious breach' before examining whether the directive provision concerned grants a right to individuals.

'Hohfeldian' sense of the word[62]) were in issue. And also in *Pafitis* the right of shareholders under Article 29 (1) of the Second Company Law Directive to subscribe to new shares on a pre-emptive basis, once an increase in capital has been decided, seems to be such a specific right. That, however, cannot necessarily be said of the 'right' that shareholders may derive from Article 25 (1) according to which any increase in capital must be decided upon by a general meeting.[63]

It is not the place here to pursue a discussion on the meaning of the concept of right, a discussion which has deep roots in both the Germanic and the Romanistic legal doctrine but which, as Hohfeld's juristic conceptions theory shows, is also not entirely absent from Anglo-American legal thinking.[64] The discussion may demonstrate that the ECJ in this instance, as in many others, will need the help of legal writers from different legal systems to clarify concepts which are inherent in its case-law.

[62] For a helpful general discussion (with references to Hohfeld's theory on 133, n. 87, and 134, n. 91), see S. Prechal, *Directives in European Community Law*, (1995) at 122 et seq. Hohfeld's analysis was first published in the *Yale Law Journal* in 1917. It has been frequently commented on, approved of or criticized. See, e.g. for a recent discussion, the articles of J. de Sousa e Brito, of M. Van Hoecke and of M. Henket in *IX International Journal for the Semiotics of Law* [1996] at 173, 185 and 202 respectively.

[63] The latter 'right' might be considered to be only the reflex of a general obligation imposed on a third party, not unlike 'rights' which individuals derive in general from provisions in environmental directives imposing the obligation on Member States to preserve e.g. the purity of ground water. See further J. G. J. Lefevere, 'State Liability for Breaches of Community Law', *European Environmental Law Review* (1996) at 237 et seq.

[64] See also G. Samuel, *Sourcebook on Obligations and Legal Remedies* [1995] at 70 et seq.

3

Comparative Law: the Challenge to the Judges

by The Rt. Hon. The Lord Goff of Chieveley

I wish to begin by saying that I believe the case for comparative law to be unanswerable. It is unthinkable that we should all continue to live under our separate legal systems, without paying any attention to the systems of law which apply in other countries, or to the different ways in which we all run our legal systems. The problem which faces us is, I believe, not whether we should strive to learn from others, but how we should set about it.

Of course, there is now a ferment at work in our universities, where professors of comparative law, and indeed many others, are dedicated to learning about other systems of law, often in relation to the area in which they specialise. There are great institutions already established, and other new ones springing into existence—like this Centre at Oxford, which is our host at this conference—which are devoted, in whole or in part, to the study and teaching of Comparative Law.

But this is only part of the picture. There remains the question; what about our judges? Is it possible for them to introduce an element of comparative law into their judicial work? It is that question which I would like briefly to consider with you this morning.

I myself have attempted to exploit comparative law in my work as a judge. But I have to admit that this has opened my eyes to the very considerable difficulties involved in this exercise. Of course, we in England are fortunate to have the benefit of assistance from distinguished judges in other common law jurisdictions—such as Canada, Australia and New Zealand. But we are not so well-placed as the common law judges in Canada, who have a civil law system within their own country, so that they are able to share their experiences with the judges of that system. Still less are we like the judges of like the judges of South Africa, with their mixed inheritance of Roman Dutch law and common law, or like the judges of Israel which is, as we all know, a hotbed of comparative law. We are simply common lawyers, with our own extraordinary history and our own extraordinary traditions. How, then, have I set about trying to take advantage of comparative law in my work?

Basil Markesinis is convinced that I first attempted to do so in a case called *The Aliakmon*,[1] years ago when I was still in the Court of Appeal, in which I attempted to formulate a principle of transferred loss. Basil is convinced that I copied this idea from German law. But he is wrong. I first discovered the German doctrine of *Drittschadenliquidation*, which is available in cases of transferred loss (*Schadensverlagerung*), a year or two later when I was browsing through a book of essays in memory of Professor Harry Lawson.[2] There I stumbled on an essay by Professor Werner Lorenz, then unknown to me but now an honoured friend, which explained the whole German doctrine to me and even, to my astonishment, referred to *The Aliakmon*. He is one of the few people I know of who thinks that I was right in that case.

My next experience occurred when Basil invited me to take the Chair at a Seminar at Queen Mary College, when papers were going to be given by two distinguished German Professors — Werner Lorenz and Christian von Bar. That was the beginning of two very important, indeed greatly treasured, friendships for me. I have forgotten precisely what they were talking about; I think that Werner's subject was Privity of Contract, whereas Christian's was more devoted to the borderland between Contract and Tort. At the end of that evening, Christian made a very rash offer to me — that if I wanted any help on German law, I could get in touch with him. This most unwise invitation has since resulted in a stream of fax messages between Chieveley and Osnabrück.

This brings me to the case in which I drew upon my knowledge of German law. This was *White* v. *Jones*,[3] a case known to some of you which raised the problem, surely known to you all, whether a disappointed legatee can recover damages from the testator's solicitor who has made a mess of the will. Those who have grappled with this problem must all have learned that it raises an acute

---

[1] *Leigh & Sillivan* v. *Aliakmon Shipping Co.* [1985] Q.B. 350.
[2] *Essays in Memory of F. H. Lawson* (Butterworth, London, 1986).
[3] *White* v. *Jones* [1995] 2 A.C. 207.

problem of analysis—how to achieve the just result consistently with legal principle. In the end,I succeeded in basing a right of recovery upon an extension of the principle in a famous English case called *Hedley Byrne*,[4] which established a form of extra-contractual liability based upon the idea of assumption of responsibility. But, in working towards that conclusion, I drew heavily upon the German principle of *Vertrag mit Schutzwirkung für Dritte* (contract with protective effects for third parties), which is the device used in German law to provide a remedy for the disappointed legatee in cases of this kind. This I had learned about from the paper which Werner Lorenz gave at Queen Mary College, and also from an excellent article published by Professor Hein Kötz in a volume of *Tel Aviv University Studies in Law*.[5] In addition I derived useful assistance from Basil's excellent book on the *German Law of Torts*, including one or two of the Judgments of the German Supreme Court which appear in the second part of the book translated into English.

So here it really happened. Comparative law actually played a useful part in a judgment of a member of the House of Lords. But, I ask myself, will it ever happen again? I must first record that, after the case was reported, a young English Queen's Counsel came up to me in one of the Inns of Court, and said: 'Hullo, Lord Goff; I see that in future we have got to provide you with all the relevant German authorities as well as all the relevant English authorities.' I have to confess that I did not know how to respond to this. It is generally accepted among the judges in this country that we do not rely on authorities which have not been cited in the course of argument, without giving counsel an opportunity to comment on them. How, then, can I rely on German authorities or writings in my judgments in future? In truth, *White* v. *Jones* was a unique case. First, all the German material on which I relied was published in the English language so that, despite my linguistic incompetence, so widely shared in this country, I was able to read it. Second, the lawyers acting for the disappointed legatees instructed Basil as one of their Counsel, so that they were able to place all this material before the Appellate Committee. It so happened that I knew it already; but this at least meant that counsel on the other side had an opportunity to comment on it.

[4] *Hedley Byrne & Co.* v. *Heller & Partners Ltd.* [1964] A.C. 465.
[5] *Tel Aviv Univ. Studies in Law* (1990) vol. 10, pp. 195, 209..

I have to admit that I have great difficulty in imagining when, in a future case of importance, a point will arise for decision on which authority from another legal system will be so directly relevant, and will be so readily available to us in the English language.

Of course, I will continue to trouble Christian with requests about the relevant German law on this and that subject. But often, I have to admit, the answers I receive, though always enlightening, are more relevant to something other than the judgment I am struggling with. For example, the answer to a question about the circumstances in which German law recognises liability in damages in respect of the negligent exercise, or failure to exercise, a power—a topic known to all the common lawyers here in relation to a famous English case called *Anns*[6]—revealed to me only how much our planning laws could be improved by adopting the structured approach to matters of this kind adopted in Germany.

Indeed, I am beginning to wonder whether it might be better if our judges concentrated more on comparative legal procedure than on comparative substantive law. This is already happening indirectly in this country. There is no doubt that, in international commercial arbitration, a system of procedure acceptable both to common lawyers and civil lawyers is developing which draws heavily on the civil law approach—with the judge or arbitrator playing a more dominant role than has been accepted in the past in this country, though the advocates have come to play a more important role than is usual in some civil law jurisdictions. This approach has infected the procedure adopted in our Commercial Court, which about five years ago adopted procedural reforms of this kind which have led to a reduction of about 50 per cent of the time involved in hearing cases. Similar reforms have been adopted in our Official Referees Court, which deals with disputes in the construction industry. These reforms, in their turn, have provided the model for Lord Woolf's reforms which are now being adopted throughout our court system. Of course, since our system of civil procedure, and indeed our rules of evidence, are the fruits of a jury system which, in civil cases, no longer exists, it was high time that we considered fundamental reforms of this kind.

Whether there has been or will be a similar cross-fertilisation,

---

[6] *Anns v. Merton London Borough Council* [1978] A.C. 728.

and reception of common law ideas, in civil law countries, I do not know, though I am hoping to find out more about this during this Conference. If this is happening, then I suspect that the most valuable example that we can offer to them will lie in an enhancement of the role of the advocate in civil proceedings, and indeed in the status of the advocate and the development of the close bond of sympathy and trust which exists between the judges and advocates in this country. But perhaps for this purpose we shall have to export to them the idea of the Inns of Court, as we are now doing to the United States of America, where nearly three hundred Inns of Court have been established in cities throughout the country in the course of the past ten years or so.

There are so many topics for us to discuss—our different methods of teaching; our different intellectual traditions; our different attitudes to scholarship, and to our practical work; our different systems of judicial appointment; our different attitudes to codification, to judicial precedent, to the form and content of judgments, and so on. There is much to be said in favour of all our systems; and as lawyers of skill and integrity, each reared within the confines of a legal system which has its own integrity and which we understand, we have an enormous amount in common. Let us therefore make the most of this Conference by seeking to learn as much as possible from each other.

4

Group Libel, Hate Speech, and other Fighting Words: Civility and the Uses of Law

by Roger Errera

To Antoine.

Freedom of expression is a paramount constitutional right in our societies. Nowhere, however, is it an absolute one. Among its limitations we find group-libel or hate-speech laws. By their very nature, contents, and scope such laws are bound to generate among legislators, governments, and judges soul-searching and much debate. The aim of this paper is to explore some of their legal and social dimensions. In this paper, I shall focus mainly on three areas: (I) the general context; (II) the question why we need group-libel and hate-speech laws and (III) Racial incitement and the uses of the law.

I THE CONTEXT

For a long time, the main legal limitations to freedom of expression related either to the rights of the individual (for example, libel), or to the protection of morality (for example, obscenity or pornography laws), or to the preservation of public order and the vital interests of the State (for example, incitement to serious crimes or protection of defense secrets).

In the course of the twentieth century, a series of new political and social factors has led to the appearance of a new form of political discourse.

A) The new social and political factors

1) The rise of political anti-semitism;
2) The expression of anti-foreign, overtly xenophobic opinions and attitudes; and
3) Writings and public expressions directed against specific minorities.

B) Hate-speech and group libel as a new form of political discourse

The content is clear enough: to denigrate certain groups, or persons belonging to them; to make these groups responsible for all kinds of social problems, evils, and dangers such as unemployment, insecurity, excessive public spending, corruption of morals, decline of the national culture, threats to national identity. After the accusation comes the 'remedy': *exclusion*, that is, the denial of certain basic rights or outright discrimination in education, housing, social services, access to certain professions, employment and the like.

II WHY WE NEED GROUP-LIBEL AND HATE-SPEECH LAWS

A) The case against and for them

Against specific legislation there exist two kinds of arguments.

i) Consequential, or utilitarian arguments:

Group-libel and hate-speech, bad as they are, express deep social and psychological currents that cannot be silenced by legislation. New legislation will give to the proponents of such doctrines the very publicity they are looking for. Such laws are a danger for freedom of expression. They may lend themselves to abuse or have a 'chilling effect' on all forms of expression. Where will the line be drawn? Such laws thus amount to a new form of censorship. Such laws might in fact damage the situation and status of the very groups we wish to protect. The best way to fight hate-speech and group-libel is a public and open discussion in what is sometimes called the 'market place of ideas'.[1]

---

[1] On the 'market place of ideas' see J. R. Pole's pungent remarks in 'A bad case of agoraphobia. Is there a marketplace of ideas?', *Times Literary Supplement*, 4 February, 1994.

ii) Arguments derived from an intrinsic and principled opposition to the idea of restricting free expression

Such restrictions are seen as deeply offensive in themselves. They represent a denial of that freedom for *all*. There is simply no right to use public power in that way, however offensive and outrageous these opinions might be, and whatever the offense, insult, or social discomfort they contain or create.[2]

B) The case for specific legislation relating to group-libel and hate-speech

I belong to those who believe that such legislation is necessary in our societies. However, I also believe that it has to be based on clear legal foundations. I shall discuss briefly these two points.

i) Why do we need such legislation?

We need it not only, and not even mainly, in order to protect or to defend certain groups or certain individuals, but for the well-being of *society as a whole*. This is a *political* issue, in the broadest sense of the word; one on which Governments and Parliaments must decide, and courts adjudicate.

The ultimate purpose for such laws is to maintain a minimum of *civility* in public discourse. Which form of civility? That which forbids us to attack an individual or a group of persons on the grounds of what they are, that is, for their identity.[3] Permitting vilification harms society as a whole. Greenawalt mentions rightly 'the long-term effects of reinforcement of feelings of prejudice and inferiority and of social patterns of domination'.[4] We live in a century and in societies where the use of legal instruments against what is, and is meant to be an aggression,[5] is fully legitimate.

---

[2] See T. Nagel, 'Personal Rights and Public Space', *Philosophy and Public Affairs*, 1995.

[3] See Note, 'A communitarian defense of group-libel laws', 101 *Harvard Law Review*, 682 (1988).

[4] K. Greenawalt, *Speech, Crime and the Uses of Language*, Oxford University Press (New York, 1989), 299.

[5] See A. Bickel, *The Morality of Consent*, Yale University Press, (New Haven and London, 1975), 71-3. Discussing Justice Brandeis's premise in *Whitney* v. *California*, that 'discussion affords ordinarily adequate protection against the dissemination of noxious doctrine' (274 U.S. 357, 375 (1927)), he writes: '... we have lived through too much to believe it.'

ii) The legal basis for such laws may be two-fold:

First, it may be seen as a constitutional one since the central principles at stake are those of equality, dignity[6] and non-discrimination. Secondly, it may be seen as resting on international law. For instance, Article 10-2 of the European Human Rights Convention allows, if certain conditions are fulfilled, restrictions of freedom of expression 'for the protection of reputation and *rights* of others'. Likewise, Article 4-a of the International Convention on the Elimination of all Forms of Racial Discrimination provides that States 'shall declare an offense punishable by law all dissemination of ideas based on racial superiority or hatred, incitement to racial discrimination, as well as all acts of violence or incitement to such acts against any race or group of persons of another colour or ethnic origin, and also the provision of any assistance to racist activities, including the financing thereof.'[7]

III RACIAL INCITEMENT AND THE USES OF THE LAW

An exploration of key legal concepts and issues will be followed by an attempt to assess group-libel and hate-speech laws.

---

[6] On the dignity of the individual in French constitutional law, see the Conseil constitutionnel's decision of 27 July, 1994, no. 94. 343/344. DC, 100; for an application in administrative law, see the two decisions of the Conseil d'Etat of 27 October, 1995, *Commune de Morsang sur Orge*, and *Ville d'Aix en Provence*, commented by the author in *Public Law* 1996, 166. On the same notion in German constitutional law, see Art. 1 (1) of the German Constitution ('The dignity of man shall be inviolable'), and K. Sontheimer, 'Principles of Human Dignity in the Federal Republic' in, *Germany and its Basic Laws. Past, Present and Future—A German-American Symposium*, P. Kirchhof and D. P. Kommers (eds.) (Nomos, Baden-Baden, 1993), 213. The dignity of man is part of the *Ewigkeit* clause in the German Constitution.

[7] On the legislative history of Art. 4 of the Convention, see W. McKean, *Equality and Discrimination under International Law*, Clarendon Press, (Oxford, 1983), 160. The French statute on hate-speech and group-libel was revised in 1972 after France ratified the Convention. See R. Errera, 'French Law and Racial Incitement: on the Necessity and Limits of the Legal Responses', in *Under the Shadow of Weimar. Democracy, Law and Racial Incitement in six countries*, L. Greenspan and C. Levitt (eds.) (Praeger, Westport, CT and London, 1993), 39. On the model law on incitement to racial, national or religious hatred adopted by the Consultative Assembly of the Council of Europe, see W. Mc Kean, op. cit., 223.

A. Key legal concepts and issues for legislators, governments and judges.

They include the following points:

i) Whether one thinks of racial incitement or of group-libel, criminal law has to be used. In certain countries, for example, France, criminal courts are empowered to award in the same judgment civil damages to the victims of such violations.

ii) The two main categories of offenses are group-libel and racial incitement. The latter may include incitement to violence, discrimination (unlawful acts in themselves) or hatred.

iii) On which grounds? What may be the scope of the offense? The key notions here are belonging (or not belonging) to a given ethnic group, nation, race, or religion.[8] Some enactments punish incitement to hatred 'against any identifiable group',[9] or 'against a certain part of the population'.[10]

iv) Should public order or public peace be taken into consideration? This is certainly the case in a number of countries.[11]

v) Should the relevant statutes mention intention? This is so in England[12] and Canada.[13]

vi) Should certain defenses be available, such as truth or the public interest? This is so in Canada.[14]

vii) Should the negation of the existence or the gross minimization of crimes against humanity or genocide be a separate offense? This is so in Switzerland,[15] France,[16] Austria,[17] and Israel.[18] In Germany the case-law relating to the implementation of art. 130 and 185 of the

---

[8] French Law on the Press (1881, as revised in 1972), art. 24, § 5, and 32, § 2; see also art. 261 *bis* of the Swiss Penal Code. In England, the Public Order Act (1986) mentions colour, race, nationality or ethnic or national origins, but not religion. The Public Order (Northern Ireland) Order (1987) includes religious belief.

[9] Canada, Criminal Code, Section 319 (1).

[10] Germany, Criminal Code, Art. 130 (1).

[11] Germany, Criminal Code, Art. 130; Canada, Criminal Code, Section 319 (1).

[12] Public Order Act, 1986, Section III, Section 18 (1) a.

[13] Canada, Criminal Code, Section 319 (2).

[14] Canada, Criminal Code, Section 319 (3).

[15] Swiss Penal Code, Art. 261 *bis*.

[16] France, Art. 24 *bis* of the Law on the Press (since 1990)

[17] Austrian Law no. 148, 1992.

[18] Israel, Denial of Holocaust (Prohibition Law) 5746–1986.

Criminal Code has led to the conviction of 'negationist' authors.
The new wording of Article 194 (1) allows a prosecution for insult
to be instituted without a petition 'if the insulted person was
persecuted as a member of a group under the National-Socialist
regime or another violent and arbitrary dominance, if the group
is part of the population and if the insult is connected with a such
persecution'.[19]

viii) Who, in addition to the State Prosecutor, may sue? This is
a key issue. To rely exclusively on State Prosecutors or on individuals is not enough. Hence the interest of allowing other bodies to
sue. Thus, under French law any association whose legal existence
has been recognized for five years at the date of the facts and whose
aim is to combat racism has *locus standi* to bring criminal proceedings (the individual's permission is needed if that person has
been attacked). In Canada the Human Rights Act (1977) allows the
Human Rights Commission to act if certain conditions are met.[20]

B. An interim evaluation of group-libel and hate-speech legislation

It is by no means easy to assess the real impact of a given legislation.
This applies to the laws mentioned above. However, a number of
valuable studies offer some guidance.[21]

i) From a legal point of view the main challenge for hate-speech and
group-libel laws (and case-law) is a constitutional one. Such a challenge has been successfully met in Germany,[22] in Canada,[23] and

[19] On the case-law and the history of the reform, see E. Stein, 'History against free
speech. The new German law against the "Auschwitz" — and other — "lies"', 85
Michigan Law Review, 277 (1986).
[20] e.g. the use of telecommunications to spread hate-messages. On Canada, see J.
Manwaring, 'Legal regulation of hate propaganda in Canada', in *Striking a Balance:
Hate-Speech, Freedom of Expression and non Discrimination*,
S. Coliver (ed.), Article XIX, International Centre against Censorship, Human
Rights Centre, University of Essex, 1992, 106.
[21] *Striking a Balance*, op. cit., studies the law and practice in Australia,
Canada, the Commonwealth of Independent States, Denmark, France, Ger-
many, India, Israel, Uruguay, Netherlands, South Africa, Sri Lanka, the United
Kingdom and the U.S.A. and offers a general evaluation; Under the Shadow of
Weimar, op. cit., studies six countries (France, England, Germany, U.S.A, Israel and
Canada). The late Stephen J. Roth has written a relevant analytical comparison.
[22] See note 17, supra and R. Hofmann, 'Incitement to national and racial hatred:
the legal situation in Germany', in *Striking a Balance*, op. cit., 159.
[23] As shown by the *Taylor* and *Keegstra* cases. The *Zundel* case related to
Section 181 of the Canadian Criminal Code punishing the wilful publication of

in Hungary,[24] thus leading to a reaffirmation of the central constitutional notions of equality, dignity, and non-discrimination.

However, there are countries which share the same constitutional values, but in which group-libel and hate-speech laws as we know them in Europe, would be unconstitutional. The U.S.A is a relevant example. We have to recognize here, a difference of legal and social attitudes and cultures.

Seen from the point of view of international law, the case is even stronger. As D. Kretzmer writes: ' [Racism] has become the one ideology outlawed by international law'.[25] The case-law of the European Human Rights Commission[26] and that of the UN Human Rights Committee[27] provides an apt illustration.

It is true that group-libel and hate-speech laws have often been seen as a 'new' body of law, entirely different from other regulations, if not somewhat alien from the classical *corpus juris*. If that is so, so be it. For such laws *are* a creation of legislators and governments in the same way that, in many countries, the rights of privacy and personality are the products of court activity. This comparison could be pursued further.

ii) This being said, it is true that there is a tension between freedom of expression and group-libel and hate-speech laws. This has to be

statements or news known as false causing or likely to cause injury or mischief to a public interest. The Canadian Supreme Court found that section unconstitutional. On the Keegstra case (*Regina* v. *Keegstra*, (1990), C.C.C. (3rd) 1 (S.C.C.), see Bruce P. Elman, '*Her Majesty the Queen* v. *James Keegstra*: the control of racism in Canada. A case-study', in *Under the Shadow of Weimar*, op. cit., 149. For a prior review of Canadian law, see Law Reform Commission in Canada, *Hate Propaganda*, Working Paper 50, Ottawa, 1986.

[24] See the Hungarian Constitutional Court's decision no. 30/1992 (V. 18) AB, in East European case reporter of Constitutional Law, 1995, 9, and A. Sajo's commentary, 'Hate-speech for hostile Hungarians', *East European Constitutional Review*, Spring 1994, 82. The Court holds unconstitutional art. 269 (2) of the Penal Code punishing the public use of 'offensive or denigrating expression', while holding constitutional Section 1 of the same article punishing incitement to hatred.

[25] D. Kretzmer, 'Freedom of Speech and Racism', 8 *Cardozo Law Review*, 445, at 458 (1987).

[26] See cases 8348/78 and 8406/78, *X* v. *Netherlands*, 21 May 1978; 9235/81, *X* v. *Germany*, 16 July 1982, *D.R.*, no. 29, 1982, 194; 7777/82, *T* v. *Belgium*, 14 July 1983 (Spreading of 'negationist' theses); *Glimmerveen and Hagenbeck* v. *Netherlands*, 10 October 1979, *D.R.*, no. 18, 1980, 187; (1979) 4 EHRR, 260. See R. Genn, 'Beyond the Pale: Council of Europe Measures against Incitement to Hatred' (1983), 13 *Israel Yearbook on Human Rights*, 189.

[27] See Communication 104/181, J. R. Taylor and the *WG Party* v. *Canada*, 6 April, 1983.

recognized by governments, legislators, and judges. The former must be careful in the drafting and wording of legal instruments; and they must take care not to change them too often. More than legal certainly is at stake here. The judges have a clear duty to implement such laws, keeping in mind their ultimate justification, through the use of appropriate reasoning.

As we all know, there is an interplay between public attitudes of governments, what Parliaments vote for, and judicial pronouncements and policy. No one here is on the side of the angels.

iii) Such laws, and the legitimate debate they give rise to, lead us beyond the classical distinctions usually employed here. We need such laws to protect certain groups and their members *and* to maintain public order (in the broader sense of the word) *and* as an affirmation of what society will not accept.

iv) One brief word about 'revisionism', outright negation or minimization of the Nazi genocide of the Jews. In a number of countries (the U.S.A, Canada, France, Britain, etc), such a negation has been the subject of books, essays, and articles.[28] There is no doubt at all that such writings are not only a perverse expression of anti-semitism, but also an *aggression* against the dead, the survivors, and society at large, aiming at the desecration or the destruction of the only grave of the former, that is, our memory, and the erosion of the very conscience and knowledge of the crime. Such an aggression is not to be tolerated.[29] However, civil law and not criminal law should be used here.

v) It is obvious that in countries which have group-libel and hate-speech laws, racial incitement will not disappear. Social attitudes and behaviour do change — for the better or for the worse—but not overnight.

The existence of these laws, their very wording and their implementation have many consequences on the public domain. In our societies as they are today, these laws express a pressing social need,

---

[28] See P. Vidal-Naquet, 'Un Eichmann de papier. Anatomie d'un mensonge', in *Les Juifs, la mémoire et le présent*, Paris, La Découverte, 1981, 193; Les assassins de la mémoire. *'Un Eichmann de papier' et autres essais sur le révisionnisme*, id, 1987; Deborah Lipstadt, *Denying the Holocaust. The Growing Assault on Truth and Memory*, (New York, The Free Press, 1993).

[29] For a study of the law and practice in France, see R. Errera, 'French law and racial incitement', *Under the Shadow of Weimar*, op. cit., at 52, and 'Sur les justes limites de la liberté d'expression', *Esprit*, 1990, 81, at 91.

'because the values of equality and dignity are so central and so *vulnerable*, and the support for these constitutional values of the community here overrides a claim to freedom of expression'.[30]

As we approach a new century, no one is in a position to overlook what Bickel wrote more than a quarter of century ago in *The Morality of Consent*: 'There is such a thing as verbal violence, a kind of cursing, assaultive speech that amounts to almost physical aggression, bullying that is no less punishing because it is simulated ... This sort of speech constitutes an assault. More, and equally important, it may create a climate, an environment in which conduct and actions that were not possible before become possible . . . Where nothing is unspeakable, nothing is undoable'.[31]

[30] K. Greenawalt, *Speech, Crime, and the Uses of Language*, op. cit., at 300.
[31] A. Bickel, *The Morality of Consent*, Yale University Press, (New Haven and London, 1975) at 72–3.

5

The Influence of the European Convention of Human Rights and the American Constitution on the English Law of Defamation

by The Rt. Hon. Sir Brian Neill

It is too early to forecast the influence which the European Convention and the American Constitution will have on the English law of defamation in the long run. At this stage one can only take note of the effects which have already become apparent and draw attention to some of the problems which await resolution in the future.

The provisions with which we are particularly concerned are Article 10 of the European Convention for the Protection of Human Rights and Fundamental Freedoms and the First Amendment to the American Constitution. In a moment I shall say something about the influence of Article 10, but first I must refer to its terms and to the terms of the other Articles which merit attention at this stage, as well as to the succinct wording of the First Amendment. I must also point to an authority of the European Court of Human Rights giving guidance as to the correct approach to Article 10.

Article 10 of the Convention provides:

1. Everyone has the right to freedom of expression. This right shall include freedom to hold opinions and to receive and impart information and ideas without interference by public authority and regardless of frontiers. This Article shall not prevent States from requiring the licensing of broadcasting, television or cinema enterprises.

2. The exercise of these freedoms, since it carries with it duties and responsibilities, may be subject to such formalities, conditions, restrictions or penalties as are prescribed by law and are necessary in a democratic society, in the interests of national security, territorial integrity or

public safety, for the prevention of disorder or crime, for the protection of health or morals, for the protection of the reputation or rights of others, for preventing the disclosure of information received in confidence, or for maintaining the authority and impartiality of the judiciary.

I should also refer to Article 8:

1. Everyone has the right to respect for his private and family life, his home and his correspondence.
2. There shall be no interference by a public authority with the exercise of this right except such as is in accordance with the law and is necessary in a democratic society in the interests of national security, public safety or the economic well-being of the country, for the prevention of disorder or crime, for the protection of health or morals, or for the protection of the rights and freedoms of others.

And Article 13 provides:

Everyone whose rights and freedoms as set forth in this Convention are violated shall have an effective remedy before a national authority notwithstanding that the violation has been committed by persons acting in an official capacity.

Finally I should set out the text of the First Amendment to the American Constitution. This Amendment was adopted in 1791.

Congress shall make no law abridging freedom of speech or of the press.

The European Court has provided guidance as to how the construction of Article 10 should be approached. In *The Sunday Times* v. *United Kingdom (No. 2)*,[1] it was said :

Argument before the court was concentrated on the question whether the interference complained of could be regarded as 'necessary in a democratic society.' In this connection, the court's judgments relating to Article 10 . . . announce the following major principles. (a) Freedom of expression constitutes one of the essential foundations of a democratic society; subject to paragraph (2) of Article 10, it is applicable not only to 'information' or 'ideas' that are favourably received or regarded as inoffensive or as a matter of indifference, but also to those that offend, shock or disturb. Freedom of expression, as enshrined in Article 10, is subject to a number of exceptions which, however, must be narrowly interpreted and the necessity for any restrictions must be convincingly established. (b) These principles are of particular importance as far as the press is concerned. Whilst it must not overstep the bounds set, inter alia, in the

---

[1] (1991) 14 EHRR 229, 241– 2, para. 50.

'interests of national security' or for 'maintaining the authority of the judiciary,' it is nevertheless incumbent on it to impart information and ideas on matters of public interest. Not only does the press have the task of imparting such information and ideas: the public also has a right to receive them. Were it otherwise, the press would be unable to play its vital role of 'public watchdog.' (c) The adjective 'necessary,' within the meaning of Article 10(2), implies the existence of a 'pressing social need.' The contracting states have a certain margin of appreciation in assessing whether such a need exists, but it goes hand in hand with a European supervision, embracing both the law and the decisions applying it, even those given by independent courts. The court is therefore empowered to give the final ruling on whether a 'restriction' is reconcilable with freedom of expression as protected by Article 10. (d) The court's task, in exercising its supervisory jurisdiction, is not to take the place of the competent national authorities but rather to review under Article 10 the decisions they delivered pursuant to their power of appreciation. This does not mean that the supervision is limited to ascertaining whether the respondent state exercised its jurisdiction reasonably, carefully and in good faith; what the court had to do is to look at the interference complained of in the light of the case as a whole and determine whether it was 'proportionate to the legitimate aim pursued' and whether the reasons adduced by the national authorities to justify it are 'relevant and sufficient'.

I should also refer to the decision of the European Court of Human Rights in *Lingens* v. *Austria*.[2] In that case the publisher of a magazine in Vienna had been convicted of criminal defamation and had been fined as the result of the publication of two articles critical of the Austrian Chancellor. The court emphasised,[3] that it had to determine whether the action taken by the national court was 'proportionate to the legitimate aim pursued.'

The attitude of the English courts to the Convention has been explained by the House of Lords. First, it is clear that the Convention may be deployed for the purpose of the resolution of an ambiguity in English primary or subordinate legislation:[3a] and that where there is an ambiguity the courts will presume that Parliament intended to legislate in conformity with the Convention, not in conflict with it.[4] It is also clear that Article 10 may be used when the court is contemplating how a discretion is to be exercised. Thus

---

[2]   (1986) 8 EHRR 407.   [3]   At 418.
[3a] See *ex parte* Brind, at 760, per Lord Acklner.
[4]   See *Ex parte* Brind, at 747, per Lord Bridge.

in *Attorney-General* v. *Guardian Newspapers Ltd.*,[4a] Lord Templeman referred to Article 10 when considering whether the interference with the freedom of expression which the grant of an interlocutory injunction would entail was 'necessary in a democratic society' for any of the purposes specified in paragraph 2 of Article 10.

Where freedom of expression is at stake, however, recent authorities lend support for the proposition that Article 10 has a wider role and can properly be regarded as an articulation of some of the principles underlying the common law. In *Attorney-General* v. *Guardian Newspapers Ltd.*[5] Lord Goff of Chieveley referred[6] to the requirement that in order to restrain the disclosure of government secrets it had to be shown that it was in the public interest that they should not be published. He continued:[7]

. . . I can see no inconsistency between English law on this subject and Article 10 of the European Convention on Human Rights. This is scarcely surprising, since we may pride ourselves on the fact that freedom of speech has existed in this country perhaps as long as, if not longer than, it has existed in any other country in the world. The only difference is that, whereas Article 10 of the Convention, in accordance with its avowed purpose proceeds to state a fundamental right and then to qualify it, we in this country (where everybody is free to do anything, subject only to the provisions of the law) proceed rather upon an assumption of freedom of speech, and turn to our law to discover the established exceptions to it. In any event I conceive it to be my duty, when I am free to do so, to interpret the law in accordance with the obligations of the Crown under this treaty. The exercise of the right to freedom of expression under Article 10 may be subject to restrictions (as are prescribed by law and are necessary in a democratic society) in relation to certain prescribed matters, which include 'the interests of national security' and 'preventing the disclosure of information received in confidence.' It is established in the jurisprudence of the European Court of Human Rights that the word 'necessary' in this context implies the existence of a pressing social need, and that interference with freedom of expression should be no more than is proportionate to the legitimate aim pursued. I have no reason to believe that English law, as applied in the courts, leads to any different conclusion.

[4a][1987] 1 WLR 1248, 1296.
[5] (No. 2) [1990] 1 AC 109.   [6] At 283.
[7] At 283– 4.

In *Derbyshire County Council* v. *Times Newspapers Ltd.*[8] Lord Keith of Kinkel referred to this passage in Lord Goff's speech and added these words, with which the other members of the House agreed:[9]

I agree, and can only add that I find it satisfactory to be able to conclude that the common law of England is consistent with the obligations assumed by the Crown under the Treaty in this particular field.

There are other authorities which reflect a similar approach. For example in *Reg.* v. *Wells Street Stipendiary Magistrate, Ex parte Deakin* [10] the House of Lords expressed the view that it would be a salutary reform in the law of defamation if no prosecution for criminal libel could be instituted without the leave of the Attorney-General. Both Lord Diplock and Lord Keith added that if such a reform were introduced the Attorney-General could then consider, in deciding whether to grant his consent in a particular case, whether the prosecution was necessary on any of the grounds specified in Article 10(2) of the Convention and that unless he was so satisfied he should refuse his consent.

It may also be helpful to refer to part of the summary given by Lord Bingham of Cornhill in his maiden speech in the House of Lords when he listed the ways in which the courts in the United Kingdom are influenced by the Convention:

1. Where a UK statute is capable of two interpretations, one consistent with the Convention and one inconsistent, the courts will presume that Parliament intended to legislate in conformity with the Convention and not in conflict with it. If the common-law is uncertain, unclear or incomplete, the courts have to make a choice. In declaring what the law is, they will rule wherever possible in a manner which conforms with the Convention and does not conflict with it.
2. When the courts are called upon to construe a domestic statute enacted to fulfil a Convention obligation, the courts will ordinarily assume that the statute was intended to achieve that effect.
3. Where the courts have a discretion to exercise, and one course open to them violates the Convention and one does not, they usually (but not invariably) seek to act in a way which does not violate the Convention.

---

[8] [1993] AC 534.   [9] At 551.   [10] [1980] AC 477.

4. When in a given situation the courts are required to decide what
    public policy demands, it may be legitimate to have regard to
    international obligations as a source of guidance.

With this introduction I should now turn to the areas of the law
of defamation where the Convention and the First Amendment
have already had an impact.

PARTIES, QUALIFIED PRIVILEGE AND PUBLIC FIGURES

I expect that you will be familiar with the *Derbyshire* case (supra)
but it may be helpful if I say something about the background to
the decision.

In 1969 Mr. Eric Campion distributed a leaflet at a meeting of a
ratepayers association which attacked Bognor Regis Urban District Council. He described their activities as *inter alia* 'Toytown
Hitlerism'. The Council brought an action for libel and was
awarded £2,000 damages after a trial lasting several weeks. The
judge at the trial upheld the contention that a local government
corporation had a 'governing reputation' which it was entitled to
protect.

Twenty years later the *Sunday Times* published articles relating
to share dealings involving the investment of monies from Derbyshire County Council's superannuation fund. The County Council
brought proceedings for libel. A preliminary issue was ordered to
be tried as to whether the Council could maintain an action for any
words which reflected upon it in relation to its governmental and
its administrative functions. The judge held that a cause of action
was disclosed because the words complained of reflected on the
local authority in the management and rectitude of its financial
affairs. The Court of Appeal allowed the Newspaper's appeal.
Balcombe LJ delivered the leading judgment. In the course of
his judgment he referred to the right to freedom of expression
enshrined in Article 10 of the Convention. He also referred to the
similar, though not identical, wording of Article 19 of the United
Nations International Covenant on Civil and Political Rights.

Balcombe LJ concluded that as there was uncertainty as to English law—the decision in the *Bognor Regis* case was in apparent
conflict with an earlier decision[11]—it was legitimate to carry out a

[11] *Manchester Corporation* v. *Williams* [1891] 1 QB 94.

balancing exercise in accordance with Article 10. Once the balancing exercise had been carried out it became clear that a right to sue for libel was not necessary in a democratic society for the protection of the reputation of the council. Adequate protection could be provided by an action for malicious falsehood or by a prosecution for criminal libel.

In the House of Lords, Lord Keith, though he came to the same conclusion, approached the matter differently. He looked west and south rather than east to Strasbourg. The ground had been prepared by the decision of the Supreme Court of Illinois in *City of Chicago* v. *Tribune Company* [12] where it had been held that the City could not maintain an action for libel. I can take a few words from the judgment of Thompson CJ who said:

> The fundamental right of freedom of speech is involved in this litigation, not merely the right of liberty for the press. If this action can be maintained against a newspaper it can be maintained against every private citizen who ventures to criticise the Ministers who are temporarily conducting the affairs of government.

A little later he added:

> ... Every citizen has a right to criticize an inefficient or corrupt government without fear of civil as well as criminal prosecution. This absolute privilege is founded on the principle that it is advantageous for the public interest that the citizen should not be in any way fettered in his statements, and where the public service or due administration of justice is involved he shall have the right to speak his mind freely.

Lord Keith noticed in his speech that the propositions enunciated by Thompson CJ had been endorsed by the US Supreme Court in *Sullivan's* case (infra). In addition Lord Keith made reference to the decision of the Supreme Court of *South Africa in Diespoorbond* v. *South African Railways.* [13] In his judgment in that case Schreiner JA said:

> I have no doubt that it will involve a serious interference with the free expression of opinion hitherto enjoyed in this country if the wealth of the state, derived from the state's subjects, could be used to launch against those subjects actions for defamation because they have, falsely and unfairly it may be, criticized or condemned the management of the country.

[12] (1923) 139 NE 86.   [13] [1946] AD 999.

Lord Keith concluded that under the common law of England a local authority had no right to maintain an action for damages for defamation. He said that he had reached that conclusion without finding any need to rely upon the European Convention, though he added that he thought it was satisfactory that the common law of England was consistent with the obligations assumed by the Crown under the treaty in this particular field.

It is to be noticed that in the *Derbyshire* case (supra) it was emphasised that, although the council could not sue, this did not prevent actions by individual councillors. For my part I wonder whether this distinction can survive. I should refer to two passages in Lord Keith's speech; first he said: [14]

It is of the highest public importance that a democratically elected governmental body or indeed any governmental body, should be open to uninhibited public criticism. The threat of a civil action for defamation must inevitably have an inhibiting effect on freedom of speech.

And later:

Not only is there no public interest favouring the right of organs of government, whether central or local, to sue for libel, but that it is contrary to the public interest that they should have it. It is contrary to the public interest because to admit such actions would place an undesirable fetter on freedom of speech.

It will be seen from these passages that the inability to sue is not based on any proposition that to do so would be *ultra vires*. The inability is based on the fact that to allow such an action at the suit of a government department or a local authority would be contrary to the public interest.

This is difficult ground where a judge must tread delicately. It seems to me, however, that once it is accepted that 'it is of the highest public importance that a democratically elected governmental body, or indeed any governmental body, should be open to uninhibited public criticism' it is not altogether clear how one can satisfactorily distinguish between the elected body itself and those who compose it.

Furthermore, one must remember the words of Thompson CJ in the *City of Chicago* case and the landmark decision of the US Supreme Court in 1964 in *New York Times* v. *Sullivan*.[15] In that

---

[14] At 547F.   [15] 376 US 254.

case, as you will remember, the plaintiff was one of three elected commissioners of the city of Montgomery in Alabama. His duties included supervision of the Police Department. The New York Times published an advertisement which stated 'Truck-loads of police armed with shot guns and tear gas ringed the Alabama State College Campus'. It was alleged that the advertisement implied that the plaintiff had acted oppressively towards those who supported Martin Luther King. Though the plaintiff's name did not appear in the advertisement it was said that he could be identified. He was awarded US$ 500,000. The verdict, though upheld in the Supreme Court of Alabama, was overturned by the US Supreme Court. The defendants relied on the First and Fourteenth Amendments to the US Constitution. The Supreme Court held that in the light of these provisions of the Constitution a State could not award damages to a public official for a false and defamatory statement relating to his official conduct unless actual malice were proved. It was therefore necessary for a plaintiff in the position of Mr. Sullivan to prove not only that the statement was false but that it had been published with knowledge of its falsity and with reckless disregard of whether it was true or not.

The decision in *Sullivan's* case has been followed and extended. It remains to be seen precisely how far the extension will go. Sullivan was a public official. But, starting with *Curtis Publishing* v. *Butts*,[16] the rule has been extended to public figures generally. Moreover, public figures have now been divided into categories— general purpose public figures and limited purpose public figures. Who is a public figure and who falls into which category is a developing jurisprudence. It was a judge in the Federal District Court in Georgia in a case against Playboy Enterprises who remarked that 'defining public figures is much like trying to nail a jelly fish to a wall'. In the time available, however, I cannot examine the limits of the rule in the United States, though it can lead to results which many English lawyers would regard as unsatisfactory. For example, in *Ocala Star-Banner Co. v.Damron*,[17] the publication complained of stated that the plaintiff who was a candidate for public office had been charged with perjury. The story was wholly false. The writer had confused the plaintiff with his brother of whom the report was substantially true. The plaintiff

[16] 388 US 130.   [17] (1971) 410 US 295.

was awarded damages but the Supreme Court reversed the decision and sent the case back so that the rule in *Sullivan's* case could be applied.

The 'actual malice' rule propounded by the US Supreme Court in *Sullivan's* case, whereby the common law of Alabama which imposed the onus of proof on the defendant to prove the truth of the libel was declared unconstitutional, was based on provisions in the US Constitution itself. Accordingly the rule, which provides a defendant with what may be called a constitutional privilege, has no direct application in England. But there are passages in Lord Keith's speech in the Derbyshire case (supra) which might provide a foundation for a modest extension of the law of qualified privilege in this country. And I can foresee an advocate in the future seeking to rely on a further passage in the judgment of Thompson CJ in the *City of Chicago* case where he said:

Municipal corporations, however, exist primarily for governmental purposes, and they are permitted to enter the commercial field solely for the purpose of subserving the interests of the public which they represent. A city is no less a government because it owns and operates its own water system, its own gas and electric system, and its own transportation system. In *Byrne* v. *Chicago General Railway Co.* (1897) 48 NE 703, this court said: 'The city is but an agency of the state and governs, within its sphere, for the state . . . The government exercised by the city is exercised as an agency of the whole public, and for all the people of the state. A municipal corporation, like a state or county, is, within its prescribed sphere, a political power.[18]

I should also notice that in *Watts* v. *Times Newspapers Ltd.*[19] it was argued, though not very strongly, that the placing of the burden of proof on a defendant to establish that the occasion of publication was privileged was inconsistent with Article 10.

I turn next to consider Article 10 in the context of damages.

DAMAGES

In *Tolstoy* v. *UK*[20] the Court in Strasbourg held that the award of damages of £1.5m. to Lord Aldington was an award which was 'prescribed by law' and pursued a legitimate aim, but that it was

---

[18] (1923) 139 NE 86 at 90, 91.   [19] [1996] 2 WLR 427.
[20] (1995) 20 EHRR.

not 'necessary in a democratic society' and therefore imposed an impermissible restriction on the right to freedom of expression enshrined in Article 10. It was also held that in the absence of the guidance given later by the Court of Appeal in *Rantzen* v. *Mirror Group Newspapers*[21] there had not existed at the date of the trial in Count Tolstoy's case any assurance of a reasonable relationship of proportionality to the legitimate aim pursued.

In *Rantzen's* case the Court of Appeal applied the principle of proportionality as expounded by Lord Goff in *AG* v. *Guardian Newspapers (No 2):*[22]

The exercise of the right to freedom of expression under Article 10 may be subject to restrictions (as are prescribed by law and are necessary in a democratic society) in relation to certain prescribed matters, which include 'the interests of national security' and 'preventing the disclosure of information received in confidence.' It is established in the jurisprudence of the European Court of Human Rights that the word 'necessary' in this context implies the existence of a pressing social need, and that interference with freedom of expression should be no more than is proportionate to the legitimate aim pursued. I have no reason to believe that English law, as applied in the courts, leads to any different conclusion.

More recently in *John* v. *MGN Ltd.*[23] the Court of Appeal has looked again at the problem of the level of damages in defamation cases and has given some further guidance for the future. In the course of giving the judgment of the Court Sir Thomas Bingham MR said:

The European Convention of Human Rights is not a free-standing source of law in the United Kingdom. But there is . . . no conflict or discrepancy between Article 10 and the common law. We regard Article 10 as reinforcing and buttressing the conclusions we have reached . . .[24]

It can be said therefore that the influence of Article 10 on the awards of damages has been indirect rather than direct. But I believe that most English lawyers would accept that Article 10 and the principle of proportionality have been of some assistance in the construction of a framework for the awards of the future.

---

[21] (1986) Ltd. [1994] QB 670.   [22] [1970] 1 AC 109 at 283.
[23] [1996] 3 WLR 593.   [24] At 619.

SOME ADDITIONAL COMMENTS

Before concluding I would like to refer to a few further matters which are of interest. I propose to consider them below under two headings: 1. The possible incorporation of the European Convention into English law, and 2. Public figures.

1. The incorporation of the European Convention into English law

In November 1996 The Constitution Unit published its Report entitled 'Human Rights Legislation'. The Report took as its starting point an assumption that if there is a change of Government at the next election, a bill to incorporate the European Convention would be introduced within the term of the next Parliament and that the development of a domestic bill of rights would follow. The Report therefore dealt with the constitutional and legal implications of the incorporation of the Convention and the introduction of a bill of rights rather than with the arguments for and against having a bill of rights at all.

The Report concluded that there would be no need to establish a constitutional court and that the ordinary courts would be able to determine issues involving Convention rights. The Report also concluded that it would be necessary for the incorporating statute to define the status of the Convention as part of domestic law. In this context three possibilities were examined:

1. The inclusion of a provision empowering the courts not to give effect to inconsistent legislation, whether pre-existing or subsequent, but subject to an express declaration in a subsequent statute that it or part of it should take effect notwithstanding such inconsistency; such a provision would be on similar lines to section 33(1) of the Canadian Charter of Rights and Freedoms, 1982.

2. The inclusion of a provision empowering the courts not to give effect to pre-existing legislation which is inconsistent with the Convention and requiring that all subsequent legislation should be construed so as to be consistent with the Convention unless this was manifestly impossible: such a provision would be on similar lines to those contained in the Hong Kong Bill of Rights Ordinance, 1990.

3. The inclusion of a provision to the effect that the Convention

should be merely a tool for use by the courts to aid interpretation; such a provision would be on similar lines to section 6 of the New Zealand Bill of Rights, 1980.

The Report recommended that any judicial powers to disapply primary legislation should be subject to control by Parliament, perhaps by means of a 'notwithstanding clause' as in Canada. It was suggested that in the alternative the Hong Kong model could be adopted. For my part, however, I am doubtful whether Parliament would wish to go further than to allow the Convention to be used as a tool of interpretation, and that the New Zealand approach might be preferred.

Though the Constitution Unit did not examine the merits of incorporation, it may be noted that one of the arguments which is sometimes deployed in favour of incorporation is that if domestic courts had to recognise and apply the Convention as part of English law the number of applications to the court in Strasbourg would be substantially reduced. Whether such a reduction would in fact take place is perhaps open to doubt, for at least three reasons:

1. The statute incorporating the Convention would attract publicity and might well bring the existence of the valuable rights enshrined in the Convention to the notice of people who had hitherto been unaware of these rights.

2. It is extremely unlikely that any statute incorporating the Convention would, or perhaps could, prevent someone who was dissatisfied with the determination of his or her claim in the domestic court from making a complaint to the court in Strasbourg.

3. Though, if the Convention were incorporated, the court in Strasbourg would be likely to allow the domestic courts a 'margin of appreciation' in their interpretation and application of the Convention, the recent decision of the European Court in *Goodwin*[25] suggests that this margin may be quite narrow.

I should say a few words about *Goodwin*, where the European Court declined to endorse the balancing exercise carried out by the United Kingdom courts, including the House of Lords, under Article 10(2) of the Convention. Mr Goodwin was a journalist in the United Kingdom. He received a telephone call in the course of

---

[25] (1996) 22 EHRR 123.

which he was given some sensitive financial information about a company called Tetra. The information appeared to have come from a confidential document about Tetra's corporate plan. Mr Goodwin decided to prepare an article for publication in the *Engineer* and communicated with Tetra to check the facts. Tetra thereupon applied for and obtained an injunction to prevent publication and the Chancery court ordered him to disclose his source. When he refused he was fined. The judge's decision was upheld by the Court of Appeal and the House of Lords. In the European Court, however, it was held that, though the remedies obtained by Tetra were 'prescribed by law' and 'pursued the legitimate aim of protecting the rights of Tetra', they were not 'necessary in a democratic society'. The judgment contained this passage:[26]

> . . . there was not, in the Court's view, a reasonable relationship of proportionality between the legitimate aim pursued by the disclosure order and the means employed to achieve that aim. The restriction which the disclosure order entailed on the appellant journalist's exercise of his freedom of expression cannot therefore be regarded as having been necessary in a democratic society . . . notwithstanding the margin of appreciation available to the national authorities.

2. Public figures

In *Manning* v. *Hill*[27] the Supreme Court of Canada considered a contention that the common law of defamation was inconsistent with the values enshrined in the Canadian Charter of Rights and Freedoms. The contention was rejected. In the course of his important judgment, however, Cory J also rejected the argument that the principle in *Sullivan* formed part of Canadian law. On the other hand, it seems that the majority view of the High Court of Australia would uphold the extension of the doctrine of qualified privilege to cover the discussion of political matters.[28] And in his decision in 1994 in *Rajagopal* v. *State of Tamil Nadu B.P.*[29] Jeevan Reddy J. was clearly much influenced by the reasoning in Sullivan's case.

[26] At 145. [27] (1995) 126 DLR (4) 129.

[28] See *Theophanous* v. *The Herald* (1994) 182 CLR 104 and *Stephens* v. *West Australian Newspapers* (1994) 182 CLR 211. These decisions have now to be read together with and as modified by the recent decision of the High Court of Australia in *Lange* v. *Australian Broadcasting Corporation* (8 July 1997).

[29] P.L.R. (1944).

The position of people in public life gives rise to particular difficulties in the law of defamation, and also in the law of privacy in those jurisdictions which recognise a right of privacy.

The limits of *Sullivan* await further elucidation. And someone may wish to examine whether the Convention can assist where there has been a possible infringement of Article 8(1) by a person or body other than a public authority. But unfortunately time does not permit any further exploration of these matters today.

6

Who is Listening to Whom?
The Discourse Between the Canadian
Judiciary and Academics

by The Hon. Mr. Justice Gerard V. La Forest

A striking feature of the current Canadian judicial scene is the constant — and fruitful — reliance on academic material, both Canadian and foreign. How could such reliance be anything but fruitful? Judges are inevitably faced with the task of deciding cases within a limited amount of time, often in areas of the law with which they may only be vaguely familiar. In consequence they may not be sufficiently aware of the broad implications a decision may have. These considerations are of particular significance in a Common Law system where precedent plays a predominant role. Traditionally, counsel for the parties are expected to produce relevant authorities to the court. There is certainly much to be said for the assumption that truth is best discovered by the strong expression of the competing views of those having a stake in the outcome of a decision. That assumption, however, is clearly more persuasive as it relates to factual issues than to the long term legal and societal implications of appellate decisions. On the latter issues, the adversarial approach to litigation is sometimes wanting owing to the lack of precedents, and its dependence on the quality of counsel and their necessarily specific perspective — winning the case.

What is often needed in our modern complex and rapidly evolving society is a more detached and broader perspective to ensure creative judicial solutions to emerging problems. Here, it seems to me, the academic has a major role to play. In his article 'The Judge and the Academic Community',[1] Kenneth Ripple has stated the

---

[1] (1989), 50 *Ohio St. LJ* 1237.

following about the importance of nurturing a relationship between the judiciary and academics:

Judicial intellectual enrichment through scholarship must not be under-
estimated. Daily judicial duties provide little opportunity to integrate
one's learning or to engage in rigorous intellectual self-criticism.
Scholarly endeavours put the jurist in touch with a broader world of
ideas and provide an important source of intellectual nourishment.[2]

We have certainly found this to be true in Canada.

I am not saying, of course, that the academic perspective is
better—only that it is different. I have found that the microscopic
examination of a specific issue I have engaged in in litigation has
required modification of views I had adopted in broader studies.
By the same token, academic work has sometimes alerted me to
the need for deeper study, that in turn led to the realization that
the narrow question on which I was working was simply the wrong
one to ask. The two approaches are not opposed; they are complementary.

POST-WAR DEVELOPMENT

The interaction between the judiciary and the academic community in Canada has grown in significance since the end of World War
II. It is today multi-dimensional. Initially, the relationship between the courts and academia was slow to emerge. This was
in part because of the influence English courts exercised over
their Canadian counterparts. The Judicial Committee of the Privy
Council was then at the apex of the Canadian judicial system, and
it was not until the abolition of appeals to that body on December
23, 1949 that the Supreme Court of Canada became the final
court of appeal for Canada. Only then did it become possible for
Canadian courts to consider deviating from English authorities.[3]

The historical link between Canadian and English courts created
reliance on English precedent. This reliance was bolstered by the
relatively small and undeveloped legal community within Canada.
As a result, strict adherence to the principle of *stare decisis* in the

---

[2] *Ibid.*, at 1241.
[3] Laskin, B., 'The Supreme Court of Canada: A Final Court of and for
Canadians' (1951), 29 *Can. Bar Rev.* 1038, at 1069.

English courts was for many years reflected in the decisions of Canadian courts. This reduced the relevance of other materials. Where a legal point had previously been decided, the courts felt bound by it and that ended the analysis, obviating the need for recourse to other sources. For example, in 1950, in *Reference Re the Wartime Leasehold Regulations*,[4] counsel for the Canadian Congress of Labour sought support for an argument from an article in the Canadian Bar Review, only to be met by the following remark from Chief Justice Rinfret: 'The Canadian Bar Review is not an authority in this Court'.[5]

Another factor influencing the early reluctance to use other sources was the English convention of not citing living authors. However, coincident with the Supreme Court of Canada becoming the final appeal court in Canada was the erosion of this convention in England, which Lord Denning bluntly criticized as 'prevent[ing] the judges having the benefit of the most up-to-date researches and discussions on a subject'.[6]

Also around this time, American legal realism, along with the concomitant recognition that law was not an autonomous realm separate and apart from political and social realities, began to have its impact felt in Canada. Legal realism, in its rejection of a restrained and conservative formalism, mandated consideration of more than legal precedent. In one articulation of it, legal realism has been referred to as 'policy analysis' that seeks an outcome that 'best promotes public welfare in non-legalistic terms'.[7] This recognition of the political nature of judicial decision-making, particularly in constitutional cases, proved to be an impetus to increased recourse to political and social theory, into which academic works could provide valuable insight.

It was in this legal climate that Bora Laskin precipitated the trend away from strict application of *stare decisis*, embracing the view that the Supreme Court of Canada had to 'adopt a simple rule of adult behaviour and to recognize that law must pay tribute to life'.[8] This, in turn required a recognition that many of the earlier

[4] [1950] SCR 124.
[5] See Bale, G., 'W. R. Lederman and the Citation of Legal Periodicals by the Supreme Court of Canada' (1993), 19 Queen' s LJ 36, at 49–50.
[6] *Ibid.*, at 51–2, where Bale cites Denning, A.T., 'The Universities and Law Reform' (1947–51), 1 *Journal of Society of Public Teachers of Law* 258, at 263.
[7] Posner, R. A., 'Legal Formalism, Legal Realism, and the Interpretation of Statutes and the Constitution' (1986–87), 37 *Case W Res. L Rev.* 179, at 181.
[8] Laskin, B., *supra*, n. 3, at 1073.

decisions, especially those of the Privy Council, were based upon a social and economic foundation that had changed dramatically.[9] Thus, *stare decisis* could not be applied inflexibly, and in Laskin's view, the Supreme Court should strive for 'empiricism not dogmatism, imagination rather than literalness' in an effort to develop its own personality.[10]

The trend away from strict adherence to precedent and the corresponding increased willingness to consider other sources was strongly influenced by the growth of law schools in Canada. The emergence of a legal academic community resulted in a rising number of full-time law professors. When Frank Scott became the first president of the new Association of Canadian Law Teachers in 1950, there were only 40 full-time teachers of law in Canada.[11] There were still only 60 when I became a law professor in 1956. By the 1980s, that number had multiplied more than tenfold,[12] a figure that does not appear to have changed significantly since.[13] With an increased number of professors dedicated to legal research and scholarship, the sheer volume of academic material available to the courts grew significantly. The creation of law journals and reviews matched the growth in membership in the legal academic community. In 1950, there were only three Canadian university law reviews; by the early 1980s, there were 18.[14] Several more have appeared since.

Law reviews proved to be a medium through which academic scholarship, the result of research and the embodiment of considered opinion and critique, heralded changes in the legal, socio-economic and political landscapes. A remark made by Justice Judith S. Kaye of the Court of Appeals of the State of New York concerning her approach has now come to be true of an increasing number of Canadian judges. She stated: 'I look to law review articles for something much different—for the newest thinking on the subject, for a sense of the direction of the law and

---

[9] Laskin, above n. 8, at 1071.   [10] *Ibid.*, at 1075–6.
[11] Consultative Group on Research and Education in Law, *Law & Learning: Report to the Social Sciences and Humanities Research Council of Canada* (Ottawa: The Council, 1983), at 18.
[12] *Ibid.*
[13] As would appear from the compilations in the *Canadian Law List, 1996*, at D-34–5, D-131–2, D-250, D-281–2, D-337–8, D-401–6, D-753–6, D-980–1.
[14] John S. McKennirey, *Canadian Law Faculties: A Report to the Consultative Group on Research and Education in Law* (Ottawa: SSHRC, 1982), at 55.

how the case before us fits within it, for a more global yet profound perspective on the law and its social context than any individual case presents.'[15] The assistance the Canadian judiciary has sought from law reviews has soared over the years.

A major factor influencing the interaction between judges and academics is the appointment of academics to the bench. An early appointment to the Supreme Court was Pierre Basile Mignault, an eminent civilian, but under the Civil Law system, of course, judges have always relied on *doctrine*. But more recent appointments of full-time or part-time academics were to have broader implications. Former full-time academics appointed to the Supreme Court include Bora Laskin in 1970, Jean Beetz in 1974, Gerald Le Dain in 1984, myself in 1985, Beverley McLachlin in 1989, William Stevenson in 1990 and Frank Iacobucci in 1991. Part-timers include Louis-Philippe Pigeon in 1967 and Antonio Lamer in 1980. Though Bertha Wilson was not an academic, her years in practice were as head of the research section in a major law firm.

The appointment of academics in courts of all levels has now become commonplace. Not only do these appointments bring an increased willingness to resort to academic materials in the course of judicial decision-making. They also generate more frequent recourse to materials other than Canadian and English.[16] One explanation for this increased use of foreign materials is to be found in the foreign training of many of our legal scholars. For example, Ivan C. Rand, who earned his L.L.B. from Harvard was the leading user of American materials in the Court during the 1950s.[17] My own willingness to resort to American authorities and periodicals stems, in part, from my graduate work at Yale. At an earlier period, virtually the only material used was Canadian or English. The latter was built into the system not only through the structural interconnection of the English and Canadian courts, but

---

[15] Kaye, J. S., 'One Judge' s View of Academic Law Review Writing' (1989), *J. Legal Educ.* 313, at 319.

[16] A study conducted over the period of 1985 to 1992 reveals that there were 990 references to law journals, of which 58.2% were Canadian, 25.1% were American, 9.7% were British, 3.6 % were French and 1.6 % were Australian. The majority of references is to Canadian periodicals and annotations, but considerable reliance on foreign materials is clearly evidenced. See Bale, G., *supra*, n. 5, at 55–6.

[17] La Forest, G. V., 'The Use of American Precedents in Canadian Courts' (1994), 46 *Me. L. Rev.* 211, at 213, referring to Bushnell, S. I., 'The Use of American Cases' (1986), 35 *UNB LJ* 157, at 169.

through the fact that at the time postgraduate studies in law by Canadians was more often English than American.

The impact of academic appointments on the Court has been felt in terms of the broader perspective with which members of the judiciary approached legal problems. It must be said, however, that perhaps the first member of our Court to be guided by such a perspective, Ivan Rand, only became an academic after he left the Court.[18] Said to be one of the most philosophically inclined judges to sit on our Court,[19] he has been praised for his ability to 'discover the broader principles of which those cases were but examples, and then to base his reasoning on those broader principles'.[20]

Of Rand it can be said that he was a practitioner with an academic bent. Of Bora Laskin, who was animated with the same awareness of the 'broader principles', it can be said that he was an academic with a practical bent. Former Chief Justice Brian Dickson in an appreciation stated that '[t]here can be no doubt that Bora Laskin the judge followed the advice of Bora Laskin the professor'.[21] In this vein, Dickson CJ remarked upon the empiricism and creativity that informed Laskin's approach to the law and noted 'his belief in the importance of a distinctively Canadian jurisprudence extended beyond the constitutional decisions'.[22]

Bora Laskin received post-graduate training at Harvard, a factor obviously bearing upon the use of foreign academic works in his judicial opinions. For example, *Reibl* v. *Hughes,*[23] a case involving the liability of a medical practitioner for battery and negligence, manifests Laskin CJ's comfort in resorting to American academics and commentators. In that case, he found an American legal periodical 'useful' for its summary of issues on which medical evidence in non-disclosure cases is significant and referred to a New York commentary in support of his formulation of the legal standard for causation in such cases. The case stands as a tribute to Chief Justice Laskin's commitment to the right of the individual to make free and informed decisions and is a lasting testament to his ethical and creative approach to the law.

[18] When he was appointed Dean of Law of the University of Western Ontario.
[19] Bale, G., *supra*, n. 5, at 59.
[20] Lederman, W. R., 'Mr. Justice Rand and Canada' s Federal Constitution' (1980), 18 *UWO L Rev.* 31, at 37.
[21] Dickson, B. G., 'Bora Laskin: An Appreciation' (1984), 6 *Supreme Court LR* xxi, at xxii.
[22] *Ibid.*   [23] [1980] 2 SCR 880.

The approach was not destined to be confined to the academics on the Court. While Brian Dickson was never a full-time law professor, his time at the Court served to contribute significantly to the trend towards greater reliance on academic materials. In his article entitled 'The Role and Function of Judges',[24] he recognized that '[j]udges do read and use legal periodicals, both Canadian and non-Canadian'; and of their utility, he stated that 'the weight to be given a citation depends upon the cogency of the argument, the intellectual honesty of scholarship, the thoroughness of the research and, yes, the reputation of the author'.[25] Dickson CJ was candid in explaining the growth in citation of legal periodicals in the Court, attributing it in part to the caseload, which left less time for independent legal analysis on the part of judges. In the result, judges became more dependent upon outside sources, including academic materials. He also noted that the proliferation of new pieces of legislation and of tribunals and boards 'forces judges to reach out to the legal periodical literature in order to keep abreast of developments'.[26] It is right to say that, today, all my colleagues routinely use academic, international and comparative material. And because we do, counsel cite them, a matter made all the easier now by their availability from computers.

The creation of the position of law clerk has also stimulated the use of academic material. The genesis of law clerks may be traced to Mr. Justice Locke of the Supreme Court of Canada, who experimented with them in 1948 and again in 1953.[27] In 1968, there were nine law clerks working for the Supreme Court. Today, there are 27. The admission of law clerks to the machinery of the Court affords it the fresh perspective of the most recent law graduates from across the country. The law clerks, usually drawn directly from universities, are familiar with the contemporaneous academic views and are inclined to rely upon law reviews and articles which they bring to the attention of the judges. I add that not only the Supreme Court but most, if not all, courts of appeal in Canada now have the benefit of law clerks. The presence of law clerks

[24] (1980), 14 *L. Soc. Gaz.* 138, at 164–5.
[25] *Ibid.*, at 165. My own comments shortly after my appointment to the Supreme Court echo these sentiments; see La Forest, G. V., 'Some Impressions on Judging' (1986), 35 *UNBLJ* 145, at 154.
[26] *Ibid.*
[27] Bale, G., *supra*, n. 5, at 58.

contributes to an academically enriched perspective on the part of the judiciary. The extent to which it does, however, is entirely dependent on the interests and approach of each particular judge.

As academic appointments to the bench accelerated the reliance on both academic and foreign and comparative materials, so too did the emergence of law reform commissions. These institutions, whose membership often include both academics and judges, rely heavily on comparative study. In exercising their mandates, they became well acquainted with American, Commonwealth and European reform initiatives sweeping across a broad range of areas, from evidence codes to the model criminal codes and codes of procedure, as well as to administrative law initiatives like those developed in Australia, often improving on these models.[28]

The provincial law reform commissions had significant success in achieving legislative reform. This was far less true of the federal Law Reform Commission of Canada. However, its activities had considerable influence on both administrative tribunals and the courts. The use of law reform commissions to familiarize the judiciary with the initiatives in, and academic commentary from other jurisdictions is clearly seen in Chief Justice Dickson's reasons for the Court in *R. v. Vetrovec*[29] where he relied heavily on the work of the Law Reform Commission of Canada in overruling the previous Common Law by holding that it was not necessary for the evidence of accomplices to be corroborated. More recently, the Court has made use of the work of that Commission and other law reform bodies in widening the exceptions to the hearsay rule. Thus in a holding favouring the admissibility of videotaped prior inconsistent statements, Chief Justice Lamer in *R. v. B.(K.G.)*[30] referred to the federal Law Reform Commission's *Report on Evidence* (1975), the Ontario Law Reform Commission's *Report on the Law of Evidence* (1976), and that of the Federal/Provincial Task Force on Uniform Rules of Evidence (1982), as well as various reports and approaches adopted in other jurisdictions, including the United States, England and Scotland, as well as academic writers.

Evidence is an acknowledged area of law in which law reform

---

[28] La Forest, G. V., *supra*, n. 17, at 213, where I discussed the importance of Law Reform Commissions in the particular context of setting the stage in Canada for the expanded use of American materials.

[29] [1982] 1 SCR 811.

[30] [1993] 1 SCR 740.

commissions have provided considerable assistance to the Court. Another area is sentencing where the work of the Law Reform Commission of Canada was informed not only by legal academics, but by academics from other disciplines. Judges throughout Canada were greatly influenced by the Commission's work in the field. Significantly, it encouraged them to seek alternatives to imprisonment and to reassess their views on the role and limits of sentencing as an instrument of deterrence. In more recent years, it has continued to play a role in shaping and defining constitutional values. An example is in *R.* v. *Lyons*,[31] where the constitutionality of the Criminal Code's provisions regarding dangerous offenders were challenged. In the course of my reasons for the Court, I had occasion to refer to several reports of various studies on sentencing by commissions in order to substantiate the view that review of sentences against dangerous offenders might require enhanced procedural safeguards to accord with the constitutional requirement of complying with the principles of fundamental justice. These included the Law Reform Commission of Canada's Working Paper 15, *Criminal Procedure — Control of the Process* (1973); the *Report of the Canadian Committee on Corrections: Toward Unity: Criminal Justice and Corrections* (Ouimet Report) (1969); and the *Report of the Royal Commission to Investigate the Penal System of Canada* (Archambault Commission) (1938). A report to the British Parliament recommending the enactment of dangerous offender legislation and concurring British academic commentary provided a broader understanding of foreign approaches to support the Court's conclusions.

Law reform commissions have also had an unequivocal impact in areas where knowledge of the particular socio-economic circumstances is crucial to the determination of the legal issues. In such cases, the judiciary may require assistance in ascertaining the nature of the socio-economic context. For example, in *R.* v. *Edwards Books and Art Ltd.*,[32] where the constitutionality of the *Retail Business Holidays Act* was in dispute, the Ontario Law Reform Commission, *Report on Sunday Observance Legislation* (1970) provided the Court with valuable insights into the retail industry, including an explanation of the competitive pressures unique to the industry, and other factors making the labour force

[31] [1987] 2 SCR 309.   [32] [1986] 2 SCR 713.

especially powerless in the face of employers. In fact, Dickson CJ stated that the 'Report accurately reflects the purposes of the Act'. The work of law reform commissions, as well as other specific studies engaged in by quasi-public bodies, constitute a significant guide to the courts. What should not be overlooked for present purposes is that their work is frequently grounded in studies by academic experts.

What should not be overlooked, either, is the influence the time spent on such reform bodies has had on judges who later returned, or were subsequently appointed to the Bench. Chief Justice Lamer, a former Chairman of the Law Reform Commission of Canada, frequently refers to work with which he was involved on the Commission. I should confess that I, too, was a member of that Commission, and my experience sometimes finds reflection in my judicial work.

THE CANADIAN CHARTER OF RIGHTS AND FREEDOMS

I have set forth many of the elements that during the post-war period played a part in creating the judicial academic dialogue that today exists in Canada. All of these have been in place for some time, but until some ten years ago they ignited only sporadically, and only a limited number of judges were involved in the dialogue. A catalyst was needed to bring all the elements into play. That catalyst was the *Canadian Charter of Rights and Freedoms,* the Canadian version of a constitutional Bill of Rights which came into effect in April 1982. The *Charter* forced the courts to look at questions differently than before as it mandated that a value judgment be made about a statute and its purposes. Accordingly, the sources to which the courts had previously turned for guidance had to change. At the time of the enactment of the *Charter*, I had stated:

I hope, too, that our search will also lead us to seek light from disciplines other than the law, for many of the questions we will have to consider transcend the legal system. Rights continue to emerge from the human experience. All of this has implications for more mundane matters like libraries and the research assistance judges should have for the proper performance of their function.[33]

The adoption of the *Charter* was a direct result of the international human rights movement that, in common with other countries, had already had profound effects in Canada. The *Charter* was but the last in a series of steps in response to this movement. The decisive step towards the adoption of a constitutional Bill of Rights began in 1968, the United Nations International Year of Human Rights, when the then Minister of Justice, Pierre Trudeau, began a campaign to bring this about. He proposed the ratification of two international treaties on human rights, the International Covenant on Economic, Social and Cultural Rights and the International Covenant on Civil and Political Rights, which sought to arouse awareness and drive governments around the world to action.[34] These treaties influenced the substance of the proposal for a constitutional human rights document ultimately put forward by Trudeau, as did the American Bill of Rights, the European Convention and the Royal Commission on Bilingualism and Biculturalism.[35] Much of this survived and was embodied in the final *Charter* document.

As I noted in a speech to the Canadian Council on International Law,[36] the connection between the *Charter* and its international context inspired Maxwell Cohen, Q.C. and Anne Bayefsky to make this comment:

The very fact . . . that the 'supreme law of Canada' represented in part by the *Charter*, is indissolubly linked by language and ideology to important international instruments and principles to which Canada subscribes, assures the inevitability of some resort to these 'external' international

[33] La Forest, G. V., 'The Canadian Charter of Rights and Freedoms: An Overview' (1983), 61 *Can. Bar Rev.* 19, at 24. In that respect, I noted in particular references to judicial decisions in other jurisdictions, notably the United States, and under the United Nations Covenant on Civil and Political Rights and European Convention for the Protection of Human Rights and Fundamental Freedoms.
[34] Trudeau, P. E., *A Canadian Charter of Human Rights* (Ottawa: Queen' s Printer, 1968), at 12.
[35] *Ibid.*, at 15–27.
[36] La Forest, G. V., 'The Use of International and Foreign Material in the Supreme Court of Canada' , *Proceedings of the 1988 Conference of the Canadian Council on International Law*, 230.

legal documents and ideas in order to be certain that on appropriate occasions the 'proper' meaning is given to that *Charter*.[37]

The authors of this comment forecast the effect the *Charter* would produce. They 'envisage[d] a generation of lawyership that, for the first time in Canadian professional history, will roam the libraries of the law schools and the government departments to find those once exotic footnotes to help define the unruly adjectives of a charging *Charter*'.[38] According to Noel Lyon, the *Charter* mandates a 'framework that gives philosophical works and empirical studies their rightful place',[39] a view that naturally advocates recourse to scholarship. These various comments have proved to be accurate predictors of the course that would be taken under the *Charter*. Professor Peter Hogg echoes the sentiment that the *Charter* indeed dictates a different judicial approach. In his view, cases under the *Charter* are more policy-laden than other cases, primarily because the rights guaranteed by it are expressed in vague terms and come into conflict with each other and other values respected in Canadian society, and thus require a balancing of competing policy choices.[40]

Given the policy considerations that routinely arise in *Charter* cases, the issues involved may extend well beyond the legal points raised and argued by the parties in a given case. Parties are primarily concerned with the issues as they relate to their interests; often, they will not have in mind the broader context required for consideration of the policy-driven matters before the court. The perspective of academia may assist in this regard by creating a more ordered world, in which the broader context may be ascertained for the resolution of these issues.

That the *Charter* has resulted in increased use of academic materials is reflected in the fact that in 1985, a section entitled 'Authors', or 'Doctrine' was added to the index of the official law reports of the Supreme Court of Canada. A study conducted by Vaughan Black and Nicholas Richter makes the same observation.

---

[37] Cohen, M. and Bayefsky, A. F., 'The Canadian Charter of Rights and Freedoms and Public International Law' (1983), 61 *Can. Bar Rev*. 265, at 267.

[38] *Ibid.*, at 275.

[39] Lyon, N., 'The *Charter* as a Mandate for New Ways of Thinking About Law' (1984), 9 *Queen' s LJ* 241, at 262.

[40] Hogg, P. W., *Constitutional Law of Canada*, 3rd ed. (Toronto: Carswell, 1992), at 797.

Of the 620 decisions rendered by the Court in the period from 1985 to 1990, the Court cited academic authority in 48 per cent, nearly half of its decisions.[41] To understand the full impact the *Charter* has had on citation of academic material, this figure must be compared with that of preceding decades. For example, in 1957, a mere 15 per cent of decisions rendered in that year referred to secondary sources,[42] most of which, I should add, were in cases dealing with the Quebec *Civil Code*, where the use of *doctrine* is a long standing tradition. In 1967, only 13.3 per cent of decisions contained citations.[43] By 1977, a small increase was perceptible, with citations in 21.6 per cent of decisions.[44]

Following the enactment of the *Charter,* a group largely made up of academics conducted a series of lectures to judges across the country, to prepare them for adjudication under this new constitutional document. Thus, from its very inception, judges were relying upon academics to inform them and provide them with an understanding of how to proceed under the *Charter*. This was accomplished by reference to what was happening elsewhere on the human rights front, for example in the United States, and internationally with treaties and conventions. The result was to create an initial cooperation between the judiciary and academics and to turn the minds of jurists outward, towards other sources, many academic, some international.

In the first case on the *Charter* to come before the Supreme Court, *Law Society of Upper Canada* v. *Skapinker*,[45] the Court made it clear that it was open to this approach. Speaking for the Court, Mr. Justice Estey made it plain that 'it is of more than passing interest to those concerned with these new developments in Canada to study the experience of the United States courts.'[46] The lesson did not go unheeded. Counsel thereafter made it a practice to resort not only to relevant American material, both judicial and academic, but to other foreign and international material. Reference to such material is replete in the reasons of the Court.[47] Most of these, of course, emanate from counsel, but

---

[41] Black, V. and Richter, N., 'Did She Mention My Name?: Citation of Academic Authority by the Supreme Court of Canada, 1985–1990" (1993), 16 *Dalhousie LJ* 377, at 382.   [42] *Ibid.*, at 383.
[43] *Ibid.*   [44] *Ibid.*
[45] [1984] 1 SCR 357.   [46] *Ibid.*, at 367.
[47] See La Forest, G. V., *supra*, n. 17; La Forest, *supra*, n. 36.

the Court has often taken the initiative unprompted, so long of course as the authority cited is relevant to the issues raised by the parties.

In adjudicating under the *Charter,* the use of international materials is especially relevant in this age of increasing global interdependence.[48] In *Reference Re Public Service Employee Relations Act,*[49] an extensive examination of international materials was undertaken by Chief Justice Dickson. Though writing in dissent, his cogent remarks on the use to be made of such material generally reflects the approach adopted by our Court in relation to *Charter* interpretation. As he stated, when the judiciary approaches the 'often general and open textured language of the *Charter*,' assistance may be sought from the more detailed textual provisions of international treaties.[50] Since Canada is a party to a number of international human rights treaties that contain provisions similar or identical to those in the *Charter*, the content of Canada's international obligations, though not of course binding, may be a relevant and persuasive source for interpreting the *Charter*.

Academic commentary on international treaties has proven useful in ascertaining the extent to which these international documents may be relied upon by the courts.[51] For example, in *Reference Re Public Service Employee Relations Act,*[52] Dickson CJ invoked the aid of British and American scholars for their discussion of general principles for the interpretation of international conventions and treaties, in the course of examining a convention of the International Labour Organization.

BEYOND THE CHARTER

The frequent use of academic material soon extended to other areas of the law. Not unnaturally, this was first felt in areas which,

---

[48] See my comments to this effect in La Forest, G. V., *supra*, n. 17, at 220. I have recently returned to the fray in an address, 'The Expanding Role of the Supreme Court of Canada in International Law Issues' delivered to the Canadian Council on International Law at its Annual Conference on Oct. 18, 1996 (to be published in the 1997 *Canadian Yearbook of International Law*).
[49] [1987] 1 SCR 313.   [50] *Ibid.*, at 349.
[51] *Ibid.*, at 355.   [52] *Supra*, n. 49.

like the *Charter*, had international roots.[53] I can illustrate this development by a case on extradition, *R. v. Parisien*.[54] There the issue was whether Parisien could be tried in Canada for offences other than those for which he had been extradited. This involved a consideration of the meaning of a common treaty provision that the state requesting extradition is confined to the prosecution of crimes for which the accused was surrendered. Having found that the fugitive had, subsequent to his surrender, remained in Canada of his own volition, I concluded, speaking for the Court, that the treaty clause was inapplicable, and that the trial on other counts could proceed. There was no previous Canadian authority, so in canvassing the international law principles applicable to extradition, I referred to the Harvard Research Project on Extradition and Israeli academic material. I also turned to case law from the United States, Venezuela, Great Britain, Switzerland, West Germany and Hungary, as well as to the Vienna Convention on the law of Treaties. The subject-matter being of an international character obviously lent itself to such treatment, but as will become evident this was a precursor of a comparative approach that has been applied generally even in areas, as apparently insular, as civil liability. And I am far from being alone among my colleagues in using a comparative approach to legal questions. Even in areas where there is considerable authority, the law may benefit from the experience of others.

Beyond this interpretive function, academic material may also alert the judiciary to the need for fundamental reformulation of principle and to the relevant international materials. Such has been the case with the rewriting undertaken by our Court in the field of conflicts of laws or private international law. The seminal case, *Morguard Investments Ltd. v. De Savoye*,[55] concerned the recognition to be given by courts of one province to judgments of the courts in other provinces in civil matters. In this field, Canadian courts had always treated the provinces as if they were in the same position as foreign countries, and on that basis followed the English approach. I was of the view, and a unanimous Court agreed, that it had been a mistake to equate English law dealing with foreign countries with interprovincial matters. The decision was based both on the ground that that approach had not been responsive to

[53] I have discussed this development in the address cited *supra*, n. 48.
[54] [1988] 1 SCR 950.   [55] [1990] 3 SCR 1077.

the underlying principles of Canadian federalism and on the conviction that the existing English approach did not fit comfortably in the modern international legal order.

In addressing the issue raised in *Morguard*, I observed that 'academic writers have now engaged the issue on a broader plane . . .' On a review of the academic commentary, I noted that 'It is fair to say that I have found the work of these writers very helpful in my own analysis of the issues'.[56] In terms of determining where to move the law in an area, academic writers can prove invaluable in pointing the way. Indeed, Kenneth Ripple reflects upon this function of academics in this remark:

It is the academic bar that has traditionally provided the intellectual 'jump spark' necessary for the law's rational growth. The scholarship of the academic lawyer identifies for both the bench and the practising bar the policy concerns that animate our law. It attempts to reconcile conflicting policies and suggests rational growth of existing legal principles to solve new problems.[57]

But the value of academic commentary is not limited to assisting in breakthroughs such as occurred in *Morguard*. It serves the important function of critiquing the courts on the issue of what techniques should be employed in arriving at decisions. In *Morguard*, for example, an academic article discussing the Court of Appeal decision highlighted some of the interests that had to be balanced in arriving at any general principles concerning the recognition of foreign judgments. In this way, its critique of the lower court decision drew our Court's attention to some of the concerns emanating from that decision which our Court was able to address on appeal.

In serving as the watchdogs of the Court, academics provide a monitoring function and ensure that adherence to principle is upheld. By providing a legal analysis of judgments, academic commentary may also assist the judiciary in resolving future cases, or cases on appeal from lower court decisions that have been the subject of academic review. That, indeed, is what occurred subse-

---

[56] *Ibid.*, at 1094.

[57] Ripple, K. F., *supra*, n. 1, at 1238. See also Kaye, J. S., *supra*, n. 15, at 319, where she says: 'Parties do not necessarily have in mind the sensible, incremental development of generally applicable principles of law; they often do not have that in mind at all. Academic writers therefore become genuine partners in the courts' search for wisdom—for determining when and where to move the law to meet the needs of our rapidly changing society.'

quent to our Court's decision in *Morguard*. The case, not surprisingly, gave rise to much academic discussion exploring its possible implications. This discussion was most helpful in refining the rationale for both jurisdiction and enforcement, and in avoiding pitfalls in dealing with cases on blocking statutes[58] and choice of law[59] that followed.

In seeking guidance on treaties and conventions, our Court has not confined itself to the general background or the internal interpretive approach inherent in them. It has sought whatever guidance may be available from the decisions of both international and national courts and institutions that have considered these documents, as well as the interpretation of Bills of Rights in other countries, notably the United States, but also the European Convention. We do not, of course, consider these decisions binding, but they are certainly helpful. A readily available source of these decisions is in the works of academics, whose commentaries are themselves useful, though increasingly we are going directly to the decisions.

The habit of consulting academic material, as well as the related practice of consulting international and foreign legal material, has continued apace. I have already mentioned this in relation to extradition and private international law, and the practice quite naturally extends to other transnational issues. For example, in *Thomson* v. *Thomson*,[60] a case involving the Hague Convention on Civil Abductions, our Court referred not only to the *travaux préparatoires*, but to academic comments by participants in the treaty and others, as well as interpretations of the treaty in Great Britain, France, the United States and Australia. A similar approach has been followed in relation to refugee law where references to academics are supplemented by decisions in the United States, and the Commonwealth and other countries.[61] The practice extends to issues involving customary international law as well.[62]

---

[58] *Hunt* v. *T & N Plc*, [1993] 4 SCR 289.

[59] *Tolefson* v. *Jensen; Lucas (Litigation Guardian of)* v. *Gagnon*, [1994] 3 SCR 1022.

[60] [1994] 3 SCR 551.

[61] See *Canada (Attorney General)* v. *Ward*, [1993] 2 SCR 689; *Chan* v. *Canada (Minister of Employment and Immigration)*, [1995] 3 SCR 593.

[62] See *Libman* v. *The Queen*, [1985] 2 SCR 178; *Re Canada Labour Code*, [1992] 2 SCR 50.

This practice, I should add, is not confined to international issues. It has long been followed in areas of constitutional and public law. Thus in examining the extent to which the executive should be immune from supplying evidence in private litigation, we again undertook an extensive examination of the experience of others.[63] In more recent years, we have substantially extended the practice to many fields of private law, including labour law,[64] insurance law[65] and even such apparently parochial matters as civil liability and family law.[66] The high water mark in the latter area was undoubtedly *Canadian National Railway* v. *Norsk Pacific Steamship Co.*[67] where in examining the issue of liability for economic loss, an extensive examination was made of academic writings covering the issue in both Common Law and Civil Law countries. In particular, I note the enlightenment obtained from German law, through the guidance of the work of the Director of this Centre, Professor Markesinis, *The German Law of Tort*.[68] The same approach was soon followed in *London Drugs* v. *Kuehne and Nagel International Ltd.*[69] involving the liability of servants for negligence in performing work in the course of their employment.

The process has led to a broad comparative approach. This has nothing to do with a feeling of dependence; quite the contrary. As I noted in *R.* v. *Rahey*,[70] in speaking of the use of American material, it would be 'no sign of our national maturity if it simply becomes an excuse for adopting another intellectual mentor'. I was alluding, of course, to our former sometimes unthinking reliance on British courts. We do not in any way feel bound by any of this material, whether judicial or academic. It must always be subjected to critical evaluation in terms of relevance to the Canadian situation. What we seek, rather, are insights others may provide, either through their own experience or through scholarly

---

[63] *Carey* v. *Ontario*, [1986] 2 SCR 637 (confidentiality of government documents).

[64] *Dayco (Canada) Ltd.* v. *CAW-Canada*, [1993] 2 SCR 230.

[65] *Scott* v. *Wawanesa Mutual Insurance Co.*, [1989] 1 SCR 1445; *National Bank of Greece (Canada)* v. *Katsikonouris*, [1990] 2 SCR 1029.

[66] *Willick* v. *Willick*, [1994] 3 SCR 670.

[67] [1992] 1 SCR 1021.

[68] Markesinis, B. S., *A Comparative Introduction to the German Law of Torts*, 2nd ed. (Oxford: Clarendon Press, 1990). A third edition appeared in 1994.

[69] [1992] 3 SCR 299.

[70] [1987] 1 SCR 588, at 639.

endeavours. It has led us, as various commentators have noted, to valuable sources of enrichment and greater sophistication.[71]

CIVIL LAW INFLUENCE

There is one further point that must be factored into the equation, and that is the place of the Civil Law of Quebec in this development, for it seems to me there are lessons in this, not only for Canadians but for Europeans as well. It should come as no surprise that the former reluctance of Canadian courts to use academic material did not extend to cases arising under Quebec Civil Law, and from its earliest days our Court, like the Quebec courts, commonly referred to such material.[72] Because Quebec Civil Law was at the time only beginning to develop its own identity, codification having occurred in 1866, French *doctrine* played a particularly important role during these early years since it offered useful guidelines to judges facing the difficult task of giving an initial interpretation to thousands of new provisions for the most part directly inspired by the French Code. But over the years, French *doctrine* has lost some of its influence amongst the judiciary.[73] This resulted from the development of a true body of Quebec *doctrine*, as well as from the fact that through the years Quebec Civil Law and French Civil Law have evolved in often very different directions, consequently diminishing the relevance of recourse to French authorities.[74] This is even more true with the recent

[71] On the issue of economic loss, for example, see Fleming, J., 'Economic Loss in Canada' (1993), *Tort Law Review* 68, esp. at 219; Markesinis, B. S., 'Compensation for Negligently Inflicted Pure Economic Loss: Some Canadian Views' (1993), 109 *LQR* 5; Sir Robin Cooke, 'The Condition of the Law of Tort' , *Frontiers of Liability Seminar for the Society of Public Teachers of Law, All Souls College*, Oxford (July 3, 1993).

[72] For example, see *Darling* v. *Brown* (1877), 1 SCR 360; *Fulton* v. *McNamee* (1878), 2 SCR 470; *Chevrier* v. *The Queen* (1879), 4 SCR 1; *Pilon* v. *Brunet* (1879), 5 SCR 318; *Giraldi* v. *La Banque Jacques-Cartier* (1883), 9 SCR 597.

[73] A recent study demonstrated that in the areas of neighbourhood nuisances, capacity to make wills and immobilisation by destination, for periods ranging from 1900 to 1939, 1940 to 1969 and 1970 to 1990, courts referred to French *doctrine* in 42%, 29% and 16% of the cases; for the same periods and in the same fields, Quebec *doctrine* was referred to in 13%, 19% and 37% of the cases; see Jobin, P.-G., 'L'Influence de la Doctrine Française sur le Droit Civil Québécois— Le Rapprochement et l'Éloignement de Deux Continents' (1992), 44 *RIDC* 381, at 386. [74] *Ibid.*

adoption of the new *Civil Code of Quebec*.[75] The *Code*, which is better adapted to today's society, is the product of a recodification process that has lasted more than 30 years. I add that, not unnaturally, academics played a central role in this process of renewal.

While the judiciary became increasingly influenced by Quebec *doctrine* to the detriment of French authorities, there is no doubt that many of the factors that increased reliance upon academic material by the judiciary in the area of Common Law have had similar effects in the Civil Law context. As a result, *doctrine* as a whole is being relied upon more than ever by courts of civil jurisdiction in Quebec as well as by the Supreme Court of Canada. Other factors more specific to the Quebec situation have also greatly contributed to this phenomenon. For instance, since the 1970s, the legal community has noted that Quebec *doctrine* has blossomed not only in a quantitative but in a qualitative manner[76] and the tremendous stimulating effect the recodification process had on all academics in Quebec is certainly responsible in large part for those developments.[77]

In spite of the increased interaction between academia and the judiciary in Common Law jurisdictions, the fundamental differences between the role played by authors in the Common Law tradition and that of *doctrine* in the Civil Law system are still palpable. It is not surprising, then, to find that the same study which revealed that academic authority was referred to in 48% of the decisions of this Court from 1985 to 1990 found that 87.5% of the decisions which dealt with Quebec's *Civil Code* matters displayed such references.[78]

Much of what I have just said may be viewed as somewhat local in importance. But what is really significant is that the two legal communities in Canada are in recent years rather belatedly really beginning to learn from one another. Thus in the new Quebec *Civil Code*, there are a number of important borrowings from the Common Law system, parts of which were originally judicially adopted piecemeal. A remarkable one is the codification of a trust regime free of the historical structural components that exist in Common

---

[75] The new *Civil Code of Quebec* came into force on 1 January 1994.

[76] Jobin, P.-G., *supra*, n. 73, at 398 *et seq.*

[77] Gaudet, S., 'La Doctrine et le Code Civil du Québec' in *Le Nouveau Code Civil—Interprétation et Application* (Montréal: 1992), 223, at 240 *et seq.*

[78] Black, V. and Richter, N. *supra*, n. 41, at 387.

Law countries. But the influence of one system on the other is increasingly apparent.[79] This is encouraged by references to academic material and the more cosmopolitan attitude that prevails on our Court. In dealing with new or evolving problems, the Common Law judges are very receptive to the views of the Civilian judges, and *vice versa*, though we are of course careful to conform to the particular mode of thought of the system in which an issue arises.

CONCLUSION

To conclude, the interaction between the courts and the academic community, though relatively recent, is integral to the intellectual well-being of the law. This partnership is increasingly necessary in light of heavy caseloads that serve to reduce the time for legal analysis on the part of the judiciary as well as to broaden the range of topics with which it is expected to be familiar. The birth of the *Charter* significantly changed the role of judges in Canada, requiring them to engage in policy-laden determinations, for which academia is integral in developing an enhanced perspective for the making of such determinations. Finally, in an era of ever-increasing global interdependence, the comparative analysis imported through academic writing ensures that our Court is enlightened by the way in which other countries deal with issues.

So far as the assistance academics may provide, this had been clearly foreseen by Sir William Blackstone at the opening of the Vinerian lectures on the Common Law at this great University on 25 October 1758. Speaking in the modest tones of the day, he had this to say:

The advantage that might result to the science of the law itself, when a little more attended to in these seats of knowledge, perhaps would be very considerable. The leisure and ability of the learned in these retire-

---

[79] See for example *Laurentide Motels Ltd.* v. *Beauport (City)*, [1989] 1 SCR 705; my reasons in *White, Fluhman and Eddy* v. *Central Trust Co. and Smith Estate* (1984), 54 NBR (2d) 293. My colleague, Justice Charles Gonthier, has discussed this development in an unpublished speech, 'Some Comments on the Common Law and the Civil Law in Canada: Influences, Parallel Developments and Borrowings' , given at the *Twenty-Second Annual Workshop on Commercial and Consumer Law*, held at McGill University, 12 Oct. 1992 (unpublished).

ments might either suggest expedients, or execute those dictated by wiser heads, for improving its method, retrenching its superfluities, and reconciling the little contrarieties, which the practice of many centuries will necessarily create in any human system; a task which those who are deeply employed in business, and the more active scenes of the profession, can hardly condescend to engage in.[80]

The academics in this and other British universities have long supplied this corrective, although the process was traditionally covert. This is of course quite understandable. English judges were the creators of the Common Law and their boldness and creativity extended to changing the law and adapting it to new circumstances, a function they have performed in an admirable way. But with the rapid and profound changes occurring in recent times, a more robust approach by academics is required, and from what I have been able to observe British academics are responding fully to the challenge.

The establishment of this Centre is a very significant step in that direction. As the establishment of studies of the Common Law at Oxford has proved immensely valuable in the rationalization and development of the law, the increasing unifying forces on a European scale make the establishment of this Centre for the Advanced Study of European and Comparative Law especially significant. When the Director, Dr. Markesinis, informed me of this momentous event, I wrote him that '[t]he creation of the Centre is an important milestone in the development of European law.' I added: 'and I am sure its work will be reflected in an even wider arena'. In this era of global rapprochement and interdependence, it is altogether right that we should seek to combine our strengths by encouraging global and regional debate on legal issues. The Centre provides a focus for this cooperation, and particularly for a means of advancing a fruitful cooperation between academics and jurists. The adaptation and development of the law can no longer be left solely to judges. There is more than enough work for all of us.

[80] Hammond, W. G., ed., *Blackstone's Commentaries*, vol. 1 (San Francisco: Bancroft-Whitney, 1890), at 31.

7

Interplay Between Judges, Legislators, and Academics.
The case of the New Civil Code of The Netherlands

by Professor Arthur Hartkamp

I INTRODUCTION

In a country with a codified system of private law the following situation will normally be found. The Code is only rarely amended and, if so, only at the fringes. The general part of private law is *aere perennius*, more durable than bronze. The legislature is merely concerned with branches of the law that are sensitive to changing developments and attitudes in society, for instance the law of landlord and tenant, labour law, and recently consumer law. In amendments of this kind the influence of case law and of academics is relatively small. The new statutory law will not often be prepared by a relevant number of court decisions; and the legislature will tend to develop the new regulations in close cooperation with interested organisations rather than with individual academics.

Once enacted, the interpretation and further development of the law will be left to the courts. As the statutory law ages, the role of the courts becomes more substantial. Since the general part of the Code is rarely amended, it is that area of private law where the courts' influence is greatest. It is also the part of the law which attracts most attention from academics involved in private law. Academic writings may influence the courts, either directly (which presupposes that judges do read such writings) or through the intermediary of barristers or, in the countries influenced by French judicial institutions, by the 'conclusions' of the Public Ministry. It may be safely assumed that such influence exists, although it is difficult to assess its weight, even in those countries where the judgments contain references to academic writing.[1]

In The Netherlands this situation of relative tranquillity continued to exist from the beginning of the 19th century, when a codification of the French type entered into force, until well into the second half of the 20th century. In 1947 the decision was taken to replace the Civil and Commercial Codes by a new Civil Code.[2] It took some time before the drafts of the new Books began to be published, but as this happened, especially after the publication of the draft of Book 6 (General part of the law of obligations) in 1961, the situation changed and a new pattern of interaction between the legislature, case law, and academic writing started to emerge.

II ACADEMIC WRITING INFLUENCING THE DRAFT CODE

Firstly, academic writers began to explore in depth the drafts presented to the Second Chamber (the Dutch Lower House) by the Ministry of Justice. This literature exerted a marked influence on the legislature, in particular through the intermediary of the Justice Commission of the Second Chamber.[3] This commission, while charged with the preliminary examination of the drafts, passed on in its written memoranda many of the questions and suggestions put to the Minister of Justice (who by standards of parliamentary courtesy, is obliged to comment in his Memorandum of Reply on all questions put to him in parliament). In this way it became precisely clear to what extent academic literature influenced the drafts. The Minister either rejected the criticism raised in academic writings, in which case he was bound to do so on explicit grounds; or he gave his reasons for accepting the criticism and changed the draft Article to which the criticisms pertained. Moreover, the the Minister's reactions could form the object of further

---

[1] See Kötz, 'Scholarship and the Courts: A Comparative Survey', in *Essays in Honour of John Henry Merryman* (1990), 183 ff. (with further references in footnote 1).

[2] See Hartkamp, 'Civil Code Revision in The Netherlands 1947-1992", in *New Netherlands Civil Code. Patrimonial law*, Translated by P. P. C. Haanappel and Ejan Mackaay (Kluwer, Deventer, 1990), XIII–XXVI.

[3] Sometimes also through the intermediary of the Supreme Court; see below for an example.

comments from academics and from the Commission in the next round of parliamentary discussion.[4]

Since the parliamentary procedure was both lengthy and intensive, so was the exchange of ideas between the legislature and the academic profession. The history of this interaction, and notably of the influence of academic opinion on the new Code, remains to be written. The future historians who will undertake this arduous task will also have to take into account the part of the debate that has not taken place in public. For the drafters at the Ministry of Justice also spent much time discussing the academic literature among themselves, often on the basis of written notes dealing with recent publications.[5] Moreover, they held many consultative sessions with academics, sometimes acting in a personal capacity, but on other occasions in their capacity as members of commissions delegated by professional organisations such as the bar or the association of judges. The relevant documents are buried for the time being in the archives of the Ministry of Justice.[6]

[4] The legislative power in The Netherlands is shared by the government and the States-General (parliament) which consist of two bodies, the First Chamber and the Second Chamber. The powers of the Second Chamber (150 members, elected directly through universal suffrage for four-year terms) comprise among others the right of amendment, which is denied to the First Chamber (75 members, elected by the provincial councils for four-year terms). For this and other reasons, the centre of gravity of the parliamentary discussion lies in the Second Chamber. The subsequent discussions in the First Chamber are confined to the general lines of the bill and therefore can be carried out much more quickly. Roughly speaking, the procedure is identical in both chambers; hereafter I will confine myself to the Second Chamber. After the introduction of the draft bill a commission of the Chamber renders a preliminary report, which the government (i.e. in the case of the New Civil Code, the Minister of Justice) answers by a memorandum in reply, if necessary accompanied by a Revised Draft. Subsequently, the Commission presents a Final Report; this Report again is answered by the Minister, who may present revisions of the Draft bill. Then there is a discussion on the floor of the House. This procedure can vary depending on the complexity of the matter and the amount of criticism and suggestions of the Commission or the Chamber as a whole. Thus, in the course of parliamentary discussions on parts of the Draft Code, hearings were held between the Minister (assisted by his advisers) and the Commission of the House, which could result in further changes of the drafts. The act being passed, this whole procedure is repeated in connection with the Introductory Act. This act prepares the promulgation of the previous one and contains transitional law, the necessary adaptations of other Codes and statutes, and if need be changes which are made in the act already passed.

[5] One of these notes was published by its author: see W. Snijders, 'Betaling per giro', in *BW-Krant Jaarboek* 1985, 29 ff.

[6] The first major study of the formative history of the new Civil Code by E. O. H. P. Florijn, *Ontstaan en ontwikkeling van het nieuwe Burgerlijk Wetboek* (Maastricht, 1994), does not address these questions.

III INTERPLAY BETWEEN THE LEGISLATURE AND THE COURTS

In addition to the above, there was and is an interplay between the legislature and the courts. This interplay may work in both directions: (A) case law may influence legislation and (B) legislation (or draft legislation) may influence case law.

A. Case law influencing legislation

Innumerable decisions of the Dutch Supreme Court (*Hoge Raad* or HR) have influenced the legislature in the sense that solutions adopted by Supreme Court judgments have been incorporated in the new Civil Code. This is most notably true for Supreme Court decisions delivered before the work started on the new Civil Code, that is, judgments delivered under the old Code interpreting Articles of that Code or supplementing gaps in the framework of the codified law. Indeed, in modernizing the codified law of The Netherlands, the drafters of the new Code habitually drew on the case law of the Supreme Court, wherever such case law was available. In this sense the case law of the Supreme Court has been the most potent source of influence in the modernization of the Civil Code.

This influence did not cease when the work on the new Civil Code started, something which is not surprising for new decisions on matters not yet dealt with in the existing drafts. As the legislative work proceeded, such decisions could, at a later stage, be incorporated.[7] More interesting are instances where new decisions of the Supreme Court deviated from solutions already adopted in the Draft Code but, nevertheless, found their way into the Code. In such cases, the solution originally adopted in the Draft Code reflected the law (codified or case law) in force at the time of its publication, whereas the Supreme Court subsequently adopted another solution which eventually was taken over by the drafters at the Ministry and then by Parliament.

---

[7] e.g. the section on Obligations to pay a sum of money (Arts. 6:111–26) for the first time appeared as part of the Revised Draft of 1976. Art. 125 was inspired by HR 8 Dec. 1972, NJ (*Nederlandse Jurisprudentie*) 1973, 377 (Ackerstaff/Van Berge Henegouwen c.s.).

The best known example relates to the doctrine of causality. The original draft of Book 6, published in 1961 and submitted to parliament in 1964, provided in Article 6.1.9.4 that the damage which qualifies for compensation, is the damage which at the time of the event giving rise to liability[8] was *foreseeable* with a sufficient degree of probability. This draft rule reflected the law in force[9] at the time. But in a number of cases starting in 1970[10] the Supreme Court abolished the requirement of forseeability, since it unduly restricted the right to claim damages, especially in the case of physical harm caused by traffic accidents. The court followed a new current in legal doctrine which emerged in the sixties[11] and which contended that the degree of probability required would vary according to the nature of the liability and the nature of the damage. This meant that one should rather concentrate upon those factors which make it reasonable (or not reasonable) to attribute the damage to the event for which the defendant is responsible. This criterion was, eventually, adopted in the Revised Draft of Book 6, submitted to Parliament in 1976, and is now found in Article 6:98.[12] In practice the new doctrine has led to an extension of the obligation to pay damages in the field of physical injury due to traffic or other accidents; in this field, therefore, the concept of foreseeability hardly plays a role any longer. In other cases, however, notably the duty to pay compensation for pecuniary losses which are not caused by material of physical damage, the concept of foreseeability is still used by the courts.

---

[8] This could be any source of liability, e.g. breach of contract or tort.

[9] i.e. the case law, since the old Code did not contain a clear rule on the matter.

[10] HR 20 maart 1970, NJ 1970, 251 (Doorenbos/Intercommunale); 9 juni 1972, NJ 1972, 360 (Risicobank/Oskam); 21 maart 1975, NJ 1975, 372 (Risicobank/Mantel c.s.); 13 juni 1975, NJ 1975, 509 (Stad Rotterdam/PNEM).

[11] H. K. Köster, *Causaliteit en voorzienbaarheid* (1962), A.R.Bloembergen, *Schadevergoeding bij onrechtmatige daad* (Kluwer, Deventer, 1965), nr. 116 ff.

[12] 'Reparation can only be claimed for damage which is related to the event giving rise to the liability of the debtor in such a fashion that the damage, also taking into account its nature and that of the liability, can be imputed to the debtor as a result of this event.' The revision of the original draft is explained in the Memorandum in Reply of the Minister of Justice; see *Parlementaire geschiedenis van het nieuwe Burgerlijk Wetboek, Boek 6* (Kluwer 1981), 343. See also A. S. Hartkamp and M. Tillema, *Contract law in The Netherlands* (Kluwer Law International, 1995), nr. 208.

B. Draft Legislation influencing case law

So much for the influence of case law on the drafts. On the other hand, the drafts of the new Civil Code have strongly influenced judge-made law. In a remarkably large number of cases the Dutch Supreme Court has interpreted rules of the old Code so as to conform to the new solutions adopted in the Draft Code or in the Explanatory Commentaries. For this mode of interpretation the term 'anticipatory interpretation' has been found. Dutch courts have, for a long time now, applied this kind of interpretation, for instance in private international law which, in The Netherlands, is for the most part not enacted law but judge-made law. Courts are known to apply the solutions of international conventions, for example, the European Convention on the Law Applicable to Contractual Obligations, well before they are ratified by the Dutch Parliament. It may even be said that one of the most important rules of Dutch private law owes its existence to anticipatory interpretation.[13] However, it is in the context of the new Civil Code that the anticipatory interpretation reached full bloom.

It is clear that there are certain limits to this kind of interpretation. The court, while invoking a draft provision, may *interpret* a codified rule but it may not *set it aside*. However, from interpretation to derogation, often 'il n'y a qu'un pas'. Perhaps this is the reason why anticipatory interpretation is considered to be more acceptable in the law of obligations, with its flexible and suppletive character, than in other branches of the law. In fact, the law of obligations offers the majority of examples of anticipatory interpretation, the law of persons and family law very few, while property law takes an intermediate position.

Nor will a court draw such rules from a draft regulation whose application requires the legislative creation of new institutions such as registers or other official devices. And courts are not likely to

---

[13] In its landmark decision of 31 Jan. 1919, NJ 1919, 161 (Lindenbaum/Cohen) the Supreme Court borrowed its definition of the concept of 'illegal act' (which from then on was also to include an act contrary to *un*written law) from a draft act, submitted to Parliament in 1911. After the Court's decision the draft was repealed and was never enacted. The Court's definition of 1919, which constituted an interpretation of Art. 1401 (corresponding to Art. 1382 French Civil Code) eventually was codified in the present Art. 6:162 para. 2.

adopt rules which do not fit in with the system of the law as it stands, or which form too radical a departure from existing law.[14]

In the European Union, comparable problems of intepretation have come to the fore more generally since the birth of 'harmonising interpretation', that is, interpretation of national rules with a view to harmonise them with a European Directive that has not yet been transformed into national law.[15] Of course, the difference is that according to the European Court of Justice the national courts are under an obligation to harmonise their national law with European law, which may allow for greater liberties with the law in force than the Dutch Supreme Court has taken when developing the concept of anticipatory interpretation.

Examples of anticipatory interpretation abound. I shall restrict myself to a number of rather spectacular cases.

One of the first examples relates to the draft Article 3.2.10 para. 4 (now Article 3:44 para. 4), presented to Parliament as part of Book 3 in 1954, which introduced the possibility of relief from juristic acts on account of abuse of circumstances (including undue influence). As early as 1957 the relevance of abuse of circumstances was recognized by the Supreme Court.[16] In the case submitted to the court, one party to a contract had been compelled to accept a very onerous stipulation because the other party was in a monopolistic position. The Supreme Court recognized in principle that a contract by which the injured party has accepted a highly unreasonable burden on account of compelling circumstances which the other party has taken advantage of, may be void, being contrary to *bonos mores*. This construction differed from the one set out in the Draft Code; apparently the court considered itself not competent to introduce new forms of legal relief on account of defects of consent. But the result was unmistakably inspired by the Draft Code, as appears also from the wording of the decision.

In a later judgment[17] the court ruled that abuse of circumstances

---

[14] See G. J. Scholten, 'Anticiperende interpretatie: een nieuwe interpretatie-methode?', *Weekblad voor Privaatrecht*, Notariaat en Registratie 5031 (1969); A. M. J. van Buchem-Spapens, *Anticipatie* (Kluwer, Deventer, 1986).

[15] See European Court of Justice 13 Nov. 1990, Jur. 1990, I–4135 (Marleasing); 14 July 1994, Jur. 1994, I–3325 (Faccini Dori).

[16] HR 11 Jan. 1957, NJ 1959, 37 (Uijting en Smits/Mozes). For this example and the next one see Arthur S. Hartkamp, 'Civil Code Revision in The Netherlands', *Louisiana Law Rev.* 1059–90 at 1085 (1975).

[17] HR 26 may 1964, NJ 1965, 104 (van Elmt/Feierabend).

does not require a certain form or amount of prejudice, which means that a financial prejudice is not essential. As a result, in the Revised Draft of Book 3, the reference to the disadvantageous nature of the juristic act concerned has been suppressed.

In several older decisions[18] the Supreme Court had held that the using of one's property will only constitute *abuse of right* and, consequently, entail liability in tort if the owner exercised his right without a reasonable interest and with the mere intention to harm another person. Thus, as soon as the owner had any interest, however small, of his own, he was not bound to take into consideration another's prejudice, great as this may have been. This narrow and individualistic view was severely criticized by legal authors. One of the critics was Professor Meijers, who afterwards expressed his opinion in Article 8 of the Preliminary Title (now Article 3:13). This Article forbids the abuse of rights and provides that a right is abused if it is used either with the mere intention to harm another person, or with the aim to pursue another object than that for which the right has been granted, or finally because of the disproportion between the interest served and the interest affected according to standards of reasonableness. In a case submitted to the Supreme Court in 1970,[19] a person had built a garage which extended thirty inches beyond his property. The neighbour sued for removal of the garage, invoking his right of ownership of the land. The court in its decision adopted almost literally the last definition of abuse of right mentioned above.

According to Article 1404 of the old Civil Code (corresponding to Article 1385 of the French Civil Code), the owner of an animal is liable for the damage caused by it. Since 1915 the Supreme Court, on historical grounds, had interpreted the Article in the sense that liability was based on a presumption of fault, so the owner was held liable unless he proved that the damage could not be attributed to any fault (negligence) on his part.[20] In the draft of Book 6 a different solution was chosen: Article 6.3.2.8 (now Article 6:178) provided for a strict liability, that is, a liability irrespective of fault.

This solution was adopted by the Supreme Court in a decision of 1980, where a farmer claimed compensation from his neighbour

---

[18] HR 13 March 1936, NJ 1936, 415 (Van Stolk/Van der Goes); 2 Dec. 1937, NJ 1938, 353 (Teunissen/Driessen).

[19] HR 17 April 1970, NJ 1971, 89 (Kuipers/De Jongh).

[20] HR 15 Oct. 1915, NJ 1915, 1071 (Municipality of Winschoten/Hogsteenge).

because when passing through the defendant's meadow he was attacked in the rear by a young bull belonging to the defendant.[21] The court adduced several reasons for its decision. In the first place the court noted that the 1915 judgment had not found a favourable reception among legal writers and that it frequently had not been followed by lower courts.[22] Secondly, it was noted that the wording of Article 1404 did not compel the court to interpret the Article with the sense that the owner could escape liability if he proved the absence of fault. In fact, the Article leaves this question open and it has been construed differently by the French Cour de Cassation.[23] Finally, reference was made to the new Article 6.3.2.8, which, according to the Court, had adopted strict liability to accomodate views in modern society which should prevail over the historical considerations in the 1915 judgment.

In a judgment of 1984[24] this decision was reaffirmed. Morover, the Court subjected the rule of strict liability to a rather complicated restriction which was also taken from Article 6.3.2.8. The restriction need not be discussed here; but it is interesting to see how the Minister of Justice, while commenting upon the Supreme Court judgments in the parliamentary discussion that took place in the framework of the Introductory Act,[25] undertook to explain the Court's decision, implying that the Court had understood the Article correctly (at the same time, indirectly, defending the Article itself).[26]

A whole string of cases in which anticipatory interpretation has been applied, is connected with the concept of good faith. In the old Code, the only provision on good faith was Article 1374 para. 3, stating that 'Contracts have to be executed in good faith'.[27] The new Code contains a whole series of provisions, absent in the old Code, which may be considered as applications of the good faith

[21] HR 7 March 1980, NJ 1980, 353 (Van de Witte/Bosch).

[22] In The Netherlands lower courts are not obliged to follow the judgments of the Supreme Court, although in practice they normally do so.

[23] B. Starck, H. Roland, and L. Boyer, *Obligations. 1. Responsabilité dilectuelle* (Paris, Litec, 1996), 289.

[24] HR 21 Febr. 1984, NJ 1984, 415 (Bardoel/Swinkels).

[25] See supra, n. 4. Book 6 was enacted in 1980; the Introductory Act was submitted to Parliament in 1981 and enacted in 1989.

[26] *Parlementaire Geschiedenis van het nieuwe Burgerlijk Wetboek, Invoering Boeken 3, 5 en 6; Boek 6, Algemeen Gedeelte van het Verbintenissenrecht* (Kluwer, 1990), 1383.

[27] Compare Article 1134 para. 3 of the French Civil Code.

principle; this may but need not become evident by an explicit reference to the concept of good faith (that is, in the new Code, to its equivalent 'the requirements of reasonableness and equity') in the text of an Article. Some of these applications are:

a) Article 6:248 para. 2 (on the 'derogatory function' of good faith), stating that a rule binding upon the parties does not apply to the extent that, in the given circumstances, this would be unacceptable according to criteria of reasonableness and equity;

b) Article 6:258 (on *imprévision* or changed circumstances), providing that the court, on the demand of one of the parties, may modify the effects of a contract or set it aside in whole or in part on the basis of unforeseen circumstances which are of such a nature that the co-contracting party, according to criteria of reasonableness and equity, may not expect that the contract be maintained in an unmodified form;

c) Article 6:233 (on general conditions), providing that a stipulation in general conditions may be annulled (either through an informal declaration by a party to the contract addressed to the other party or by judgment) if, taking into consideration all the circumstances of the case, it is unreasonably onerous to the other party;

d) Articles 6:52 and 6:262 on the right to suspend the performance of an obligation, not only in a contractual relationship (*exceptio non adimpleti contractus*), but also outside the scope of contract law; and

e) Article 6:94, providing that the court may reduce a stipulated penalty if equity clearly so requires.

All these Articles have been anticipated by the Supreme Court. This began with a case of 1966,[28] continuing in a number of cases until the formal entering into effect of the new Code in 1992.[29] In fact, anticipatory interpretation could always be expected to take place when an Article of this group in modern scholarly opinion (and possibly in the judgments of lower courts) was considered to contain a just and equitable solution. As in the case of liability for animals (discussed above), it was not felt to be an impediment that the Supreme Court had to come back from decisions taken in the

---

[28] HR 19 May 1967, NJ 1967, 261 (Saladin/HBU).
[29] And even afterwards: 'anticipatory interpretation' is still applied in cases which according to transitional law have to be decided according to the old law.

past, which in fact was often the case, most obviously so in the doctrine of changed circumstances.

The only exception to this practice has been a decision[30] in which the Supreme Court has refused to apply the rule of Article 6:109, which grants the courts the power to reduce a legal obligation to repair damage on the ground that awarding full reparation 'would lead to clearly unacceptable results'. Among the factors to be taken into consideration are the nature of the liability (for example, risk versus fault), the juridical relationship between the parties, and their respective financial capacity. There is no power to reduce damages if the debtor's liability is or (by statutory duty) should have been covered by insurance. The Court refused to anticipate because the provision was considered too radical a departure from existing law. Indeed, the new rule on mitigation of damages has been harshly criticized by some legal scholars who considered it to be a rule of social security law rather than a rule of private law.[31]

An extremely interesting example of interplay between judges and legislators[32] may be found in the doctrine of precontractual liability. At the end of the work on Book 6 the Justice Commission of the First Chamber asked the Minister of Justice whether it would not be desirable to add a section on precontractual liability. The Commission referred to Professor H. Drion of Leiden University, who in several publications[33] had proposed to accept, in some circumstances, an obligation to pay damages in the case of breaking off negotiations; the measure of damages was to be restricted to the reliance interest. The Minister of Justice and his advisers rejected this proposal: such an obligation might hamper a party's freedom to collect freely offers for concluding a contract.[34]

Next, the Supreme Court—with Drion sitting as one of the judges—accepted liability in case of breaking off negotiations. Out of several relevant cases, most important is a 1982 judgment,[35] in

[30] HR 13 Oct. 1995, RvdW 1995, 205 (Davidson/Helling).

[31] C. J. H. Brunner, *Aansprakelijkheid naar draagkracht* (Kluwer, Deventer, 1973).

[32] As well as academics and, probably, commercial interest groups.

[33] 'Het tot stand komen van overeenkomsten. Afd. 6.5.2 van het Ontwerp BW', *Weekblad voor Privaatrecht, Notarisambt en Registratie* 4829 (1964); 'Precontractuele verhoudingen naar Nederlands recht', *Preadvies voor de vergelijkende studie van het recht van België en Nederland*, 1967, 43 ff.

[34] *Parlementaire Geschiedenis van het Burgerlijk Wetboek, Boek 6* (1981), 71 and 878–9; *o.c.* Boek 3 (1981), 38, 42, 49.

[35] HR 18 June 1982, NJ 1983, 723 (Plas/Municipality of Valburg).

which the Court even went so far as to accept the possibility of a measure of damages including expectation losses. Briefly, the facts of the case are as follows.[36]

Plas, a construction firm, tendered for the building of a municipal swimming pool in the small town of Valburg. Its proposal came out best—there was no official tendering—and the mayor and its eldermen agreed to the plans which were within the budget available. Their decision, however, still had to receive the approval of the city council, where a member of the council proposed an alternative tender made by another company at a lower price. The latter plan was thereupon accepted by the city council and Plas was set aside. His claim for damages led to a landmark decision by the Dutch Supreme Court. The Court made a distinction between three stages in the negotiating process of parties:

1) initial stage: parties are free to break off negotiations, without any obligation to compensate the other party;
2) continuing stage: a party may be free to break off negotiations, though he is under an obligation to compensate the other party for expenses incurred;
3) final stage: a party is not allowed to break off negotiations since this would be against good faith. Violation of this obligation gives rise to compensation of the other party's expenses and also, if deemed appropriate, the profits that would have been made by that party.

Some years later, the Justice Commission of the Second Chamber when examining the Introductory Act[37] relating to Book 6, asked the Minister of Justice to comment on an opinion expressed by Professor Schoordijk of Tilbug University. Schoordijk, in an influential book on the subject,[38] had urged the legislature to take account of the Plas/Valburg case law in Book 6 of the Civil Code. This time, the Minister agreed, and he proposed an Article stating that parties when negotiating a contract must take into account each others' justified interests;[39] and that both parties are free to

---

[36] Quoted from Jan M. van Dunné, 'The Prelude to Contract, The Threshold of Tort. The Law on Precontractual Dealings in The Netherlands', in Ewoud H. Hondius (ed.), *Pre-contractual liability. Reports to the XIIIth Congress International Academy of Comparative Law 1990* (Kluwer 1991), 230.

[37] See *supra*, n. 4.

[38] H. C. F. Schoordijk, *Onderhandelen te goeder trouw* (Kluwer, Deventer, 1984), 62 ff.

[39] This rule had already been adopted by the Supreme Court in a 1957 judgment on error (misrepresentation), in which case the contract had been concluded but

break off the negotiations, unless this would be unacceptable either because the other party justifiably relied on a contract coming into existence or because of other circumstances.[40] However, during the plenary deliberations in the Second Chamber on the Introductory Act, the proposal was rejected by a majority of the House, which considered the matter to be still in a state of evolution and thus better left to the judiciary for further crystallization rather than to be codified by parliament.[41]

The reaction of the Supreme Court came swiftly. In a judgment delivered some months later,[42] the Supreme Court had to decide on an appeal against a decision of the Court of Appeal of The Hague

was subject to annulment (rescission). See HR 15 Nov. 1957, NJ 1958, 67 (Baris/ Riezenkamp).

[40] Other circumstances may include, for example, the case in which the negotiations are of great importance to the national economy (in which case they should not be terminated before every conceivable opportunity for reaching consensus has been tried), and the case in which parties have undertaken an obligation to negotiate.

[41] It has been suggested that the majority of Parliament that opposed the proposal (at the time a right-wing majority consisting of the Liberal and the Christian Democrat parties) were under the influence of a lobby of commercial interest groups, who disliked the case law of the Supreme Court and hoped that it would eventually be reversed. The same majority was unsympathetic to some other proposed additions to Book 6, such as the regulation on standard terms of contract, which, however, eventually was not rejected but merely slightly amended.

[42] HR 23 Oct. 1987, NJ 1988, 1017 (VSH/Shell). The case concerned a corporate take-over. Shell conducted negotiations with VSH about taking 60% of the shares in a daughter company of VSH in order to develop a joint venture. Agreement had been reached subject to Shell board approval. While the negotiations continued on some minor points, it turned out that it was difficult for VSH to finance her part of the deal; it would be preferable that Shell took over 100% of the shares. Shell broke off negotiations and VSH sold the daughter (100%) to another company (which by the way was partly a daughter of Shell) at a much lower price. VSH claimed the loss from Shell, i.e. the expectation interest (profit that would have been derived had the originally intended contract with Shell been concluded). The court ruled that parties in a negotiating process are under the obligation to take into account the justified interests of the other party; as a consequence the freedom of a party to break off negotiations (which in principle exists) is barred if that would be unacceptable either because of the justified reliance of the other party on the conclusion of the contract or in consideration of other circumstances of the case. A minimum condition is that it must be *plausible* that the contract would have been concluded if the negotiations had not been broken off; it is not necessary that all the details of this contract have been worked out already. In this case the court was not satisfied of this condition; moreover it ruled that there was no justified reliance on the side of VSH.

that had anticipated on the proposed Article cited above.[43] The Supreme Court rejected the appeal, quoting the second part of the proposed Article *literally*. Although it is true that parliament had left the matter to the Supreme Court for further development, especially this literal citation of the Article (the only word that the Court of Appeal had 'changed' was 'restored' by the Supreme Court) may be considered as a rebuke of the two parliamentary spokesmen who, it seems, were considered by the Court to have opposed the draft Article unconvincingly.

IV THE CODE AND THE COURT SINCE 1992

Since the new Civil Code has come into force on 1 January 1992, nearly five years have elapsed. Five years is too brief a period for an assessment of the interplay between the Code and the Supreme Court. In fact, the court has had to decide only a limited number of matters of interpretation of the new Code, since it takes several years for a case to come up for its final decision by the highest court in the land. Most of these cases do not warrant particular attention. This is natural, since courts are supposed to apply faithfully the provisions of Codes and statutes in force, that is to say in accordance with their wording or, if that is impossible (for reasons of age or otherwise), at any rate in accordance with the intention of the legislature. However, the Dutch Supreme Court, although normally following this precept, has already in several instances shown a critical attitude vis-a-vis the new Code, indicating that the Court does not shrink from a liberal interpretation of the Code or from further developing the law where the legislature remains passive. I shall give three examples.

The first comes from the well-known DES case[44] of 1992, where

---

[43] Most attention for 'anticipatory interpretation' has focused on the case law of the Supreme Court, but the lower courts have also frequently adopted this mode of interpretation.

[44] HR 9 Oct. 1992, NJ 1994, 535. A summary in English is published in Tijdschrift voor Milieuaansprakelijkheid 1993, 19–20. See on the case (in English) E. H. Hondius, 'A Dutch case: Pharmaceutical Companies Jointly and Severally Liable', *Consumer Law Journal* 1994, 40; J. G. Fleming, 'Mass Torts', *AJCL* 1994, 507 ff, 512; T. Koopmans, 'Comparative Law and the Courts', *International and Comparative Law Quarterly* 1996, 545 ff at 551; 'Case Notes', in *European Journal of Private Law*, 409 ff. My present remarks are based on the fuller treatment of

the Court liberally applied Article 6:99 to a case of product liability. Six DES-daughters sued ten pharmaceutical companies and claimed compensation for illnesses resulting from the fact that between 1953 and 1967 their mothers took tablets of DES (diethylstilbestrol) while they were pregnant with these daughters. The defendants had marketed these tablets in The Netherlands. The lower courts confined themselves to the preliminary question whether the plaintiffs, who were not able to prove which individual defendant had produced the tablet(s) used by their respective mothers, were allowed to claim full compensation from each of the defendants. The courts denied such a claim but the Supreme Court has quashed this decision. To this decision (as well as to the Plas/Valburg decision dealt with above), one could apply Cicero's famous exclamation *'Quam aequum, nihil dico; unum hoc dico: novum'*.[45]

The Supreme Court based its decision on Article 6:99, which provides that where the damage may have resulted from two or more unlawful acts[46] for each of which a different person is liable, and where it has been determined that the damage has arisen from at least one of these acts, the obligation to repair the damage rests upon each of these persons, unless he proves that the damage is not caused by the act for which he himself is liable. The Article did not appear in the old Civil Code, but the Court held that it also reflected the legal views obtaining in the period from 1953 onwards. This view was based on the fact that the Article was included in Meijers' Draft of Book 6, published in 1961, and that the rule was not disputed in or outside Parliament. In itself this is correct, but it must be borne in mind that the rule in legal literature, if discussed at all, was only connected with traditional cases like the one in the Californian case of *Summers* v. *Tyce*,[47] where several persons fire a rifle or throw stones in the same direction and a person is hurt by one of the projectiles. The question to be decided was whether and to what extent the rule could be applied also in a case like the one

the case by A. S. Hartkamp and M. Tillema, 'Mass Torts. The Netherlands', in *Netherlands Reports to the Fourteenth International Congress of Comparative Law, Athens 1994* (Asser Institute, The Hague, 1995), 51 ff, at 57.

[45] Cicero, *Pro Quinctio* VIII, 30.

[46] The article is framed in a more generic way, because it applies to other grounds of liability as well.

[47] 33 Cal. 2d 80; 199 P. 2d 1 (1948).

at hand, which had not been discussed during the parliamentary deliberations of the provision. Three views have been advanced on the matter.

The first view was that the Article does not apply and that the claim must be rejected because the plaintiffs are not able to prove which manufacturer is the actual tortfeasor in each individual case. This view was taken by the lower courts in the DES-case.

Another view was that Article 6:99 did not apply in the sense that it might support a claim for full compensation of the loss suffered by each plaintiff. This, however, would not preclude a claim directed at receiving a compensation that would correspond to the market share of each of the manufacturers of DES in the relevant period. This view was defended by a number of legal authors in The Netherlands and was also put forward by the present author, as Advocate-General, in his 'conclusions' to the Court. For the policy arguments used, I must refer to the Article mentioned in the first footnote to this section.

A third view was that Article 6:99 allowed for the award of full compensation, just as in the more traditional cases mentioned above. This view was taken by the plaintiffs and accepted by the Supreme Court. The Court based its view on a strongly teleologic reasoning: the Article aims at removing the unreasonableness that the injured party would have to bear the damage itself because he is unable to prove whose act was the cause of his damage. It would be unacceptable if—supposing that each of the defendants was at fault by marketing DES and that the plaintiffs sustained serious injuries as a result of the use of DES by their mothers—the plaintiffs would nevertheless be denied full compensation.

To its policy arguments the Court added that the situation occurring in the present case is also covered by the text of the Article. However, it proceeds by considering a case which in my view is clearly not within the wording of the Article. The court (pre)supposes a case that will establish that in the relevant period DES was also marketed by one or more producers who (due to the absence of fault)[48] are *not liable* and that the damage of the DES-daughter in question may also have been caused by such DES. According to the text of Article 6:99, the Article would not be applicable, because it requires that it has been determined that the damage has

[48] The DES-case was not yet subject to the strict liability, introduced by the 1985 EC-Directive.

arisen from at least one of several unlawful acts for each of which a different person *is liable*. However, the court ruled that this will not release the other producers from their liability for the entire damage, unless, in the given circumstances which include the degree of risk that the damage of the DES-daughter in question was caused by DES originating from a producer who is not liable, such liability would be unacceptable according to criteria of reasonableness and equity.

The decision has been commented upon by many Dutch authors. Their opinions are sharply divided. A number of authors favour the result reached by the Supreme Court; but many critical remarks have also been voiced. The latter group of authors sustain the proposition of market share liability; the view of the lower courts denying any responsibility whatever has not found any favour. The interesting aspect of this discussion is that it concentrates on policy matters, not on the question whether or not the decision of the Court has transgressed the textual bounds of the Article.

My second example relates to the law of securities on movable objects (personal property), and more precisely to fiduciary ownership. The old Civil Code did not recognize this institution, allowing merely the right of pledge to be used for the purpose of granting a security right by a debtor to his creditor. However, according to the relevant rules of the old Code, pledge required dispossession of the debtor: the goods had to be handed over to the creditor or to a third party.

In order to accomodate the need, strongly felt in commercial practice, for a form of conventional security on movables that could remain in the power of the debtor, the Supreme Court, under the influence of German case law, allowed in 1929 the so-called *fiducia cum creditore (Sicherungsübereignung)*, according to which movables could be transferred to the creditor for security purposes without dispossession of the debtor/transferor.[49] Since the legislature abstained from adapting the Code to this innovation, the Court, in a long series of decisions, had to work out the particulars of its own creation, laying down for example, its relation to statutory securities (*'privilèges'*), its functioning in the case of bankruptcy, the powers vested in the creditor (in case of non-performance by the debtor, the creditor was not allowed to keep

[49] HR 25 Jan. 1929, NJ 1929, 616 (Mr.Haan/Heineken) and 21 June 1929, NJ 1929, 1096 (Hakkers/Van Tilburg).

the goods for himself, but had to sell them just like property given
in pledge) and the effect of performance of the debt (resulting in a
return of the property *ipso iure* to the debtor). In the same vein, the
Court accepted the transfer of claims for security purposes.

In one of its most sweeping ruptures with existing law, the new
Code has prohibited the transfer of property for security purposes
(Article 3:84 para. 3). It has been replaced by a regulation of non-
possessory pledge, which may be constituted by an authentic deed
or a 'registered deed under private writing' (meaning that the date
of the act is registered by an official authority, which is something
quite distinct from registration in public registers). The reason for
the change is that the legislature disapproved of the practice of
transfer for security purposes which could be effected in secrecy,
enabling business people and companies to uphold an appearance
of creditworthiness which was based, not on the property of goods
but on the mere factual possesion of them.

Of course, the wisdom of this decision has been questioned
by many authors, taking into consideration, firstly, the fact that
the granting of a non-possessory pledge is hardly less secret than
the old transfer for security purposes, secondly, the wide-spread
practice in business circles of encumbering goods and claims with
security rights and, thirdly, the fact that as far as movables are
concerned property can also effectively be held as security through
retention of title.[50] This latter construction was already known in
the old Code (in hire-puchase transactions) and had been generally
accepted by the Supreme Court; and it has been retained in the
new Civil Code, albeit subject to certain restrictions that purport to
prevent that in practice it will take the place of the abolished
transfer for security purposes (Article 5:92). The real reason for
the abolition of property for security purposes is the legislator's
dislike of granting the creditor full title to the goods transferred
whereas he only needs his security interest to be protected.

In 1995 the Supreme Court for the first time was called upon to
interpret the new provision. The case involved a sale and lease
back of personal property. Two printing presses had been delivered
by Mahez to The Zaaiers. The latter concluded a sale and lease-
back transaction with Sogelease: the presses were sold and the

---

[50] Another problematic aspect is that Dutch law has alienated itself from the
neighbouring major legal systems, which all know the transfer for security purposes, either in general, or for specific categories of property.

property transferred by the Zaaiers to Sogelease; Sogelease undertook to pay the purchase price (Dfl. 1.5 million) to Mahez; Sogelease leased the presses to the Zaaiers for a seven year period, after which the lessee was allowed to acquire them for a price of Dfl 100. After De Zaaiers had gone bankrupt, the trustee in bankruptcy alleged that the lease contract was null and void because it violated Article 3:84 para. 3: it clearly was 'a juridical act intended to transfer property for purposes of security'.

The Supreme Court rejected the claim by means of a very narrow interpretation of the provision. It decided that the provision merely intended to prohibit transactions which intended to protect a creditor in his *typical creditor interest* as against other creditors. This interest was defined by the Court as the right to take recourse against the property and then to be paid from the proceeds of the property before the other creditors. As the Court noted, such a creditor (for instance a pledgee or a mortgagee) is not allowed to stipulate that he may appropriate the property (Art. 3:235 forbidding the old Roman *lex commissoria*). But according to the Court, in the present case things were different. Here, the 'sale part' of the transaction purported to transfer the thing to the creditor and to vest the full right of ownership in him right from the outset; and this gave the creditor, in case of non-payment of the debt, the right to set aside the 'lease part' of the transaction and to dispose of the property freely.

Of course, this reasoning provokes many questions and the decision has come as a surprise to many observers in the Netherlands. However, the strong and weak sides of the argument do not concern us here. For present purposes it is enough to note that the Supreme Court, through the well known device of restrictive interpretation, does not hesitate to come down severely on a provision of the new Code which it considers to be an obstacle to the needs of commercial development. In this, it is not put off by the pivotal position of the provision in property law and by the heated discussions which it has occasioned—and survived—during its long parliamentary history.

My final example appertains to the law of matrimonial property. In the Netherlands spouses are typically subject to the matrimonial regime of community of goods, the community including all present and future property and also all debts. However, the spouses may exclude or restrict this community by an agreement normally concluded before the marriage. One of the possibilities is total exclusion of community of goods. The disadvantage to the wife of such a settlement is clear in those cases where the husband earns more money than she does; or even earns *all* the money, while the wife stays at home, looking after the house and the children. This disadvantage may be balanced by a stipulation, obliging the spouses to divide every year the net proceeds of their income(s) earned in that year. Such a clause is frequent in the Netherlands, but so is, unfortunately, the addition that a claim for division lapses three months after the end of each year. Since most wives during marriage do not bother to ask for division, at the end of the marriage their rights are gone, which is particularly harsh in the case of divorce.

According to some legal authors the clause prescribing lapse in three months is null and void, because it is seen as running contrary to public policy or against a provision of the Code which limits the possibility of prescription of actions between spouses.[51] However, this reasoning is not strong and it has been rejected by the courts.[52] As time went on and the legislature failed to intervene, the Supreme Court developed an ingenious device to remedy the problem. This device consists of two layers.[53] The first is the provision of Article 6:248 para. 2, covering the whole of contract law, and indeed the whole of patrimonial law:[54] a rule binding upon the parties does not apply to the extent that, in the given circumstances, this would be unacceptable according to criteria of reasonableness and equity. This means that good faith may, in a given case, extinguish rules prevailing between the parties or exclude their application. The second layer of the device is that the time stipulation was considered by the Court, in view of the balance of interests of husbands and wives *in general*, to be *normally* contrary to good faith. This latter decision implies that it is the husband who, in order to rely on the time stipulation (and so to escape the division), has to take the initiative by alleging and proving that the

---

[51] Article 3:321 para. 1 litt. *a*.

[52] HR 18 Febr. 1994, NJ 1994, 463 (A./Estate of V.). Article 3:321 is not mandatory law; moreover, here we are not concerned with prescription, but with a stipulation concerning lapse of right, which is allowed subject to the general limits posed by the regulation on standard terms.

[53] HR 19 Jan. 1996, RvdW (*Rechtspraak van de Week*) 1996, 37 (R./P.).

[54] See Arthur Hartkamp, 'Judicial Discretion under the New Civil Code of The Netherlands', 40, *The American Journal of Comparative Law*, 551 ff at 554 (1992).

stipulation in *his* case is not unreasonable. Absent the second layer, the wife, in order to discard the stipulation, would have had to allege and prove its unreasonable character.

This device had been used by the Supreme Court only once before, in anticipation of (what has become later) Article 6:237 on standard terms.[55] This Article enumerates a number of standard terms that are presumed to be unreasonably onerous to the adhering party, which means that where this latter party challenges a term the party relying on it has to prove that it is reasonable in the case under discussion. The interesting thing is that, although the matrimonial contract involved was not a standard contract in the sense of the relevant section of the Code, the type of interests concerned lent themselves to the same judicial approach. The decision may be aligned with an addition to Article 6:237 and it shows that the Court intends to continue, wherever necessary, the innovative role which has fitted it so well in the past.

V CONCLUDING REMARKS

Under the old Civil Code of the Netherlands, enacted as early as 1838 and (in its general part) essentialy unchanged until 1992, the Supreme Court has taken an active stand in modernizing the law and adapting it to changing economic and societal developments. Some scholars have expressed their concern that recodification might hamper the court in doing so in the future and eventually lead to a period of stagnation and literal ('legalistic') interpretation which the country has known for the better part of the 19th century and which would run contrary to the trend of judicial activism that can be witnessed in the surrounding countries of Europe. Elsewhere, I have set forth my view, based on the structure and the spirit of the new Civil Code, that such apprehensions are unfounded.[56] The three judgments discussed above underpin this argument and show that the Supreme Court is far from taking a legalistic approach.

[55] HR 25 April 1986, NJ 1986, 714 (Van der Meer/Municipality of Smilde).
[56] 'Statutory Law-making: The New Civil Code of The Netherlands', in *Towards Universal Laws. Trends in National, European and International Law-making* (Uppsala 22–26 March 1995), in De lege, Juridiska Fakulteten i Uppsala, Arsbok, Argang 5, 1995, 151–78, at 172 ff. (with further references).

Nor are academics trapped in a narrow-minded concentration on the new Code. Of course, there is a keen attention for the new regulations, and part of academic writings is devoted to their interpretation. But there is at least as much interest as there has always been for the case law of the Supreme Court. Finally, it is gratifying to note a remarkably increased interest for comparative law, first kindled by the work on the new Civil Code and subsequently stimulated by the European unification movement and by recent undertakings such as the principles of European Contract Law and the UNIDROIT Principles of International Commercial Contracts. It is my firm belief that the future interplay between judges, legislators and academics in the Netherlands will increasingly be inspired by international developments.

8

This Heap of Good Learning:
The Jurist in the Common Law Tradition

by Professor Peter Birks QC, FBA

'*But when I saw That many Parts of Our* Common *and* Statute *Laws were* Disused *or* Abrogated; *That the* Niceties *in* Pleadings *and* Practice *were lessen'd by Statutes or New Inventions; I Entertained Hopes that* Now *It might not be Impossible to* Sort, *or put in some* Order, *this Heap of Good Learning; and that a* General *and* Methodical *Distribution, Preparatory to a more Large and Accurate Study of Our Laws, might now be made, as well as an Institute of* Civil *or* Canon *Law, or of the Laws of* Other *Nations; which were Once too Heap'd up together without Beginning or End, before they were unravell'd and rescued from their first Confusion and Intricacy.*'[1]

Authority in interpretation of the law naturally derives from learning combined with good judgment and discretion in its deployment. Paul, Papinian and Ulpian were great men in their day, but, amongst lawyers, they owed their authority to their learning in the law. Today everyone with a problem in contract turns to Professor Treitel, to the man himself if they are lucky enough to have that opportunity, but otherwise to his books. The reason is the same. Nobody knows more. In the Roman system this natural foundation of authority was very little interfered with. Those who believe that the emperor took to putting a star on foreheads of chosen jurists, allowing them to answer *ex auctoritate principis*, will be minded to deny this, at least in part. If that is what happened, an element of artificiality did enter into the structure of authority after the collapse of the republic. For who was to say that the man with the star was indeed the most learned in the law?

In our law it is somewhat different. Combining the functions of adjudication and interpretation, the common law has always put its

[1] Thomas Wood, *An Institute of the Laws of England* (London, 1722) preface.

jurists on the bench. If we stop the clock before Blackstone wrote
the *Commentaries*,[2] we will find ourselves in a world in which the
judges had no competitors. There was virtually no learned literature of the common law outside the law reports. The most learned
in the law became judges, and they uttered through the cases. An
element of artificiality was of course built in from the beginning.
No more than it would guarantee the grant of the imperial *ius
respondendi,* learning would not, in itself, make you a judge.

Nowadays the artificiality is more pronounced. The reason is
that there has been a huge growth of learned literature outside
the cases, which is as much as to say in the number of jurists who
are not judges. We have reached the 112th volume of the *Law
Quarterly Review*. In the years since 1885 the law library has been
transformed. This transformation has passed some important subjects by, for there are those, such as civil and criminal procedure,
which have been killed dead by the pernicious division between
academic and vocational learning or, more precisely, by their allocation to the vocational stage and thus to institutions which have
repudiated the obligation to conduct research and write. But all
those which have escaped that fate have been enriched by rigorous
extra-forensic literature and, much as in all the other sciences, all
are now in a certain sense dominated by the professoriate, by teams
of professors (not necessarily cooperating) and by their books. This
would be true even if there were no superstars, no Treitels, Goodes,
Cornishes or Craigs. Despite this transformation of the very nature
of the common law, the history of our system commits us to an
artificial differentiation between the binding authority of the cases
and the merely persuasive authority of the other literature. And
the artificiality goes one step further. The same judge whose utterances bind in the law reports is merely persuasive in the *Law
Quarterly Review* or between the hard covers of a leading textbook. In the midst of these and other artificialities we also know
that, when the chips are down, they count for less than their articulation suggests to the new law student. The ultimate reality is
that the law library is one body of learning and bears on difficult
problems as one body of learning. The artificialities in the structure
of authority tend to melt away.

[2] Sir William Blackstone, first Vinerian Professor in Oxford and first ever
professor of the common law at any university, published *The Commentaries on
the Laws of England* from 1765 to 1769. The four volumes found their origin in his
lectures.

Changes in social phenomena, even quite dramatic changes, are not always easy to recognize until after the event. Although this change in the nature of interpretative authority in the common law has been happening for more than a century, we are still in the midst of it. And curious devices, such as the rule that university jurists should never be mentioned in court until they were dead, delayed its recognition. The credit for opening our eyes goes in large measure to Lord Goff's Maccabaean Lecture, which was given at the British Academy in 1983.[3] The main theme of that lecture was the need for the law to face up to the rapidity of change and to find in a sound grasp of essential principles a reconciliation between inescapable fluidity and the imperative for stability. The sub-theme was that judges and university jurists had become partners in that enterprise. This recognition by a leading judge that the old judicial monopoly of interpretative authority had given way to a new partnership and division of labour was an event of legal-historical importance in its own right.

An essay, written so to say in the shadow of Lord Goff's Maccabean, appeared in a previous volume edited by Professor Basil Markisinis.[4] That essay may account for this second invitation to address the role of the the jurist in the common law. It would have been possible to elaborate aspects of what has in the main been a success story. The partnership between the universities and the courts is now an evident fact of legal life. The law and the law library would be unrecognizably different if, which is unthinkable, that symbiosis were suddenly interrupted. But, far from being interrupted, it in fact strengthens. In the very week of this conference the Master of the Rolls has announced that there will for the first time be a team of young associates to assist the judiciary, much as in Australia and Canada. There are many arguments in favour of that development. One is the more direct contact which it will facilitate with the periodical literature and the most recent monographs. As La Forest, J., remarks in this volume, judges need this help with keeping in touch with the latest university thought and cannot safely rely on the necessarily partisan accounts pre-

---

[3] Lord Goff of Chieveley (then Sir Robert Goff), 'In Search of Principle' (1983) 69 Proceedings of the British Academy 169.

[4] P. Birks, 'Adjudication and Interpretation in the Common Law: A Century of Change', in B. S. Markesinis, ed., *The Clifford Chance Lectures* (Oxford, 1996), 135–63.

sented by counsel. However, I hope I shall be forgiven for putting the success story on one side and taking the opportunity to deal with one matter which the revolution in our law library seems to have left behind.

The Roman jurists did not go in for theory. They did not even devote much energy to the very practical kind of theory which has made Gaius immortal. Gaius was exceptional in his interest in rational classification. He worked out, and in his *Institutes* presented, a method of organizing the whole law in a coherent manner, so as to give a systematic overview, not just a random or alphabetical list. Gaius succeeded, if we may borrow Blackstone's famous metaphor, in constructing 'a general map of the law' and in 'marking out the shape of the country, it's connexions and boundaries, it's greater divisions and principal cities.'[5] Some three hundred years later, in the early 530s, the commissioners through whom the Emperor Justinian worked produced what was essentially a second edition of Gaius's *Institutes*. Gaius's own text was lost. It was not rediscovered until modern times, in 1816, just after the battle of Waterloo and the end of the Napoleonic wars. But Justinian's *Institutes* has some claim to be the most influential secular book in the history of western civilization.[6] It has formed the minds of lawyers to this day, and it has shaped the codes which, in most civilian countries, have largely displaced the old *ius commune*.

The institutional overview was not confined to civilian jurisdictions. The common law also used it. But it is being more and more forgotten. We now need to reawaken the organizing and systematizing spirit of Gaius. Despite the flourishing state of legal literature in the common law jurisdictions, those learned in our law, whether in the courts or in the universities, appear to have given up the challenge thrown down by Thomas Wood in 1722 that it might now be time '*to* Sort, *or put in some* Order, *this Heap of Good Learning'*.

This paper therefore has a very simple aim. It seeks to draw attention to the indifference of common lawyers to taxonomy. Halsbury encourages us to think of the law as an alphabetical list of subjects. University law schools advertise lists of courses. Precious

---

[5] W. Blackstone, 1 *Commentaries* 1, 35.
[6] This claim is discussed in more detail in P. Birks and G. McLeod, *Justinian's Institutes* (Duckworth, London, 1987), 18–26.

little effort goes into seeing how it all fits together. This brings our law into disrepute. It also creates unnecessary intellectual problems which, though they arise from discreditably simple errors, multiply litigation and work practical injustice. Neither law schools nor courts can claim to be free of this fault, but the law schools are more to blame. It is peculiarly the business of the university lawyer to draw the map of the law. But this business is not being done.

In the first part, the paper sets up a civilian glass and some raw common law material to study. In the second it tries to comment on the specimen under examination, so to say through civilian eyes. In the third, some specific examples of taxonomic disorder are reviewed. These are taken from the same body of raw material as will have been discussed more generally in the second part. In the fourth and last part a brief attempt is made to say what might be done to improve things and to reawaken some sense of the import- ance of taxonomy.

I. A SPECIMEN UNDER A CIVILIAN GLASS

Early last year the two practising professions published a new statement of the areas of law which they require to be studied by anyone wishing to proceed to the second, vocational, stage of legal education.[7] A great deal of ink has been spilled on the merits and demerits of the policies underlying that statement. There is no need here to reopen any of those questions. Nor to dwell on the style and standard of its draftsmanship. The statement will be used here simply as a conveniently serious example of an overview of a large part of our law. The document itself refers to the list which it contains as 'The Foundations of Legal Knowledge'. It will be necessary to set out that list in full. However, the prior step must be to set up the civilian glass through which to look. Rather than state the scheme of the code of one jurisdiction, it seems best to step behind the codes and to use a modernized version of the scheme of Justinian's *Institutes*, which, with different degrees of variation,

---

[7] Council of Legal Education and The Law Society of England and Wales, *Notice to Law Schools Regarding Full-Time Qualifying Law Degrees* (January, 1995). The full document is reproduced in the 1995 Yearbook of the *WEB Journal of Current Legal Issues* 43–47 and can be accessed on http://www.ncl.ac.uk/~nlawwww/

underlies the modern structure of every modern civilian jurisdiction. And in fact, as we have already observed, the institutional
scheme is not alien to our own legal thought. Though we have
largely forgotten doing so, we have leaned on it heavily in the not
very distant past.

It may be helpful to set out the institutional scheme in the form
of a diagram and in a somewhat modernized version. There is not
space to discuss all the ways in which the modernized version
departs from the original, let alone to consider why those devia-
tions have seemed necessary. All we want for this purpose is a
scheme, recognizable to anyone brought up in a civilian system,
through which to look at the disordered condition of our own law.

The most important differences from the Roman original are
that the law of 'things' is described as the law of 'rights', so that the
trichotomy 'persons, things and actions' has become the law of
persons bearing rights, of the rights which they bear and of the
procedures by which they realize and protect those rights. Then,
within the law of things, the Roman line between corporeal and
incorporeal things has been moved over, so that the main division
is drawn between *rights in rem* and *rights in personam*, producing
the rigid separation of *PROPERTY* and *OBLIGATIONS*. This
ordering, separating property and obligations, is almost univers-
ally thought to be essential even though, apart from the *numerus
clausus* point, the structure of the subsequent inquiry is similar in
both cases: How do the rights arise? From what events? A third
class of rights has been added. Many would say that there is no
room for that. But, without engaging in argument about it, I will
say that I include it in order to avoid having to categorize primary
rights such as the right to physical integrity or the right to reputation or the controversial right to privacy as rights *in rem* or rights *in
personam*.

At a lower level, the events which give rise to obligations are not
as Justinian stated them. His *Institutes* says that every obligation
arises from a contract, from a wrong, quasi from a contract or quasi
from a wrong. The last two categories have been found to be
taxonomic disasters. This modern version merely takes one
nominate event, namely unjust enrichment, out of the miscellany
of obligation-creating events beyond contract and wrongs. It is
then content to leave a reduced but perhaps still large residual
miscellany as its fourth category. It will be noticed that no attempt

A MODERNIZED VERSION OF THE INSTITUTIONAL MAP

Law is either **public** or **private.**

PUBLIC	PRIVATE

Private law is about **persons** who have rights, the **rights** which they have, and the **procedures** through which those rights are realized.

PERSONS	RIGHTS	PROCEDURE

The **rights** which people have are **proprietary (in rem)** or **personal (in personam)** or **neither** of these. The third category is controversial.

PROPRIETARY RIGHTS =RIGHTS IN REM = LAW OF PROPERTY	PERSONAL RIGHTS =RIGHTS IN PERSONAM =OBLIGATIONS =LAW OF OBLIGATIONS	OTHERS

Proprietary rights, of which there is a *numerus clausus,* then require to be classified by their **content** and by the **events** from which they arise.

PROPRIETARY RIGHTS	WHAT KINDS (by content) EXIST?	HOW ACQUIRED?

Personal rights by contrast have no *numerus clausus* so that there is no practical purpose in classifying by content. Hence they—**obligations (rights in personam)**—are categorized by reference to the events which bring them into being.

OBLIGATIONS	HOW ACQUIRED?

FROM

CONTRACTS	WRONGS	UNJUST ENRICHMENT	OTHER EVENTS

is made to refer property rights, rights *in rem*, to that series of events or indeed to any other identified series of causative events. It would be logically possible, though it might be pedagogically inconvenient, to make the causative events absolutely dominant, pausing only to generalize 'contract': rights, of whatever kind, are born of consent, wrongs, unjust enrichment or other causative events. Whether one makes the division between property rights and personal rights before or after the division between causative events, it is a fact that all rights have to be understood by reference to the events which bring them into being. Property rights must be referred to the events from which they arise, and so also must personal rights (obligations).

The Seven Foundations

The professions' 1995 statement proposes that there are seven foundations of legal knowledge,[8] or eight if one counts, as we shall not, the all-pervading skills gathered under the head of Legal Research. The seven foundations are stated in this way:

Obligations I

The foundations governing the formation and enforceability of contracts, together with their performance and discharge, including the remedies available to parties and the doctrine of privity. An outline of the law of restitution.

Obligations II

The foundations of tortious liability (including vicarious and joint liability) and the remedies in respect of torts (including damages). There should be a sufficient study of the major torts (such as negligence, nuisance, intentional interference with the person and defamation) to exemplify the application of the general principles and the defences, and to familiarise the student with the principal torts and their constituent elements.

Foundations of Criminal Law

The general foundations of criminal liability and a sufficient study of the major offences (such as homicide, non-fatal offences against

[8] The Law Society and the Council of Legal Education, *Joint Notice to Law Schools Regarding Qualifying Legal Degrees* (London, January 1995).

the person and theft) to exemplify the application of the general principles and familiarise the student with the principal offences and their constitutive elements.

Foundations of Equity and the Law of Trusts

The relationship between Equity and Common Law. The trust as used for family or commercial or for public charitable purposes. Express, resulting and constructive trusts of property. Trustees' powers and obligations. Nature and scope of fiduciary obligations. Nature and scope of equitable rights and equitable remedies, especially tracing, Mareva injunctions, Anton Piller orders, specific performance, imposition or personal liability to account as a constructive trustee, estoppel entitlements to property or compensation, the developing principle of unconscionability.

The Foundations of the Law of the European Union

The political institutions and processes of the European Communities. The European Court of Justice and its jurisdiction. Sources and general principles of the Law of the European Union. The relation between the Law of the European Union and National Law. An introduction to the main areas of the substantive law of the European Union.

Foundations of Property Law

The foundation concepts of land law, the relationship between the common law and equitable rights, the scope, nature and effect of estates and interests in land. An introduction to the strict settlement, trusts for sale and co-ownership and, in essentials, the relationship of landlord and tenant. An introduction to registered conveyancing.

Foundations of Public Law

The basic features and characteristics of the constitution. Constitutional law should cover the main institutions of government (Parliament, Executive and courts) in the United Kingdom and the European Union; Civil Liberties and the European Court of Human Rights; the sources of law and the law making processes. Administrative Law should cover administrative powers and their control, especially by judicial means (including judicial review).

2. THE SPECIMEN OBSERVED

The historical dependence of the common law on the institutional map is immediately, albeit fitfully, apparent. But the first thing a civilian would want to do would be to reorder the list, or at least to ask upon what principle the order is based. It is clearly not the alphabet. The list passes from obligations to equity to European Union, thence to property and on to public law. It would be unprofitable to spend too long trying to crack the problem. There is no principle at all, unless we invent the principle of the heap. The list perfectly demonstrates the common law's innocence of order and the prevailing indifference to it.

Public Law Foundations

The law is either public or private. If, first giving Diceyan warnings as to the common law's difficulties with this division, we accept that public law includes all the law concerning the structure of the state and its relations with its citizens and with other states, then three of the Foundations belong or largely belong on the public side of the line. The foundation which is actually called Public Law should stand with Criminal Law and with at least the structural part of European Union. However, it is a complicating factor that in the description of that foundation the general inclusion of the substantive law of the Union clearly imports a large quantity of private law. There are, of course, well-known arguments for distributing this foundation to others. The counter-argument is that, at least in the short term, law schools must be compelled to take special and hence separate notice of the European dimension of anything. However, we must not here pursue that debate. Impurities aside, we seem to have three units of public law. No two of those three are even juxtaposed.

Private Law Foundations

Subject to the mixed nature of the foundation called European Union, the separation of those three now leaves four private law foundations. It easy to pick out and reassemble the principal elements of the law of things or rights, most obviously Property and the double helping of Obligations. The remaining foundation, namely Equity and the Law of Trusts, has to be brought in here too, though more will have to be said of it below. Somewhat foxed by Equity, the observer might suggest an order which would run thus: Property, Obligations (×2), Equity.

Within the double unit of Obligations the civilian eye will easily detect the two principal categories of obligation-creating event. For Obligations I is nearly all described in terms of contract, and Obligations II is clearly tort. Under instruction the observer will also accept that we currently call our law of unjust enrichment by the response-oriented name of 'restitution'. 'An outline of the law of restitution' in Obligations I thus provides the third category of obligations. No reference is made to the fourth, namely 'Other (Obligation-Creating) Events'.

What is not foundational?

One advantage of a shared system of classification is that it enables lawyers to see and reflect upon matter that does not appear. This is one aspect of the central advantage of an efficient system of classification, namely that it allows the lawyer to make a rapid review of the whole law in a way that an alphabetical list does not, much less a heap. It is, of course, not a criticism to find that something has been omitted from this particular document. The professions' document is selective; it was never intended to be comprehensive, and there would have been shouts of pain if it had been. We are not concerned to criticise the scope of the document but only to demonstrate the intellectual advantage of having a map. Whatever form of legal utterance is in question, a good taxonomy lodged in the reader's mind — or, as the French would say, in his *formation* — will reveal what is not being said or what has being missed out.[8a]

[8a] At the 1995 Conference of the Society of Public Teachers of Law several speakers claimed to have diagnosed in the product of the law schools a deficiency which they called 'stovepipe mentality', the condition of being unable to move from one category to another. They prescribed an abolition of categories, a prescription previously recommended to the author by a senior member of the education office of the Law Society of England and Wales during the preparation of the 1995 document. One might as well abolish thought. The cure for 'stovepipe mentality' lies in the opposite direction, in making the categories and the relations between them explicit. Those who cower in the first available bolthole do so because they have no map.

Here the civilian glass reveals that what the professions count as foundational are some parts of public law and some parts of the law of things (rights). From the former, there are large omissions: public international law, for example, is not foundational, nor is the law of taxation. On the private side of the line, they do not count any part of the law of persons as foundational, hence not the law relating to differences between natural and artificial persons, citizens and aliens, men and women, husbands and wives, parents and children, and so on. The decision to omit all of family law might cause the raising of the odd eyebrow, but this is not the place to do more than observe. Then, the professions do not count any of the law of actions as foundational, hence no mention is made of pleading or evidence or anything to do with procedures for protecting or realizing rights, unless perhaps one were to treat tracing, Mareva injunctions and Anton Piller Orders as small fragments within that third main division of private law.

Below the large divisions, one generally needs to know more than the bare outline of the taxonomy in order to pick up omissions; or, more accurately, one needs to know the smaller, subsidiary categories within the taxonomy. We have already noticed, however, that within obligations the event unjust enrichment, under the name 'restitution,' is to be studied only in outline, and the fourth, residual and miscellaneous category of obligation-creating events is not noticed at all. Within Property there is no reference at all to events which bring rights in rem into existence, until at the very end reference is made to registered conveyancing. This puzzles. The *Institutes* tells us that property rights have to be explained in terms of their creation and acquisition, in other words in terms of causative events. The civilian eyes have barely begun to screw up when they perceive a more startling omission. There is nothing said about property rights in things other than land. Hence it is not just modes of acquisition which are omitted, but all aspects of property in chattels and in money.

Has this matter been included elsewhere? It has not, except so far as it is covered, more or less by chance, in the jurisdictionally determined category of Equity and Trusts. Stocks and shares and paintings and money, and all other forms of wealth other than land, are brought into consideration there, but only to the extent that they are the subject of trusts and other equitable rights. But even a common lawyer will appreciate, once the systematic civilian has drawn attention to this curiosity, that to include the equitable contribution to the law of property in assets other than land, while excluding the common law, is to invite an audience to listen to the sound of one hand clapping.

Intersecting categories

It is necessary at this point to recall yet again that this is not an exercise in trying to determine what the professions should or should not prescribe as obligatory subjects of study. The purpose is only to illustrate, from one serious pronouncement upon our law, our astonishing indifference to orderly organization. We have just seen that, uncorrected by such university jurists as they consulted, the professions, not by design but simply by the habit of not thinking through the relationship between categories, have invited students only to the dark side of the moon of personal property. That point took us into Foundations of Equity and the Law of Trusts. If we stay there for one moment we will see that the inclusion of this category causes difficulties across the board.

The problem arises because, not surprisingly a century and quarter after the Judicature Acts, there survives in this list no category called Common Law. Let us confine attention to private law and, more narrowly to the law of things or rights. Just as happens in all our law schools, the law of private rights, so far as it is represented in this statement, is committed to a distinction between proprietary and personal rights (i.e. property and obligations) and then, albeit fitfully, to a division by causative events. But that commitment, fragmentary and subliminal as it is, competes with a quite different division according to jurisdictional origin: all the law derives either from the royal courts of common law or from the court of chancery and the lesser courts of equity. This competing division is expressly represented in the statement only as to one limb, namely Equity. The consequence is that the foundation called Equity must and does cut across the others, as a category of animals determined by colour must cut across categories determined by eating habits: all animals are herbivores, carnivores, omnivores, yellow or of other kinds. A child of eight can spot the intellectual trap.

We have seen that the failure to reflect on the likely consequences of dealing in intersecting categories produces in relation to personal property a situation of near absurdity in which equity is in and common law out. More generally, this intersection of Equity and other foundations perfectly expresses our failure to think in a coherent series of categories. Thus, notwithstanding there being a double allocation to the law of obligations (rights in personam, personal claims), the word 'obligation' expressly appears twice under Equity, for there are trustees' obligations and there are fiduciary obligations to be considered under that head. And there is more. There is a line for 'imposition of personal liability to account as a constructive trustee'. This looks different. The language is different. But in fact a personal liability to account as a constructive trustee is no more than an obligation recognized by equity which comes into existence other than by consent. There are obligations recognized by the common law which come into existence other than by consent, as where they arise from wrongs, unjust enrichment or miscellaneous other events. These personal liabilities to account are of the same kind, only equitable. Evidently, therefore, but surprisingly and unannounced, Obligations I and Obligations II are not intended to represent the whole field of obligations.

That is not the end of it. The study of contract in Obligations I will inevitably include, inter alia, the study of the remedy of specific performance, the supplementation of the doctrine of consideration by detrimental reliance (estoppel), the setting aside of contracts on many grounds, including 'unconscionability'. Yet these matters are repeated under Equity, though, curiously, innocent misrepresentation and undue influence are not, unless generically within 'equitable rights'. The intersection of categories entails repetition. Obligations I includes restitution (unjust enrichment). Anyone teaching that subject without its equitable component would be wasting the students' money. Non-express trusts, not all of them but many of them, belong in the law of restitution. Obligations II is obligations arising from torts or, we might think, from wrongs. But breaches of trust and breaches of fiduciary duty are wrongs too. They figure under Equity. The statement tacitly accepts the historical restriction of 'tort' to the common law. And so do most law schools.

So long as we spoke in terms of contract and tort we had to look hard to see the anomaly, but, now that we once again see contract and tort as subsets of obligations when obligations are divided by their causative events, we ought to spot at once and in full daylight the fact and the danger of our defective taxonomy. A category of jurisdictional origin cannot be fitted into or sit beside a classification, or a fragment of a classification, which is based on types of right, subclassified by causative event, no more than a classification of animals by colour can fit into a classification of animals by eating habits.

The reader will be tempted to explain the list by saying that it assumes the distinction between equity and common law as categories of jurisdictional origin. It only mentions one limb of that distinction, but it assumes that all will understand that the other private law foundations are all common law, as though it had first said that rights were either legal or equitable and had then proceeded to deal with each jurisdictionally determined category separately. There is no hope down this path. We have already seen that in relation to chattels the common law has been omitted altogether. And nobody construing the law relating to property in land would understand that only the common law side was contemplated in that foundation. The same of contract in Obligations I. Nobody would dream of saying that the equitable contribution to the law of contract must be contemplated as excluded from contract and belonging under Equity and the Law of Trusts. There is no intellectual order, merely a heap of historically determined subjects.

The same taxonomic problem of intersecting categories recurs, on a more restricted scale, in relation to the contextual category of the law of the European Union: all the law about the EU. A contextual classification is as alien to a classification by rights and events as is a classification by jurisdictional origin. Hence, some of the matter listed under European Union belongs also and equally in Public Law and some—the substantive law of the Union—intersects with private law categories, some of which are present in this list while others are not mentioned at all.

3. MORE PARTICULAR DEFECTS

This part picks from the professions' 1995 statement four specific illustrations of taxonomic carelessness, again merely as examples of the indifference of the entire common law thinking machine to the elementary requirements of intellectual orderliness. We have hitherto noticed the failure of the list to present its subjects in a coherent order and its failure to take notice of the intersecting nature of the categories which it uses. What follows is of the same kind but on a somewhat smaller scale.

(1) An outline of the law of restitution

Obligations I requires the aspiring lawyer to learn the bare bones of restitution. By the law of restitution we mean to identify the law of unjust enrichment. It may seem a matter of indifference whether it is called one thing or the other, but in fact we cannot continue to call our law of unjust enrichment the law of restitution. There are good reasons why, when Professors Scott and Seavey made the *Restatement of Restitution* in the 1930s they preferred the remedial orientation of 'restitution'.[9] 'Unjust enrichment' and 'unjustified enrichment' irritated common law judges, as being invitations to redistribute wealth according to abstract principles of justice, the very last thing that any judge would wish to do at any time, let alone in the aftermath of the Bolshevik revolution. However, this fear, always unreal, has abated, not because the fear of communism and revolution has died down, but because it has at length been realized that the language never extended any such invitation. The word 'unjust', it is now accepted, initiates an inquiry into the state of the law in the cases and statutes. It has nothing to do with abstract speculation about distributive justice. There is now no doubt that we do have, as Scott and Seavey saw, a law of restitution of, and because of, unjust enrichment. But we must move to calling it the law of unjust enrichment.

Professor Burrows, now a Law Commissioner, wrote an important, and justly famous, article under the title: 'Contract, Tort and Restitution: A Satisfactory Division or Not?'[10] The argument shows that the substance of the division is not only satisfactory but necessary. But the form, as expressed in the trichtomy of the title, is wholly unsatisfactory. For one thing, we cannot do without the residual miscellany. For another we cannot do with a classification

[9] *Restatement of Restitution* (American Law Institute, St Paul, 1937). Scott and Seavey were the reporters responsible for the work. See A. W. Scott and W. A. Seavey, 'Restitution' (1938) 54 LQR. 29.
[10] A. S.Burrows, (1983) 99 LQR 7.

which starts with causative events and then suddenly turns a corner into types of response. Contract, and all the contracts, such as sale, hire, partnership and agency, are events which happen in the world and give rise to rights. Tort, and all the specific torts, such as defamation, battery, false imprisonment, are likewise events which trigger rights. Restitution does not fit, for restitution is a response made by the law to an event or a purpose pursued by the law because of an event. And the event is, generically, unjust enrichment. As sale is to contract and species to genus, so mistaken payment is to unjust enrichment.

The statement that rights arise from contract, tort and restitution is of the same kind as as the proposition that birds are seed-eaters, insect-eaters, yellow, or of other kinds. My canary is yellow and eats seeds. It counts twice. There may seem to be two birds. There is only one. The same simple trap can catch the law. Let us consider a claim for the money received by a wrongdoer through his wrong. In *United Australia Ltd.* v. *Barclays Bank Ltd.*[11] it was held that, the language of waiver of tort notwithstanding, when a plaintiff brings an action for the money received by a wrongdoer through his wrong, rather than to recover his own loss, his cause of action remains the wrong. What he is seeking is a gain-based remedy, rather than the more familiar loss-based award. Some people say that we should not call that gain-based claim 'restitutionary'. They would prefer to call it a claim to disgorgement, confining 'restitution' to 'giving back' and excluding 'giving up'. Unless we go down that route, *United Australia* tells us that there are claims to restitution which arise from wrongs. And there is no doubt about it. In the field of intellectual property, for example, it has been recognized by statute that an account of profits lies for breaches of copyright and infringement of patent, as it does, without statute, for the tort of passing off. But (overlooking the ineptness of 'arise from') if obligations arise from contract, tort, restitution and other events, the restitutionary award for a wrong threatens, like my canary, to count twice. The cause of action is the wrong. But does it not also belong under Restitution in column 3? It does not, because 'restitution' is there an inept synonym for autonomous unjust enrichment, where the word 'autonomous' is added precisely to show that, in column 3, 'unjust enrichment' is a genus of causative event distinct

[11] [1941] A.C.1.

from and independent of the events named in the other three columns. 'Tort or restitution?' is a bad question. There can be restitution triggered by a tort. Just like the canary, the *United Australia* claim struggles to be counted twice, but only because the cages have been ineptly labelled.

The objection might be made that Scots law has inherited from Viscount Stair the habit of classifying a wide range of obediential obligations according to their purpose and effect, reducing to a lower level the reference to causative events. Thus reparation, restitution, repetition, recompense, and relief are all familiar categories.[12] Does not this show that a system can deal in categories of response, distinguished according to a particular remedial aim? Why should it not do so? Of course, a system can proceed in this way. The real danger arises when the categories are mixed. Given a firm commitment to one or other basis of classification, the argument must then be about efficiency. Which is the more efficient taxonomy? This is not the place to argue the point, but it seems to me that the commitment of Scots law to this basis of classification has not been firm enough, and that, firm or not, its experience shows that it is a kind of classification which is inefficient and not very accessible. These points are not for now. The only point which matters is that classifications which turn corners, because the categories change their base, set dreadful intellectual traps.

(2) Negligence, nuisance, intentional interference with the person and defamation

Obligations II is, as we have seen, the law of tort. As described, it comes close to saying that the student must study the major torts enough to become familiar with the major torts. On the way it makes an illustrative list. 'There should be a sufficient study of the major torts (such as negligence, nuisance, intentional interference with the person and defamation) . . .' Even this short illustrative list reveals that our law of tort has something rotten in its foundations. It is built on a bent taxonomy.

Three of the torts mentioned are conceived as infringements of protected interests. This is obvious in relation to intentional interference with the person, pretty obvious in relation to defamation

---

[12] Stair, *Institutions*, 1.7-8; cf. Erskine, *Institutions*, III.1.10–11.

(infringement of the interest in reputation) and true but not obvious without additional knowledge in the case of nuisance (infringement of the interest in the enjoyment of land). Other torts are also of that kind, as very obviously interference with chattels; and 'negligence' can be made to belong in that series if it is redescribed as, for example, negligent injury, negligent damage, negligent infliction of economic loss, and so on. But a tort of negligence, *tout court*, cannot stand in that series. It aligns only with principles of or bases of liability, such as strict liability, recklessness and malice.

The House of Lords recently decided *Spring* v. *Guardian Assurance*.[13] An employer wrote a reference which made incorrect assertions of fact about a former employee and thus caused that employee pure economic loss. Was the employer liable in negligence? The answer was yes. This is somewhat surprising. The reference was a communication which was subject to qualified privilege as being written as a matter of duty to a person with an interest to receive it. In defamation the employer could not therefore have been liable without proof of malice. One commentator asks whether, if the case had been argued in defamation, the House of Lords would have changed the law applicable to that tort.[14] Since the law seemingly was that such a defendant could not be liable except for malice and since the law now is that he can be liable for negligence, one might equally put the question differently. Has the decision in negligence changed the law of defamation?

This is just another example of miscounting canaries. If all birds are seed-eaters, yellow, or others, my canary counts twice. The double vision is due to the bent classification. There is only one bird. Two categories intersect. Defamation is a wrong, like inducing breach of contract or interference with chattels, which is manifestly named by reference to the interest infringed. Defamation is the infringement of the interest in reputation. Negligence is a wrong named by reference to a kind of fault. It follows that the two categories must often intersect. In other words infringement of the interest in reputation will often be negligent. Is there one wrong or two? There is only one wrong. A decision that there is a public interest in cutting down liability for defamation in the cases within what we therefore call qualified privilege is a decision that there

[13] [1994] 3 W.L.R. 354 (HL).
[14] T. Allen, 'Liability for References: The House of Lords and *Spring* v. *Guardian Assurance*' (1995) 58 M.L.R. 553, 560.

shall be no liability for negligence, and a decision that there shall be liability for negligence is a decision that there is no public interest cutting down the liability for defamation in these contexts. There is only one wrong, just as there is only one canary.

The law of tort raises very difficult problems of analysis and of policy. It cannot be right to exacerbate those problems by seeding the whole discussion with the intellectual traps which arise from criss-crossing categories. We ought to have decided long ago whether we wanted tort organized by bases of liability or by interests infringed or according to some other single principle.

(3) Equitable wrongs

In the Foundation of Legal Knowledge called the Foundations of Equity and Trusts the professions make mention of fiduciary obligations and accountability as a constructive trustee, also of the obligations of trustees. We have already noticed this in drawing attention to the difficulty of having a double unit of the law obligations which still leaves obligations outstanding in other categories. The professions' statement does not identify by name any equitable wrongs, but breach of trust, breach of fiduciary duty, abuse of confidence, and knowing assistance are all by implication present behind the words which are actually used.

There are great dangers in separating one family of wrongs from those which, by chance, happen to have grown up in the common law and acquired the name 'torts'.[15] The simplest form of trouble is the lop-sidedness which is illustrated at the moment by knowing assistance. If someone knowingly assists a breach of trust, our law, drawing on equity precedents, is perfectly sure that that person commits an actionable wrong. If the same acts and intents operate to assist a common law wrong, the confidence dissipates. There is certainly no wrong under that name in the common law. Hence, the question becomes whether there is the same thing in effect, under

---

[15] Of a contrary opinion is J. D. Davies, who thinks that classification is merely a convenience for the teacher and the text-writer and 'can so easily produce artificiality': J. D. Davies, 'Restitution and Equitable Wrongs' in F. D. Rose ed., Consensus as Idem, Essays on Contract in Honour of Guenter *Treitel* (Sweet and Maxwell, London, 1996), 158, 176. However, what is at stake is not expository elegance but clear thinking in the courts and, ultimately, the capacity of the courts to decide like cases alike.

other language; and, if so, under what language.[16] Equivalent results can be constructed. But the lop-sidedness is absurd, and fraught with the probability of erratic decision-making.

More sinister is the possibility of developing a parallel law of tort, in which difficult policy decisions are taken differently and difficult analyses are worked through by alternative methods. Plaintiffs are already exploiting the mine of fiduciary obligations to achieve ends which the common law has decided are out of reach. Already, it is being said that the analysis of causation and remoteness may proceed in equity on different lines from those used at common law.[17] If French or German law differs from English law, the differences can be instructive. If English law differs from English law, alarm bells ought to ring. We do not allow different judges to go their own way; nor is the law allowed to be applied differently on Wednesdays. An equitable origin is not in itself a reason justifying a difference from the common law.

The reason we welcome the wrong of abuse of confidence is that we are sure that it is filling a gap left by the common law which we want filled. It does not matter whether we remind ourselves of its equitable origins or not. It is essential that we always have that conviction about equitable wrongs and the analyses associated with them. Are the differences really wanted? The only way to answer that question is to keep comparing the common law position and the alleged equitable addendum. That cannot be done if the wrongs are kept in different packets. A simple example is provided by the equitable account of profits. If the account of profits (equity) is kept right out of the books on damages (common law) it can be made to seem completely anomalous unless and until the court is somehow put into equitable mode. In common law mode a court will say that profits of wrongs are never awarded; in equitable mode it will assume that an award of profits is absolutely normal.

(4) Express, resulting and constructive trusts

When we study obligations, we ask what events bring them into existence. When we study property rights, we do the same, pausing

[16] On this exercise, P. Sales, 'The Tort of Conspiracy and Civil Secondary Liability' (1990) 49 *C.L.J.* 491.

[17] As in *Target Holdings Plc* v. *Redferns* [1996] 1 A.C. 421, 438-9; cf. Sir Anthony Mason, 'The Place of Equity and Equitable Remedies in the Contemporary Common Law World' (1994) 110 *L.Q.R.* 238, 245.

first to enumerate the recognised kinds of rights *in rem*. The law of trusts poses two kinds of problem. One is that trusts really add nothing to rights *in rem* and rights *in personam*, property rights and obligations. For a trust is a relationship which supposes some of both. We may put that problem on one side. The other is that when we think about trusts we use a terminology which averts our eyes from the very inquiry which we most want to make, namely that same inquiry as to the facts which bring trusts into being.

Justinian did the same when he said that obligations, such as do not arise from contract or wrongs, arise quasi from contract or quasi from wrongs.[18] The 'quasi' terminology hides the true facts, merely telling us not to look for a contract or a wrong. Similarly with trusts, we know that they can arise by consent (express declaration) but as for such trusts as do not arise expressly, we only know two bits of gobbledegook, that they are resulting or constructive. These words turn out to tell us, so far as they tell us anything at all, something entirely negative, namely that in non-express trusts the intentions of the parties play no part at all (constructive trusts) or a minor role in rebuttal of presumptions (resulting trusts). Meanwhile all we actually want to know is the facts on which non-express trusts do arise. We might at this stage apply a presumption that the events from which trusts arise will resemble those which give rise to obligations and property rights when obligations and property rights are not combined together in the particular manner which produces what we call a trust. Do trusts arise from consent? We know they do. Do they arise from wrongs? Do they arise from unjust enrichment? And do they arise from any other events?

If we do not ask those questions, but pretend instead that trusts is a law unto itself,[19] we will never avoid contradiction with the law of rights *in personam* (obligations) and rights *in rem* (property rights). The contradictions will happen because (a) trusts are rights *in rem* and *in personam* and therefore are not capable of being sealed up in a container of their own, (b) all such rights have to be explained in terms of the events which bring them into being, and (c) if we search for those facts in the case of trusts in language quite different from the language which we use elsewhere we will

---

[18] J. *Institutes* 3.13.
[19] Which seems to be the spirit of *Westdeutsche Landesbank Girozentrale* v. *Islington L.B.C.* [1996] 2 WLR 802.

inevitably come up with groupings of facts which, semantically and perhaps also substantially, contend with the categories of facts which are used in relation to other rights. And the end will be that we have built two tunnels through the same hill, a pointless and wasteful labour.

4. WHAT IS TO BE DONE?

Judges can encourage or discourage, but this is not really a judicial responsibility. It belongs to the law schools. If diktats from the educational bureaucracy of the professions currently exacerbate the problem, the law schools have only themselves to blame for tolerating intellectual disorder for so long and advertising syllabi in which each subject appears as an island in an archipelago. 'What is to be done?' therefore becomes, 'What are the universities to do?'

Legal philosophers ought not to think taxonomy beneath them. Where Jurisprudence, in the sense of legal philosophy, is taught, legal taxonomy ought to be taught. But in many law schools Jurisprudence is not taught, or only to a very few enthusiasts and only towards the end of their tour of the archipelago. And most legal philosophers are now engaged exclusively on supposedly larger and higher problems. Nevertheless, just as Darwin would have achieved nothing if he had been indifferent to taxonomy, so those who care deeply about legal rationality must take seriously the need to eliminate the traps and fallacies latent in careless classification. Some responsibility must therefore lie with those who profess to be philosophers of law.

It falls to all teachers of law to explain where their subjects fit in the order of the law as a whole. Yet the task cannot be done unless legal education prepares both the teachers and the taught to expect it to be done and to participate in the debate. The way Justinian saw it was that the first year lawyers in the university law school should be taken up to a high place and made to look down on the law below, so as to see how it all fitted together. That is to say, in their first year they should be taken through the whole law, quickly, to familiarize themselves with its main features and understand the interrelation of the different subjects. That is the taxonomic purpose for which the *Institutes* was produced. It provided the map of the law.

The mind which had internalized that map would later always know where it was, however dark and dense the detail of the immediate subject-matter. In the same way, and equally important, that same mind, looking not at the law but at raw life and the problems thrown up by it, would know how to relate that raw material to the law, how to review the law in order to find the solution to problems thrown up, unlabelled, by life. It is difficult for a lawyer to analyse a real live problem against an alphabetical list or a random collection of legal topics. A heap can be turned over, knowledgeable friends can be called in to help identify things that turn up. A rational map of the law is much more useful. It directs analysis, and it provides a means, as we have seen, of checking whether any possibility has been accidentally omitted. Far from locking people into categories, a good taxonomy enables the lawyer to move over them with confidence. Anti-formalism, so far as it has been anti-taxonomic, has handicapped the diagnostic capacity of many legal minds. Justinian's educational system was calculated to build in the necessary sense of structure from the beginning.

So long as the basic Roman law course remained in place, English lawyers were never left without a map. In effect the *Institutes* continued to do for us what Justinian intended them to do for the *cupida legum iuventus,* the young eager for the study of the law, in the great law schools of Constantinople and Beirut. In throwing out Roman law, the law schools of common law jurisdictions have failed to think through the various goods that that study was doing. They have therefore failed to put in place new means to those old ends. There is unending debate about what ought best to be taught by way of an introduction to law. For my part I have no doubt at all that the best introduction is still Justinian's *Institutes.* Even now it best provides the bird's eye view. It gives entry to every legal system in the western tradition. At the same time it should go without saying that, just as beginners should look down at that map, so they should also be taught to view it with vigilant scepticism. Inert acceptance is no good to anyone. What is needed is a keen taxonomic awareness and a continuing debate. The *Institutes* is merely the best starting point.

If the book itself is rejected, its content must nevertheless somehow be communicated. There ought to be a place in the syllabus, and an early place since this matter is needed when beginners are indeed laying the foundations of their legal knowledge, in which law students become acquainted with the history of legal classification, from the *Instititutes* of Gaius and Justinian to the modern civil codes. In its early paragraphs this paper drew attention to the importance of the Maccabaean lecture given more than a decade ago by Lord Goff.[20] The most recent Maccabaean, given in November 1995 by Professor Peter Stein, was devoted precisely to the history of the struggle for intellectual order in the law.[21] That lecture could, given the chance, play an important role in enabling every lawyer both to have a map of the law and to continue the taxonomic debate. Nobody thinks that the *Institutes* got the taxonomy exactly right, and Professor Stein's story is partly the story of attempts to improve on the Roman original. It may not be possible to draw the map perfectly and permanently right. The crucial thing is that the legal mind, individual and national, must have a department of critical taxonomy.

There must be a map. And the map must always be regarded as highly suspect. The suspicion must, however, be directed to improvement, not destruction. In the absence of this taxonomic awareness the law cannot but be a heap of good learning. So what? So what if it is just a heap? Unfortunately law which is intellectually disorderly is also law which is unreliable and unpredictable. Where the law is '*Heap'd up together without Beginning or End*'[22] intellectual accidents cannot be avoided and, more often than is inevitable, people will win cases they ought to lose and lose cases they ought to win. Intellectual order and a high quality of justice go hand in hand.

Our habit has been to celebrate experience in preference to logic,[23] historical continuity in preference to systematic coherence,[24] but in the fluid and fast-moving world of 'In Search of Principle' we can no longer take secret pride in these priorities. It is not at all fashionable to insist on the autonomy of law and legal science. Yet, however much the law opens up to other disciplines, it will never escape the special responsibilities which set it apart from

---

[20] N. 3, above.

[21] P. G. Stein, 'The Quest for A Systematic Civil Law' given on 28th November 1995.

[22] See the quotation from Wood, text to n. 1 above.

[23] Most famously in the dictum become mantra of Oliver Wendell Holmes, *The Common Law* (Boston, 1881), 1.

[24] O. Kahn-Freund's essay introducing K.Renner, *The Institutions of Private Law and their Social Functions* (London, 1949) 10–13.

them and profoundly colour the nature of its peculiar rationality, namely the duty day by day to decide difficult cases, the obligation to give convincing reasons for those decisions, and the requirement of justice that like cases be decided alike. In a changing world in which sheer authority counts for less and less in the absence of the legitimation which derives from tight reasoning, common lawyers cannot hope to discharge those responsibilities if they persist in regarding careful taxonomy as an artificial and faintly distasteful obsession of those too clever and too theoretical lawyers from civil law jurisdictions.

9

Politics and Courts in Europe:
From an Old to a New Lack of Balance

by Thijmen Koopmans

1 In European Community law, it is difficult to find a triangular relationship between legislation, case law and academic writing. The main problem is the relationship between the political institutions and the Court of Justice, or, to put it in different terms, between the legislative and the judicial branch of the Community. Academic writing followed the Court's case law, rather than paved the way for it. It may be true that, among lawyers, there are more signs of a prevailing opinion at a European level than among politicians;[1] but, generally speaking, this opinion is not very critical of the performance of the courts. Perhaps, that reveals more about the distinguishing features of lawyers than about those of the European Community.

2 In speaking about 'legislative and 'judicial' bodies of the Community, one seems to assume that comparisons between national legal systems and the institutional system of the Community can be usefully made. That is, however, the first question which needs to be addressed. For does not the comparison imply that the European Community, or now the European Union, is considered as a state-like entity, rather than as an international organization with some particular characteristics of its own?

In order to avoid debates on political philosophy, we might as well look at the evidence, that is, at literature aimed at comparing the Community system to national legal systems. Some authors have indeed tried to make these comparisons, but they have done so with varying degrees of success. At one end of the scale, we find the doctoral thesis of Koenraad Lenaerts on courts and the Con-

---

[1] See my 'Europe and its lawyers in 1984', *C.M.L. Rev* 22 (1985), 9.

stitution in the United States of America and in the European legal order.[2] In a detailed study, the author argues very convincingly that parallels can be drawn between American case law, particularly the case law of the United States Supreme Court, and the case law of the Court of Justice of the European Communities and of the European Court of Human Rights, at least as far as the courts' role is concerned in protecting constitutional values. The book focuses on the division of powers (*'la délimitation du pouvoir'*) but, more generally, it does show how euro-american comparisons can be made. At the other end of the scale, we find Hjalte Rasmussen's book on 'law and policy' in the case law of the Court of Justice.[3] It is based on the American debate on judicial activism, but it has selected only one possible explanation of activism, that is, that which one might call the 'greed for power' argument, while neglecting other elements of the American debate. It is certainly an argument which deserves to be considered carefully. Robert Bork did so very elaborately with regard to the United States.[4] When presented in isolation, it gives, however, a very poor picture of judicial attitudes. The difficulty Rasmussen's book presents to the reader is, indeed, that it does not show any willingness to consider the particular characteristics of the Community legal order.

It seems to me that at least three reservations, or *caveats*, should accompany efforts aimed at comparing the Community legal order to national legal systems.

The first is that general comparisons cannot easily be made: there is a limited 'comparability'. In the Community, there is no legislative power in the same sense as in its Member States. Rule-giving activities of Community institutions are founded on limited powers as embodied in the European treaties. National parliaments, or national legislative bodies, have what is called in French legal parlance, *'la plénitude des pouvoirs'* — the fullness of powers (the term 'sovereignty' is too vague to serve as a substitute). French lawyers usually take the view that the concept of 'legislative power' does not apply in the Community. In accordance with the logic of

---

[2] K. Lenaerts, *Constitutie en rechter* (Antwerp, 1983). French translation, by F. Hubeau, *Le juge et la constitution aux Etats-Unis d'Amerique et dans l'ordre juridique européen* (Brussels, 1988).

[3] Hjalte Rasmussen, *On Law and Policy in the European Court of Justice* (Dordrecht and Lancaster, 1986).

[4] Robert Bork, *The Tempting of America; the Political Seduction of the Law* (New York and London, 1990).

their own national system, they see a clear distinction between the regulatory powers of Community institutions, submitted to judicial review, and the real legislative powers which are exercised by national parliaments. Lawyers from other national systems do not always adhere to the strictness of this view; but they encounter, nevertheless, the same problems when they try to draw comparisons.[5]

The second observation is that the Court's jurisdiction, when compared to the 'legislative' powers of the political institutions, is couched in very general terms. According to Article 164 EC-treaty, the Court of Justice 'shall ensure that in the interpretation and application of this Treaty the law is observed'. And although the Treaty does not define the notion of 'the law', it does gives some indications as to how it is to be found. In particular, the Treaty provision on tort liability of the Community refers to 'the general principles common to the laws of the Member States' as a source of law for the Court.[6] From the very beginning of its case law on the EEC-treaty (as it was initially called), the Court of Justice has held that Article 164 must mean that the application of Community rules, as well as decisions, directives, and regulations of Community institutions, must respect general principles of law, such as are common to the legal systems of the Member States.[7] As a result, there is a marked contrast between the specific rule-giving powers of the political institutions and the generality of the Court's possibilities to elaborate 'the law'.

The third remark is that the legislative power of the Community—whether or not it can properly be called 'legislative'—works very poorly in practice. This is, of course, well known. There is an incredibly complicated decision-making mechanism, which varies according to the subject which has to be dealt with;[8] but the subjects are circumscribed in such a way that the boundaries between them are often far from clear.[9] In spite of the applicable rules, decision making is, in fact, normally based on consensus. This is particularly

[5] See also, with some qualifications, T. C. Hartley, *The Foundations of European Community Law*, 3rd ed. Oxford, 1994), 110–19.

[6] Art, 215, par. 2, EC-treaty.

[7] See already the famous case 26/62, *Van Gend en Loos* [1963] ECR 12. A good example is also case 155/79, A.M.& S. [1982] ECR 1575.

[8] See, for example, 189a–189c EC-Treaty.

[9] Compare Art. 100C EC-treaty to Art. K. 1, par. 1, Treaty on European Union (TEU, or 'Maastricht').

true in the exercise of regulatory powers by the Council, where Member State delegations often negotiate as if engaged in the process of preparing diplomatic agreements. To make matters worse, the Council is often unwilling to leave the implementation of its rules to the Commission (except in some matters, such as agriculture), although the Treaty rules appear to impose delegation of executive powers to the Commission.[10] In practice, the Council prefers to look after the implementation of its rules itself, but the consequence of it is that many decisions, although announced in Council regulations, fail to be issued.

3 This brings me to my first problem: should the Court of Justice make up the Council's failures to act? In other words: should the Court stand in, as a kind of substitute, for the legislative bodies, in particular for the Council, if these bodies fail to act where action is legally necessary?

The answer of the Court of Justice has often been in the affirmative. That is particularly true for decisions which are part of the common agricultural policy. In agricultural matters, there is sometimes an urgency which is lacking in other areas of Community legislation. On the one hand, there is a strong mutual connexion between the different decisions: for example between rules on prices, on interventions, on import levies and on export subsidies. On the other hand, the common organization of the agricultural markets shows a high degree of integration, which makes it difficult for national authorities to intervene when the common rules do not provide an adequate answer to their problems.[11]

A very eloquent case concerned the failure of the Council to fix, at the appropriate moment, the dairy prices for the new season.[12] The applicable regulation, the basic regulation on dairy products, provided that the 'indicative price' for milk was to be fixed at a certain date, before the start of the new agricultural season (the 'campaign'). This indicative price was the basis for other prices to be fixed, for example the intervention price, as well as for the system of levies and subsidies for different dairy products. The ministers of Agriculture had not been able to agree on the indicat-

[10] Art. 155, last indent, EC-treaty.
[11] See Kapteyn-Verloren van Themaat, *Inleiding tot het recht van de Europese Gemeenschappen*, 5th edn. (Deventer, 1995), 667–9.
[12] Case 10/79, *Gaetano Toffoli* [1979] ECR 3301.

ive price in this case, although they were legally obliged to fix it. The Italian government considered that there was a gap in the price system, with the result that Member States regained their freedom to determine their own price level. Italian farmers had assumed that the new price would be the same as the old price, with the addition of a certain percentage, corresponding to earlier price increases within a given period. In a preliminary ruling on questions put to it by an Italian court, the Court of Justice held that the old price continued to be applicable after its expiration date, until the moment the Council would fix the new price. Powers of intervention in economic life, once transferred to Community institutions, do not revert to Member States for the sole reason that these powers are not exercised, or not exercised in due time, said the Court.

The same reasoning was applied by the Court in a somewhat more dramatic situation. The Accession treaty of Denmark, Ireland, and the United Kingdom provided that existing conservation regimes for North Sea fish would continue to apply until a certain date, and that they were to be replaced, on that date, by a common conservation regime adopted by unanimous decision of the Council.[13] The Council failed to reach unanimity, because of the continued opposition of one Member State, the United Kingdom. After the expiration date, the British authorities tried to impose their own national regime which, it was said, was more favourable to British fishermen. French, Belgian, and Danish fishermen alleged that they were subjected to discriminatory measures, and the Commission commenced an action against the United Kingdom for infringement of Treaty rules. The Court considered that, after the date fixed by the Accession treaty, Member States were no longer entitled to exercise their own powers with regard to this subject.[14] Therefore, they had no power to change the regulations which were applicable on that date; the regime was, in a certain sense, frozen as from that moment. However, the Court considered that this legal situation did not imply that the applicable rules could not be modified at all in order to be adjusted to the evolution of biological and technical data. And, referring to the duty of Member States to facilitate the achievement of the Community's tasks and

[13] Art. 102 Accession treaty (Denmark, Ireland, Norway and United Kingdom).
[14] Case 804/79, *Commission* v. *United Kingdom (British Fishery case)* [1981] ECR 1045.

to abstain from measures which could jeopardize its functioning,[15] the Court held that the necessary adjustments of national conservation regimes could only be decided in close collaboration with the Community institutions, particularly the Commission. Here again, the Court of Justice stepped in where the political institutions had been unable to provide for the rules which were legally necessary, even for interim rules. Of course, the Court could not, itself, fix the permanent rules to be applied; but it was able to show the way to an interim regime and thereby to facilitate the eventual decision of the Council on conservation measures.

This attitude of the Court is not restricted to agricultural cases. Thus, it was the Court of Justice, not the Council or the Commission, which drew the consequences from the Treaty provisions on equal pay for equal work of male and female workers.[16] The full effect of these provisions had been hampered by the fact that the main rule was not expressed as a right of workers but as an obligation of Member State authorities. 'Member States shall . . . ensure and subsequently maintain . . .'. Relying on this particular wording, national authorities treated the Treaty obligation only as a guideline, to be implemented in the future, a future which seemed always to recede. And although the Commission and the European Parliament urged the Member States to proceed more quickly to the realization of the aim of equal treatment, these institutions assumed likewise that action had to be taken by the authorities, and that underpaid female workers, or trade unions acting in their name, could not seek redress by applying directly to the courts. In 1976, however, the Court of Justice held that the Treaty embodies a clear and unconditional prohibition to discriminate between male and female workers and that, therefore, these workers had a right to equal pay.[17] In other words, the Treaty provision was directly applicable in such a way that there was no need for political action in order to have the rights of the workers implemented. As women were actually largely underpaid in much of economic life, notwithstanding the prohibition of unequal treatment, the consequences of this judgment have been far-reaching. A substantial part of the Court's case law in the eighties was indeed devoted to the practical effects of its bold affirmation of the workers' rights under the non-

---

[15] Art. 5 EC-treaty.
[16] Art. 119 EC-treaty.
[17] Case 43/75, *Gabrielle Defrenne (Defrenne II)* [1976] ECR 455.

discrimination rule.[18] And, interestingly, the legislative machinery began to move, as the Commission proposed directives on equal treatment which have been ultimately adopted by the Council.[19] It was, in a way, the Court's attachment to the purpose of the Treaty provisions which finally unleashed the Community's legislation on non-discrimination between men and women.

4 It is also possible to look at the role of the Court of Justice from a quite different perspective, by examining who can be considered as having given shape to Community law, who has been the 'law maker'. There is little doubt that, from this point of view, the contribution of the Court has been more important than that of the political institutions.

This role of the Court started already in early 1963, with the famous *Van Gend en Loos* judgment.[20] The Court held that the Treaty could not simply be considered as an agreement creating mutual obligations between the contracting States. The Community constitutes 'a new legal order', said the Court, which also imposes obligations on individuals and confers rights upon them, independently of the legislation of the Member States. One year later, the Court put the same idea in a somewhat different wording. It said succinctly that the Member States have 'created a body of law which binds both their nationals and themselves'.[21] The very idea of Community law as an autonomous body of law, created by the Treaty establishing the EEC but independent of the traditional rules of public international law, was thus developed by the Court.

That was by no means the Court's sole contribution to the evolution of an independent body of Community law: the Court not only proclaimed the concept, it also slowly, and step by step, began to elaborate the implications of this autonomous legal system. By thus drawing the consequences of its own case law, the Court has been able to give meaning to important parts of the construction of the economic union as intended by the Treaty and to show the coherence of that construction.

[18] See S. Prechal and N. Burrows, *Gender Discrimination Law of the European Community* (Aldershot 1990), ch. 1–3.
[19] Directives 75/117 on equal pay, 76/207 on equal treatment in employment, 79/7 on equal treatment in social security (OJ 1975, L 45; 1976, L 39; 1979, L 6).
[20] Case 26/62, *Van Gend en Loos* (see n. 7).
[21] Case 6/64, *Costa* v. *ENEL* [1964] ECR 593.

The most famous example is the *Cassis de Dijon* line of case law, named after a case concerning dissimilar national legislations on requirements to be met for certain alcoholic beverages.[22] On the basis of Treaty provisions forbidding import and export restrictions in intra-Community trade,[23] the Court had already construed the concept of free movement of goods as one of the central tenets of the economic union as embodied by the Treaty. It held from the very beginning that the requirement of free movement of goods has a much wider scope than the mere avoidance of protectionist measures: it concerns 'any' hindrance to intra-Community trade.[24] In *Cassis de Dijon*, the Court said that import restrictions occasioned by dissimilarities between national food and drugs legislations ('disparities', in Community language) are to be overruled by the requirement of free movement of goods. The Court was aware that some of these national restrictions were to be upheld, for example if inspired by urgent considerations of public health, consumer protection, protection of the environment etc. In the Court's view, however, the general rule was that products legally manufactured in one Member State, under the national provisions as applied in that State, can be exported to any other Member State, even if the applicable national provisions in that State are completely different. As a result, national provisions on a minimum degree of alcohol for certain liquors, on the use of durum wheat for pasta, or on the compulsory use of certain ingredients for beer, could be validly imposed by the Member States for goods produced on their own territory; they could not, however, be considered as an obstacle to the import of liquors, pasta or beer validly manufactured in a different Member State.[25]

The upshot of this line of case law is that dissimilarities of national production rules can not only be overcome by the harmonization process the Treaty envisages for these situations;[26] the Court of Justice also reads a 'recognition principle' in the free movement of goods provisions of the Treaty, and considers that this principle applies during the period in which harmonization has

---

[22] Case 120/78, *Rewe* (*'Cassis de Dijon'*) [1979] ECR 178.
[23] Arts. 30, 34 and 36 EC-treaty.
[24] Case 8/74, *Dassonville* [1974] ECR 837.
[25] Example: case 178/84, *Commission* v. *Federal Republic of Germany* (*'Reinheitsgebot'*) [1987] ECR 1227.
[26] Already in Art. 100 of the old EC-treaty.

not yet been realized. It is not unlikely that harmonization of food and drugs legislations appeared nearer at hand at the time than it does nowadays; but even so, this case law made a major contribution to the realization of free movement of goods, by showing an alternative way of achieving this end. In its later case law, the Court began to apply similar principles of recognition to the freedom to provide services.[27]

This chapter of the Court's case law is not only important from a point of view of economic law: it also gave a major boost to the position of the judiciary in the European Community. The *Cassis de Dijon* way of reasoning leaves indeed a wide discretion to the courts. Some disparities are to be accepted under this doctrine, even though providing obstacles to intra-Community trade; but this can only be the case if these disparities are either incorporated in the Treaty or founded on urgent considerations which are recognized as such by the courts. This power assigned to the courts strengthened the position of the Court of Justice; but in that way it reinforced indirectly (*'par ricochet'*) the powers of national courts with regard to their own national legislation.

A further reinforcement of the position of the judiciary was achieved when the Court held that Community legislation is to respect human rights and fundamental freedoms. The Treaty is silent on the matter (probably because it was drafted when political leaders of the original six Member States still considered the prospect of concluding a 'political' community after the entry into force of the EEC). In the Court's view, however, protection of human rights forms part of the general principles of law to be upheld by the courts. It referred to the constitutional traditions which are common to the Member States, and to the international obligations Member States have subscribed to.[28] In later judgments, the Court referred in particular to the European Convention on Human Rights. More recent case law shows that the Court assumes, more or less implicitly, that the human rights which must be respected by Community institutions are those enumerated in the European Convention.[29] More generally, rules of Community law will have to be interpreted in the perspective of the provisions of the

---

[27] Case 279/80, Webb [1981] ECR 3305; case C–76/90, Säger [1991] ECR I–4421.

[28] Example: case 44/79, *Liselotte Hauer* [1979] ECR 3727.

[29] Example: case 374/87, *Orkem* [1989] ECR 3283.

Convention and the values they are intended to protect. Thus, the position of the individual citizen with regard to the powers of the authorities is strengthened; but by the same token, the influence of the judiciary with regard to the political institutions increases.[30]

A comparable development took place when the Court of Justice began to give a general scope to the non-discrimination rules of the Treaty. The first move in this direction was the doctrine, developed by the Court, that the different non-discrimination rules of the Treaty embody a general principle of equal treatment. Thus, the rule of equality was to be observed in staff cases, although the applicable staff regulations made no reference to it.[31] Equal protection also became a guiding principle in matters of economic law, for example when relations between different products, or groups of consumers, were at issue. In a later stage, the Court gave a wide scope to the prohibition of discrimination founded on nationality, by considering that access to vocational training was a subject covered by different provisions of the Treaty. The educational authorities of the Member States could not, therefore, charge a higher tuition fee to citizens of other Member States than to their own nationals.[32] These two developments, combined with the equal pay case law, amount to the establishment of a genuine equality law of the European Community.

The Court certainly did not have the monopoly of developing Community law. However, the role of the other Community institutions was less general and more limited to specific themes. Thus, the common agricultural policy has been developed by the Council and the Commission, and it has been gradually leading to the development of a common set of standards for foodstuffs. Although the Court's contribution to competition law has been important, this part of Community law has been made jointly by the Commission and the Court. In a long series of decisions, and by a practice of non-deciding on particular issues, the Commission has been giving shape to a large part of competition law. The Commission played a major role in defining the precise limits of such vague concepts as 'state aid', 'concerted practice', 'restricting competition

---

[30] See also C. N. Kakouris, 'La Cour de Justice des Communautés europee nes comme cour constitutionnelle: trois observations.', in: O. Due, M. Lutter, a. J. Schwarze (eds.), *Festschrift für Ulrich Everling* (Baden-Baden, 1995), I, 629.

[31] Joint cases 75 and 117/82, *Razzouk and Beydoun* [1984] ECR 1509.

[32] Case 293/83, *Gravier* v. *Ville de Liège* [1985] ECR 593.

within the common market', 'abuse of a dominant position' etc.[33] Community legislation has been important in certain areas: agriculture, fishery, transport, and protection of the environment. If one looks, however, at the Community legal order as a sibling of national legal systems, comparable to these systems from a point of view of substance, the influence of the Court of Justice has been pervasive. When we look at the Court of Justice solely from this point of view, its role might be compared to that of the United States Supreme Court, perhaps to that of the German Federal Constitutional Court, the *Bundesverfassungsgericht*, as it has evolved during the last ten or fifteen years. A more appropriate comparison would perhaps be that with the English courts in medieval times ('time immemorial'), when they developed the common law of England, or with the French *Conseil d'Etat* in the 19th century, when it hammered out the general principles of law to be respected by the administration in its regulations and decisions. There is, however, no common ground with the contribution to the evolution of the legal system of courts such as the present House of Lords or the French *Cour de cassation*: that contribution is infinitely more modest.

5 Looked at from this point of view, the Community legal order seems to show a certain lack of balance in the relationship between the judicial and the political institutions. It presents a somewhat 'dicastocratic' element, which is absent in the Member States— except, perhaps, in Germany.

This characteristic is also apparent when we look at the reactions of the political institutions to the innovations accomplished by the Court of Justice. There was, at least initially, a tendency to accept that, henceforth, the law of the Community was as the Court had said it was: Community legislation could only serve to codify or to elaborate it. Case law was often followed by legislation; not the other way round. I referred already to the Community directives on equal treatment of men and women in employment and in social security, which were issued after the Court had clarified the legal situation.[34] A similar evolution occurred after the Court had held that the protection of human rights and fundamental freedoms,

[33] See the annual surveys on competition law in *Yearbook of European law* (Clarendon Press, Oxford).

[34] See n. 19.

though not expressed in the Treaty, is a general principle to be respected by the Community. Subsequently, representatives of Member States, as well as the European Parliament, adopted solemn declarations to the same end. The Maastricht treaty finally incorporated the rule that Community institutions shall respect 'fundamental rights, as guaranteed by the European Convention for the protection of human rights and fundamental freedoms signed in Rome on 4 November 1950 and as they result from the constitutional traditions common to the Member States, as general principles of Community law'.[35] In its typical meandering way the Community decision making system came to exactly the same result as the Court's case law had indicated fifteen years earlier.

In this way, the Court's case law also contributed to the creation of the *'acquis communautaire'*. This term, a typical example of Community jargon, indicates the state of Community law at a given moment. It is used in particular when new Member States intend to join the Community: they have to accept the treaties, and everything which has been done on the basis of the treaties, lock, stock and barrel. This implies that new Member States have also to accept the Court's case law as it stands on the moment of accession. That, in its turn, has its particular importance for such general rules or principles as equal treatment and the protection of fundamental rights.[36]

In a still broader sense, the observer of European developments could also come to the conclusion that the Court's specific contribution to Community law was to impose and to accentuate the requirements of the rule of law (*'Rechtsstaatlichkeit'*). By comparison, its contribution to the evolution of substantive economic law of the Community was more in line with the situation at the national level: there is an interaction between legislative, administrative, and judicial activities. The regime on fishing quota provides an excellent example of such interplay. Nevertheless, in purely

---

[35] Art. F, s. 2, TEU. See Giorgio Gaja, 'The protection of human rights under the Maastricht treaty', in: Curtin-Heukels (eds.), *Institutional Dynamics of European Integration (Essays in Honour of Henry G. Schermers*, II, Dordrecht-London, 1994), 549.

[36] See R. J. Goebel, 'The European Union Grows: the Constitutional Implications of the Accession of Austria, Finland and Sweden', *Fordham Int. Law J.* 18 (1995), 1092.

constitutional matters, it is more difficult to find instances of this interaction.[37]

6 A new evolution may be on its way. There have been signs, recently, that the importance of the Court's role is no longer taken for granted. First, Member States' governments show more and more openly their dissatisfaction with certain parts of the Court's case law, and they sometimes balk at their duty to implement the rules and principles resulting from it. Secondly, and perhaps more importantly, Member States sometimes try to turn the wheel back, especially when getting together in order to revise the treaties. I shall give some examples of each of these tendencies.

The most illustrative example is the Barber protocol, as it is called, annexed to the Maastricht treaty. In its Barber judgment, the Court had held that benefits under complementary occupational pension schemes are to be considered as 'remuneration' in the sense of the equal pay rule of the EC-treaty.[38] As a result, benefits for pensioned male and female workers had to be equal, and the implication was that this would also have to be the case if premium contributions to the pension funds in the past had been made on a different basis. This could mean that financial claims might have a disrupting effect on pension funds, a result which would ultimately turn to the disadvantage of the pensioners. In order to avoid such a result, the Court limited its interpretation of the equal pay rule in such a way that it only applied for the future, except when the claims had already been brought before the courts prior to the date of the Barber judgment.[39] In other words, the new interpretation was not to have retroactive effect in principle. The judgment did not say explicitly, however, whether the lack of retrospectivity applied to benefits paid before the date of the judgment or to benefits based on periods of employment prior to that date. A protocol agreed upon during the Maastricht negotiations opted for the latter alternative. It was a clear expression of the national governments' mistrust of the Court's possible intentions, as there was no obvious link with the other provision of the Union treaty.[40]

[37] See also Ami Baraw, 'Omnipotent courts', in: Institutional Dynamics (quoted n. 35), 265.   [38] Case C–262/88, *Barber* [1990] ECR I–1889.
[39] See Art. 174, par. 2, EC-treaty.
[40] Protocol concerning Article 119 of the Treaty establishing the European Community (second protocol annexed to TEU).

There are more examples of this mistrust. The German federal government openly showed its dissatisfaction with the case law on social security for migrant workers and their families. It seems that the competent ministry in Bonn is very upset by the duty of the German institutions to pay child benefits to Italians working in Germany according to German standards—even if the children are living in Italy where, it is alleged, living standards are much lower. The Court considered that this rule follows very clearly from the provisions of the regulation on social security for migrant workers and their families,[41] and on this point, the regulation has not been changed so far. Recently, the British Prime Minister threatened to block revision of the Maastricht Treaty because the Court of Justice refused to annul a directive he had been opposed to.

Another example is the propensity of the national governments to appoint 'politically coloured' judges to the Court of Justice. To the astonishment of most observers, the German government took the initiative of replacing the German judge, who was not a member of a political party but a well-known expert in European Community law, by a member of the socialist party; this new judge was 'sacked' at the end of his term of six years, to be replaced by a member of the Bavarian Christian Social party. For a country which prides itself upon its devotion to constitutional values, this was not behaviour one would have expected. In the latest round of appointments, the Belgian government nominated its own minister of Justice. As far as Italy is concerned, political appointments have already been customary for more than twenty years. Sometimes, government leaders spread rumours to the effect that they discussed, at a summit meeting, the possibility to consider Treaty revisions intended to reduce the power of national courts to put questions for preliminary rulings to the Court of Justice.

Efforts at turning the wheel back are exemplified by the Maastricht protocol on Danish summer cottages. It provides that, notwithstanding the Treaty, Denmark is allowed to 'maintain the existing legislation on the acquisition of second homes'.[42] Press reports have it that the Danish population was to be lured into accepting Maastricht by the government's promise that German

---

[41] Regulation 1408/71 (OJ 1992, C325), Art. 10 s.1. See already case 32/77, *Giuliani* [1977] ECR 1857; case 92/81, *Camera-Caracciolo* [1982] ECR 2213.

[42] Protocol on the acquisition of property in Denmark (first protocol annexed to TEU).

holiday-makers would continue to be excluded from the market for summer cottages in Jutland. Be that as it may, the protocol is a clear infringement of the market freedoms which characterize the common market in the view of the Court of Justice; it is also a violation of the prohibition of discrimination founded on nationality. Moreover, the protocol may set a bad example for future negotiations: one would not hope to see future protocols closing London to the Irish or forbidding the sale of French or Dutch newspapers in Belgium.

There are more efforts aimed at putting a stop to the influence of the Court's case law. Some of the Member States refuse to consider a role of the Court in the application and interpretation of new conventions to be concluded between them. Examples are Europol, the convention on bankruptcy, and the Community patent convention. This is in particular, though by no means exclusively, the attitude of the United Kingdom. As other Member States, like the Netherlands and Italy, insist on recognizing jurisdiction of the Court of Justice in the framework of these new conventions, the negotiations are fruitlessly dragging on. It is a very discouraging spectacle. In the new 'pillars' of the European Union, the one on a common foreign and security policy and the one on cooperation in the fields of justice and home affairs, the Commission and the European Parliament are associated to the co-operation between the national governments in the framework of the Council; but no role has been assigned to the Court.[43] There may be intrinsic reasons for such a choice as far as foreign and security policy is concerned. For justice and home affairs, however, which are so close to many Community activities, it is difficult to devise such reasons.[44] The governments probably did not want the Court to continue its 'law-making' activities.

7 From the very beginning, there has never been a proper balance between the judiciary and the political institutions in the Community. At present, it seems likely that we are moving from one lack of balance to a different lack of balance. Sampling the political atmosphere of the moment, one is tempted to think that the governments of the Member States, or some of them at least, should like to warn the Court that it ought not to overstep the boundaries they

---

[43] See, however, Art. K. 3, s. 2 under *c*, TEU.
[44] See n. 9.

have assigned to the Court's jurisdiction and to the scope of its activities.

The governments are able to emphasize this intention in different ways. They can do so by their policy of judicial appointments; that is, however, a very unreliable solution, as any student of American constitutional law knows. Chief Justice Warren was a case in point; he was appointed by President Eisenhower because of being a 'middle of the road man', but developed, according to his opponents, to one of the 'radical' judges in the Supreme Court.[45] The governments could also try to make more 'Barber protocols' in coming negotiations on (what is presently called:) Maastricht II and Maastricht III. There is already some pressure on the governments to make a 'Kalanke' protocol, some supporters of affirmative action and 'positive discrimination' being dismayed by the way the Court interpreted, in its *Kalanke* judgment, the directive concerning equal treatment on this point.[46] A final, and perhaps most appealing, possibility for the governments is to construct new phases of the European integration process outside the institutional framework of the European Community; for example by extending the existing second and third pillars to new policy areas, or by constructing new pillars.

There are, of course, countervailing powers. Some Member States tend to combat efforts aimed at reducing the Court's role in the life of the European Union; that is particularly the case of the Benelux States and Italy. Moreover, the Court of Justice has friends in the non-political world. In particular, it has established a kind of intellectual authority among the lawyers, national judges included.[47] There is no doubt, however, that there has been a clear swing of fashion during these last five or ten years.

Member State governments should perhaps reflect before making the next move in the direction of dismantling the Court. They, or their experts, might ponder over the reasons for judicial review as elaborated in American literature on constitutional law.[48] Com-

---

[45] See A. H. Kelly & W. A. Harbison, *The American Constitution, Its Origins and Development*, 5th edn. (New York, Norton, 1976), 805–6.

[46] Case C–450/93, *Kalanke* v. *Freie Hansestadt Bremen* [1955] ECR I–3069. See Linda Senden, 'Positive Action in the EU Put to the Test: A Negative Score?', *Maastricht J. of Comp. and Eur. Law* 3 (1996), 146.

[47] This statement is partly founded on personal experience.

[48] See, in particular, John Hart Ely, *Democracy and Distrust, a Theory of Judicial Review* (Cambridge, Mass. and London, Harvard Univ. Press, 1980 ch. 3–6.

bining American and European experience, we could refer, for example, to the way courts discovered values, rather than interests, as the proper approach to the interpretation of constitutional and legal provisions; to the judges' task of facilitating representation of minorities in the political process and in social and cultural life; to the courts' role in clearing the political channels and in guaranteeing the soundness of the political process. This is not merely an American problem; without judicial control, the strongest political actor will always tend to neglect the rights of weaker political actors. The rights attributed to the European Parliament by the European treaties have only been realized because the Court of Justice had the courage to draw the consequences from infringement of essential procedural requirements in the sense of the Treaty[49] and to annul regulations or directives issued in disregard of these requirements.[50] Politics should be played according to the rules of the game; in the European Union, only the Court can ensure that these rules will be respected.[51]

8 The time is ripe, it seems to me, to discuss these fundamental issues. The debate on the 'autonomous legal order' of the Community started after the Court's ruling on the existence of such a legal order. It is more appropriate, or at least intellectually more satisfactory, to start the debate before the decisions are taken. The future of the European Union is too important to be left to diplomats and politicians.

[49] Art. 173, par. 1, EC-treaty.
[50] Case 138/79, *Roquette* [1980] ECR 3333; case C–65/90, *European Parliament* v. *Council* [1992] ECR I–4593.
[51] See also Gil Carlos Rodríguez Iglesias, 'Zur "Verfassung" der Europäischen Gemeinschaft', *Eur. Grundrechte Zeitschr.* 23 (1966), 125.

10

The Law-Making Power of the Legislature and the Judicial Review*

by Professor Jutta Limbach

I. JUDICIAL REVIEW

To speak about judicial review at the Clifford Chance Conference does not seem to get right to the point since our general topic is the question: Are judges and legislators getting their act together. But judicial review means the authority of a court to declare laws of the legislative branch void and unenforceable if they are judged to be in conflict with the constitution. On the surface, this judicial activity seems to be a sort of control and not cooperation. Yet in the background of the concept of checks and balances, this examination implies cooperation—provided of course, that it is well done. For interpreting a statute in the light of the fundamental principle of separation of powers implies a restriction for the judges as well. That means that the court has to exercise the power without usurping the function of the legislature. Before I speak about the intricate relationship between the judiciary and the legislature in the development of the law, I will offer some general remarks concerning judicial review.

This power is possessed chiefly by constitutional courts. In Germany this is the Federal Constitutional Court. In the United States, since *Marbury* v. *Maryland* (1819) the power of judicial review is given to the US Supreme Court, which is an appellate court as well as constitutional court. This special authority is a chief judicial instrument in the system of checks and balances. Nevertheless, it is not a common or necessary element of a democratic constitution. As we all know, our hosts have a different system: The British system knows neither a constitutional judiciary nor a judicial

*Iain L. Fraser translated this chapter for publication.

review, even though — or perhaps because — the British constitution is firmly based upon the separation of powers.

I think that each democracy has to face the problem of how to decide a conflict between laws of different rank or authority. Take the relationship between the national and supranational law in the European Community. Though each system will develop tools to perform judicial control of legislative acts, for example by interpretation in the light of a fundamental principle. According to Rob Bakker, the British courts are applying a kind of implicit constitution-conformable interpretation. This means, that if the wording of the statute so allows, the court will interpret parliamentary legislation in such a way that a violation of fundamental principles will be avoided. But if the explicit wording of the statute does not allow such an interpretation in accordance with the constitution, a British court has to apply the statute, even if it finds the result grossly unfair.[1] This is the consequence of the supremacy of the Parliament which forbids the judge to overrule acts of Parliament explicitly.

In the German system all constitutional organs have to respect the priority or prerogative of the constitution. It is stated in the first article of the Basic Law, that the following basic rights shall bind the legislature, the executive, and the judiciary as directly enforceable law. The acknowledgement of human rights as the fundamental elements of our constitutional system is a response to the disdain shown towards human dignity during the period of 1933–1945. Even the establishment of the Federal Constitutional Court has such historical reasons. It should be a safeguard against dictatorship and disregard of human rights. And you can observe in recent history that the experience of preceding totalitarian regimes inspired the framers of constitutions not only to formulate a Bill of Rights but to establish a kind of constitutional court and judicial review, as well. You will find many such examples in East-Europe as well as in Africa.

The Federal Constitutional Court decides on the interpretation and application of the federal constitution, the Basic Law. It is thus not a court of appeal which decides on questions of constitutional law arising in the course of civil or penal proceedings. Instead, it is a court of first and last instance. Its exclusive responsibility is to decide questions of constitutional law and to interpret the Basic

---

[1] Rob Bakker, 'Verfassungskonforme Auslegung' Rob Bakker *et al.* (eds.), *Judicial Control — Comparative Essays on Judicial Review*, (Antwerp, 1995), 20.

Law with final, binding force. The scope of the Court's responsibilities is very broad, but I will draw your attention only to those competences, which are important in relation to the law-making power. An appeal may be made to the court in three cases.

First, any citizen after exhausting his legal remedies, can file a complaint alleging that a statute has violated his constitutional rights.

Second, whenever a court considers a law or statute unconstitutional it has to bring the case before the Constitutional Court, under the condition, however, that the law considered to be unconstitutional is relevant in the case.

Third, but even apart from a concrete case a government—be it the federal government or a government of a country—or one third of the members of the federal parliament may require a review of a statute by the Constitutional Court. This happened, for example, in 1992, when one third of the deputies of the federal parliament brought the new legislation on abortion before the Constitutional Court. It held the regulation of the respective statute permitting an abortion within the first three months of pregnancy unconstitutional. The US Supreme Court does not know such an abstract review of statutes upon the request of political factions or governments. There, the judicial review is only exercised under the impact of a lively conflict between antagonistic demands, which make, as justice Frankfurter said, the resolution of the controverted issue a practical neccessity.[2] I think Rob Bakker is right in saying that this restriction is a manifestation of the wider concept of judicial restraint by the US Supreme Court.

These functions, which are not exhaustive, illustrate the extent of the court's power in the interplay of constitutional forces in the separation of powers. In all seriousness one must admit that the Federal Constitutional Court is an outstanding factor in the political process.[3] It may sound provocative to describe the Federal Constitutional Court as a political power factor. Yet it is merely putting a legal finding into words. The Court adjudicates in the name of the Basic Law. Its operations extend into the political sphere because its criterion is the Constitution of a political

---

[2] Citation from Rob Bakker, above, n. 1 at 12.
[3] Cf. Christoph Gusy, 'Das Bundesverfassungsgericht als politischer Faktor', in: *EuGRZ* 1982, 93, 99.

community.[4] As we all know: 'The checking of power is necessarily itself power.'[5]

2. THE FEDERAL CONSTITUTIONAL COURT AS A JUDICIAL ORGAN

Given this political influence, can one still talk of adjudication in the traditional sense? Or do we have to do with a *'Fourth Power'*, additional to the triad of the separation of powers among legislature, executive, and judiciary?

The Constitutional Court, as the highest settler of disputes, ranks above all State bodies, legislative or executive as well as judiciary. It has the last word on all questions of interpretation of the Basic Law. We like to speak of the Federal Constitutional Court as *'supreme guardian'* of the constitution.[6] The Basic Law sets the criteria, in the form of its norms, for the Court's work. Of course, the other powers of government, too, have to be guided by the constitution, respect fundamental rights and safeguard the free democratic constitutional order. But the Federal Constitutional Court decides, with ultimate constitutional force, how any constitutional question is to be answered in the event of differences of opinion of clashes of competence between constitutional organs.

Nonetheless, it is not endowed with *'suprema potestas'*. For first of all, it cannot act on itself but only in response to an application. It always needs an impulse from outside. A catalogue of competences and procedures lays down in detail when and how the jurisdiction of the Court may be invoked. Outside these requirements, the Court has no competences.[7]

---

[4] Peter Häberle, *Verfassungsgerichtsbarkeit zwischen Politik und Rechtswissenschaft* (Königstein, 1980), 59.

[5] As Adolf Arndt tellingly puts it in relation to judging in general, in: *Das Bild des Richters* (Karlsruhe, 1957), 15.

[6] Cf. here and below Gerhard Leibholz, 'Der Status des Bundesverfassungsgerichts, in: *Das Bundesverfassungsgericht 1951-1971* (Karlsruhe, 1971), 32 ff. This *'status memorandum'*, as it is called, is obligatory reading for every new judge on the Federal Constitutional Court needing intellectual underpinnings as the *'noblesse de robe'* in the gamut of constitutional bodies. It was instances of lack of respect for the Federal Constitutional Court, and the consequent loss of reputation he feared that impelled him to create a 'constitutional obligation on the constitutional organs to show the mutual respect that any constitutional organ is legally entitled to' (p. 47); here 31, 34 ff.

[7] See Leibholz, op. cit. n. 6, 46, and Klaus Schlaich, *Das Bundesverfassungsgericht*, 3rd ed. (Munich, 1994), 27, 296, 303.

Secondly, the Court performs a predominantly checking function, delimiting and restraining power. Its task is to tie policy to law, and subordinate it to law. For the Basic Law has 'resolved the age-old tension between power and law in favour of the law.'[8] The Court's task is the limited one of interpreting the Constitution in Court proceedings; the expediency considerations of politics are not its concern.[9] The Federal Constitutional Court is *'designed as an organ of law, not of politics';* even if its decision may, inevitably, have political repercussions.[10]

3. THE GUIDING POWER OF NORMATIVE TEXTS

Nonetheless—or on that very account—particular attention should go the question whether adjudication can at all be separated with logical distinctness from the field of political action. Despite contradictory views, it is still readily held that: *'Judging means finding, not shaping.'* This is to assert a qualitative difference between adjudication and lawmaking: in the ideal pattern, finding the law is a matter for adjudication, while making law is by contrast a task for politics.

The debate on the judge's creative relationship to the law is older than the Federal Republic's jurisdiction. Montesquieu's saying that the judge is the mouth that utters the words of the law is still often quoted; but only to locate a cheap point of attack for doubts. Over a century ago, enlightened jurists were already rejecting the view of the judge's task as a 'purely intellectual operation, like any other judgement; a logical operation with the statutory

---

[8] Helmut Simon, 'Verfassungsgerichtsbarkeit', in: Benda, Maihofer, and Vogel (eds.), *Handbuch des Verfassungsrechts*, 2nd ed. (Berlin, New Yok, 1994) 1637 at 1661.

[9] So the Federal Constitutional Court refrains from considering whether the legislature has chosen the wisest, most just and most expedient solution. Cf. 36 BVerfGE 174, at 189; 38 BVerfGE 312, at 322.

[10] As rightly put by Thomas Clemens in his 'Das Bundesverfassungsgericht im Rechts- und Verfassungsstaat: Sein Verhältnis zur Politik und zum einfachen Recht; Entwicklungslinien seiner Rechtsprechung', in: Michael Piazolo (ed.), *Das Bundesverfassungsgericht—ein Gericht im Schnittpunkt von Recht und Politik* (Mainz, Munich, 1995), 13, 16 et seq.; and Deiter C. Umbach, 'The German Demoncracy and the Federal Constitutional Court as Promoter and Guardian of the Rule of Law', in: Dobers, Goussous, Sara (eds.), *Democracy and the Rule of Law in Germany—in Jordan* (Amman, Jordan, 1992) 25 et seq.

provision as major term and the facts to be adjudicated on as minor term'. If that were so, the judge would need nothing but 'a reliable edition of the law, the art of reading, care, and sound, clear human reason'.[11] Yet the legal order is neither without lacunae, free of contradiction, linguistically unambiguous nor above social change.[12] This is particulary true of constitutional law, which is marked by a low density of regulation and vague wordings.[13]

Not just general clauses but a multiplicity of undefined legal concepts delegate actual norm making to the judge. They open up semantic room for manoeuvre, allowing not just one correct decision. Judicial decision is not only finding, but always also law-making. 'In every act of judicial application of law . . . cognitive and volitional elements form an indissoluble combination'.[14] The judge creates law in the process of finding a decision. Adjudication accordingly always has a political dimension too.

This is certainly true of constitutional jurisdiction. For the Articles of the Basic Law are marked by a low degree of definiteness. They are norms with great openness, and margins of interpretation that are hard to delimit.[15] The Basic Law essentially contains—apart from the law on the organization of the State—principles that must first be spelled out before they can be applied.[16] One example is the constitutional principle that the Federal Republic is a social State (Art. 20 (1) Basic Law). But in the fundamental-rights context too, terms are used whose content can be made definite only by using interpretation or even evaluation, sometimes through recourse to extra-legal notions and historical experience.[17] Consider, say, the dignity of the person protected by Article 1 of the Basic Law, or the family, which by Article 6 of the

---

[11] Oskar Bülow, *Gesetz und Richteramt* (Leipzig, 1885), iv ff., 14.

[12] Dieter Grimm, 'Politik und Recht', in: *Grundrechte, soziale Ordnung und Verfassungsgerichtsbarkeit* (Heidelberg, 1995), 91, 99.

[13] Hesse, *Grundzüge des Verfassungsrechts der Bundesrepublik Deutschland*, 20th ed. (Heidelberg, 1995), 11.

[14] Grimm, op. cit. n. 12, 100.

[15] Hesse, op. cit. n. 13, 20, and Wolfgang Zeidler, in: *Verfassungsgerichtsbarkeit, Gesetzgebung und politische Führung, Ein Cappenberger Gespräch* (Köln, 1980), 46.

[16] Ernst-Wolfgang Böckenförde, 'Die Methoden der Verfassungsinterpretation,' in: *Staat, Verfassung, Demokratie*, 2nd ed. (Frankfurt a.M., 1992), 53, 58, and Willi Geiger, *Verfassungsentwicklung durch die Verfassungsgerichtsbarkeit* Karlsruhe, 1965) 4.

[17] Geiger, ibid.

Basic Law enjoys the special protection of the State. The openness and breadth of the Basic Law ought not to be pointed to as defects. On the contrary: a constitution can generally be regarded as successful if it is couched tersely and vaguely. For a constitution that were not open and therefore 'to some extent capable of ever-new interpretation' would, as Willy Geiger rightly says, 'inevitably soon come into hopeless contradiction with its object, and reach the critical point where the only choice left open would be to break it, i.e. to disregard it, or else continually and very quickly adapt it formally to changing needs'.[18]

4. ATTEMPTS AT DRAWING THE LINE

If, however, interpreting the constitution cannot be reduced to textual exegesis, then law and politics as elements in judicial decision-making cannot be strictly separated either. Nonetheless, the question where constitutional jurisdiction's area of action ends and that of politics begins demands an answer, however imperfect. For an institution which, like the Federal Constitutional Court, reviews the functioning of the constitutionally set limits must in turn be mindful of the limits to its own decisional power.

4.1. Judicial self-restraint

The maxim often recommended to the court—judicial self-restraint—is, if taken literally, more misleading than persuasive. The call for judicial self-restraint serves neither to locate grey areas of law and politics, nor to clear them up. Nor can restraint be a general strategy for a court whose prime duty is to check power and assert the protection of fundamental rights. The latter task may, as Konrad Hesse rightly stresses, call for resolute intervention rather than restraint—even at the risk of affronting some other constitutional organ.[19] As regards the formula of judicial self-restraint, Benda rightly calls it an attitude or a virtue: the court cannot limit its own power and function, but has to carry out its tasks. Of course,

---

[18] Geiger, ibid., 5.

[19] Konrad Hesse, 'Funktionelle Grenzen der Verfassungsgerichtsbarkeit', in: *Recht als Prozeß und Gefüge, Festschrift für Hans Huber* (Bern, 1981), 261 ff., 264.

it may not extend these either, having regard to the principle of separation of powers that has to be respected.[20]

The Federal Constitutional Court's Second Senate has explicitly stressed that the principle of judicial self-restraint does not mean diminishing or weakening the Court's powers, but its refraining from 'playing politics'. The principle is seen as aimed at keeping open for the other constitutional bodies the latitude for free political action guaranteed to them by the Basic Law.[21] So understood, the demand for judicial restraint is just as correct in practice as the contrary call on lawmakers to display more 'political self-confidence'.[22] But both maxims have no informative function: they merely formulate a problem, but do not offer any criteria for solving it.

4.2. The 'political question' doctrine

Often, the formula of judicial self-restraint acts only as another label for attempts at drawing the line discussed in the literature under the heading of the 'political question' doctrine. The term 'political question' denotes a number of cases in which the US Supreme Court, on constitutional, functional or pragmatic considerations, has exercised abstinence and sent the problem for decision to other powers of State. Examples are cases where the State power involved in the constitutional conflict is acting within its margin of discretion, or the court fails to find usable criteria to decide the legal question.[23] Apart from the fact that scholarship has scarcely been able to discover a system in the adjudication of the US Supreme Court, even answering the question how the term 'political' is to be understood in the sense of the 'political question' doctrine raises difficulties. For at bottom every constitutional question is politically significant, since it always also affects the legal order of a political community. To be sure, the Supreme Court

---

[20] Ernst Benda, 'Constitutional Jurisdiction in West Germany', in: *Columbia Journal of Transnational Law*, Vol. 19 (1981), 1, 11 f.

[21] 31 BVerfGE 1 at 14 f..

[22] Christine Landfried, *Bundesverfassungsgericht und Gesetzgeber* (Baden-Baden, 1984), 175.

[23] Henry J. Abraham, *The Judicial Process*, 6th ed., (Oxford, 1993), 358 ff., David P. Currie, *Die Verfassung der Vereinigten Staaten von Amerika* (Frankfurt a. M., 1988), 20, and Winfried Brugger, *Einführung in das öffentliche Recht der USA* (Munich, 1993), 20.

does not see a question as 'political' just because it is politically important or controversial.[24] Scholarly analyses of the judgements have however led only to attempts at definition that are more stylistic exercises in irony than offers of information that can be taken seriously. For instance, Peltason viewed political questions as those the judges choose not to decide; they become political by the judge's refusal to decide them. Post regarded the term 'political question' as simply an 'open sesame word'.[25]

Justice Powell sought to condense the investigation of a political question into three questions: 1. Does the issue involve resolution of questions committed by the text of the Constitution to a co-ordinate branch of the government? 2. Would resolution of the question demand that a court move beyond areas of judicial expertise? 3. Do prudential considerations counsel against judicial intervention?[26] However attractive this formulation may be in theory, comments Abraham, 'the "political question" maxim is a treadmill; perhaps to a fatal degree its supporting logic is circular'.[27] This is so even if one confines oneself to its essence of being a function of the principle of separation of powers.

5. THE CASE LAW OF THE FEDERAL CONSTITUTIONAL COURT

One must therefore warn against unthinking adoption of the 'political question' doctrine, if only because it offers no clearly recognizable and binding criterion.[28] Additionally, simply borrowing it would be out of the question because the tasks of the Federal Constitutional Court do not necessarily coincide with the US Supreme Court's jurisdiction. The Federal Constitutional Court has to follow a precisely formulated catalogue of competences. Once an application is admissible, it must be decided on. For the question that then arises as to the content of the decision, it may certainly be important that, say, a question under discussion cannot be decided on the basis of legal criteria and considerations, or concerns areas of activity belonging to the sphere of responsibility of other constitutional bodies.

24 Abraham, Currie and Brugger, ibid.   25 Abraham, ibid.
26 Abraham, op. cit. n. 23, 362.   27 ibid.
28 Brugger, ibid., 21.

This sort of conflict situation has repeatedly been discussed in decisions of the Federal Constitutional Court. Constitutional theorists have sought, on the basis of these—self-restraining—judicial utterances to derive normative guidelines. But in this attempt to mark the boundaries of the judicial areas of responsibility, they have had no more success than their colleagues in the USA. They have not managed to demonstrate a system of criteria and methods, but only to name some problematic groups of cases.[29] These relate either to particular decisional structures or to subject areas. Thus, the Court exercises restraint, and is expected to, in cases involving forecast decisions or expediency considerations. The same applies to review of acts of the legislature or executive in the sphere of foreign or economic policy.

The most prominent example of a forecast decision is the Federal Constitutional Court's *Kalkar* decision on the Nuclear Act, which regulates the peaceful use of nuclear energy and protection against its hazards. The background to the decision was the protest by a citizen against the building of a nuclear power station. The Federal Constitutional Court had been presented with the question whether Parliament had regulated the permit procedure sufficiently precisely. Was it enough to bind the authority, in relation to the dangers, only to the given state of scientific and technical progress? Or ought the legislator to have set more precise standards and unambiguously marked the boundary of the bearable residual risk?

The Federal Constitutional Court answered the second question negatively, and found that the basic decision for or against the legal admissibility of the peaceful utilization of nuclear energy was a matter for the legislature alone. Its primacy resulted not just from the far-reaching repercussions of the decisions for the citizens, but also from the limits to human cognitive capacity. In such a 'situation necessarily loaded with uncertainty' it lay 'primarily in the political responsibility of the legislature and the government . . . to take the decisions they saw fit. Given this position it is not the court's task to stand in for the appointed political institutions with their own assessment. There are no legal criteria for that'.[30] Of course, uncertainty as to the side-effects of a law 'in an uncertain future' does

---

[29] Cf. e.g. Gunnar Folke Schuppert's worthy attempt at classification, in: Selfrestraints der Rechtsprechung, in: (1988) *DVBl*, 1191, 1194.

[30] 49 BVerfGE 89 at 127, 131.

not require refraining from enacting the law. For the assessment of the hazards of nuclear energy the Court points to practical reason, which it evidently sees as better left up to the legislator.[31]

In a decision shortly thereafter (the Codetermination judgement), the Court made two points clear. First, uncertainty as to the repercussions of a law did not rule out empowerment to enact it, even where the object of regulation was of broad scope. Secondly, such uncertainty did not justify *per se* a predictive margin for the legislator that would be inaccessible to constitutional review. The legislator's assessed forecast, and thus the intensity of review, depended on various factors — the specific nature of the topic, the possibilities of knowledge, and the importance of the objects of legal protection involved. Pointing to many examples from case law, the Court distinguished review of certainty from review of justifiability, going as far as to acknowledge intensive review of content.[32]

Neither this pattern nor the case groups listed should lead one to the hasty conclusion that reliable machinery can be derived from the decisional practice of the Court, enabling an a priori clean separation of the areas of responsibility of constitutional court and legislator. It is essentially a matter of topic like those developed by Scharpf in his analysis of the US Supreme Court's case law: primarily the court's limited means of cognition and respect for specific areas of responsibility of the political institutions. In both cases Scharpf's insight applies, that adjudicatory practice cannot be made the starting point of a general theory of judicial self-restraint.[33]

The non-binding nature of the verificatory criteria postulated in the *Codetermination* judgement[33a] can readily be shown on the basis of other case-law examples listed there. Take the area of foreign policy, often cited as an example of judicial self-restraint. Thus, in the judgement on the Basic Treaty with the GDR the Court wished neither to exercise criticism nor to express its views on the prospects for the then Federal Government's reunification policy.

[31] The Court stresses that in view of the limited empirical knowledge one could not demand of the legislator a regulation that would rule out endangerment of fundamental rights with absolute certainty. Cf. 49 BVerfGE 89 at 143.

[32] 50 BVerfGE 290 at 332.

[33] Fritz Wilhelm Scharpf, Grenzen der richterlichen Verantwortung, Die political-question-Doktrin in der Rechtsprechung des amerikanischen Supreme Courts (Karlsruhe, 1965), 404 ff., 417.

[33a] 50 BVerfGE 230.

Responsibility for choosing the political ways and means towards this State objective of the Basic Law lay with the political bodies alone.[34] By contrast, in the *Maastricht* judgement the Court discussed critically the political ways and means chosen by the Federal Government towards the goal of European integration.[35] The *Masstricht* decision has been cited by a voice in the academic sphere as 'a good example of how the Federal Constitutional Court copes with the German tendency to constitutionalize foreign policy questions'.[36] For a prominent example where the importance of the object of legal protection at issue demanded intensive judicial review, the protection of nascent life intended by the abortion law is frequently cited.[37] By contrast, in the Kalkar decision, the Court saw no occasion for intensive review of the Nuclear Act despite the far-reaching possible consequences of the option in favour of the peaceful use of nuclear energy for the life and limb of citizens.[38]

We need not go into whether other viewpoints have justified judicial self-restraint or activism in this or that case. We wish only to show that the principle of judicial self-restraint the Court strove for in the Codetermination judgement has indeed been properly described in its generality. It 'is aimed at keeping open for the other constitutional organs the room for free political action guaranteed them by the constitution'.[39] Yet it has not been possible to give this precept shape against the background of the leading cases with a catalogue of criteria. The formula of judicial restraint offers nothing more than a rhetorical structure of argument that only gives information about the problem to be solved and the intellectual effort proposed.

Despite this at first sight disillusioning perception, it should not be ignored that the Federal Constitutional Court has continually striven to uphold the sphere of responsibility of the other organs of government.[40] Long-range sensitivity by the court to the limits of judicial responsibility is the self-evident work ethos of the guardian of a constitution that has opted for power-separating democracy;

---

[34] 36 BVerfGE 1 at 18.   [35] 89 BVerfGE 155.
[36] Vgl. Juliane Kokott, 'German Constitutional Jurisprudence and European Integration', in: *European Public Law*, 2, Issue 3, 413, 416.
[37] 39 BVerfGE 1 at 51; cf. also 88 BVerfGE 203 at 340 f..
[38] 49 BVerfGE 89 at 127.
[39] 50 BVerfGE 1 sub 2.
[40] This is substantiated by the examples listed in 59 BVerfGE 290 at 333, and in Simon (n. 8, 1668).

for that democracy forbids unlimited constitutional interpretation.[41]

6. FUNCTIONAL LIMITS TO CONSTITUTIONAL JURISDICTION

Even the Court's most passionate critics have so far not managed to draw any line of demarcation between the overlapping competences of legislation and jurisdiction. This is not, say, a consequence of intellectual laziness, but has to do with the amalgamation of law and politics, which cannot be puristically dissolved. Accordingly, attention is increasingly being paid to the theme of the relation between constitutional jurisdiction and the other organs of State laid down in the Basic Law.[42] What could be more natural than to look for the information, or better the stimulus to thought, in the constitutional principles whose infringement is continually alleged in cases of boundary disputes? In the forefront here are the principle of the separation of powers and the democratic principle. Those who choose this approach make clear from the outset that one cannot somehow read off from these structural principles criteria that promise simple formulae.

6.1. The Separation of Powers

Attention should be directed first to the principle of separation of powers, which is not to be understood in the sense of a strict separation of legislature, executive and judiciary. The organizational and functional structure of powers inherent to the Basic Law serves to distribute power and responsibility and to put a check on the bearers of power.[43] Bryde points first and foremost to the freedom-guaranteeing aspect of the separation of powers, aimed at moderating the use of power and securing the citizen against

[41] Cf. Simon, op. cit. n. 8, 1670.
[42] Cf. e.g. Brun-Otto Bryde, *Verfassungsentwicklung* (Baden-Baden, 1982), 325 ff.; Grimm, 'Verfassungsgerichtsbarkeit—Funktion und Funktionsgrenzen im demokratischen Staat', in: Wolfgang Hoffman-Riem (ed.), *Sozialwissenschaften im Studium des Rechts II, Verfassungs- und Verwaltungsrecht* (Munich, 1977), 83 ff., 98 ff.; Konrad Hesse, 'Funktionelle Grenzen der Verfassungsgerichtsbarkeit', in: *Recht als Prozeß und Gefüge, Festschrift fhr Hans Huber* (Bern, 1981), 261 ff., and Simon, op. cit. n. 8, p. 1665 ff.
[43] 68 BVerfGE 1 at 86.

government interference. No substantive criteria can be derived from this negative viewpoint for drawing the demarcation line, only the effort not to let any constitutional institution become all-powerful.[44]

Of special importance to resolving boundary disputes, however, is the functional aspect. For the principle of separation of powers is aimed primarily at having 'government decisions taken as correctly as possible, that is, by the organs best meeting the requirements for them, because of their organization, composition, function and procedures'.[45] This allocation of tasks is made according to priority areas, but without any claim to exclusivity. Functional overlaps, for instance in creative legal interpretation by courts, are part of it from the outset. Creative and therefore social-patterning elements in constitutional case law are thus not illegitimate *per se* either. Nonetheless, the Court always has to bear in mind that the Basic Law has made the legislature the 'central actor' in shaping the political community.[46] Its autonomy of action is comprehensive and it can, in contrast to the Federal Constitutional Court, act of its own volition. The Court can only act on the basis of an external impetus, reactively, to review decisions already taken. Its perspective is substantively determined by the application. This vision, necessarily restricted through the judicial procedure of acquisition of law, always contains the danger that the social situation may be perceived too narrowly and consequential problems overlooked. By contrast, the legislature can observe the effects of its decisions and, should these be undesirable, make corrections if necessary; for it remains 'master of its work'. This advance by the maxim of trial and error, of great importance in decisional situations necessarily fraught with uncertainty, remains barred to the Court. It cannot revise its judicial pronouncements by itself.[47]

6.2. The binding force of precedents

The Federal Constitutional Court is dependent, when new perceptions emerge, on the legislature's spirit of contradiction. The latter should not fail in its willingness and capacity to learn just because

---

[44] Bryde, op. cit. n. 41, 333 f.
[45] 61 BVerfGE 1 at 86.
[46] Bryde, op. cit. n. 41, 335.
[47] Bryde, op. cit. n. 41, 337; Simon, op. cit. n. 8, 1672.

the court has already declared unconstitutional a statutory provision under discussion; otherwise, it would be showing impotence in the face of new knowledge and radical change in the circumstances of life. The Federal Constitutional Court has seen this problem in all its sharpness and made the binding effect of its decisions relative. In a judgement from 1987 it found that the legislature could venture a 'second go' and challenge the Court to take a stance again. The verdict that a provision was unconstitutional did not prevent the legislature from deciding on one with the same or similar tenor. Just as there was no binding effect for the Federal Constitutional Court itself, so the legislature was not barred from pursuing its creativity and responsibility by enacting a new regulation with the same sense if it was deemed necessary.

The Court bases this possibility on the special responsibility of the democratically legitimated legislature to adapt the legal order to 'changing social requirements and altered conceptions of order' and avert rigidification of legal development.[48] For if the legislator were bound in perpetuity by decisions of the Federal Constitutional Court, that would lead to petrification of the law. There would be no openness to changes in the conditions of life or in social thinking. Such stagnation would be incompatible with the concept of democracy. For this State, form is not something static; instead, it organizes the process of political change. The unceasing competition for the electors' votes, the struggle for social progress and for parliamentary majorities to make it possible, and not least alternation in power, characterize the functioning of democracy.[49]

7. THE DEMOCRATIC PRINCIPLE

7.1. The Openness of the Political Process

The democratic principle in itself also requires respect, irrespective of its separation-of-powers component, particularly when

---

[48] 77 BVerfGE 84 at 104. The Court makes explicitly clear that the Federal Constitutional Court's task of legally binding interpretation of the Basic Law and of guaranteeing effective constitutional legal protection is not impaired by the legislature's capacity to repeat norms.

[49] Cf. Kurt Lenk on the specificity of democracy as a State form, as being not a system closed in on itself, but a *'future-open, risky project'*, in: 'Probleme der Demokratie', in: Hans-Joachim Lieger (ed.), *Politische Theorien von der Antike bis zur Gegenwart* (Bonn, 1991), 933 ff., 934.

legislative measures come onto the test-bench of the Federal Constitutional Court. This principle calls for restraint to the extent that the issue is *how* a regulatory need ought to be met by the legislator. It is not the Federal Constitutional Court's business to decree a detailed regulatory programme *qua* Basic Law. For the finer the Court makes the net of constitutional postulates and requirements, the more it ties down the legislature's possibility for action and cripples its political imagination.[50]

The openness of the political process essential to democracy takes account of the fact that the Basic Law leaves political decision-making up to as broad as possible a political debate, in which the common weal is defined.[51] This applies above all in questions where the Basic Law is not very eloquent. For in all areas not adequately provided for in constitutional law, as Grimm says, 'the democratic principle requires that only those who can be called to account again through the vote may decide'.[52]

Response by the citizens in regular elections does not apply to the members of the Federal Constitutional Court. The judges are outside the day-to-day political struggle. Their personal and material independence, guaranteed in the Basic Law, is intended to make them specifically immune to political pressures, and guarantee that the law alone counts. Judgement as to the optimum realization of the common weal is by contrast to be a matter for politics.

7.2. Value conflicts in the pluralist social order

If conflicts between values are made the object of abstract constitutional review, then account has also to be taken of the fact that the Basic Law has opted for a pluralist social order. In conflict situations where fundamental rights positions clash, the verdict on the constitutionality of a law is not a matter purely of judicial acuity or the art of constitutional interpretation. Instead a weighing up, that is, an evaluation, is called for.

As an example we may take the conflict over abortion law that occupied the Federal Constitutional Court in 1993: here the con-

---

[50] Simon, op. cit. n. 8, 1670, and Wahl, 'Der Vorrang der Verfassung', in: *Der Staat*, Vol 20 (1981), 485 ff., 505 ff.

[51] Bryde, op. cit. n. 41, 343.

[52] Grimm, op. cit. n. 41, 100.

stitutionally protected right to life of the unborn and the mother's fundamental rights position had to be weighed against each other. The legislature had resolved this value conflict in 1992 with a time-limit concept. According to this, termination of pregnancy within twelve weeks of conception was not unlawful and therefore exempt from punishment. Hardly any statute has been so thoroughly debated in the Bundestag or so massively underpinned academically by the securing of expert opinions as this one. This final text of the act was a hard-fought compromise in the Federal Parliament based on many competing preliminary drafts.

The Federal Constitutional Court, invoked by the defeated minority in the Parliament, nonetheless quashed the law and decided that termination of pregnancy is to be treated as wrong for the whole duration of the pregnancy. It declared admissible a consultative model that combined the time-limit solution with compulsory counselling.[53] The parliamentary majority defeated in court responded—it could hardly do otherwise—with the accusation that the Court in Karlsruhe was once again presuming to do the legislator's job.

Certainly, it is a matter for the Federal Constitutional Court to decide authoritatively questions of the constutitionality of provisions brought before it. Yet it must be mindful of the fact that the answer to the question of a law's constitutionality is the outcome of a multi-layered process of evaluation. There is no absolute rightness of the decision; or at least that is not attainable for us here on earth. The dissenting opinions of judges on many decisions are proof of this preception.[54]

Differences of opinion among judges are not just random. Historical, cultural and socially divergent views as to values held by those adjudicating play a part. Since Gadamer and Esser[55] we know that there is a prior understanding that also more or less consciously influences the acquisition of law. This has nothing to do with bias or prejudice. Instead, we are all marked by this sort of basic attitude preceding any legal cognition, which is more experienced with intuitive conviction than acquired rationally. It is a

[53] 88 BVerfGE at 203.   [54] 88 BVerfGE at 38, 359.
[55] Hans-Georg Gadamer, *Wahrheit und Methode*, 2nd ed. (Tübingen, 1965); Josef Esser, *Vorverständnis und Methodenwahl in der Rechtsfindung* (Frankfurt a. M., 1970), 7, 10 ff., 134.

mixture of moral, legal, philosophical, and political convictions that include a particular conception of reality.

The Court has accordingly to bear in mind that the election of parliamentary representatives has ensured a particularly broad spectrum of such interpretations. This compels reticence in relation to the products of parliamentary work. The Federal Constitutional Court ought therefore in a case of conflicting value judgements to pay attention not so much to the outcome as to the procedure of lawmaking; that is, the process of political opinion-forming and decision-making that led up to the statute that is under test.[56] If there is nothing to take exception to as regards the solidity and rationality of the parliamentary work, then it deserves respect. This should be the case particularly where the question of constitutionality has been thoroughly brought up for debate, against the background of the constitutional law developed by the Court. Where, however, information, expert advice and reflection have been lacking, the Court may return to the legislators a value judgement that the Court in its majority does not agree with. It should however guard against laying down regulatory contents for the authors of statutes.[57] For that does more than just browbeat Parliament. It breeds pusillanimity and inaction, and ultimately brings about unwillingness to communicate and to reach compromise. It tends rather to give a lift to those forces that 'spice' every political argument with the threat to take the road to Karlsruhe if they end on the losing side in the legislative process.

8. THE COURT'S PERCEPTION OF ITS TASK

Intellectual honesty compels us to state that there is no usable catalogue of criteria that could serve as a signpost in the ridge-walking between law and politics. The two fields of action partly overlap, and cannot unambiguously be separated from each other. As the constitutional review body, the Court has a share in politics. The problem to think about is the scope of the Court's area of

---

[56] Wiltraud Rupp-von Brhnneck, 'Verfassungsgerichtsbarkeit und gesetzgebende Gewalt,' in *AÖR* 102 (1977), 1 ff. 18; Simon, op. cit., n. 8, 1672 f.

[57] This means that the writer takes very seriously the criticism by Hans-Jochen Vogel ('Gewaltenvermischung statt Gewaltenteilung', in: *NJW* 1996, 1505, 1510 f.) and others.

responsibility. The test criteria, or better maxims, that present themselves are the structural principles of the Basic Law, which have as their object the interplay and antagonism of judicial review and political activity. These are necessarily very abstract, and denote only stages in a thought process. The horizon of reflection marked out by the principle of separation of powers and the democratic principle has to be paced off in thought for *every* decision. Although these principles are only topics of reflection, they ought not to be misinterpreted as more or less nonbinding appeals to constitutional judges. For what is at stake here is not voluntary self-restraint, but the fulfilment of a constitutional precept.[58] The sensitive definition of its own sphere of responsibility is a self-evident duty for an organ of government which according to the Constitution must, through the separation of governmental powers, watch over their balanced exercise.

[58] As Grimm rightly says, op. cit. n. 41, 107.

The EU Investment Services Directive
The Impact on Cross-border Business

by Timothy J. Herrington

I. INTRODUCTION

In this article I shall focus briefly on some of the practical issues which affect global banking and investment corporations seeking to comply with the new regulatory systems within the European Union (EU). I shall concentrate in particular on the effect of the Investment Services Directive (93/22/EEC) (ISD) on these entities.

Although I consider the effect of the ISD on entities incorporated within the EU ('EU entities') and on those incorporated outside the EU ('non EU entities') separately, it should be understood that the distinction which is drawn at a regulatory level between EU and non-EU entities can be misleading. Often non-EU entities will establish a branch within a European member state *and* incorporate a subsidiary so that their European presence comprises both EU and non-EU entities. Such groups may gain advantages, for example in terms of regulatory capital costs since they are able to conduct business directly through their non-EU entities (which usually have larger capital bases).

It should be borne in mind, therefore, that regulatory rules affecting non-EU entities do not necessarily leave EU entities unaffected, rather, they are likely to impact on the ways in which global financial groups structure their business as between their EU and non-EU entities.

2. THE LIBERALISATION PARADOX

More than a year has now passed since the 31 December 1995 deadline for national implementation of the EU Investment

Services Directive (93/22/EEC) ('ISD'). Most EU[1] member states have now implemented the Directive.

The ISD was a key element in the EU single market programme designed to open European markets to EU investment firms in a similar way to that achieved for banks by the earlier Second Banking Coordination Directive (89/646/EEC) ('2BCD'). In a nutshell, investment firms and banks authorised in one member state (the 'home state') are now both given a 'passport' enabling them to establish branches and to conduct cross-border business (of the types specified in the Annex to ISD or the 2BCD respectively) in another member state (the 'host state') free from host state licensing requirements, but subject to host state conduct of business ('CoB') rules and other rules imposed by it which may be justified in the interests of the '*general good*'.

It is a paradox that a liberalising measure should be seen as resulting in restrictions, but the ISD has now become synonymous with restrictions on cross-border business (as well as with widespread legal uncertainty). The explanation can be found in three main features of the ISD.

New licensing requirements

The ISD, unlike the 2BCD, requires member states to impose licensing requirements on a broad range of securities and derivatives-related business. A number of member states (such as Denmark and Ireland) had not previously imposed comprehensive licensing requirements on financial services. In a number of other member states the implementation of the ISD has resulted in a broadening of the scope of licensing requirements (to apply to over-the-counter derivatives business) or has highlighted the importance of existing restrictions.

This has focused attention on whether non-EU entities (including EU branches of non-EU entities, such as the London branches of US banks) require a local licence to conduct cross-border business with customers and counterparties in the EU. After all, the fact that EU banks and investment firms need the passport implies

---

[1] The Directive not only applies in the member states of the European Union (EU) but also in those states which are members of the wider European Economic Area (EEA). References to the EU in this article should be read as including a reference to the EEA, unless the context otherwise requires.

that there are 'immigration controls' on the cross-border activities of non-EU entities.

In addition, even though EU banks and investment firms (including the EU-incorporated banking or securities subsidiaries of US banks) should generally be able to rely on their passport to avoid the need to comply with local licensing requirements, the passports are not fully comprehensive. For example, commodity and commodities-derivative business falls outside the scope of the passports and investment firms only have a limited passport for foreign exchange services. An EU bank or investment firm may still require a local licence to conduct non-passported business with customers and counterparties in another member state where that member state extends its licensing requirements to cover activities falling outside the scope of their passport.

Most member states do not either clearly define when their licensing requirements apply to business conducted by a foreign entity with local customers and counterparties or provide clear exemptions for cross-border business conducted with banks, investment firms, governmental entities, corporations or other sophisticated customers and counterparties (notable exceptions include Ireland and the UK which both provide relatively broad exemptions for certain categories of cross-border business). Thus, local licensing requirements may represent a real barrier to cross-border business even in the wholesale markets.

New conduct of business rules

In addition, the ISD, unlike the 2BCD, requires each member state to adopt CoB rules in relation to activities covered by the ISD and to apply these to both EU investment firms *and* banks conducting cross-border business within the territory of that member state.[2] By requiring member states to create CoB rules (when many previously had none) and establishing the principle that it is the host, rather than home, state CoB rules which apply to cross-border business, the ISD raises the spectre that, for example, a UK bank or investment firm conducting cross-border business from London throughout Europe could be required to comply with seventeen sets of CoB rules in addition to the rules applying to it in London.

---

[2] Article 11 ISD. Article 11 applies to banks as well as investment firms by virtue of Article 2(1) ISD.

These rules might regulate in differing, and perhaps conflicting ways, matters such as the terms of customer agreements. The CoB rules might also apply to cross-border business conducted by non-EU entities in the EU.

Although the ISD requires member states to apply these rules taking into account '*the professional nature of the person to whom the services are provided,*'[3] in many cases the rules adopted by member states do apply to business conducted with sophisticated customers and counterparties.

Solicitation restrictions

The ISD (and the 2BCD) also appear to permit member states to continue to apply and enforce some restrictions on solicitation and other marketing activities. A number of member states have unclear and broad-ranging rules restricting the marketing of investments, through telephone calls or distribution of marketing literature, which may even apply to solicitation of sophisticated customers and counterparties. For example, France maintains a number of overlapping and confusing laws regulating *démarchage* (solicitation) in relation to investment services as well as laws (the *loi Toubon*) requiring the use of the French language in marketing materials and certain contracts. Although the ISD specifically states that it does not prevent EU investment firms advertising their services '*through all available means of communication*,'[4] member states are free to regulate advertising in the interests of the '*general good*'. The Directive also specifically states that the regulation of certain solicitation restrictions remains a matter for national provision.[5]

Impact of barriers to cross-border business

The potential barriers to cross-border business created by licensing requirements, CoB rules and solicitation restrictions have to be taken seriously.

---

[3] Article 11(1) ISD.
[4] Article 13 ISD.
[5] 8th Recital ISD. Although the English language version of the ISD only states that 'door to door selling' remains a matter for national provision, the French language version refers to '*démarchage*'.

Because of the ISD, EU regulators may increasingly focus on the activities of foreign entities (both EU and non-EU) conducting cross-border business with local customers and counterparties (even in the wholesale markets). While there may have already been barriers at the borders, there may now be police guarding those barriers.

In addition to the risk of regulatory enforcement action and attendant publicity, there are concerns, in a number of countries, that contravention of local licensing requirements, CoB rules or solicitation restrictions may give local customers or counterparties grounds on which to avoid their liabilities under contracts or to claim damages. In the current climate, where even apparently sophisticated customers and counterparties may dispute liability under derivatives contracts or other transactions the natural first line of defence for a local customer or counterparty would be to argue that the foreign entity violated local law in executing the transaction in question.

3. IMPACT ON EU ENTITIES

The ISD and the 2BCD, however, for all their drawbacks, still represent a significant liberalisation of the EU market for EU banks and investment firms.

So long as the activities fall within the scope of a passport, the Directives should sweep aside any need for any EU passported entities to comply with local licensing requirements for cross-border business within the EU, leaving only the issues of the application of CoB rules and solicitation restrictions. However, licensing concerns remain for business falling outside the scope of the passports, in particular, for commodities and commodity derivatives business and, for investment firms, some foreign exchange business.

Passported business

Once an entity has established that it is an EU incorporated bank or investment firm falling within the Directive definitions, the next key question is whether the business falls within the scope of the Annex to the relevant Directive. EU banks must look to the Annex to the 2BCD to determine whether their activities fall within the scope of their passport; investment firms must look to the Annex to the ISD. There is considerable overlap between the scope of the two passports. Both passports cover securities broker-dealer business, trading in financial derivatives, most fund management and investment advice, underwriting and distribution of new issues and corporate finance advisory business. However, there are also important differences.

For example, investment firms do not get the ISD passport for:

(i) *Foreign exchange services* (other than currency options, currency swaps and financial futures), except where connected with the provision of core investment services (as defined — the ISD). In contrast, banks have an unrestricted passport for foreign exchange services.

(ii) *Lending or credit activities*, except where an investment firm involved in a transaction in financial instruments grants credit to an investor to enable the investor to carry out the transaction in financial instruments (for example, margin credit). In contrast, banks have an unrestricted passport for lending or credit activities, including financial leasing.

(iii) *Fund management and investment advisory services* which are not related to ISD financial instruments (for example, foreign exchange or commodities investment advisory services). In contrast, banks have an unrestricted passport for portfolio management and advice.

(iv) *Deposit-taking.* This can raise questions as to the extent to which host states can restrict the ability of investment firms to hold client money without segregation into separate client accounts, although the ISD does provide that client money is a matter which falls to the home state to regulate. In contrast, banks have an unrestricted passport for deposit-taking.

(v) Only banks get the passport for *certain other services* such as money transmission services, issuing and administering means of payment (credit cards, etc), money broking and credit reference services.

There are few areas where the passport available to banks is narrower than that available to investment firms, although there are some doubts as to whether banks receive the passport for the services of *reception and transmission of customers' orders* (that is, the arranging of transactions as opposed to execution of transactions for the account of customers) or business related to *equity swaps* (as these are specifically mentioned in the Annex to the ISD, but not in the Annex to the 2BCD).

In addition, neither the ISD nor the 2BCD passport covers trading in commodity or commodity derivatives.

Whether these limitations cause problems of course depends on the law in the state where the customer or counterparty is located. If business outside the scope of a passport is not regulated in that state, then an EU bank or investment firm is unlikely to be troubled by the fact that the passport does not apply.

If it is regulated, however, then additional issues arise, which are much the same as those which arise for non-EU entities (see Section 4 below).

Has the activity been notified under the Directives?

Two further conditions need to be fulfilled before an EU bank or investment firm can rely on its passport for cross-border business. First, the activity in question must be *'covered by'* its home state authorisation. This is unlikely to be an issue in relation to most cross-border business. Secondly, the entity must have *notified its home state regulator* that it intends to conduct that activity in the other member state. The home state regulator will then pass on that notification to the host state regulator concerned and in the case of investment firms (but not banks) the passport does not become effective until the notification has been received by the host state regulator.

However, the notification requirement has proved to be controversial. Under both Directives, the bank or investment firm is only required to notify its home state regulator where it intends to conduct the activity *'within the territory'* of the other member state. When the 2BCD was implemented many EU banks assumed that simply doing cross-border business with customers and counterparties in another member state did not trigger the notification requirement. However, by the time the ISD was being implemented the attitude to notification had changed, at least in the UK.

Investment firms were increasingly conscious of the risks of being found to have contravened local licensing requirements in other member states even if the business fell within the passport. The only way of being sure of avoiding a contravention was to notify their home state regulator and to ensure that notification was passed on to the host state.

In addition, the European Commission had published for consultation a draft communication on the 'freedom to provide services and the interests of the general good in the Second Banking Directive' dealing with the notification requirements under the 2BCD. This suggested that cross-border services would be regarded as provided '*within the territory*' of another member state, triggering notification requirements, if the bank had engaged in '*commercial canvassing*' within the territory of another member state such that the bank (rather than the customer) could be regarded as having '*initiated*' the relationship. This initiation test was widely criticised as impractical, in particular because banks and investment firms would find it impossible to determine whether they had 'initiated' a particular relationship.

Accordingly, a number of investment firms adopted, as a matter of prudence, the practice of providing their home state regulator with 'blanket' notifications covering all activities which they might wish to conduct with customers in all other member states, while not admitting that they were in fact providing services '*within the territory*' of any other member state.

However, it now appears that the European Commission, as a result of its consultations on its draft communication, may adopt a different test to determine where a service is provided. The new test would focus on where the '*characteristic performance*' associated with a particular service takes place and it would be presumed that the characteristic performance generally takes place where the service provider is located. Under this test, the service would not normally be regarded as provided '*within the territory of*' the state where the customer or counterparty is located except where personnel of the service provider travel to that country to provide the service. This test is obviously helpful to banks and investment firms, although it remains uncertain as to how far it will go (if adopted) to eliminate uncertainties, in particular because it would not be binding on host state regulators.

As a result, banks and investment firms will probably continue the practice of giving 'blanket' notifications under the Directives until the situation is clarified, in particular because of the risks of unenforceability of contracts or civil claims for damages.

Application of local CoB rules and solicitation restrictions

The other principal concern for an EU bank or investment firm is that by dealing with customers or counterparties in another member state it will be subject to CoB rules, solicitation restrictions or other requirements in the host state.

The ISD specifically allocates responsibilities between the home state and the host state in relation to investment services provided by EU banks and investment firms. It is the home state's responsibility: to determine whether the bank or investment firm meets the relevant authorisation criteria; to monitor its regulatory capital requirements; and, to adopt rules regulating administrative procedures, internal controls, custody of client assets, safeguarding of client money, record keeping and the organisational structure necessary to minimise the risk of conflicts of interest.[6] In contrast, Article 11 of the ISD requires member states to adopt CoB rules and states that implementation and supervision of these rules shall be the responsibility of the state *'in which a service is provided'*, that is, the host state.[7]

This again raises the issue of 'where' a service is provided. If the service is treated as being provided in a place other than the home state, then EU banks and investment firms conducting cross-border business from a single location are exposed to the risk of having to comply with multiple sets of CoB rules.

At this stage of the implementation of the ISD, the following observations can be made:

(i) The Commission's proposed *'characteristic performance'* test, if adopted in relation to notification requirements, should (but will not necessarily) apply equally to the scope of application of CoB rules adopted under Article 11 of the ISD.

(ii) The ISD (but not the 2BCD) requires a member state to respond to a notification from an investment firm of its intention to provide cross-border services by providing details of the CoB rules and other rules adopted in the interests of the *'general good'* which

---

[6] Articles 10 and 20 ISD.   [7] Article 11(2) ISD.

may apply to that firm. However, it is questionable whether any reliance can be placed on the scope of these responses as a defence to an allegation of non-compliance.

(iii) Member states appear to be taking very different approaches to the implementation of Article 11. Some states have adopted rules which broadly restate the general principles in Article 11; others have adopted detailed rule books. Few states (other than the Netherlands and the UK) seem fully to accept that there should be a clear divide between wholesale business, to which only general principles should apply, and retail business, where more detailed rules may be justifiable, even though the ISD specifically requires that CoB rules should '*take account of the professional nature of the person to whom the service is provided*'.

(iv) A number of states seem to be disregarding the distinction between host state and home state responsibilities by imposing requirements on passporting entities which appear to be home state responsibilities under the ISD.

(v) There may in some cases be uncertainty as to when any new CoB rules apply to particular types of business. The ISD only requires that CoB rules be applied to 'core investment services' and only if 'appropriate' to 'non-core services.' There is clear scope for confusion as to when and how any CoB rules do apply, even if a member state sticks to the bare minimum requirements of the ISD.

Finally, states remain free to impose restrictions on marketing and other solicitation activity and to maintain other rules which can be justified in the interests of the 'general good'. Under existing case law of the European Court of Justice, such restrictions must not be discriminatory, duplicative, disproportionate or unduly burdensome, but there is considerable margin of appreciation for member states—a margin which some would like to see used, in particular, to 'protect' consumers from new products and services being offered to them from other member states.[8]

---

[8] For example, the proposed ISDN Directive may require restrictions to be placed upon certain forms of telemarketing without consent from the person contacted. Amendments proposed by the EU Parliament would require member states to apply the new rules to all activities whether or not targeted at individuals.

4. IMPACT ON NON-EU ENTITIES

It seems reasonably clear that the real victims of the ISD are non-EU entities, including those operating through EU branches. The ISD has led to new, or has highlighted existing, licensing barriers to cross-border business, in many cases without any appropriate exemptions for cross-border business conducted with banks, investment firms, governmental entities, corporations or other sophisticated customers and counterparties. Unlike an EU bank or investment firm, a non-EU entity cannot rely on a passport to overcome or mitigate the effects of such licensing barriers.

In theory, many non-EU entities could avoid this issue by ensuring that all cross-border business with European customers and counterparties is conducted by an EU incorporated affiliated bank or investment firm entitled to a passport under the Directives.

However, customers and counterparties may often prefer to transact their business with the non-EU entity rather than its EU affiliate, perhaps for credit reasons (for example, where the non-EU entity has a larger capital or an established credit rating) or simply because there is an existing business relationship with the non-EU entity or because the non-EU entity's personnel are perceived as being closer to a particular market or as having particular expertise in the product concerned.

In addition, the EU affiliate may itself not have sufficient regulatory capital to support the proposed business. Many EU banking or investment firm affiliates of non-EU entities have a relatively small capital base which would, for example, materially restrict their ability to assume significant derivatives positions with a single counterparty.

Requiring all business to be booked into EU affiliates would also prevent a group using a non-EU entity as a central booking entity (with traders in a number of time zones able to commit the central entity to transactions). Use of a central booking entity facilitates the centralised risk management of positions and enhances the effectiveness of netting rights.

Thus, non-EU entities will have to examine whether licensing restrictions are in fact a real restriction on their ability to conduct cross-border business with European customers and counterparties. This means looking at the following key issues in the countries where their customers or counterparties are located.

Is there a licensing requirement?

The first issue is whether the particular type of business is subject
to any licensing requirement in that country. To comply with
the ISD, all member states should now have introduced licensing requirements covering at least the 'core investment services'
specified in the ISD. Some states may also require licences for
activities outside the scope of the passport.

What is the territorial scope of that licensing requirement?

If there is a licensing requirement, it is necessary to determine
whether or not it applies to cross-border business. A few countries
take the view that the licensing requirement only applies to entities
operating through an establishment in that country. Other countries (such as the Netherlands) have taken a broad view such that
any contact with local customers and counterparties may be
enough to trigger the application of their licensing requirements.
In most countries, however, the law does not adequately define
when business is conducted that country so as to trigger the application of local licensing requirements.

It may be that one of the most significant benefits of the Commission's adoption of the proposed '*characteristic performance*' test (if
adopted and applied by member states) would be to limit the
territorial application of licensing laws to cross-border business by
non-EU entities. After all, it may be inconsistent to hold that a
particular service is not provided 'in' a particular member state
(and thus does not trigger a notification requirement or the application of CoB rules) where that service is provided cross-border by
an EU entity, but to hold that the same service is provided 'in' that
country (so as to trigger licensing requirements) when provided
cross-border in the same manner by a non-EU entity.

Is there a 'professionals' exemption?

In some countries, there are broad exemptions from local licensing
requirements which apply to cross-border business. For example,
in Ireland there are broad exemptions which may be available to
entities conducting cross-border business otherwise than with individuals. In the UK, there is an exemption for 'overseas persons'

who conduct cross-border business with a locally licensed entity or with other customers and counterparties without violating UK cold-calling and investment advertising rules (which themselves contain exemptions for solicitation of sophisticated customers and counterparties).

Is the business sheltered by an existing branch licence?

If a non-EU bank already has a locally licensed branch in a particular country, it may not require an additional licence to conduct cross-border business from, say, its head office with local customers and counterparties (even if the branch is not involved in either originating or executing the transaction). Whether this approach works may depend on whether the local regulators regard the existing licence as covering the entity as a whole or only the activities of the branch.

Is it possible to obtain a cross-border licence?

It may be possible for a non-EU entity to obtain a licence to do cross-border business in a particular state without establishing a locally licensed branch or subsidiary (and without becoming subject to onerous local regulatory capital or other requirements).

Does 'intermediation' shelter the non-EU entity from local licensing requirements?

It may also be possible for the non-EU entity to avoid the application of local licensing requirements by dealing with local customers or counterparties through the 'intermediation' of a local bank or investment firm or an EU bank or investment firm exercising the passport in that country (for example, where the passported bank or investment firm either introduces business to the non-EU entity or is authorised to trade in its name). A passported entity should not generally be subjected to local licensing requirements as a result of acting as an intermediary between the local customer or counterparty and the non-EU entity (except where the business falls outside the scope of the passport altogether, for example, where it involves commodities or commodity derivatives).

However, it seems that the UK may be unique in explicitly

addressing the question of whether the non-EU entity is subject to licensing requirements in these circumstances.[9] UK law clearly exempts an 'overseas person' from local licensing requirements where it deals with local customers and counterparties through the agency of a UK authorised person or passported entity. While regulators in some other countries may be willing to accept that this should be the result, in many cases the position is uncertain and in any event may depend on exactly how the business is structured. Obviously, there may be particular concerns where the non-EU entity is conducting cross-border business through an intermediary with individuals, highlighting the particular difficulties faced by non-EU entities conducting cross-border private banking business in Europe.

In some countries, there may also be a concern that where the non-EU entity is acting through the agency of a local entity or a local branch of another entity, it may itself be treated as having established a local 'establishment' which would itself require a licence.

What is the impact of solicitation restrictions and CoB rules?

Non-EU entities will also need to address the scope and application of any local solicitation restrictions as well as any local CoB rules which may apply to them. Again, it will be necessary to determine how CoB rules apply to cross-border business conducted by the non-EU entity, in particular as CoB rules may apply even though the non-EU entity does not obtain (or require) a local licence.

5. CONCLUSIONS

The ISD has a dual effect in that it enhances the ability of EU entities to conduct certain forms of investment business within Europe while it also imposes certain restrictions (or rejuvenates existing restrictions). These restrictions operate not only on EU entities in respect of other forms of business, but also on non-EU entities in respect of all types of business. This effect on non-EU entities has the potential to harm the EU financial services

---

[9] Compare Rule 15a-6 under the US Securities and Exchange Act of 1934.

market because of the potential restrictions on choice for EU customers (who may prefer to deal with non-EU parent entities) and increases in costs (which may arise from the effects on regulatory capital costs for the service providers).

The Directives highlight the need for international financial groups to address the compliance and structural impact on cross-border business of the re-regulation of European markets triggered by the ISD. This, however, may prove to be a difficult task simply because it is not always clear whether (or how) licensing or notification requirements (or CoB rules) will apply in relation to any particular kind of business in any given country. Legal uncertainty is always an unnecessary evil. Nevertheless many crucial issues such as the territoriality of host state regulation are likely to remain unresolved.

The result of the Commission's initiative to issue interpretative guidance on the 2BCD is at the time of writing expected shortly. Nevertheless, even when it is available, it cannot be assumed that this non-binding compromise text will resolve all the issues (even for EU entities), although it holds out some prospect of reducing some uncertainties.

12

Legislation, Regulation, and Judicial Review

by Prof. Paul Craig

The interplay between legislators, judges and academics within the sphere of public law is particularly significant at present. In recent years there has been a renewed interest in both the intensity of judicial review in the UK and in the conceptual foundations of this review power. What is particularly interesting in this respect is the nature of the principal protagonists in this debate. Hitherto this was a debate carried on largely within academia, with some academics questioning whether the traditional *ultra vires* doctrine could continue to furnish the appropriate foundation for what the courts had been and were actually doing within this area.[1] More recently the challenge to that doctrine has been taken up by members of the judiciary themselves, notably by Sir John Laws, Sir Stephen Sedley and Lord Woolf.[2] This challenge has prompted a defence of the ultra vires principle by Christopher Forsyth[3] and Lord Irvine.[4]

The purpose of this paper is not to engage directly in this debate. Suffice it to say for the present that I fall into the camp of those who do not believe that *ultra vires* can provide a fitting basis for judicial review. A detailed analysis of the arguments why this is so can be found elsewhere.[5]

[1] Craig, *Administrative Law*, 3rd ed., (London, Sweet & Maxwell, 1994), 3–17; Oliver, 'Is the *Ultra Vires* Rule the Basis of Judicial Review?' [1987] *P.L.* 543.

[2] Sir John Laws, 'Illegality: The Problem of Jurisdiction', in Supperstone and Goudie (eds.), *Judicial Review* (1992), Chap. 4 and 'Law and Democracy' [1995] *P.L.* 72; Sir Stephen Sedley, 'Human Rights: A Twenty-First Century Agenda' [1995] *P.L.* 386; Lord Woolf, 'Droit Public-English Style' [1995] *P.L.* 57.

[3] 'Of Fig Leaves and Fairy Tales: The *Ultra Vires* Doctrine, the Sovereignty of Parliament and Judicial Review' [1996] *CLJ* 122.

[4] 'Judges and Decision-Makers: The Theory and Practice of *Wednesbury* Review' [1996] *P.L.* 59.

[5] Above, n. 1, and Craig, '*Ultra Vires*, Judicial Review and Sovereignty' (forthcoming).

The object of this paper is rather different. The normal focus on judicial review is to consider the scope of the courts' power, with the object of determining whether they have strayed beyond their proper review role and have intervened on the merits of a particular dispute. This is indeed an important issue and it will be discussed within the first part of the ensuing analysis. It will be argued that the courts are generally well aware of the limits to, and appropriate intensity of, judicial review. In the second part of the analysis it will, however, be argued that the interrelationship between legislators and courts within the sphere of public law has another dimension. It will be suggested that the legislature itself has certain responsibilities in the way in which it frames legislation, or in the manner in which it effectuates more general administrative changes. The judiciary may well have to fashion appropriate tools of review to deal with these novel institutional changes. Certain recent developments in the pattern of government which have posed new problems for the courts when applying the classical doctrine of judicial review will be analysed within this section. These alterations have been put into effect either by the executive or through the passage of legislation with scant regard for any broader constitutional or administrative law implications.

The interrelationship between the courts and the legislature within the area covered by public law should, therefore, be seen as two-dimensional. The courts must be aware of the appropriate limits to their judicial role. Yet the legislature itself has responsibilities in the way in which it enacts legislation, whether particular or general; and the courts may well have to be creative in order to mould doctrine to meet the needs of a changing administrative environment.

I. THE COURTS AND THE BOUNDARIES OF JUDICIAL REVIEW

It is commonly acknowledged that the courts should not, in the context of an action for judicial review, substitute their views on the merits for that of the original decisionmaker. All legal systems have to find the appropriate balance between legal controls over the exercise of discretion and the avoidance of judicial substitution on the merits of the case. Where differing legal systems draw this line is often of crucial importance. Two recent decisions show that the courts in the UK are fully aware of the need to avoid judicial substitution of judgment, whether directly or indirectly.

One such case is *R.* v. *Cambridge Health Authority, ex p. B*.[6] The problem was rendered more challenging by the tragic nature of the fact situation. The applicant, B, was a 10 year old girl who was extremely ill. She had received varying treatments for this illness, including a bone marrow transplant, but the treatment had not proven to be effective. As a result the hospital, on the advice of the relevant specialists, decided that B had only a short time to live and that further major therapy should not be given. B's father sought the opinion of two further specialists who thought that a second bone marrow transplant might have some chance of success. Such treatment could, however, only be administered privately because there were no beds in the National Health Service public sector within a hospital which could carry out such therapy. The proposed treatment would take place in two stages, the first of which would cost £15,000 and have a 10-20 per cent chance of success; the second stage would cost £60,000 with a similar 10-20 per cent chance of success. B's father requested the health authority to allocate the funds necessary for this therapy. It refused to do so, given the limited nature of the funds at its disposal and the small likelihood that the treatment would be effective. B's father then sought judicial review of this decision. This application succeeded in part at first instance, but the decision was overturned by the Court of Appeal. The judgment of the latter court was delivered by Sir Thomas Bingham MR.

He began his judgment by recognising the tragic nature of B's situation, but stressed also that the courts were not the arbiters of the merits in cases of this nature. It was not for the courts to express any opinion as to the likely success or not of the relevant medical treatment.[7] The courts should, said the Master of the Rolls, confine themselves to the lawfulness of the decision under scrutiny. The Court of Appeal then evaluated the four criticisms which had been made of the health authority by the judge at first instance, Laws J.

The Court of Appeal had little difficulty in rejecting the first two of these criticisms, which were that the health authority had given insufficient attention to the wishes of the patient, and that it had described the suggested therapy as experimental. Both of these

[6] [1995] 2 All E.R. 129.   [7] *Ibid.*, 135-6.

reasons for overturning the health authority's decision were rejected on the facts of the case.

The other grounds for the decision of Laws J at first instance in favour of the applicant are of more general interest. The basic rationale for the health authority's refusal to press further with treatment for B was, of course, the scarcity of resources. Health authorities do not have limitless budgets. They are subject to financial constraints and have to make difficult choices as to how to expend these limited sums. Laws J. had accepted that this was so, but had felt that it was incumbent on the health authority to provide a more detailed explanation as to why they could not fund this treatment, given that the life of a child was at stake.

Sir Thomas Bingham MR, giving the judgment for the Court of Appeal, differed. He believed that it was unrealistic to demand of the health authority the type of detailed financial explanation which had been required by Laws J. Bingham MR expressed the matter as follows.[8]

I have no doubt that in a perfect world any treatment which a patient . . . sought would be provided if doctors were willing to give it, no matter how much it cost, particularly when a life was potentially at stake. It would however, in my view, be shutting one's eyes to the real world if the court were to proceed on the basis that we do live in such a world. It is common knowledge that health authorities of all kinds are constantly pressed to make ends meet. They cannot pay their nurses as much as they would like; they cannot provide all the treatments they would like; they cannot purchase all the extremely expensive medical equipment they would like; they cannot carry out all the research they would like; they cannot build all the hospitals and specialist units they would like. Difficult and agonising judgments have to be made as to how a limited budget is best allocated to the maximum advantage of the maximum number of patients. That is not a judgment which the court can make. In my judgment, it is not something that a health authority such as this authority can be fairly criticised for not advancing before the court.

The force of this quotation clearly reveals the danger of the courts intervening in a way which would affect these difficult allocative decisions which must be made by any health authority. The Master of the Rolls rightly stressed that decisions of this nature concerning the merits are not for the courts. Implicit in this quotation is a further message as to how far one can expect the health

[8] [1995] 2 All E.R. 129, 137.

authority to be able to provide a reasoned financial breakdown justifying its decision. While the courts in the UK have made great strides in demanding reasoned decisionmaking from public bodies,[9] there are limits as to the degree of detail which can be demanded of them, particularly in this type of case. This is brought out forcefully by Sir Thomas Bingham MR in the following passage.[10]

I furthermore think, differing I regret from the judge, that it would be totally unrealistic to require from the authority to come to the court with its accounts and seek to demonstrate that if this treatment were provided for B then there would be a patient, C, who would have to go without treatment. No major authority could run its financial affairs in a way which would permit such a demonstration.

The outcome of this case was, in all events, better for the applicant B that might be imagined from a simple reading of the preceding analysis. Her plight was reported in the national press, with the result that a private party came forward with the funds for her treatment. This does not, course, mean that the decision of the Court of Appeal was wrong. It was not. The reasoning of the court and the result which it reached are, I believe, unassailable. Allocative decisions of the kind which were in issue in this case are not for the courts. They have no basis, constitutional or pragmatic, for making the kind of decisions on the merits which arose in this case. To have required the health authority to fund this treatment would have necessarily meant that some other area covered by the health authority would have gone short of funding. Nor, for the reasons indicated by Sir Thomas Bingham MR, would it have been realistic to expect the health authority to provide the type of detailed financial explanation which Laws J appeared to demand. The macro-financial budgetary provisions of such an authority do not lend themselves to this type of analysis. The fact that the story had a happy ending is wonderful for the child and her family, but it does not serve to show that the Court of Appeal was wrong.

R. v. *Chief Constable of Sussex, ex p. International Trader's Ferry Ltd.*[11] provides our second example of the UK courts being mindful of not substituting judgment on the merits of the case. The applicant, ITF, transported livestock across the channel. It attempted to

---

[9] Craig, 'The Common Law, Reasons and Administrative Justice' [1994] *CLJ* 282
[10] [1995] 2 All E.R. 129, 137H–J.   [11] [1995] 4 All E.R. 364.

do so from a port in Sussex. The company's operations were impeded by large scale protests from those who were against the export of livestock in these conditions. As a consequence the local police force had to deploy very large numbers of police in order to ensure the safe passage of the vehicles: during the first ten-day shipping period, 1,125 police were required at each sailing of ITF's lorries; thereafter for three months this number was reduced to 315 police for each sailing because the number of protesters had dropped. This placed a considerable financial burden on the Sussex police, since it had to call on other police forces for assistance at a cost of £1.25 million during the initial period alone. The Sussex force did not actually seek special financial assistance from the Home Office, but statements from the Home office indicated that this would probably not be forthcoming. The Sussex police were also under strain because the number of men being deployed to cover the port meant that there were far fewer police to deal with all the other calls on their services. As a consequence the chief constable of Sussex wrote to ITF stating that he intended to reduce the level of policing at the port. Police cover for ITF's vehicles would only be available on a limited number of days, twice per week or four times per fortnight. ITF's lorries would be turned back if they could not be safely boarded onto ferries at other times. ITF sought judicial review of this decision. The case came before the Divisional Court and Balcombe LJ gave the judgment. ITF failed on domestic law, but succeeded under Community law.[12]

The reasoning in the case concerning domestic law was, it is believed, correct. ITF claimed that the Sussex police were in breach of their duty to keep the peace and enforce the law. The firm recognised that the police have a discretion as to how to deploy their limited resources, but argued that the way in which the police force had done so in this instance was unreasonable.[13] Balcombe LJ, giving the judgment of the court, disagreed. He held that while the courts would ensure that the police fulfilled their duty to uphold the law, the courts would not normally interfere with the manner in which the police exercised their discretion. He recognised that a chief constable must have regard to the resources available to

---

[12] It is questionable, to say the very least, whether the argument based upon Community law should have been successful.

[13] [1995] 4 All E.R. 364, 372.

him,[14] and that it was proper for the chief constable to take into account the cost of providing certain types of police coverage.[15] As Balcombe LJ stated,[16]

The essential point is that the chief constable has finite resources in man and woman power; the financial resources available to him are equally finite and are not under his direct control.

While the courts are, therefore, properly mindful of not substituting their judgment on the merits of the case, they are equally aware of the need to maintain appropriate controls over the legality of administrative action.[17] What has become more apparent in the jurisprudence is the way in which the intensity of the review will vary depending upon the subject matter which is in dispute. This development is to be welcomed and is exemplified by the way in which the courts deal with cases involving fundamental human rights.

A key conceptual step in this process has been the courts' acknowledgement that rights which exist under the European Convention are not different in principle from those recognised at common law.[18] The modern approach to matters of this kind is evident in *R. v. Secretary of State for the Home Department, ex p. McQuillan.*[19]

The applicant was a national both of the UK and the Republic of Ireland who was living in Belfast in Northern Ireland. During the 1980s he had occupied a prominent position in the Irish Republican Socialist Party (IRSP), but had resigned from the IRSP in 1992. From 1987 onwards the Home Secretary had issued exclusion orders against him under the Prevention of Terrorism (Temporary Provisions) Act 1989, prohibiting him from entering Great Britain on the ground that he was or had been involved in acts of terrorism. The applicant, M, sought review as he was entitled to do under the

---

[14] *Ibid.* 372J, citing *R. v. Cambridge Health Authority, ex p. B* [1995] 2 All E.R. 129, with approval.

[15] [1995] 4 All E.R. 364, 372–3. See further, *R. v. Metropolitan Police Commissioner, ex p. Blackburn* [1968] 2 Q.B. 118; *R. v. Chief Constable of the Devon and Cornwall Constabulary, ex p. Central Electricity Generating Board* [1982] Q.B. 458; *Harris v. Sheffield United Football Club Ltd.* [1988] Q.B. 77, 95.

[16] [1995] 4 All E.R. 364, 373C. This reasoning was affirmed by the Court of Appeal, [1997] 2 All E.R. 65, 77–79.

[17] See generally, Craig, above n. 1, Chap. 11.

[18] *Att.-Gen. v. Guardian Newspapers (No. 2)* [1990] 1 A.C. 109, 283–4.; *Derbyshire County Council v. Times Newspapers Ltd.* [1993] 1 All E.R. 1011.

[19] [1995] 4 All E.R. 400.

legislation and he was duly interviewed by a nominee of the Home Secretary. At this interview the applicant maintained that he was no longer a member of the IRSP, that he had never been involved in terrorist activities and that his life was in danger if he continued to live in Northern Ireland. The Home Secretary was not persuaded and refused to revoke the exclusion order. In refusing to revoke the order the Home Secretary merely stated that he was satisfied that M was or had been involved in acts of terrorism, and that the exclusion order appeared to be expedient to prevent further such acts. The Home Secretary also stated that it was not possible to reveal further details of why the order had been made, because this might lead to the discovery of relevant sources of information which could compromise security operations in this area. The applicant, M, sought judicial review of this decision. The case came before Sedley J who reasoned as follows.

Sedley J recognised that freedom of movement, subject only to the general law, was a fundamental value *of the common law*.[20] The power given to the Home Secretary to restrict this freedom, not by modifying the general law, but by depriving certain persons of the full extent of this right, was a draconian measure which could be justified only by a grave emergency. Such a power could create a form of internal exile. It was for this reason that Parliament had only sanctioned use of such a power to counter the grave threat of terrorism. It was for this reason also that,[21]

. . . the courts would enforce rigorously the requirement that the Secretary of State is to take into account 'everything which appears to him to be relevant' so as to ensure that nothing of real relevance is discounted by the Secretary of State solely because it appears to him not to be relevant: in other words, the courts would scrutinise his reasoning closely and draw the boundaries of rationality tightly around his judgment.

Sedley J went on to hold that what was true of the right to freedom of movement was true also for the right to life. This too was recognised and protected *by the common law* and 'attracted the most anxious scrutiny by the courts of administrative decision-making.'[22] It was held that the right to life encompassed a prohibition on inhuman treatment, even though this was an enlargement of the relevant provision contained in the Bill of Rights 1689.

[20] [1995] 4 All E.R. 400, 421–2.   [21] *Ibid.* 422.   [22] *Ibid.* 422D.

Sedley J then proceeded to consider the relevance of the ECHR. The strict doctrinal position was that, because the Convention has not been incorporated into domestic law, it could not be relied on as a matter of right in cases which arose within our domestic courts. Nonetheless, in line with much recent academic and judicial thinking, Sedley J concluded that the Convention could be taken notice of by common law courts when they set their own standards. Drawing upon an important paper by Laws J,[23] Sedley J agreed that the ECHR could be used as a text to inform the common law, and as a yardstick against which to test domestic public law principles. From this it generally followed that whenever rights recognised as fundamental were in issue, the standard of executive justification for the interference with those rights was commensurately more exacting.[24]

Thus far the case for the applicant appeared to be promising. However, in order for the applicant to succeed he needed to obtain further information from the Home Secretary as to why the latter still felt that the applicant posed a threat. The Home Secretary was, as noted above, unwilling to reveal this information. Ostensibly, this was for reasons of national security, but, as Sedley J noted, in reality the executive's reluctance to disclose more was based upon grounds of public interest immunity.[25] The judge made it clear that had the matter been free from binding authority he would have held that the arguments proffered by the executive did not fall into the category of national security, but fell to be assessed on the grounds of public interest immunity. There was, however, authority directly on point in the form of prior decisions in which the courts had been satisfied with executive 'explanations' which were identical with those given by the Home Secretary in the instant case. Given that this was so the applicant could not proceed further as a matter of domestic law.

All was not, however, lost for the applicant. A feature which is becoming increasingly common in administrative law pleadings is reliance on both domestic public law principles *and* those derived from the European Community. Important issues of Community public law concerning the scope of Article 8a(1) of the EC Treaty and the compatibility of the UK legislation with Article 9 of Directive 64/221, were raised by the case. Questions of this nature

---

[23] Sir John Laws, 'Is the High Court the Guardian of Fundamental Constitutional Rights?' [1993] *P.L.* 59.
[24] [1995] 4 All E.R. 400, 422J.   [25] *Ibid.* 423.

had already been referred to the ECJ in other related cases and therefore Sedley J stayed the present action, pending the outcome of those actions. He did not feel able to grant interim relief to the operation of the exclusion order while waiting for the answers from the ECJ.

The decision in *McQuillan* is instructive in a number of respects. It demonstrates the current approach of the UK courts to cases involving fundamental rights and the review of administrative discretion, indicating the willingness of the courts to use the common law to fashion appropriate degrees of control for cases of this kind even in the absence of a written Bill of Rights. It shows also the importance of the interplay between substantive protection and access to documentation and evidence. At the end of the day the applicant in *McQuillan* could not gain redress via domestic law alone because of prior authorities which were binding upon the judge in that case, which authorities had shown themselves to be satisfied with 'brief explanations' of the kind which had been proffered by the executive in *McQuillan* itself. While the courts must of course be wary of intervening in cases of national security, they must also, as Sedley J indicated in *McQuillan*, be able to assess whether there really are reasons which can plausibly be regarded as coming within this area. If explanations from the executive are to be accepted when they are as exiguous as that which was given in the instant case then the substantive protections afforded by the common law will not be as effective as they might otherwise have been.

2. THE LEGISLATURE, INSTITUTIONAL DEVELOPMENTS AND JUDICIAL REVIEW

(a) Next Steps Agencies: The Background

The last five years have seen the most major revolution in the pattern of administration in this country since the Northcote-Trevelyan reforms. Those nineteenth-century reforms instituted a unified and uniform service, with governmental functions being organised in and through departments.[26]

---

[26] This was in contrast with the pattern of administration in the earlier part of the nineteenth century when public functions were often undertaken by boards which operated outside the confines of the now traditional departmental organisational norm.

By the 1960s strains had begun to appear in what had become the accepted organisational structure. These became apparent in the Report of the *Fulton Committee*.[27] Two major themes are evident in the Committee's Report. One was the need for improved efficiency within traditional departments, and this entailed a structure in which different units had clearly defined authority for which they could be held responsible. The other theme was that we should reassess precisely which activities required to be undertaken directly within the department at all. Many activities might work better if they were 'hived off' and run by bodies which existed outside the departmental framework, albeit subject to overall ministerial guidance.

The proposals of the Fulton Committee were one of the catalysts for the hiving off of a number of functions to newly created agencies: the Civil Aviation Authority was formed from the Department of Trade and Industry in 1971; the Manpower Services Commission, the Advisory and Conciliation and Arbitration Service (ACAS) and the Health and Safety Commission were split from the Department of Employment in 1974. These agencies were *regulatory* in nature, even though part of their brief might also include the giving of advice.

Other attempts at improving efficiency and effectiveness in the civil service were to follow, but it was the establishment of the *Rayner Unit* in 1979, (later known as the *Efficiency Unit*), by the Prime Minister after her election victory that was to sow the seeds for more major reform. Rayner headed a small team which undertook a number of efficiency scrutinies of particular departmental activities. In this sense Rayner operated through the medium of the laser beam rather than the arc light.[28] Sir Robin Ibbs succeeded Lord Rayner as head of the Efficiency Unit and began by undertaking an overview of the achievements of the Rayner scrutinies.[29] This was followed by a more radical study, which culminated in the *'Next Steps' Report*.[30] The radical nature of its proposals led to it

[27] *Report of the Committee on the Civil Service 1966–68*, Cmnd. 3638 (1968).
[28] Hennessy, *Whitehall* (London, Fontana Press, 1990), Chap. 14; McDonald, *The Future of Whitehall* (London, Weidenfeld & Nicolson, 1991), Chap. 1.
[29] *Making Things Happen: A Report on the Implications of Government Efficiency Scrutinies* (HMSO, 1985).
[30] *Improving Management in Government: The Next Steps* (HMSO, 1988); Goldsworthy, *Setting Up Next Steps: A Short Account of the Origins, Launch, and Implementation of the Next Steps Project in the British Civil Service* (HMSO, 1991).

being concealed until after the 1987 election. The object of the study was to discover what had been achieved by the scrutiny exercises, and what should be the next steps in civil service reform. The *Next Steps Report* proposed two fundamental changes. Firstly, there should be a split between service delivery and the making of policy. As a consequence there should be a real devolution of power to executive agencies in the area of service delivery, which would cover approximately 95 per cent of civil service activity. Secondly, there should be an end to the fiction that the minister was responsible for everything done by officials in his or her own name. The recommendations in the Report began to be acted upon in 1988-89. A project manager, Peter Kemp, was appointed to carry forward the Report's proposals, with reference to the creation of executive agencies responsible for service delivery. Government departments were required to review their activities and to consider five possibilities: abolition, privatization, contracting out, creation of an agency, and preservation of the status quo. If the agency route is chosen then the matter will be put into effect by a Project Executive made up of representatives from the Project Team, the Treasury, the Efficiency Unit and the sponsoring department itself. Large parts of the civil service have been hived off and have agency status. As of October 1996[31] 72 per cent of the Home Civil Service now work in agencies which operate on Next Steps lines. There were 125 such agencies, not counting those parts of the Inland Revenue Service and Customs and Excise which function as Next Steps agencies. Many, but not all, of the bodies which have been created are *service delivery agencies*.

Agencies which have been established independently of the Next Steps initiative will almost always be based upon statute, or on occasion the prerogative. The empowering legislation for bodies such as the Civil Aviation Authority, the Monopolies and Mergers Commission, the Gaming Board, and the regulatory authorities created to oversee the privatized industries, will normally state in some detail the composition and powers of such bodies. This legislation will also indicate what role the minister is to have within that particular area. The minister may, for example, be able to give statutory directions to the agency, or ministerial approval may be required before certain courses of action can be taken. Any legal

---

[31] *Next Steps Briefing Note* (Office of Public Service, October 1996), 1.

action for judicial review will normally be brought against the agency in its own name, unless the applicant is seeking to impugn a particular decision taken by the minister.

The position with respect to Next Steps agencies is markedly different. The powers of such agencies are defined not by statute, but through 'framework agreements'. These agreements will be made between the sponsoring department and the agency, and the Treasury will often be a party. The agreements cover a number of important topics: they set out a corporate plan defining current and future objectives; they dictate the financial arrangements for the agency, including accounting and auditing procedures; and they detail the agency's personnel and staffing policy. Once the agency is established the Chief Executive is responsible for its day-to-day running and he or she can be removed if goals are not met. While the agency is meant to be concerned with service delivery rather than policy the Chief Executive will inevitably have some input into the latter, if only to pass comment upon its workability. Framework agreements are reviewed on average every three years, but adjustments can be made within this period.

It is clear that the creation of Next Steps agencies has significant implications for traditional notions of ministerial accountability. As Drewry and Butcher note,[32] 'how can ministers credibly cling to their virtual monopoly of accountability to Parliament, via traditional models of ministerial responsibility that (according to Mrs Thatcher) were to remain unaltered by the *Next Steps*, in respect of agencies whose chief executives are expected to take managerial initiatives at arm's length from ministerial control?' Notwithstanding this problem it should not be thought that the creation of these agencies has necessarily diminished accountability. The problems of rendering the minister accountable for the operations in his or her department are well known. The formation of agencies which have annual targets, and which have to publish annual reports, business plans etc can enhance accountability, more particularly given that the Chief Executive of these agencies may be called to account before the appropriate select committee.[33]

The revolution in Whitehall has, nonetheless, generated a number of legal questions which require analysis. Agencies which have been created prior to, or independently of, the Next Steps initiative

[32] *The Civil Service Today*, 2nd ed. (Oxford, Basil Blackwell, 1991), 228.
[33] *Next Steps Briefing Note* (Office of Public Service, 1992), para. 20.

will almost always be founded upon statute. The relevant legislation will set out the agency's powers and responsibilities. Applications for judicial review can be brought against the agency itself in the normal way if an individual feels that the agency has exceeded its powers. Actions against bodies such as the Monopolies and Mergers Commission, the Commission for Racial Equality or the Gaming Board have been brought not infrequently. The relevant minister may also be a party to any such action if the applicant claims that ministerial powers granted under the legislation have been exceeded.[34]

The position with respect to Next Steps Agencies is markedly different. They owe their existence to administrative reorganisation of the civil service.[35] The basis of their powers is laid down in the relevant framework documents, and they are clearly intended to operate as largely independent entities with the Chief Executives being responsible for the attainment of targets or corporate goals. This sense of independence has been enhanced by statutory changes which have further emphasised the separateness of the agencies.[36]

(b) Contracting Out: The Background

In recent years there has been an increased use of contractual language over a broader area. Contractual ideas have influenced the relationship between Next Steps Agencies and their sponsoring departments, notwithstanding the fact that there cannot be a real contract because the agency possesses no separate legal personality.

Contracting-out of government functions has, however, now

[34] Baldwin and McCrudden, *Regulation and Public Law* (London, Weidenfeld and Nicolson, 1987).

[35] There may be statutes which are of relevance for a small number of Next Steps Agencies in circumstances where the body which has now attained agency status was subject to some statutory provisions.

[36] For example, a number of these agencies are now financed as trading funds pursuant to the Government Trading Act 1990, which in essence allows certain activities to be run through moneys obtained from the provision of goods or services. This method of financing increases the autonomy of such institutions. The other important legislative innovation is the Civil Service (Management Functions) Act 1992. The effect of the statute is to increase agency autonomy in relation to the discharge of its functions, and to facilitate separate appointment and management practices by agencies.

been employed in an ever growing range of areas.[37] When a department reviews its existing activities it considers five options. The activity can be abolished, privatized, contracted-out, given to a Next Steps Agency or the status quo can be maintained. The contracting-out option can apply both to activities performed in-house and to those for which agencies are responsible. These five choices will apply to a general sphere of activity. It may, for example, be decided to create an agency for the payment of social welfare benefits, or for social welfare contributions. It may be decided to preserve some of the more general policy matters in the social welfare field in-house. Contracting-out as an option will be considered for more particular activities irrespective of whether they are currently done by the agency or the department itself. The criterion for deciding whether an activity will continue to be undertaken in-house or contracted-out is market testing,[38] which operates as follows.[39] A department will establish a special project team to carry forward the market testing process. This will then decide which activities in a service area are appropriate for market testing and the way in which they can best be packaged to stimulate competitive bids. A detailed specification of the service required will be prepared, and bids will then be invited from in-house and selected external contractors. These bids will then be evaluated to assess the quality and cost of offers, and the contract will be awarded appropriately. If the external bid is successful then the in-house service will be closed down, or it may be transferred to the new contractor to manage.

---

[37] The reasons for contracting-out are said to be that: public sector 'in-house' monopolies are inefficient and this is reflected in low productivity; there is 'open-ended' financial commitment to public sector 'in-house' units and such units do not take sufficient account of costs; competition generates new ideas, techniques, etc.; and contractors can be penalised for defective performance and late delivery. The reasons against contracting-out are said to be that: private contractors are unreliable, and may well default; contractors use low bids to eliminate the in-house capacity, thereby making the public body dependent on a private monopoly; competitive tendering entails monitoring costs; and private contractors in areas such as the Health Service can place patients at risk. See generally, Hartley and Huby, 'Contracting-Out Policy: Theory and Evidence', in Kay, Mayer and Thompson, *Privativation and Regulation*, 289.

[38] *The Government's Guide to Market Testing* (HMSO, 1993).

[39] *The Citizen's Charter, First Report*, Cm 2101 (1992), 60–4, contains a detailed breakdown of market testing being carried out by different government departments and agencies.

(c) Institutional Developments and Judicial Review

Next Steps Agencies do not have any formal legal status of their own.[40] Legal actions will in general have to be brought against the relevant minister under whose aegis the agency functions. The application of principles of judicial review to such agencies is not, however, unproblematic. Because of the very informal way in which these agencies were created the courts will perforce have to decide on a case-by-case basis how standard principles of judicial review will apply to such entities. Similar problems exist in the context of contracting-out, as will be seen from the ensuing discussion.

(i) Issues of Principle: Which Matters can be Contracted-Out?

Legal doctrine within the UK places no formal constraints as such on the nature of the subject-matter which can be contracted-out. This general statement must be broken down into a series of more specific propositions.

Firstly, the doctrine of Parliamentary Sovereignty, as understood in the UK, means that, in principle at least, it would always be open to Parliament to contract-out any task, provided that a statute made it clear that it was Parliament's will that this should be done. One can of course posit extreme examples, where a statute purports to contract-out a 'core governmental function', such as the general practice of adjudication currently undertaken by the ordinary courts, to a private party. In such an instance the established judiciary would certainly *construe* such legislation extremely narrowly, and apply it in the most limited fashion possible. If this interpretative technique did not suffice to blunt the force of the hypothetical legislation, then the established judiciary would have to decide whether to *refuse to apply* such a statute, and thereby create a qualification to the traditional idea of Parliamentary Sovereignty in the UK. Subject to this caveat, administrative and constitutional law doctrine does not place impediments upon the nature of the subject matter which can be contracted-out.

Secondly, a statute may not even be necessary in order to effectuate the desired changes. Thus the reforms which instituted the Next Steps Agencies were not even enshrined within a statute, the

[40] Harden, *The Contracting State* (Buckingham, Open Univ. Press, 1992), 44, 46.

assumption being that this was merely a species of administrative reorganisation of the civil service, a matter within the prerogative of the government of the day.

Thirdly, it is open to the government of the day to enact a general statute which will facilitate the discharge of government functions by bodies to which power has been contracted-out. This is, in effect, what the Deregulation and Contracting Out Act 1994 has done. The effect of this legislation will be considered in more detail below. Suffice it to say for the present, that the passage of this legislation was not felt to entail any issue of constitutional principle by the ministers which introduced and piloted the statute through Parliament.

(ii) The Susceptibility of Next Steps, Agencies and Contract to Judicial Review

The UK does not, as is well known, have a separate legal system to deal with public law matters of the kind which exists in many civil law countries. However, the reforms in the law of remedies which were introduced in the late 1970s in the UK have led to a public/ private divide, at least for the purposes of seeking judicial review. Detailed examination of this regime can be found elsewhere.[41] One consequence of these reforms has been that it is now necessary to show that the case 'concerns' public law in order to be able to make use of the procedures for seeking relief contained in Order 53 of the Rules of the Supreme Court and the Supreme Court Act 1981. Space precludes a detailed study of the criteria used by the UK courts to determine whether a case really is 'about' public law for these purposes. In general the courts adopt a test which is in part formalistic, placing emphasis upon the source of the relevant power, and in part functional, looking to the nature of the power which is in issue in a particular case.[42] What is of particular concern for the purposes of the present analysis is the application of these criteria to cases concerning the use of contract. In this respect it is necessary to draw a distinction between three different types of case.

Firstly, Next Steps Agencies do not have any formal legal status of their own.[43] In principle it is therefore clear that such Agencies

---

[41] Craig, above n. 1, Chap. 15.   [42] *Ibid.* 564–6.
[43] Harden, *The Contracting State* (Buckingham, Open Univ. Press, 1992), 44, 46.

must be subject to the procedures for seeking the application for judicial review contained in section 31 of the Supreme Court Act 1981. The formal statutory duty or power still rests with the relevant government minister, and the legal action will in general have to be brought against the minister under whose aegis the agency functions.

Secondly, it is equally clear in principle that companies to whom business has been contracted-out must also be susceptible to the public law procedures for seeking judicial review for the following reason. The relevant statutory power or duty has been imposed upon the government department or agency. The fact that it has chosen to fulfil that obligation by contracting-out some of the work to a private undertaking cannot, as a matter of principle, alter the fact that it is a statutory power or duty which is being exercised. It remains to be seen whether the appropriate defendant in any such case is the private firm as well as the government department or agency.

Thirdly, what is less certain is whether the courts will regard the process of choosing the relevant contractor as itself subject to challenge under the public law procedures for seeking judicial review. The traditional stance of the UK courts has been to treat the making of such contracts as coming within the purview of private as opposed to public law. This approach is in the process of transformation. Procurement decisions made by local authorities have, for example, been held to be amenable to judicial review.[44] Which procurement decisions will be susceptible to judicial review is less certain. Thus in *R. v. Lord Chancellor's Department, ex p. Hibbit and Saunders*[45] the Lord Chancellor's Department invited tenders for court-reporting services. The applicant, who was unsuccessful, sought judicial review, on the ground that it had a legitimate expectation that discussions would be held with some of the tenderers to enable them to submit lower bids. The court held that the decision itself was not amenable to judicial review because it lacked a sufficiently public law element. Such an element could, said the court, be found in cases either where there was some special aim being pursued by the government through the tendering process which set it apart from ordinary commercial tenders; or

---

[44] *R. v. Lewisham BC, ex p. Shell UK Ltd.* [1988] 1 All E.R. 938; *R. v. Enfield LBC, ex p. Unwin* [1989] C.O.D. 466.
[45] [1993] C.O.D. 326.

where there was some statutory underpinning, such as where there was a statutory obligation to negotiate the contract in a particular way, and with particular terms.

(iii) The Application of Public Law Principles to Next Steps, Agencies and to Bodies to which Power has been Contracted-Out: The Delegation Problem

It will be assumed during the ensuing analysis that the body to which power has been contracted-out is amenable to judicial review in accord with the discussion in the previous section. This does, however, still leave open the question as to how far the normal procedural and substantive principles which comprise public law will be applied to such bodies. Whether all such principles will be applicable in the normal way in which they would be applied to public bodies *stricto sensu*, or whether they will have to be modified to take account of the fact that the relevant body is private rather than public, will be considered in the course of the subsequent discussion.

One of the standard principles of administrative law in the UK is the rule against delegation of functions to a body other than that to which the power has been granted by statute.[46] The general starting point is *delegatus non potest delegare*. One of the standard qualifications of this doctrine is known in UK law as the *Carltona* principle, named after the case which is authority for the legal point.[47] The basic idea behind this principle is simple and sensible. When power is given to a minister it cannot realistically be expected that he or she will be able deal with every detailed exercise of the power; many matters will, of necessity, be decided by civil servants working within the government department. The most convincing explanation for the operation of the *Carltona* principle is that when such decisions are made by civil servants there is not, in reality, any delegation at all. The responsible officer merely acts as the *alter ego* of the minister who retains ultimate political and legal responsibility. How then will this idea be applied when power has been given to a Next Steps Agency, or has been contracted-out?

The recent decision of the Divisional Court in *R. v. Secretary of State for Social Services, ex p. Sherwin*[48] provides guidance as to

[46] Craig, above n. 1, 386–91.
[47] *Carltona Ltd.* v. *Commissioner of Works* [1943] 2 All ER 560.
[48] 16. 2. 96.

how the judiciary will respond where the relevant power has been exercised *de facto* by a Next Steps Agency, as opposed to a civil servant within the parent department. Regulation 37 of the Social Security (Claims and Payments) Regulations 1987 gave the Secretary of State power to suspend the payment of a benefit where there was an appeal pending on a point which affected payment of that benefit. Regulation 37A gave the Secretary of State the same suspensory power where another case was being used as a test case on the same point. A decision to suspend payment had to be made within one month. The applicant's benefit was suspended by a District Manager of the Benefit Agency in Birmingham and this agency was a Next Steps Agency operating within the Department of Social Security. It was argued on behalf of the applicant that notice was not given within the requisite period of one month, because the District Manager of the Agency could not be said to speak for the minister within the context of the *Carltona* principle.[49]

The Divisional Court disagreed, holding that the *Carltona* principle could indeed apply notwithstanding that the officer who made the decision operated within a Next Steps Agency. This decision clearly has much to recommend it. These agencies do not have any separate legal status, and powers are still formally vested in the name of the minister. Given that this is so, the policy underlying the *Carltona* principle can be seen to have continuing force in this context: the minister cannot literally be expected to address his or her mind to each such decision and must, of necessity, act through officials. Moreover, the result serves to ensure that it will be the minister who will continue to have ultimate legal responsibility for the decision which has been taken.

This may well be so. The invention of Next Steps Agencies has, however, created a tension in this area. These agencies are, as we have seen, designed to have authority over operational matters. They are meant to function *de facto* more independently from the minister as compared to the situation when all matters were carried on in-house within a unitary government department. The idea of the framework agreement, the appointment of a Chief Executive and the growing autonomy which these agencies have over pay and conditions of those who work therein, are all factors which serve to reinforce this sense of separation. The particular framework agreement which governed this area expressly emphasised the idea that

[49] *Carltona Ltd.* v. *Commissioners of Works* [1943] 2 All E.R. 560.

there was a delegation of operational autonomy to this agency.[50] At the very least this leads to difficulties in accepting that a decision taken by an official in a case such as this can really be regarded as a decision taken on behalf of the Secretary of State.

The application of the *Carltona* principle to situations where power has been contracted-out to a private undertaking is both legally clearer and at the same time more alarming as a result of the Deregulation and Contracting Out Act 1994. Part II of this legislation makes provision for the contracting-out of certain functions by government to bodies which will normally be private. It should be made clear that government departments have frequently contracted-out functions independently of this Act. The statute was passed in order to enable the body to which the power has been contracted-out to operate in the name of the minister, by analogy with the *Carltona* principle.

Section 69 enables functions which, by virtue of any enactment or rule of law, can be performed by an officer of a minister, to be contracted-out to an authorised party. Section 69(5)(c) makes it clear that the minister may still exercise the function to which the authorisation relates; section 71 imposes some limits upon the functions which can be contracted-out; and section 72(2) is contracted out designed to render the minister ultimately responsible for action taken by the body to whom the power has been contracted-out, although the meaning of this particular section is not free from doubt.

It is readily apparent from the discussion of the legislation while it was in the House of Commons that the government regarded these sections as merely technical amendments involving no issue of principle as such. They were depicted as minor changes designed to facilitate contracting-out by sweeping away unnecessarily restrictive distinctions as to what had to be done by civil servants as opposed to outside contractors.[51] It is nonetheless difficult to regard these changes with such equanimity for two reasons.

On the one hand, although Part II of the legislation is entitled 'Contracting-Out', section 69 is actually framed so as to empower an outside body to exercise the functions of the minister. The donee

---

[50] See, e.g., para. 4 of the Framework Agreement.
[51] Freedland, 'Privatising *Carltona*: Part II of the Deregulation and Contracting-Out Act 1994' [1995] *P.L.* 21, 22.

of the power is not simply the *alter ego* of the minister, but the
actual repository of the statutory power.[52]

On the other hand, the very idea that one can transfer the
Carltona type principle and apply it to private bodies to which
power has been contracted-out is itself contentious. In formal legal
terms this can of course be achieved, given that Parliament is
sovereign and has passed the 1994 legislation which stipulates this
result. This should not, however, serve to mask in substantive terms
the shift in thinking which has occurred in this area. The point is
captured well by Freedland,[53]

One cannot read the unanimous judgment of the Court of Appeal in the
Carltona case without concluding that it would have been unthinkable to
that court that their doctrine could be extended so that the functions of a
Minister could be exercised by a private sector employee linked to the
minister only by a chain of contracts and not by any public service
relationship. They would have been amazed that the Minister could be
expected on the one hand to seek and maintain a commercial relationship
with an outside contractor, while on the other hand treating that contractor as the very embodiment of himself. It requires some ingenuity thus to
treat somebody as standing in one's shoes, yet at the same time to keep
that person at arm's length.

(iv) The Application of Public Law to Bodies to which Power has been Contracted-Out: Procedural and Substantive Principles of Judicial Review

Procedural principles in this context connote, for a common lawyer,
the application of those rules concerning a fair hearing, unbiased
adjudicators and the like. Substantive principles of judicial review
include concepts such as unreasonableness, propriety of purpose,
relevancy, proportionality and, in some instances, legitimate expec-
tations.

As a matter of principle the position should be as follows. If the
parent department or agency is fulfilling a statutory function, as
will normally be the case, then it will be subject to the usual public
law norms. If it chooses to fulfil part of that statutory remit by
contracting-out certain tasks to a private undertaking then it would
be contrary to principle for the citizens' protections to be reduced
as a result of this organisational choice. Given that this is so there
are then two ways of proceeding. Either the parent department

[52] *Ibid.* 24–5.   [53] Freedland, above n. 51.

maintains a residual public law responsibility for the tasks which have been contracted-out. Or the private contracting party must itself be subject to the rigours of the public law controls where this is appropriate. Thus, if the parent department would, according to normal public law principles, have had to comply with the requirements of natural justice before disbursing benefits or deciding upon the allocation of a licence, then so too should a private party to which the task has been contracted-out. The same must also be true of the application of substantive public law norms of the kind mentioned above. The courts in the UK have shown themselves to be willing to apply public law principles in circumstances where a private undertaking is performing a regulatory role with the backing, directly or indirectly of the government.[54] Given that this is so, the situation where power has been contracted-out would, *a fortiori*, demand the same conclusion. The fact that many of these contracts are concerned with service delivery rather than regulation should make no general difference, although it might well affect the number of occasions when public law would, in practice, be invoked.

(v) *The Application of Public Law to Bodies to which Power has been Contracted-Out: Damages Actions*

Interesting and difficult questions can arise concerning damages actions which might well be brought when activities have been contracted-out. Imagine that a tort has been committed by a prison officer who works in a prison the running of which has been contracted-out to a private firm. An action would clearly lie against the individual officer, and also against the employer, subject to the normal rules on vicarious liability. The interesting issue would be whether any action could be brought against the department which had contracted-out out the work. This might well be of some importance if the private undertaking turns out to be insolvent. The answer may well depend upon the nature of the duty or discretion, the fulfilment of which has been contracted-out to the private firm. A court might well interpret the governing statute as imposing a residual primary duty on the department which cannot ultimately be divested.[55] On this view, it would be open to the

[54] Craig, above n. 1, Chap. 15.
[55] For general discussion of damages liability see, Craig, above n. 1, Chap. 17. For discussion of the distinction between primary and vicarious liability see the decision of the House of Lords in *X (Minors)* v. *Bedfordshire County Council* [1995] 2 A.C. 633.

department to contract-out the activity if it wished to do so as a matter of organisational choice, but this would not necessarily serve to divest it of legal responsibility. Further interesting questions would arise if the private party to which the power had been contracted-out were to argue that it would be wrong or unfair to hold it negligent if the terms of the contract agreed with the parent department could not, objectively, have enabled it to perform its tasks at the level being demanded by the imposition of the legal duty.

3. CONCLUSION

Public law, by its very nature, entails the possibility of conflict between the legislature and the courts. The very existence of judicial review means that administrative action, including delegated legislation and executive decisions, can be struck down. The review power must perforce be exercised with care in order to ensure that the judiciary do not venture beyond their assigned role within our constitutional structure. However, as argued above, the relationship between courts and the legislature is two-dimensional. The legislature itself has responsibilities, more particularly when it is introducing significant changes to the pattern of administration. Developments of this nature may well require the courts to be legitimately creative as to the types of bodies which are regarded as susceptible to judicial review, and creative also in the way in which those principles are applied within the changing administrative landscape.

Appendix

Clifford Chance Conference
15–16 November 1996

Baade, Professor H. W. (University of Texas at Austin)

Bar, Professor Dr Christian von (Osnabruck, Germany)

Beloff, The Hon Michael J, QC, Master of Trinity College, Oxford.

Bingham, The Rt Hon The Lord Bingham of Cornhill, Lord Chief Justice for England and Wales

Birks, Professor Peter, QC, DCL, LL.D, FBA (All Souls College)

Birt, Simon (Brasenose College)

Blair, William, Esq. QC

Bonell, Professor M. J. (University of Rome)

Browne-Wilkinson, The Rt Hon The Lord Browne-Wilkinson (House of Lords)

Brunink, Harold (Lady Margaret Hall)

Burca, Grainne, de (Somerville College, Oxford)

Burrows, Professor Andrew (Law Commission)

Caldwell, Emma (University College, Oxford)

Carter, P. B. Esq. QC (Wadham College, Oxford)

Cartwright, J., BCL, MA (Christ Church, Oxford)

Carver, J. P. (Partner, Clifford Chance)

Child, G. (Lincoln College, Oxford)

Clark, K. (Senior Partner, Clifford Chance)

Craig, John (Lincoln College, Oxford)

Craig, Professor Paul (Worcester College, Oxford)

Cranston, Professor Ross (London School of Economics)

Crossley, Helen (Christ Church)

Dannemann, Dr G. (Deputy Director of CASECL)

Darbon, C. (Jesus College, Oxford)

Davies, Edward (St Edmund Hall)

Davis, S. (Partner, Clifford Chance)

Delamotte (St Peter's Oxford)

Deroche, Jean-Charles (St Catherines College, Oxford)

Douglas, Countess Magdeleine

Driesson, M. (Lincoln College)

Errera, Professor Roger (Conseil d'Etat, France)

Forest, Mr Justice G. la Forest

Mrs G. la Forest

Freedland, Professor MR, MA, D.Phil (St John's College, Oxford)

Gandhi, S. (St Hugh's College, Oxford)

Galligan, Professor Dennis (Director, Centre for Socio-Legal Research, Wolfson College, Oxford)

Gerven, Professor Walter van, University of Leuven, Belgium, former Advocate General, Court of European Communities, Luxembourg

Gardner, O. R. (Keble College, Oxford)

Gibson, The Rt Hon Lord Justice Gibson (Court of Appeal, London)

Glidewell, The Rt Hon Sir Ian Glidewell(Worcester College, Oxford)

Goff, The Rt Hon The Lord Goff of Chieveley, PC, DCL, FBA, Lord High Steward of the University of Oxford

Lady Goff

Goode, Professor Roy, CBE, QC, LL.D. FBA (St John's College, Oxford)

Grainger, L. (Partner, Clifford Chance)

Greatorex, Paul (Christ Church)

Grierson, Sir Ronald

Hackney, J. (Wadham College, Oxford)

Harel, N. (Trinity College, Oxford)

Hartkamp, Professor Dr Arthur (Advocate General, Supreme Court, The Netherlands)

Herrington, T. (Partner, Clifford Chance)

Hoffman, The Rt Hon The Lord Hoffman PC (House of Lords)

Horvay, Karl (Wadham College, Oxford)

Ichikana, T. (Brasenose College, Oxford)

James, S. (Partner, Clifford Chance)

Johnston, Angus (Brasenose College, Oxford)

Jones, Emma (St Hugh's College, Oxford)

Karanja, Peter (Brasenose College, Oxford)

Kennedy, The Rt Hon Lord Justice P. Kennedy (Court of Appeal, London)

Kohner, Debbie (Jesus College, Oxford)

Koopmans, Professor Tim, LL.D. (Advocate General, Supreme

Court of The Netherlands)
Lee, Gareth (Christ Church, Oxford)
Leveque, Philippe (Pembroke College, Oxford)
Lever, Jeremy Esq. Q.C.
Limbach, Professor Dr Jutta (Präsidentin des Bundesverfassungs-
gerichts, Germany)
McMahon, M. (Partner, Clifford Chance)
Markesinis, Professor B. S, Ph.D., LL.D., DCL., D.Iur.h.c. (Clif-
ford Chance Professor of European Law, Director of CASECL)
Martinelli, Thomas (Brasenose College, Oxford)
Matthews, M. H. (Chairman of the Faculty Board of Law)
Michalik, Paul (Worcester College, Oxford)
Moor, Anne de (Somerville College, Oxford)
Neill, The Rt Hon Sir Brian
Lady Neill
Nix, Jenny Ms.
Pasquini, Nello Esq. (Partner, Radcliffe & Co.)
Perrin, C. (Partner, Clifford Chance)
Picard, Professor Etienne (Professor University of Paris 1; Deputy
Director of CASECL)
Pipe, Daniel D. (Christ Church, Oxford)
Price, Nia (Trinity College, Oxford)
Proukaki, E. (St John's College, Oxford)
Reker, Tim (Exeter College, Oxford)
Reynolds, Professor F.M.B., QC, DCL, FBA (Worcester College,
Oxford)
Ries, Anne Catherine (St John's College, Oxford)
Ripka, Ondine (St John's College, Oxford)
Rudden, Professor Bernard Rudden, DCL, LL.D, D.Iur.h.c., FBA
(Brasenose College, Oxford)
Sabania, Ariano (Brasenose College, Oxford)
Sandelson, J. (Partner, Clifford Chance)
Schonberg, S. (St Edmund Hall, Oxford)
Scola, Nick (Jesus College, Oxford)
Scorey, David Esq.
Sedley, The Hon Mr Justice Sedley (High Court of Justice, Lon-
don)
Lady Sedley
Silber, S. R., QC (Law Commision)
Smith, Matthew (St Edmund Hall, Oxford)

Smyth, M. (Partner, Clifford Chance)
Snook, Mrs Irene
Trindade, Francis A., Sir Owen Dixon Professor of Law, Monash University, Australia
Tur, R. (Oriel College, Oxford)
Veeder, V. V., QC
Voong, Peng (Wadham College, Oxford)
West, Matthew (Corpus Christi, Oxford)
Wright, Abigail (St Hilda's College, Oxford)

Index